Interlover

Evelyn D'Arcy

NEW ENGLISH LIBRARY
Hodder and Stoughton

Copyright © 1997 by Evelyn D'Arcy

First published in 1997
by Hodder and Stoughton
A division of Hodder Headline PLC

A New English Library paperback

The right of Evelyn D'Arcy to be identified as the Author of
the Work has been asserted by her in accordance with the
Copyright, Designs and Patents Act 1988.

10 9 8 7 6 5 4 3 2 1

All rights reserved. No part of this publication may be
reproduced, stored in a retrieval system, or transmitted,
in any form or by any means without the prior written
permission of the publisher, nor be otherwise circulated
in any form of binding or cover other than that in which
it is published and without a similar condition being
imposed on the subsequent purchaser.

All characters in this publication are fictitious
and any resemblance to real persons, living or dead,
is purely coincidental.

British Library Cataloguing in Publication Data.
A CIP catalogue record for this title is available
from the British Library.

ISBN 0 340 66645 5

Typeset by Avon Dataset Ltd, Bidford-on-Avon, Warks
Printed and bound in Great Britain by
Cox & Wyman, Reading, Berks

Hodder and Stoughton
A division of Hodder Headline PLC
338 Euston Road
London NW1 3BH

SATISFACTION FOR SALE...

The idea of laying one hand on Ruth's thigh and slowly letting it drift upwards under the hem of her skirt made Mark shiver with longing. 'What do you do?' he asked, having difficulty in controlling his voice.

'I'm setting up Interlover,' she replied crisply.

'Dare I ask what made you think of the idea?'

'I realized that there was a niche market out there. Career women without a partner, divorcees or people who've just split up with a long-term lover, and women whose husbands can't – or won't – fulfil their needs. Women who want good sex, delivered in the way they want it – not a quick and tacky bonk with some himbo or other. We're targeting professional women. Lawyers, accountants, teachers.' She shrugged. 'Hence the need for good conversation skills as well as your skill between the sheets...'

Also in New English Library paperback

Arousal
House of Lust
The Uninhibited
Submission!
Haunting Lust
Depravicus
The Splits
The Degenerates
Rock Hard
Midnight Blue

For Brian . . . a leader of true inspiration!

ONE

'It was a dream job,' Ruth said, draining her glass. 'Marketing Manager for Romulus Books . . .' She shrugged. 'Ah, well. I suppose all dreams have to end, one day. This one just ended a bit sooner than I'd expected, that's all.'

Aidan's blue eyes were sympathetic as he looked at his lover. She'd loved her job so much: and she'd been good at it. 'I'm sure you'll find something else soon. Something just as good.'

'Mm.' She wasn't convinced. 'And in the meantime?'

'Look, you know I'll support you.' He squeezed her hand. 'You don't have to worry about money, or anything like that.'

He was surprised, not for the first time, at just how icy brown eyes could be. Ruth's were particularly glacial as she glared at him, removing her hand abruptly from his. 'I'm not going to sponge off you, Aidan.'

'I didn't mean that.' He refilled her glass. 'Look, if I'd been the one who'd been made redundant, you'd have supported me, wouldn't you? Both emotionally *and* subbing my half of the mortgage, until I'd got another job and could pay my way again – not to mention paying you back, when I was on my feet again. I'm simply saying that I'll do the same for you. As your equal partner.'

She nodded, smiling ruefully at him. 'Sorry. I'm a bad-tempered cow. Not to mention ungrateful.'

'No, you're not. Anyone would be the same, in your shoes. I'd be difficult to live with, too – being made redundant isn't exactly the world's nicest experience,' he told her, rubbing his nose affectionately against hers. 'Look, Ruth, don't worry. I know the job market's tough nowadays, but with your qualifications and experience, you'll be snapped up before you know it. I bet as soon as the news hits the grapevine, someone will ring you and beg you to join them.'

'I don't really know,' she admitted, brushing her straight dark hair out of her eyes, 'if I want to be snapped up, actually.'

He frowned. 'Then what are you going to do? Do you want to go back to university, do a PhD? Or stay home and write poetry, or paint? Or set up on your own, making designer tapestries or something?'

She shook her head. 'Nothing like that.' University had been an attractive idea, for a while – a chance to wallow in nostalgia and remember how much fun she'd had as an undergraduate, with Laura and Shelley – but she couldn't face being a student again. Not after working for nearly ten years, earning money and being out of the academic rat-race. Being a student, with no money, and having to fight for a research position when she'd finished her doctorate, wasn't what she wanted. What she had in mind was something very...

'Then what do you want to do?' Aidan asked, cutting into her thoughts.

The idea which had been formulating in her mind for the past couple of weeks, since she'd first learned that Romulus Books was going under, wasn't something she could discuss with her live-in lover. Not without an extreme amount of tact – or an extreme amount of courage, fuelled by an equally extreme amount of wine. She wrinkled her nose. 'Oh, I don't know,' she lied. 'I'm sure I'll think of something, given a little more time.'

He stroked her hair. 'Why don't we eat out tonight? My shout, because it's my idea.'

'I've got a better idea,' she said. 'Let's get a takeaway, and go to bed.'

He grinned. 'Tut, tut, Ms Finn. Think of the sheets.'

She grinned back. 'How about bed first, and takeaway later?'

'Sounds good to me.' He stood up, drawing her up with him, and pulled her into his arms. At five feet eight, Ruth was only about four inches shorter than he was: though she wasn't the scrawny model type, all skin and bone. He loved the softness of her generous curves.

It turned him on, just thinking about her: sometimes, if he called her from work, he ended up fantasizing about making love to her on his desk, and had to spend the rest of the afternoon with an aching hard-on. He'd relieved himself in the office, once, unable to bear the frustration, and had nearly been caught by his secretary: the memory still had the power to make him wince. And yet he couldn't help himself, where Ruth was concerned.

Nor custom stale her infinite variety, he thought, letting his hands drift down her back to trace the soft swell of her buttocks. The more time he spent with her, the more he desired her. Boredom had never set in between them: even the most common erotic acts were somehow special between them. The more often his cock sank into her warm wet flesh, the more he wanted her. 'Mm. Nice,' he breathed.

She moved closer, so that her breasts were pressed hard against his chest, and slid one thigh between his. Aidan could feel the hard points of her nipples through her soft black lambswool sweater; her lower lip was swollen and reddened and her eyes were a tell-tale gold. Ruth's eyes always changed colour when she was aroused.

He nibbled at her bottom lip until her mouth opened; with a sigh of contentment, he kissed her, sliding his hands under her sweater and stroking her back. His hands moved slowly upwards until he reached the clasp of her bra; murmuring with pleasure against her mouth, he undid it. He drew his hands along her sides and finally nudged her bra away, replacing the lacy cups with his hands. 'I love the way you feel,' he said.

She nibbled his earlobe. 'You're not so bad yourself.'

'I'd like to sin, with Ruthie Finn, upon a tiger skin,' he quipped.

As he'd hoped, she started laughing, her problems forgotten. 'That's terrible, Aidan,' she said.

'OK, bed it is,' he said, waltzing her out of the room to the bottom of the stairs. 'If I was a macho man, I'd carry you up.'

'But because you're not fit enough,' she retorted, 'I'd better walk it.'

'You wait. Give me six months at the gym—'

'When you don't have yet another good excuse to skip it,' she interrupted, 'like a good film on the television, or football, or you've been working late and you're too tired.'

He ignored her. 'Six months, and I'll be strong and muscular.'

'Actually,' she said, 'I think I rather like you as you are. Love handles and all.'

'*Love handles?*' In mock affront, he chased her up the stairs, finally catching her in their bedroom. 'I ought to spank you for that,' he said, stripping off her black sweater and letting it fall to the floor, together with her bra.

'Don't you dare!' she warned, her eyes sparkling.

'Or tie you up,' he said ruminatively, eyeing their Victorian brass bedstead. 'Using a black silk scarf.'

She pulled a face at him. 'Why don't you just shut up and fuck me silly?'

'What a good idea . . .' He stripped quickly, leaving his pale green chinos and black sweater in a heap on the floor. Ruth watched him with a surge of mingled affection and desire as he took off the rest of his clothing, standing naked before her.

Sometimes Fate could be bloody wonderful, she thought. Like the day she'd been late for work and dropped her briefcase on the platform of Holborn station. It had burst open, spilling papers everywhere. The tall blond-haired man who'd been standing next to her – and whom she'd already dismissed as being the boring accountant type – had helped her gather the papers together again. They'd ended up having dinner together that evening, and she'd discovered that Aidan Shaw was indeed an accountant. But he was very far from boring. And he was extremely good in bed.

'What are you thinking about?' he asked gently, seeing the faraway look in her eyes.

She smiled at him. 'I'm not fretting about my job, if that's what you were worrying about. Actually, I was thinking about when we met – and the first time you took me to bed.'

'Mm.' He nuzzled her shoulders. 'I remember. That night.'

'I'm not given to leaping into bed with just anyone,' she reminded him, her tone slightly frosty.

'I know. I think you must have been still in shock at dropping your briefcase.' He grinned. 'I remember that you hogged the duvet all night.' He peeled off her leggings with practised ease, swiftly following with her black lacy knickers. He pushed the duvet aside, then drew her down onto the bed. 'I was bloody freezing – but it was worth every goose pimple.' He shrugged. 'Otherwise I suppose neither of us would be here now.'

'No.' She stroked his flanks. 'Just think of what we'd have missed. I'd never have known that the man standing next to me in his boring grey suit and white shirt and sober tie—' Aidan, seeing her eyes like molten gold with desire, let the remark pass without argument '—could kiss so well. And stroke, and lick, and caress . . .' Her hands wandered round to his stiffened penis, her fingers curling round the shaft. 'Not to mention having an extremely gorgeous cock.'

'And I'd never have known that the woman with the power suit and power bob had such a come-hither smile. Or that she virtually purrs when she comes. Or that she has such gorgeous breasts.' Aidan cupped them, pushing them up and together to deepen the vee of her cleavage, then buried his face in the soft pillowy flesh, breathing in her scent. He traced their outline with the tip of his tongue, noting the way the texture of her skin changed as he licked her areolae, and finally set to work on her nipples. He sucked on the hard flesh, nipping the sensitive tissue gently at first, and then drawing hard on it until she gasped with pleasure.

Ruth stretched, cat-like, lifting her ribcage; Aidan, taking the hint, slowly tracked downwards, avoiding the ticklish spots by her hip bones and nuzzling the soft planes of her abdomen. She sighed with pleasure as he parted her legs, kissing the soft pale skin of her upper thighs, then moving upwards to slide his tongue along her satiny cleft. As the tip of his tongue moved along her labia, she closed her eyes, tipping her head back and shifting her hips so that she lay more comfortably.

At last, his mouth found her clitoris and he began to tease the hard bud of flesh from its hood, alternately circling it and flicking rapidly across it. She reached down to slide her hands into his hair, the pads of her fingertips massaging his scalp; as pleasure began to bubble through her veins, the pressure of her fingertips grew deeper, and she gave small murmurs of pleasure.

Her flesh grew liquid under his ministrations, and she pushed her pubis hard against him, wanting more. He kissed her nether mouth lovingly, then shifted to lie between her legs, his glans butting against her entrance. Ruth's legs came up to lock round his waist, and she pushed upwards.

Aidan gave a sigh of contentment as he entered her, her flesh encasing him like warm wet silk.

'I love the way you feel,' he murmured against her ear. 'Your cunt's warm and wet and tight, and I love the way it clings to me.'

'Mm. And I love the way you fill me,' she said softly. With most men, it would have been just a pretty compliment, a sop to his ego: with Aidan, it was true. He'd been endowed with both quality and quantity, she thought dreamily: a man with a long and thick cock, and the knowledge of how to use it to its full potential.

He supported his weight on his hands and knees, his body just brushing hers as he thrust into her; the light covering of hair on his chest created a delicious friction against her breasts as he moved. His thrusts were slow and measured; as she grew more aroused, pushing back against him, his pace quickened.

At last, he felt her quim rippling round his cock, tipping him into his own release; she made a small sound, like a cat purring, and he smiled against her skin. Ruth Finn had a reputation for being a tiger in business: but she was a complete pussycat in bed, her eyes gold slits of passion as she came.

He withdrew from her and shifted onto his side, tucking her into the curve of his body. She rested her head on his shoulder, tracing complex patterns on his skin with her fingertips.

'What a way to relax,' she quipped.

'The perfect present for a stressed-out businesswoman?' he suggested.

Ruth's eyes widened. It was almost as if he'd picked up on what she was thinking. Maybe he wouldn't be so upset about her idea, after all. Though she still thought that she needed to tread carefully when she finally told him what she was planning. She made a non-committal murmur of agreement and nestled closer, hoping that he'd drop the subject.

He did. 'Ruthie?'

'Mm?'

'Are you hungry?'

'That depends.'

He stroked her hair. 'On what?'

'On who's actually going to get the takeaway.'

He laughed. 'Meaning that if I'm going, you're hungry; and if you are, you'd rather have cheese and biscuits?'

She laughed back. 'Something like that. I'm too warm and lazy to move.'

'OK, I'll go.' He kissed her lingeringly. 'What do you fancy?'

'A Chinese would be nice.' She ran her fingernails lightly over his thigh. 'Peking duck and crispy seaweed. Chow mein. And *lots* of sesame prawn toasts.'

'Sounds good to me.' He played with her breasts. 'You're not intending to get dressed while I'm gone, are you?'

'Only in a bathrobe.'

'Good.' He kissed her again and got out of bed, dressing almost as swiftly as he'd stripped earlier. 'I'll see you in a minute, then.'

'OK.' She smiled at him, and he left the bedroom. Rather than getting up straight away, she settled herself back against the pillows. It wasn't going to be easy, telling Aidan what she was planning to do. She knew that it would make him feel threatened – which was crazy. Since the first time they'd made love, she'd felt no need to look at anyone else, let alone fantasize about them, or act on her fantasies.

She'd refused to marry him – despite having several happily married friends, she was convinced that having that little bit of paper would spoil what they had between them – but she loved him, and didn't feel the need to chase around after other men. Aidan knew that, too: but at the same time, she had a gut feeling that the Interlover idea would make him feel insecure.

Then she remembered the dinner party. Laura and Shelley, her oldest friends from her college days, were coming to dinner, with their respective husbands. If she could get the two of them in the kitchen on the pretext of making coffee, and have a quick confab with them, they might have some bright ideas about how she could tell Aidan.

'Are you sure that you're really up to this?' Aidan asked, coming to stand behind her and sliding his arms round her waist, resting his chin on her shoulder. If he'd been the one who'd just lost his job, he wouldn't have felt like entertaining friends – even if they were as close as Ruth's old college pals. He would just have mooched around the house, snarling at anyone who tried to encourage him and brooding on how unfair it all was. Ruth, on the other hand, had been remarkably calm. No tears, no tantrums: apart from the odd sharp comment, it was hard to tell that she had anything on her mind.

'I'm sure they'll understand if we call off this evening. We could postpone it for a couple of weeks, say. Until you've sorted things out.'

She tipped her head back to look at him. 'How did I manage to find myself such a New Man?' she asked teasingly. 'Aidan, it's really sweet of you, but there's nothing to worry about. I'm over the shock of it now; and, to be honest, I'd much rather carry on life as normal, instead of crawling into a corner and brooding about how unfair it all is.' She smiled. 'I'm fine – and it'll be nice to see them all again. I don't often see Nicholas or Carlo.' She stroked his face. 'I'm looking forward to it, Aidan. Really.'

He nodded. 'Well, if you're sure . . .'

'I'm sure,' she said firmly.

'Do you need a hand with anything?'

'No, thanks, I'm fine.' She began folding the cream into the base of the white chocolate mousse. Aidan couldn't resist dipping a finger into the mixture, and promptly had his hand slapped.

'Get out of my kitchen, Aidan Shaw,' she ordered, her smile softening the harshness of her words.

He grinned. 'Yes, ma'am!' He kissed the back of her neck, released her, and went out of the kitchen; as he reached the door, he paused. 'By the way . . . the pudding's not quite up to scratch. I think you ought to make another batch, and let me have that one.'

Ruth didn't believe a word of it. 'Apart from the fact that it's a pathetic excuse, your executive paunch doesn't need any more pampering.'

Aidan sucked his stomach in. 'Paunch? What paunch?' He coughed. 'Maybe I'll just nip down to the gym for a workout, then . . .' He blew her a kiss, and left her to finish sorting out dinner.

Ruth watched him as he walked out of the room, and was half-tempted to follow him and lure him upstairs to bed. On the other hand, if she did, dinner would definitely be on hold. The sensible side of her won; pursing her lips, she turned back to the white chocolate mousse.

Laura and Nicholas arrived at half-past seven precisely; Shelley and Carlo, as usual, were late.

'You'd think that, being a teacher, she'd have a thing about being punctual,' Nicholas observed, his grey eyes amused.

'She is, when she's on her own,' his wife said tartly. 'You know what Carlo's like. No sense of time at all – he never even wears a watch! He's probably still in his darkroom, fiddling about with some arty shots or other.'

'Well, it's a cold starter and a cold pudding, and casseroles are impossible to spoil,' Ruth said equably. 'It wouldn't matter if they were an hour late.'

'It smells gorgeous, anyway,' Nicholas said, sniffing the air.

'And now to get the tactless bit over with,' Laura said. Her blue eyes were rueful. 'I'm really sorry about the job, Ruthie.'

'It's OK. Really. I'm over the worst, now.' Ruth poured her friend a glass of wine. 'Cheers.'

'Cheers.' Laura sipped the wine, and tossed her fair hair out of her eyes. 'So dare I ask what you're going to do?'

Ruth smiled. 'I've got one or two ideas.'

'Oh come on, don't be so secretive.'

'I'll explain later.'

Laura was intrigued by the mischievous smile in her friend's eyes. Ruth was definitely up to something. Aidan didn't seem perturbed, so either he knew about it and approved – or Ruth knew that he wouldn't like whatever she was planning, and hadn't told him about it yet. The wicked look on Ruth's face made Laura fairly sure that it was the latter.

The conversation veered onto theatre, and they were arguing the merits of the latest RSC production when the doorbell rang.

'Sorry we're late,' Shelley said breathlessly, hugging Ruth and handing her a bottle of wine.

'Stuck in the darkroom, were you?' Ruth asked Carlo teasingly, greeting him with a kiss.

'Men!' Shelley said feelingly, rolling her eyes. 'Next time, I'll tell him that we have to be here an hour before we really do. Then, maybe, we'll be here on time! I take it that Nicholas and Laura are already here?'

Ruth nodded. 'Go through, and I'll sort out the drinks. I take it you're having the usual?'

'Please,' they said in unison.

Ruth was feeling mellow enough to be reckless by the time that they reached coffee and Carlo asked her what she was planning to do. She smiled. 'Actually, I'm thinking about setting up on my own.'

'Freelance marketing? Great idea. I might be able to put something your way,' the good-looking Italian said. 'I've a few contacts at the advertising agencies, and they're always on the lookout for outside help. Someone with your talent could make a fortune, going freelance – and you get the best of all worlds. An interesting job, but no office politics.'

She shook her head. 'It's very sweet of you, Carlo, but that's not really what I was intending to do.'

Again, Laura was intrigued by her friend's slightly wicked smile. 'What are you plotting, then?'

'Put it this way – I was reading this article about women

who pay men for sex.' Ruth looked at her friends. 'Would you?'

Shelley coughed, nodding at the men. 'Great timing, Ruthie.'

'No, seriously. I want to know – just supposing that you were single and dedicated to your career, or you'd just split up with the love of your life, with no hope of getting back together again. Single men – *nice* single men, who don't have any hang-ups or a broken marriage and a few debts – are bloody hard to find. They've all been snapped up at the age of twelve. Now, masturbation's all right for a while, but then you start wanting the real thing. Would you consider paying a man for good sex?'

Carlo laughed, his dark eyes sparkling. 'Wow. And to think that you lot are always telling us how men can be replaced by six inches of plastic!'

'Some men, maybe,' Shelley retorted, pulling a face at her husband.

'I'll remind you of that later,' he warned, still laughing.

'Seriously,' Ruth interrupted, 'there are a lot of women out there on their own who could do with a good fuck. No strings, no worries about disease – and definitely a man with a brain, not just a himbo she'd picked up in a bar somewhere. Someone who can talk to her as well as give her physical pleasure. Someone who'll make a fuss of her.'

'Hm.' Laura was interested. 'Go on.'

'I'm not just talking about single women, either. What about women who are married, but maybe their husbands can't give them what they want? I don't mean temporary impotence here.' Ruth waved her hands expansively. 'I'm talking about men who don't like giving oral sex, say – or women who want to try something mildly kinky, but their partners aren't comfortable with the idea of light bondage or spanking or whatever.'

'Actually, I read that article as well,' Shelley said, pushing her hair back from her eyes. 'You've got a point, Ruthie. I know quite a few single women who just suppress their sexual urges because they don't want to go to a club or some other meat-market, just to pick up a bloke. There's certainly a market out there.'

Ruth smiled delightedly. 'So, Shelley, would you do it? If you were in that position, that is?' she added hastily.

'I don't know,' Shelley said. 'Maybe.'

'Laura?'

Laura shook her head. 'I don't know, Maybe. If I wasn't married to Nicholas.'

Ruth nodded. 'And would any of you let women pay you for sex?' she asked the men.

'What, you mean be a male prostitute?' Carlo asked, faintly shocked.

She nodded. 'If you want to put it in those terms, yes.'

He shrugged. 'Isn't that the average man's dream job? Being paid to perform?'

'But only if they were good enough in other areas. Like I said: I don't want men who are all cock and no brain, and I definitely don't want the arrogant sort. We're talking about kind, considerate, bright – and good in bed.' She coughed. 'Present company excepted, of course, it's hard to find men like that.'

'So what are you really up to, Ruthie?' Nicholas asked. 'Are you intending to send us all out as rent boys?'

She laughed. 'Definitely not! Think about it, Nicholas. What do you give the woman in your life for Valentine's Day? Or on special anniversaries?'

'Flowers,' he said.

'Carlo?'

He thought about it. 'Chocolates.'

'Aidan?'

'Perfume, nice undies.'

She grinned. 'And don't forget dinner out. But you get my drift. You spoil her rotten, with sensuous things – and she appreciates it.' She paused. 'Shelley. Suppose one of your friends splits up with a long-term lover. What would you do for her?'

'I'd go round to her place with a sympathetic ear, tissues, large supplies of chocolate, and listen while we drink either coffee or wine,' Shelley said promptly.

'And later, when it's your friend's birthday, and she's really down in the dumps? What would be the perfect present?'

'Yeah. You have a point,' Shelley admitted. 'A night of being spoiled by a gorgeous man, and all the sex she wants.'

'Exactly. Now, imagine that there was an agency which didn't deliver flowers or chocolates, but delivered conversation and good company. Including sex, if you wanted it. Good sex, with someone who'd been trained in the art of giving a woman pleasure.' Ruth paused. 'And that's what I'm going to do. Set up the agency.'

There was a stunned silence around the table. Aidan was the one to break it. 'Are you serious, Ruth?'

'Absolutely. In fact, you said to me last night that an orgasm was a perfect present for a stressed-out businesswoman.'

He flushed, unable to argue with her comment. 'Yeah.'

Laura's lips twitched. 'An orgasm-a-gram. Well, I suppose it makes a change from lingerie parties.'

'Mm.' Shelley raised her eyebrows. 'At least your demonstrators won't be telling women that the tip of their nose is the most sensitive part of their body, after the clitoris, and advising her to test her vibrator on it . . .'

Carlo's eyes widened. 'You're kidding! Is it really?'

'So they say,' she said lightly, stroking his thigh under the table. 'I haven't been to one of those parties for years. And, before you ask, I can't remember what I felt when I *did* try putting a vibrator on the end of my nose!'

'Maybe you ought to have a lingerie party.' He nibbled her earlobe. 'A private one, you and me. Or maybe I could get a commission to do the photography for a brochure, and use you as my test model . . .'

Shelley swallowed hard, her sex going liquid at the thought of Carlo trying a full range of sex toys on her, and forced herself to concentrate on the people round her. 'So what are you going to call this service of yours, Ruth?'

'Interlover.'

'Not spelt with an A, I hope,' Laura said. 'You'll be in hot water with a certain florist.'

'Traditional spelling,' Ruth confirmed. 'Though it's still at the idea stage, at the moment.'

'And what an idea.' Shelley looked approving. 'I can think of a few people at school who could do with your service. Especially a certain old bat of a headmistress. Having an orgasm might actually make her human.' She turned to Laura. 'What about in your office?'

The solicitor nodded. 'Definitely. Half a dozen – including my boss's dragon of a secretary.' She paused. 'Is it a women-only service, Ruth?'

'Yup.'

'Sexist,' Carlo said lightly.

'Is it legal?' Shelley asked.

'I dunno. I suppose it's like massage parlours and the like – you can have as much of the service as you like. If you just want dinner, conversation, and a little light flattery, fine: if you want more, then it's up to you to say so.' She shrugged. 'I'm still looking into that aspect of it.'

'I'll check up for you next week, if you like,' Laura offered.

Ruth smiled. 'Thanks.'

Shelley, noticing that the men – Aidan in particular – had suddenly gone very quiet, changed the subject, telegraphing with her eyes to Ruth and Laura that as soon as they had a girly evening they'd be able to discuss it further.

The rest of the evening passed without reference to Interlover; when the others had gone, Aidan headed for the kitchen. Ruth followed him, catching him by the waist. 'Leave that. I'll do the washing up in the morning,' she said. 'Come to bed.'

Aidan said nothing; he merely wrinkled his nose at her.

'What's up?' Ruth asked, shifting round so that she faced him.

'This Interlover idea of yours . . . Are you serious, or were you having us on?' he asked.

'I was serious,' she said quietly. 'Think about it, Aidan. There'll be quite a high demand for it. Given the current divorce rate, and the trend for more and more women to stay single . . . There are a lot of women out there who'd like good sex, but don't want to have complicated relationships to go with it.'

'I see,' he said drily. 'Does that include you?'

'No, of course it doesn't!' She stroked his face. 'Don't feel threatened by it, Aidan. You know I love you, and I'm not looking for anyone else.'

'Hm.' He didn't sound convinced.

'I'm merely meeting a customer need. Providing a professional service of good sex, good conversation, and no need to worry about catching some gross disease.' She took a deep breath. 'If I set up a database and have a questionnaire – for the person who gave the order *and* the person who received the service – I'll be able to see where my main market is, and tailor my promotional strategy accordingly.'

Aidan was silent. It sounded like she was looking at it purely from a business angle – but what if one of her young studs took her fancy? Would she try him out?

'If you're worrying,' Ruth said, 'that I'm going to be so wrapped up in the business that I'll neglect you, then don't.' She grinned. 'And if you think I'm not giving you enough attention, you could always send yourself to me, via Interlover . . .'

'Yeah. I suppose so.'

She rubbed her nose against his. 'Come to bed,' she repeated, taking his hand and leading him out of the kitchen. Aidan allowed her to lead him upstairs, and stood completely still while she undressed him.

Ruth, sensing that he needed more than verbal reassurance from her, caressed every inch of skin that she uncovered, from his broad shoulders, down over his firm pectoral muscles, to his waist. She fumbled slightly with his belt, then traced the outline of his hardening cock through the fine material of his dark trousers, curling her fingers round it and feeling it grow under her hand.

Slowly, she undid his zip and eased his trousers down. Aidan stepped out of them, and allowed her to peel off his socks. She tossed her hair back, and then knelt before him. She smiled up at him, and removed his silk boxer shorts so that he stood naked before her.

He was magnificent. Three years of living with him hadn't made her grow tired of his body – or even take it for granted. Every time she saw him, she still felt that same ripple of desire that started somewhere at the base of her spine and had her nipples rock-hard and her quim hot and moist within a matter of seconds.

'God, you're lovely,' she breathed, cupping his balls in one hand and taking his cock in the other. The thick rigid muscle trembled slightly at her touch, and she saw a tell-tale drop of moisture at its eye. Aidan was as bewitched by her touch as she was by his, she thought: so deliciously responsive.

She let her fingers play along his shaft, tantalizing him, before bending her head and taking his glans into her mouth. She traced its surface with the tip of her tongue, flicking over the sensitive spot in its groove. Aidan tangled his hands in her hair, the massaging movements over her scalp urging her on; she began to suck him in earnest, her lips working up and down his thick rigid shaft until he cried out, and she felt a warm salty fluid filling her mouth.

She swallowed it, then kissed the end of his cock before standing up again. Aidan pulled her into his arms, kissing her gently.

'I love you,' he whispered, stroking her face. 'And I don't want to lose you.'

'You're not going to. It's simply a business venture,' she said, her voice firm yet gentle. 'Besides, I haven't finished yet.' She gave him a sultry look, and nodded to the bed.

Smiling, he pushed the duvet aside and settled back against the pillows. Ruth swayed at the foot of the bed, undressing very slowly; Aidan watched her with obvious enjoyment as first her shirt was discarded, then her skirt, leaving her clad in a white lace bra, matching knickers, and black lacy-topped hold-up stockings.

Next, she shed her bra, letting the flimsy garment fall to the floor, and finally her knickers; she left the stockings on, and moved round to the side of the bed. Aidan blew her a kiss as she knelt next to him on the bed, then shifted gracefully so that she was straddling him. She pressed her quim against his cock, making sure that he could feel how hot and wet it was. She slid her hand behind them so that she could fondle his balls and stroke his perineum; his eyes were hot and very blue, she noticed, and his blond hair was tousled. There was a faint flush on his cheeks which betrayed his arousal – even if she hadn't been aware of the fact that his cock was rock-hard again.

Smiling, she bent down to kiss him, running her tongue along his lower lip before sinking her teeth into it. His mouth opened, and she slid her tongue inside to explore its contours.

Both of them were shaking when she lifted her head. She guided his cock to her entrance, and pushed down so that her pubis was grinding against his own. His hands came up automatically to cup her breasts, his thumbs circling her areolae and rubbing the sensitive flesh until the rosy buds became hard. She lifted herself up until he was almost out of her, then pushed down hard, repeating the movement again and again. Pleasure lanced through her, pooling in her solar plexus, and she felt her internal muscles spasm around his rigid column of flesh.

He cried out her name, and she felt his cock throb inside her; slowly, she lowered her upper body so that her breasts were against his chest, and he enfolded her in his arms. She rested her cheek against his, content to lie there in silence; he stroked her back with absent-minded affection.

'I love you, Ruthie,' he said softly.

'Me too,' she said, nuzzling her cheek against his.

'As long as you don't get so wrapped up in these young studs that you forget me.'

She lifted her face away from his so that he could see her eyes. 'I won't. And that's a promise.' She smiled. 'Besides, who else am I going to try out all my ideas on?'

'Hm.' He still wasn't one hundred per cent convinced, but it would do for now.

TWO

'Wanted: broad-minded individuals, with good conversation skills, for exciting new business venture. Send CV and photograph, plus a list of interests and hobbies, to Box 69.' Laura chuckled. 'Oh, Ruthie! What a box number!'

'It was totally deliberate,' Ruth admitted, a wicked smile on her face. 'As I'm sure half of the applicants realized!'

Shelley was puzzled. 'I thought you only wanted men?' She twirled the ends of her red curls around her finger. 'Or are you catering for the male market, too? Or lesbians?'

Ruth smiled. 'Interlover's aimed at the professional heterosexual woman. But I can't advertise for men only, because that's sexist: it's against employment legislation. So—' Ruth spread her hands '—my hands were pretty much tied. But some of the women might consider helping to train the lovers, so I'm killing two birds with one stone, I suppose.'

'Fair enough.' Shelley nodded. 'So what did you get? You said you needed our help to sift through them.'

'I do.' Ruth handed them each a pile of letters. 'These are just the men. If we put them into three piles – absolute no-nos, possibilities, and definites – it'll help us whittle down the applicants to a manageable number.'

'OK.' Her friends nodded, and began reading.

There was nothing but the rustle of paper and the occasional chink of glass for a while: and then Laura burst out laughing.

'What?' The others looked up.

'This one.' She waved the paper at them, still giggling. 'I think he's an ex-yuppie with a cash-flow problem. His hobbies are yachting, walking around the estate with the Labradors – he calls them "labs" – and drinking champagne.'

Ruth groaned. 'No. Absolutely no. He'll spend all evening talking to our clients about himself and his enormous credit card bills, and bore them silly!'

'What do you mean, *our* clients?' Laura picked up on the word immediately.

'Um.' Ruth coughed. 'I was going to ask you. Would you both like to be part of the agency? I mean, the lovers are going to need training.'

'You mean, you want *us* to train them?' Shelley asked, her green eyes surprised.

'Well . . . not the whole training program. Just the parts you like best,' Ruth said hastily.

Shelley's lips twitched. 'Technically, you're asking us to be unfaithful – making love to a man other than our husbands.'

Ruth sighed. 'Sorry. I didn't think. Look, just forget I asked, OK? I'll find someone else to help me out.'

'Hang on, you've got a point. You need to make sure that the lovers *are* trained, like you say,' Laura interrupted. 'And you need to be sure that you can trust the trainers to do their job properly. So it has to be someone you know well, or someone who has a stake in the agency.'

'Or both,' Ruth added.

'Are you up for it, then?' Shelley asked Laura, slightly surprised.

'In principle, yes. I'll talk it over with Nicholas. If he says he doesn't mind, then I'm in.' Laura's eyes were sparkling. 'Actually, I rather like the idea. Being in complete control, and telling men what to do!'

'Hang on, Laura – it's not going to be a thrashing frenzy every time they get something wrong. *Gentle* training works best, doesn't it, Shelley?' Ruth said, laughing.

'It does indeed.' Shelley pursed her lips. 'OK. If Carlo's happy about it, then I'm in.'

'Great.' Ruth topped up their glasses.

'Just out of interest, what did Aidan say?' Laura asked.

Ruth coughed. 'He's not wonderfully pleased about it, but he accepts that it's what I want to do. I expect he'll sulk a bit, when the business gets started, but I'll deal with that as and when it happens.' She picked up another letter. 'Right. Well, we might as well finish this pile first.'

Half an hour later, the letters had been sorted into three piles. The 'nos' was the largest pile, and there were only about ten in the 'definites'.

'So what now?' Laura asked.

'How about if we pick the best one, and ask him to be our pilot Interlover?' Ruth asked. 'If you decide what you want to do with him and then, when you've seen him, report back to me about whether you think he's suitable . . .'

Shelley burst out laughing.

'What's so funny?' Ruth asked.

'You sound like you're trying out a new printer or a designer – not a super-stud!' Shelley chuckled.

'It's not so different, you know,' Ruth said seriously. 'So we're down to ten. How about if we give each one marks out of ten, and the one with the highest total is our pilot?'

The others nodded. 'Fair enough.'

Ruth handed them a piece of paper and a pen, swiftly numbered the letters, and placed them on the table. 'Pick a letter, any letter,' she quipped.

Shelley and Laura smiled, and took a letter each. They read them through carefully, and thought for a while before giving them a mark. Eventually, all the letters had been marked. Ruth swiftly totted up the scores.

'It looks like it's number seven, by quite a margin,' she said.

'Mark Beasley.' She looked at the letter and photograph. 'A semi-professional musician. He's got a nice face.'

She passed the letter and photograph to Laura, who smiled. 'If I didn't know you better, Ruthie, I'd say that you cheated.'

'Hm?' Shelley's brow cleared as Laura passed her the photo. 'Oh, I see what you mean. Tall, blond, blue eyes, big nose.' She gave the photo back to Ruth. 'The typical Finn type, in fact!'

Ruth coughed. 'Now, now, girls. *You* gave him high marks as well.'

'True,' Shelley agreed. 'So what now?'

'I'll ring him to arrange an interview. If he's good enough, then I'll ask him to be our pilot.'

'It's quite appropriate, really,' Laura said. 'Interlover, Mark One.'

Shelley and Ruth groaned. 'That's terrible!'

'But true.' Laura raised her glass. 'To Mark Beasley. And may he live up to our expectations!'

The others echoed the toast.

Ruth put the photo back on the table. Mark was very attractive indeed – as Shelley had said, the sort of man that Ruth usually went for. She would have to remind herself that this was strictly business. And the interview would definitely have to be in a public place. Being on her own with him, in private, would be too dangerous.

Mark Beasley had a pleasant phone manner, she thought. He didn't answer with the gruff 'Yeah?' which was as good as 'Sod off, I'm too busy to talk to you just now'; or with the sycophantic 'How can I help?' which always set her teeth on edge.

'Hello, Mark. I'm Ruth Finn.'

There was a surprised silence, followed by a cautious, 'Ruth Finn?'

'You answered my ad. Box 69,' she replied.

'Oh.' His voice was suddenly full of interest.

'I wondered if we could meet for an informal interview. Say, Thursday lunchtime?'

'Thursday lunchtime. Do you mind if I just check my diary?' he asked politely. There was a rustle of paper, and then a pleased, 'Thursday lunchtime will be fine. What time, and where?'

'One o'clock.' She named a wine bar near her office. 'I'll carry a copy of the *Financial Times*,' she said.

He laughed. 'I'll carry a red rose. And no doubt you'll be sitting under the clock?'

She laughed back. 'If I can find one!'

'I'll look forward to meeting you then,' he said softly.

'Fine.' She replaced the receiver. He had a dangerous voice. Soft, smoky, and extremely sexy – and that was just on the phone! What he'd be like in the flesh . . . She shivered. Maybe this Interlover idea wasn't such a good one, after all. It could blow her relationship with Aidan wide apart. On the other hand, it could teach her to value what she had. She bit her lip. She'd just have to chance it.

Thursday lunchtime found Ruth in the wine bar, waiting for Mark. She glanced at her watch. She was ten minutes early. So much the better: she could see his arrival, too, and make sure that he wasn't just putting on an act for her sake. She ordered herself a mineral water from the bar and settled herself in a comfortable chair, where she had a good view of the door. She had the advantage of knowing what he looked like, whereas Mark Beasley had to rely on her description of herself.

Exactly one minute before he was due to meet her, Mark Beasley walked into the bar, carrying a red rose. Ruth's eyes widened. His photograph hadn't done him justice. He was tall, with blond, slightly curly hair and blue eyes – and the big nose that Laura had noticed was a feature of all Ruth's lovers.

He reminded her slightly of Aidan, bar the fact that Mark had slightly broader shoulders than her lover and his muscles were more toned. He had a sensual mouth, and his face was quite serious; Ruth found herself wondering exactly what he'd look like when he smiled.

Or when he came.

She blanked the thought out of her mind. She was the service provider, not the service user! Besides, it was bad for business to be involved with your staff, she reminded herself crossly. Even if she hadn't already been involved with Aidan, Mark Beasley was off limits.

He looked like a musician, she thought: although his hair was neat and clean rather than greasy grunge-style locks, the brown leather jacket and the tightness of his faded stone-washed jeans gave him away. Nice, she found herself thinking, and smiled wryly. That was precisely what she wanted her customers to think. So he'd passed the first test.

Mark glanced round the bar, and eventually saw a woman with dark straight hair held back with an Alice band, dark eyes, and the proverbial copy of the *Financial Times*. He walked over, and Ruth's eyes widened. He not only looked good, he moved well: fluid and graceful. She gave him another mental brownie point. If all her trainees turned out to be as good as Mark . . . Interlover would turn out to be the best career move she'd ever made.

'Excuse me, please. Would you be Ruth Finn?' he asked politely.

And a nice voice, she thought. Even nicer than he had sounded on the phone. The sort of voice that, saying the right words, could virtually bring you to orgasm. She smiled, standing up and offering him her hand. 'Yes. Mark Beasley, isn't it?'

He took her hand, but instead of shaking it, he kissed the inside of her wrist, keeping his eyes firmly fixed on hers. 'Hallo,' he said softly. He handed her the red rose. 'For you.'

Ruth swallowed hard. She hadn't been expecting him to be quite this practised! 'Thank you,' she said, sitting down again, aware that her voice was slightly shaky and her skin was tingling where his lips had touched it.

'Would you like another drink?' he asked, indicating her glass.

She shook her head. 'I'm fine, thanks.'

'I'll be back in a minute,' he said.

Nice bum, Ruth thought, watching him as he walked to the bar. Very nice bum. The way he moved was enough to make her shiver. If she hadn't been with Aidan, she would definitely have pounced on Mark Beasley. To make things worse, he was wearing Aramis – the same aftershave as Aidan, and a scent that always managed to make her feel horny. She squeezed her thighs together, trying to ignore the pulse beating hard in her quim. This is business, Finn, she told herself sternly. You're interviewing him for a job – so use your brain, not the more intimate parts of your anatomy!

Mark came back to join her, and sat down next to her. She noted approvingly that he, too, was drinking mineral water. Obviously he was taking this as a serious interview: he didn't look like the teetotal type. She could see him more as a real-ale drinker. Or maybe he preferred good champagne, letting it trickle over his lover's body and then licking it off... She swallowed hard. This was meant to be an interview, not a time for her to start fantasizing about a man who was off limits in any case.

'So, you're a musician?' she asked.

'Struggling,' he admitted. 'That's why I replied to your advert. It looked like a part-time job, so I could continue working in the band as well.'

She nodded. 'What do you play?'

'Instruments, you mean?' She nodded. 'Guitar, though I'm

also lead vocals. Our band plays soft rock, mainly.' He smiled. 'I'm a little too old for grunge.'

'Thirty-two.' She knew his CV virtually by heart.

He nodded. 'Plus I was intrigued by the "broad-minded" bit.'

Ruth smiled. 'And you'd like to know more about the job?'

He raised an eyebrow. 'Well, that's why I'm here.'

'I'm setting up a delivery agency,' she told him.

He frowned. 'You mean, a courier service?'

'Not quite. You'll deliver flowers or champagne and chocolates, and also conversation.'

'And?' He picked up on the glint in her eyes.

She smiled. 'An orgasm.'

He seemed completely unfazed, to her secret disappointment. 'And how often might this be?'

'It depends on customer demand. We'll be in pilot stage for a while.'

'So you want me to be the pilot.'

Ruth nodded. 'We had quite a few replies. There's a shortlist of ten.'

'So you're interviewing others as well?'

'Yes,' she lied, not wanting to give everything away. 'So how do you feel about the idea?'

'Delivering orgasms?' He took a sip of mineral water. 'Well, I'm not married, and I don't have a steady girlfriend at the moment, so it wouldn't cause any problems in my personal life.' He glanced at her left hand, and was pleased to find it bare. She wasn't married, then. She was very attractive; if he'd had to describe her, it would have been as a dark-haired and taller Marilyn Monroe, all lush curves. He liked the way she smiled, the fullness of her lower lip. He couldn't help wondering what she wore beneath her navy business suit and severe white shirt. A white stretch lace body, perhaps, and navy lace-topped hold-up stockings . . .

He shifted in his seat, uncomfortably aware that his cock was hardening at the thought of removing her clothes, and hoping that she hadn't noticed. Having an erection during an interview was hardly likely to get him the job. Though on the other hand, bearing in mind what sort of job was on offer – maybe it *would* help. He smiled wryly to himself. He'd been in a lot of difficult situations in the past – but none as bizarre as this. What made it even more bizarre was that he could see Ruth as a manager in a more conventional line of business. Why had she decided to set up this service?

'So you'd be quite happy to work for us, then?'

He nodded. 'Provided that standard protection was used, of course.'

'Of course.' Ruth was impressed that he had thought that far ahead.

He suddenly realized that she'd been using the plural. 'Who's "us"?'

'Me, plus a couple of friends.' She took a sip of mineral water.

'So what now?' he asked. 'The last interview I had, I had to do some tests.'

'Personality questionnaires and interest inventories?' Ruth pursed her lips. 'I don't think this job really calls for that – or numeracy and verbal reasoning tests.' She smiled. 'Mind you, if you want to talk to me about films or books or theatre or quantum physics, to prove your conversational skills . . .'

There was definitely a glint of interest in those beautiful dark eyes, Mark thought, and decided to risk it. 'How do you know that I'm going to perform up to your standards? Sexually, I mean?'

He was surprised by her answer. 'Training.' She grinned at the look on his face. 'You didn't think I was going to ask you for a quickie in the middle of a public place to prove yourself, did you?'

He flushed. 'Well. I wondered if you . . .'

'Wanted to try out the wares, or take a few vital measurements?' She smiled. 'I'm very flattered but, like I said, we have a training programme worked out for you. If you want the job, that is.'

'I'm surprised,' he said, 'that you didn't pick someone younger. Someone with more – well, stamina.'

Ruth shook her head. 'Twenty-year-olds might have a faster recovery rate, and be able to do more assignments per night, but that's not what Interlover's all about. Our clients will expect conversation and a lot of personal attention, not just a pretty face and "wham, bam, thank you, ma'am, gotta go to the next bird now, so see ya later, babe". Breaking in virgins has its place, I suppose—' she smiled '—but not in Interlover. We want men who know what to do, and where and when to do it.'

Mark was impressed by her frankness. 'Are your friends like you?'

She shook her head. 'Laura's blonde and stately, and Shelley's a redhead: either quiet or bubbly, depending on her mood and the sort of day she's had. Shelley teaches music, actually, so you've got a lot in common with her.'

'What about Laura?'

'She's a lawyer.'

'And you?' he asked, wondering if he dared to take her hand and start stroking her palm. Or maybe slip off one of his shoes and slide one foot between hers, caressing her ankle. The idea of laying one hand on her thigh and letting it drift slowly upwards under the hem of her skirt made him shiver with longing. 'What do you do?' he asked, having difficulty in controlling his voice.

'I'm setting up Interlover,' she replied crisply.

The frostiness of her tone made him decide that the time to make a move wasn't right now. 'Dare I ask what made you think of the idea?'

'Apart from being made redundant, as from three weeks' time—' no wonder she'd reacted so badly when he'd asked what she did, he thought, wincing inwardly '—I realized that there was a niche market out there. Career women without a partner, divorcees or people who've just split up with a long-term lover, and women whose husbands can't – or won't – fulfil their needs. Women who want good sex, delivered in the way they want it – not a quick and tacky bonk with some himbo or other. We're targeting professional women. Lawyers, accountants, teachers.' She shrugged. 'Hence the need for good conversation skills as well as your skill between the sheets.'

'And which of the three are you?' he asked softly.

She frowned. 'What do you mean?'

'A career woman without a partner, a woman who's split up with her husband or long-term lover, or a married woman whose husband won't indulge her?'

'None of them, actually.' She smiled wryly. 'Who's interviewing whom?'

'Point taken. The boss's private life is out of bounds,' he said quietly.

She nodded. 'Did you have any other questions about the job?'

'Apart from the obvious – payment – what about the training programme?'

'The pay depends on the job. There'll be a sliding scale, depending on what you're expected to do. We'll pay you per assignment. As for the training: you'll visit various different women, all of whom have a different "speciality". They'll train you up to their standards.'

Part of him was amused that she could be so matter-of-fact about it: the way she spoke about training, they could have been talking about computer programming or cookery, not sex. 'Will Laura and Shelley be among the trainers?' he asked softly.

She nodded.

'And you?'

She smiled. 'Now *that* would be telling.'

His glance slid over her. She really was lovely. Generous breasts, and a full lower lip which invited him to kiss her. Good legs. A curvy waist. Hair he'd like to bury his face in. I'd like to taste every inch of your skin, Ruth Finn, he thought, kiss you all over – and then some.

'I beg your pardon?'

Mark suddenly realized that he had spoken the last few words aloud. He flushed. 'I was trying to pay you a very clumsy compliment. No doubt whoever does the conversational training would give me a black mark for that.'

'Fishing?' She grinned. 'Well, I can tell you now – I'm not going to train you in the art of conversation. I don't think Shelley or Laura will, either, unless they think you need it.'

'Just the sex side.' He nodded. 'So when will I know if you want me to join you?'

She glanced at her watch. 'How about now?'

Was she asking him to take her to bed, or offering him the job? He wasn't sure, and decided to play safe. 'Pardon?'

She smiled. 'Would you like to be our first Interlover, Mark?'

He smiled back. 'Accepted, with pleasure.'

She held out her hand and he took it, sealing the contract in the conventional way. He would have liked to seal it in a much more unconventional way: but he knew that if he ever went to bed with Ruth Finn, it would be on her terms, and on her invitation. Pushing his luck right now wouldn't just lose him the job, it would lose him her respect as well.

'I'll send you a formal letter,' she said, 'together with a note of your training program. Plus your travel expenses, of course.'

'Travel?'

'We're London-based, but our clients will live in different

parts of the city,' she explained. 'So you'll need petrol money or Tube fares. I don't expect you to pay for your travel expenses. Well – good luck.' She stood up.

He stood up. 'Thank you, Ms Finn.'

'Call me Ruth.' She smiled at him. 'I think we'll be seeing each other soon.'

'I look forward to it,' he said huskily, wondering just what her 'speciality' was. A dozen erotic possibilities swept through his mind, each of them delightful.

He watched her leave the wine bar. Not married, not divorced, and not a career woman without a partner. Which meant what? If she was living with someone, Mark thought, he was a lucky bastard. And he was either completely crazy to let her run this Interlover project, or extremely sophisticated. Either way, Mark felt a twinge of jealousy. There had been a definite attraction between him and Ruth – he knew that it hadn't been his imagination – but she'd also more or less told him that she was off limits.

'One day, Ruth Finn, I'm going to make love to you,' he said softly. 'Maybe when I've completed my "training". And I'll give you pleasure that you won't forget.'

The strains of a Bach cello concerto – the adagio of the G minor – greeted Ruth as she opened the front door. She was surprised. Aidan wasn't usually home before her, and he hadn't mentioned taking any time off work. Had something happened at the office?

She sniffed. He was obviously in the kitchen, judging by the scents of garlic and lemon. She hung her coat on the bentwood coat stand, kicked her shoes off, and padded into the kitchen.

'What's all this in aid of?' she asked, sliding her arms round his waist.

'I just decided to cook dinner tonight,' he said, taking the pan off the heat and turning round to kiss her. 'Had a good day?'

'Mm. Ish.' She didn't want to bring up the subject of Mark Beasley. 'And you?'

'Fine. I managed to get away early.' His hands slid down to cup her buttocks. 'Mm. Ruthie, I suggest you get out of the kitchen, otherwise I'm not going to be able to keep my hands off you for long enough to cook dinner.'

She kissed the tip of his nose. 'Is that my cue to slip into something more comfortable?'

He groaned, pressing his pelvis against her so that she could feel the strength of his erection. 'Now look what you've done. Go and have a bath, or something. And lock the bathroom door!'

Ruth gave him a sultry pout, and sashayed over to the kitchen door. 'Sure you don't wanna join me, big boy?' she asked, in her best Mae West voice.

He grinned, suddenly feeling more secure than he'd felt all afternoon, knowing that she was interviewing the first of the Interlovers. 'Maybe after the candle-lit meal and the bottle of champagne . . .'

'Champagne?' She turned round, leaning against the door-jamb and staring at him, her head tipped slightly to one side. 'Aidan, seriously, what's all this in aid of?'

'Because today has a "y" in it,' he retorted. 'Off you go, or dinner will be ready before you are.'

She smiled, blew him a kiss, and left the room. Champagne. He was obviously feeling insecure, worrying about the Interlover project – which was crazy. He didn't need to worry. She'd already told him that. Maybe, she thought, running the bath, she needed to prove it to him.

As she lay in the hot foamy water, she grew thoughtful. She'd always known that she needed to handle the subject carefully where Aidan was concerned; she didn't want to hurt him. Particularly as she'd found Mark Beasley so attractive. At the same time, the opportunity of Interlover was too good to miss.

The problem would just have to resolve itself, she thought crossly, and hauled herself out of the bath again. When she'd finished drying herself, she padded into the bedroom. Aidan was obviously going to a lot of trouble over the meal; the least she could do was go to some trouble over her appearance.

She decided to dispense with underwear, and put on a midnight-blue bias-cut dress which she knew he liked, teaming it with a black chiffon wrap. She added the Armani perfume which he loved her wearing, and put her hair up into a sleek knot at the top of her head, leaving the odd tendril of hair to soften the severity of the style. She added a light touch of make-up, then glanced at the finished ensemble in the cheval mirror, and smiled. Just the effect she wanted.

Aidan whistled when he saw her. 'Wow. What's all this in aid of?'

'Because today has a "y" in it.' She echoed his earlier comment, adding a teasing grin.

'You look gorgeous.' He drew her closer, burying his face in her neck. 'And you smell gorgeous, too.'

He kissed the sensitive spot at the side of her neck, and Ruth felt her knees go weak. It never ceased to amaze her just how deeply Aidan could affect her; no matter how much time she spent with him, the attraction never palled.

'I'd like to take you to bed right now,' he murmured against her ear, 'but I don't want to spoil all my hard work.'

'Then the quicker you feed me, the better,' she said, equally softly.

He smiled, and kissed her lightly. 'If madam would like to come through to the dining room?' He ushered her through to the table, lit the candles, and poured her a glass of champagne.

'What's on the menu?' she asked.

'Garlic mushrooms, chicken with lemon and cream – and ice-cream, because I'm hopeless at puddings,' he said. 'Followed by coffee.'

'Sounds wonderful,' she said – revising her opinion to 'tastes wonderful', by the end of the meal.

Aidan carefully avoided the subject of Interlover until coffee. 'You were interviewing someone today, weren't you?'

'Mark Beasley,' she confirmed.

'How did it go?'

'OK. He's accepted the job.'

Aidan nodded, but said nothing.

Ruth reached across to take his hand. 'Do you want me to give up the idea of Interlover?'

He sighed. 'Yes. I hate the idea of you putting all these men through their sexual paces. Though if you give it up, you'll resent me for it. Either way, we're going to end up rowing.' He shrugged. 'So it looks like I'll just have to put up with it, and shut up, doesn't it?' His eyes met hers. 'Did you sleep with him, Ruth?'

She shook her head. 'It was an *interview*, Aidan, in a wine bar. Of course I didn't sleep with him! Though it'll probably be on his training program, at some point.'

Aidan, realizing from the slightly guilty look on her face that she fancied Mark Beasley, glowered.

'Laura and Shelley are going to be trainers on the programme, as well,' she told him quietly. 'Nicholas and Carlo know about it, and they accept that it's not the same as having an affair.'

'Isn't it?' Aidan's voice cracked. 'You obviously fancy him.'

'In exactly the same way that I fancy Kenneth Branagh, Charlie Sheen and Jon Bon Jovi. Besides, if I don't find the guy attractive, how can I expect my clients to find him attractive?'

Aidan, focusing on the first half of her statement, scowled.

'Apart from the fact that you're not likely to meet *them*, and you're going to see *him* regularly.'

She sighed. 'This is business, Aidan. I'm not intending to string him along until I'm sure of his commitment, and then dump you for him. Or for any of the others, once the business gets going.'

'No?'

'No.' She drew her fingertips across his palm. 'If you're that worried about it, Aidan, then marry me.'

His eyes widened. 'Am I hearing things, or did you just propose to me?'

'I asked you to marry me,' she confirmed.

'What if I say no?'

'Then—' her lips curved '—I'll seduce you into it.'

'Is that a promise?'

She nodded.

He smiled back. 'In that case, my answer's no.'

'I see.' She stood up, drawing him up with her, and blew the candle out before leading him through to the sitting room. She paused for a moment by the CD player, finally selecting some Bach, then led him over to the silk Turkish rug by the fire.

Without another word, she began to undress him, removing first his black cotton poloneck sweater, and then his dark trousers. He kicked his shoes off, allowing her to remove his socks and underpants.

She curled her fingers round his already erect cock. 'Mm. So do *you* want to marry me?' she addressed the rigid muscle.

Aidan made it nod at her; she grinned. 'Then let's persuade the rest of you, hm?' Ruth stepped back and let the chiffon wrap fall to the floor. She unzipped her dress, letting the garment go the same way. Aidan took a sharp intake of breath as he realized that she was completely naked beneath, apart from her stockings. Her breasts were full, and her nipples erect; he itched to touch her, but forced himself to refrain. She was supposed to be seducing him, after all.

She lifted her hands to her hair, loosening the knot and then shaking her head so that her hair fell about her shoulders, then turned round, bending over to roll her stockings down. She made sure that he could see her moist puffy labia as she did so, then wiggled her bottom slightly, and stood up again.

She walked back towards him, sliding her arms round his neck and tangling her fingers in his hair. She drew his face down to hers and kissed him hard, nipping at his lower lip with her teeth until he opened his mouth, then sliding her tongue against his. She pushed one leg between his; he could feel the moist heat of her quim against his skin, and shivered, remembering the beautiful sight he'd been treated to only moments before.

Gently, she drew him down onto the rug, straddling his thighs and supporting her weight on her hands so that the hard tips of her breasts grazed his chest. The ends of her hair brushed against his face, and her eyes were dark and glowing.

'So are you going to marry me, Aidan Shaw?' she asked huskily.

He shook his head. 'Nope.'

She lowered her face, kissing him again, and moved slightly so that her satiny cleft was positioned just over his cock. 'Are you sure about that?'

'Sure,' he breathed, desperately wanting to push up and into her wet velvety sex-flesh. But his need for her to make all the running was stronger. Just.

She smiled, and lifted herself slightly, positioning his cock at her entrance and then pushing down hard. Aidan gasped as her flesh enclosed his cock; she sat up straighter, changing the angle of his penetration to give them both the most pleasure, and began to lift and lower herself

Aidan reached up to cup her breasts, caressing the soft

undersides and rolling her nipples between thumb and forefinger. Unable to resist their lure, he lifted his upper body so that he could nuzzle the deep vee of her cleavage, then, taking her nipples into his mouth in turn, sucked hard on the puckered rosy flesh.

Ruth began to move in small circles, using her internal muscles to the full; he muttered hoarsely against her skin, and she felt his teeth grazing her sensitive flesh. She slid her hands into his hair, the soft pads of her fingertips digging into his scalp.

He drew her back down with him to the floor, then rolled over so that he was on top of her, careful not to let his weight rest on her. Her legs came up automatically to lock round his waist, letting him penetrate her more deeply. He thrust hard, and she felt bubbles of pleasure roll through her veins, warmth rising from the soles of her feet up to her quim.

'Marry me, Aidan,' she urged huskily as she came, her internal muscles flexing hard around his cock.

Aidan rubbed his nose against hers. 'Yes.'

She couldn't help pressing home the small victory. 'What about Interlover?'

He rested his cheek against her hair. 'As long as I come before any of the men you take on, that's all that matters.'

'Even if I train them?'

He sighed. 'Even if you train them. Just call out my name when you come, OK?'

She smiled. 'OK.' She stroked his hair. 'I do love you. Otherwise I wouldn't have asked you to marry me, would I?'

'True.' He lifted his head again, looking into her eyes. 'You won't regret it, Ruthie. I promise.'

'I know.' She drew her nails down his back as she felt his cock begin to grow firm again inside her. 'Now, where were we?'

THREE

Mark locked the door of his slightly battered Beetle and glanced at the piece of paper in his hand, to check the address. He was in the right street, at least. He walked down the road, looking at the numbers on the houses, and eventually found number seventeen.

It was a tall Georgian building – a typical Hampstead residence, with elaborate wrought-iron holders for window boxes, and perfectly clipped bay trees in terracotta pots acting as miniature porticoes. The door was painted a glossy navy blue, with a polished brass knocker and letter box, and the windows were long and graceful, in pristine white.

He opened the wrought-iron gate and smiled to himself. There wasn't a weed in sight, and the borders and tubs were crammed with white narcissi and blue parrot tulips. These people were either keen gardeners, or were rich enough to employ someone to tidy the grounds for them. The tulips were unusual enough to make it the former; but as they lived in Hampstead, he had a feeling that it was more likely to be the latter. Laura was a solicitor, so Ruth had said, and her husband was a barrister.

There was a wrought-iron bell pull – not a plastic buzzer such as most houses he knew had. He pulled it gently, and heard a bell clang. Probably the original bell of the house, he thought. No doubt, inside, all the original features had been lovingly restored – everything from the coving to the picture rail.

A few moments later, a tall and statuesque blonde woman, dressed in a calf-length pleated skirt and a matching silk shirt, opened the door.

'Mrs Rivers?' he asked.

Laura smiled. 'Yes.'

'I'm Mark Beasley. I hope I'm not too early for my appointment?'

She glanced at her watch. He was five minutes earlier than she'd expected. Still, better that he was early than keeping her waiting. In common with Ruth, she hated waiting for things. 'No, that's fine. Do come in.'

'Thanks.' He followed her into the hall. As he'd expected, the house was furnished in period style – he guessed that the tables and cabinets were the real thing, rather than clever reproductions – yet, although the place was immaculate, it also had a sense of being lived in. It was a home, not a showpiece.

'Would you like a coffee, or would you prefer a glass of wine?'

'I'm driving, so it had better be coffee, please, Mrs Rivers.'

'Laura,' she corrected.

He smiled. 'By the way – these are for you.' He handed her the carefully wrapped flowers.

Her eyes widened with delight as she unwrapped the flowers. 'Irises – my favourites. Thank you.' She sniffed them. 'That's very sweet of you.'

'Pleasure,' he said diffidently. There was something about Laura that made him feel a little shy; on the other hand, he found her very attractive. He itched to touch her. But he knew that it would be best to leave her to set the pace.

'I'll just put them in water, and make us some coffee. Come into the kitchen and talk to me.'

He did as she asked. As he had half expected, there was an Aga in the corner of the kitchen, finished in blue; the floor was tiled in white ceramic, with tiny blue diamonds where the corners of the tiles met. The units were gleaming white, with pale grey worktops, and expensive-looking stainless-steel pans hung from a butcher's rack above the sink. Yet the kitchen wasn't fitted out just for style's sake: the terracotta pots of herbs on the windowsill looked as though they were used.

Laura switched on the kettle, then took a white vase, filling it with water and arranging the irises in it. She shook coffee into the cafétière and looked at Mark, her head tipped to one side. 'Milk and sugar?'

'Neither, thanks.'

She grinned. 'Good. A man after my own heart — one who doesn't like his caffeine adulterated.'

'Mm.' He grinned back, and handed her a small and beautifully wrapped box. 'Except with these.'

She opened them, and smiled. 'Belgian white chocolate truffles. Wow. Either Ruth primed you, or you have excellent taste.'

'A bit of both,' he admitted. 'They're my favourites, too.'

'Right.' Laura made the coffee and handed him one of the mugs, tucking the chocolates under her arm and picking up the vase of flowers. 'Shall we go and sit down?'

'Fine.' He followed her through to the sitting room, and sat on one end of the sofa.

Laura put the vase on the mantelpiece and the chocolates on the coffee table, then sat down next to him. 'So. Here we are, then.'

'Mm.' He smiled at her. 'I must say — this isn't a situation I've been in before. I don't know whether I'm supposed to treat this as an initiative test, or let you set the pace.'

'As your trainer, you mean?' Laura sipped her coffee. 'A bit of both, I suppose. Well, before we start, I'd like to know a little more about you. And I suppose you really ought to know more about me, too.'

'Yeah.' Mark smiled wryly. 'Which gives me nil out of ten, so far, in the chatting-up stakes.'

Laura laughed. 'I'm not marking you – yet.' She tipped her head on one side. 'So, you're a musician?'

'Yes. Guitar and vocals.' He shrugged. 'The band plays mainly soft rock, with a bit of blues and a ballad or two. I've been with the same band for about three years.' He grinned. 'I can't ever see us being teeny-bop idols – we're about ten years too old! – but the living's OK.'

'As long as you supplement it a little?'

He nodded. 'Mainly through giving private music lessons; though I've done bar work in the past, and the odd stint selling hamburgers. Now the band's established on the pubs-and-clubs circuit, it'll be easier. Even so, I need to make sure I cover my part of the rent. That's why I answered Ruth's ad.'

'Right.' She paused. 'Would it make you feel less awkward if we put some music on?'

He nodded. 'Yes, I think so.'

'Then help yourself.' She indicated the rack of CDs and the small system in the corner. Mark looked quickly through the discs, then turned to her. 'Would you prefer classical or rock?' he asked politely.

'Either. Well, rock, really.' She grinned. 'Nicholas is the classical freak. He drives me mad, playing opera all the time. I like the odd aria, but I really don't like screechy divas. With the exception of Maria Callas, I suppose.'

'I know what you mean,' Mark said feelingly. 'I like light classics, but nothing too heavy. Just the sort of stuff they use in films, really.' He turned back to the discs, and chose a Paul Rodgers compilation. 'Is this OK?' he asked, holding it up.

Laura nodded. 'That'd be lovely.' She grinned. 'I never let Ruthie have free run of my CDs. She always picks chamber music. She, Aidan and Nicholas sit there discussing the phrasing of the cellists and being ultra-pretentious. They're even worse if Shelley's over as well; in the end, Carlo and I head for the kitchen and play very loud rock music while we're making coffee, to get our own back. I sing, and he plays air guitar.'

'Right.' He felt a small stab of jealousy as he slid the CD into the holder. From the way Laura spoke about him, Aidan was obviously Ruth's man – and on very good terms with Ruth's friends. 'Did you just call her "Ruthie"?' he asked.

'Mm.' Laura gave him a serious look. 'But that's because I've known her for years and years, since we were at university together. I can get away with it – most people can't. If you want to see Ruth in glacier mode, just try soft-soaping her. She has an inbuilt bullshit detector.'

'Warning heeded,' Mark said, pressing the 'play' button and coming back to sit beside her on the sofa. 'So how did you get involved in all this?'

'Interlover?' Laura sighed. 'Ruth's one of my best friends. I assume you know why she's setting it up?'

He nodded. 'More or less. She said that she'd been made redundant, and she'd had the idea of filling a gap in the market.'

'Exactly.' Laura spread her hands. 'Well, she asked Shelley and me to help on the training side. We're her oldest friends, so we couldn't let her down.'

Mark frowned. 'But your husband – doesn't he mind you doing this?'

Laura grinned. 'Nicholas is extremely broad-minded. He did say something about wanting to hide in the wardrobe . . .'

Mark, realizing that he was being teased, smiled back at her. 'Ruth described you as stately.'

'That's because I'm taller than she is, by all of half an inch.' Laura's lips twitched. 'But don't confuse "stately" with "staid", will you?'

He laughed. 'I don't think you're the staid and pompous type, somehow.'

'Thank you.' She opened the box of chocolates, offering them to Mark.

'Cheers.' He took one.

Laura ate a chocolate, too, and smiled at him. 'So. What else is there to know about Mark Beasley?'

'Not a lot. I share a house in Walthamstow with two of the others from the band, my sister, and a couple of her friends. I have half-shares in a car – actually, it lowers the tone of your street admirably.'

'Oh?' She tipped her head on one side, intrigued.

He grinned. 'It's an elderly orange Beetle – orange, so you can't see the rust.'

'And sounds like a pneumatic drill?' she guessed, laughing.

'Something like that.' He smiled. 'My parents are both alive, living in Sussex; I have one older brother, Adam, who's very sensible and works in a bank, and a younger sister, Louise, who's an actress and owns the other half of Roach—'

'Roach?' Laura asked.

'The car. Roach, as in cockroach, as in beetle.' He grinned. 'Could have been worse. Though Lou's a bad influence on me.'

Laura was intrigued. 'How do you mean, a bad influence?'

'I used to work in an office. She was the one who persuaded me to give up the day job and spend more time on the band. Lou believes in following your heart.'

Laura nodded. 'She has a point. You spend nearly half your waking hours working – so why do a job you hate?'

'As my parents see it, to bring in enough money for the rent.' Mark shrugged. 'But, like I said, things are picking up a bit, with the band.' He paused. 'And that's really about it. I assume you already know my interests and whatever from my application letter.'

Laura nodded. 'We all liked the sound of you.'

Mark just about stopped himself from saying, *including Ruth*? 'Thanks,' he said. 'So, what about you? All I know is that you were at college with Ruth, you're married to a broadminded opera fiend called Nicholas, and you're both lawyers. Oh, and that you like irises, white chocolate and soft rock.'

'I'm thirty, an only child, and I'm ridiculously happy in my job.' Laura crossed her legs. 'I have a mad streak – that's why I let Ruth talk me into helping her with the Interlover project. I like reading and watching old films, and I can't sing or play an instrument or paint. Unfortunately, I'm not the creative type.' She sighed. 'Shelley's a music teacher, and she plays the piano, flute and violin. Ruth writes – at least, she used to. Mainly poetry and very literary short stories, though she says they were never up to publication standard. We also have mutual friends who paint; so I'm the odd one out.' She shrugged. 'Though I make much better coffee than either of them.'

He smiled back at her. 'I'll bear that in mind.' He took her hand, rubbing his thumb against her palm. 'I really ought to quote some poetry at you now. Byron, or something seductive.'

'Actually, Donne's the most erotic poet. According to Ruth, that is. She has a real passion for him, and she can be incredibly boring on the subject. Don't ever get her talking about seventeenth-century poetry!'

Mark made a mental note to pay a visit to Charing Cross Road and hunt down some Donne, to surprise Ruth. 'Sadly, I don't know any Donne. And most of the songs I know aren't really that romantic. Not if they're spoken, anyway.' He grinned. 'I suppose I could always sing to you . . .'

Laura grinned back. 'And how did you spend your day today, dear? Well, I had that young man round from Interlover. He sang to me,' she said, in a mock-quavering voice.

'And is that all he did?' Mark asked.

'I do hope not,' Laura said, reverting to her own voice, 'or Ruth will have my guts for garters.'

'She doesn't seem the aggressive type.'

'She's not. It's a figure of speech,' Laura said. 'Ruthie's probably one of the nicest people I know. She's as stubborn as a mule, when she gets an idea into her head – but she's nice with it, so you can't hold it against her, even if you don't agree with her. That's probably why she's such a good negotiator. She persuades the other person that what she wants is actually their idea, or something like that.' She sighed. 'Actually, I'm surprised that she hasn't been snapped up, since the demise of Romulus Books. She's got a good reputation in the business.' She took another chocolate. 'I think she just wants a break from the rat race for a bit. Hence Interlover.'

'Right.' Mark's thumb stroked her wrist. 'And that's why she talked you and Shelley into helping out.'

'Mm.'

'So how does this training programme work?' he asked, moving a little closer.

'You give me a demonstration of what you know. Then I'll tell you how you could make it even better.'

'I see,' he said.

'That's if you need to be improved, of course,' Laura said with a grin. 'You might be perfect already.'

He laughed. 'Now that's very flattering of you. And today's topic is . . . ?' He tipped his head on one side, waiting for her answer.

She smiled. 'Stroking and kissing.'

'Right.' He glanced at the curtains. 'Do you think we should draw these? Or go into another room?'

Laura shook her head. 'Apart from the fact that it's the middle of the afternoon, and this is a very quiet road, you definitely can't see through the curtains.'

How did she know that? Mark wondered. Unless she and Nicholas had ended up making love in front of the fire, one Sunday afternoon, or something like that. 'In that case . . .' He leaned over, sliding one hand beneath her hair, and drew her face over to his. He touched his lips to hers, very gently, and rubbed his nose against hers. Laura closed her eyes, tipping her head back slightly, and he kissed her harder, nibbling at her bottom lip until she opened her mouth, then sliding his tongue against hers.

He eased one hand between their bodies, slowly undoing the buttons of her shirt while he continued to kiss her. Tugging gently at the material, he managed to pull it free of the waistband of her skirt, then tossed it to one side.

Laura shivered. 'OK?' he asked softly.

'Mm.'

'You're not cold?'

She shook her head.

'Good.' He kissed her lightly on the lips, then began a trail of kisses down her throat, pushing her back against the sofa. He eased one hand under the white lace of her bra and pushed the material downwards, releasing one breast and stroking its soft underside. Laura shivered, and Mark quickly released her other breast.

Her nipples were erect, the areolae dark and puckering with her arousal; Mark smiled, cupping her breasts and rubbing the nipple between thumb and forefinger. Laura gasped, and he bent his head, burying his face in her cleavage and breathing in her scent for a moment. Then he took one nipple into his mouth, sucking gently.

Laura thrust her fingers into Mark's hair, the pads of her fingertips digging into his skin and urging him on. He drew harder on her nipple, using his teeth just enough to make her cry out in pleasure, while he continued to massage its twin between his thumb and forefinger. He slid to the floor, deftly manoeuvring her so that she lay prone on the sofa, then lifted her hips gently so that he could remove her skirt and petticoat. She was wearing lacy-topped hold-up stockings; he smiled, and stroked the smooth skin above the lacy welts.

She shivered.

'Is that how you like it?' he murmured softly against her ear.

'Yes. Nice and gentle. But firm, at the same time.'

'With pleasure. What would you like me to do next?' His fingers drifted along the gusset of her knickers; he could feel the heat of her quim through the thin material and he wanted to touch her, feel the warm moist flesh sliding against his fingertips. 'After all, you're my teacher.'

'Use your imagination,' Laura groaned.

Mark smiled. The impeccably dressed lawyer who'd met him at the door was lying on the sofa, nearly naked. The little that she was wearing was pushed lewdly awry; her hair was mussed, and her lips were reddened and swollen with arousal. A successful assignment, so far, he thought: all he had to do was persuade her to talk to him, tell him exactly what she wanted. 'I'm afraid, Laura, that my imagination's completely deserted me.'

'You're supposed to be kissing and stroking me,' she reminded him.

He hid a grin. Her voice was cracking slightly; it was an effort for her to stay in control. When she came, he thought, it would be explosive. 'Where, precisely, would you like me to stroke you and kiss you?'

She twisted her head to look at him. 'Mark. Don't tease me.'

'How about here?' He stroked her thighs. 'Or here?' He hooked aside the gusset of her knickers, and trailed his finger along her quim, parting her labia. 'Or even here . . .' He slid one finger deep inside her, and rested his thumb on her clitoris, massaging it lightly.

Laura's hips bucked. 'Oh, my God!' she muttered.

Mark withdrew his hand, cupping her chin gently with his other hand and making her look at him. Then he slid his finger into his mouth, tasting her arousal. 'Mm. Honey and vanilla,' he proclaimed. 'A good Chardonnay, I'd say.'

Laura chuckled. 'You wicked tease,' she informed him,

her grey eyes sparkling with a mixture of arousal and good humour.

'So you'd prefer me to stroke you some more?' He brushed her erect nipples with his fingertips, making her arch her back and push against him. 'Or kiss you here?' He dipped his head, taking one nipple into his mouth again. 'Or kiss you here?' He began a trail of kisses southwards, over her abdomen.

She groaned as he eased her knickers down towards her ankles and blew on her quim. 'We're not supposed to be doing this, Mark – just kissing and stroking. You're supposed to be doing *that*—' as he ran his tongue experimentally over her labia '—with Shelley.'

He sat back on his haunches, his eyes crinkling at the corners. 'I won't tell, if you don't.'

'It's not fair, Mark. It's cheating Ruth.'

'OK. We'll play it your way,' he said amenably, licking the soft skin of her inner thighs.

She couldn't help thrusting her pelvis towards him, widening the gap between her thighs.

'I wish I could paint,' Mark said. 'I'd like to paint you as you are now, your head thrown back and your mouth open in abandonment, your hair mussed and your nipples sharp, and your underwear in gloriously lewd disarray. I'd like to paint you with your eyes open, watching yourself in the mirror, with your hand working hard between your legs. I'd like to watch you as you come, your teeth bared and your quim turning liquid and the perfume of your arousal filling the room.'

Laura shivered. 'My God. I can imagine it, too,' she said, her voice growing husky.

'Do you have any idea how good you look?' he asked. 'I wonder what your clients would think, if they could see you now? Or your colleagues, your staff?'

'They'd probably be shocked,' Laura admitted.

'And Nicholas?'

'If he were sitting where you're sitting,' Laura said, 'he wouldn't be talking to me.'

'What would he be doing?'

'Using his mouth on me, for starters.'

'You just told me not to,' Mark reminded her. 'So what would you like me to do?'

'Touch me,' Laura said. 'Stroke me.'

'Make you come?' he offered.

She nodded.

'Then that,' he said softly, 'is exactly what I'll do.' He leaned over to kiss her again, sliding his hand back between her thighs and rubbing the soft skin. She slid her arms round his neck, tangling her fingers in his hair, and pushed her pelvis up towards him.

Mark began to rub the hard base of his thumb against her quim, a slow rhythmic stroking that made her quiver and push harder against him. He broke the kiss and licked his way down the side of her neck, making her shiver.

'Oh, God, yes,' she moaned softly, as he nuzzled her breasts, taking one rosy tip into his mouth and sucking gently. She moaned again as he eased one finger inside her, dabbling it in her juices, then brought his finger up to anoint her other nipple. She shivered uncontrollably as he slid his finger back inside her, adding a second and a third, and began to suckle the nipple he'd just anointed with her musky juices.

She was beautiful, Mark thought. So very responsive. But she wasn't Ruth. Had she been Ruth . . . He began to pump his fingers into her, rubbing her clitoris with his thumb at the same time. Had it been Ruth under him, he would have driven them both to the edge, maybe holding back to make her want him more, then drowned his senses in the way she felt and tasted . . .

Laura cried out as she felt the beginnings of her orgasm, a slow rolling heat through her veins that gathered momentum as it travelled up from the soles of her feet, then exploded gloriously in her solar plexus. Mark stilled his hand, liking the feel of her quim contracting hard round his fingers, and shifted position slightly so that he could kiss her.

Her eyes were closed, and he could see a tear glistening on her lashes; he touched the tip of his tongue to the bead of moisture. 'Laura. Are you all right, sweetheart?' he asked softly.

She opened her eyes. 'Mm,' she said, not trusting herself to speak.

Gently, he raised his hand and stroked her face. 'Are you sure?'

'Yes.'

She sat up, and he put his arms round her, holding her close. 'Nicholas is a very lucky man,' he said softly. 'You're lovely.'

'Thank you.'

He pulled back so that he could look her in the eyes. 'I mean it, Laura. You're very lovely. So responsive, so sweet. Making love with you would be a privilege, as well as a pleasure.'

She flushed, slightly embarrassed, and he grinned. 'Don't go shy on me, now. Not after what we've just done!'

She couldn't help smiling back. 'Mm, you do have a point.'

He stroked her hair. 'Would you like me to run you a bath, and wash your back?'

She shook her head. 'No, I'll be fine.'

'Would you like me to go?' He rubbed his nose against hers. 'What I'd really like to do is to be grossly macho and pick you up, carry you upstairs, and make love to you properly for the rest of the afternoon.'

'Apart from the fact that you'd give yourself a hernia, hauling me up the stairs . . .' Her voice trailed off.

He nodded, understanding immediately. 'I get the picture. This is as far as you'll go, right?'

'Mm.' She kissed him lingeringly. 'Not because you're unattractive – I think you're very attractive. But I made a promise – to Nicholas, as well as to Ruth.'

'I thought as much.' He smiled at her. 'I'll leave you now, then.'

She flushed. 'I suppose I ought to—'

'Offer to return the compliment?' he finished. 'No. That's not really the point of Interlover, is it?'

Her flush deepened. 'Put like that, it makes it sound so – so . . .' She sighed. 'Selfish, I suppose.'

'And why shouldn't you be selfish, once in a while?' He kissed her cheek. 'Maybe I'll take you up on your offer, one day. If our paths cross again.'

'Yes.'

'It was – er – nice, meeting you.'

She laughed, her equanimity returning. 'Likewise. Well, good luck with the rest of your training programme.'

He tipped his head on one side. 'Do I get my marks now, or later?'

'That's down to Ruthie, I'm afraid.'

'Cruel woman,' he teased, kissing the tip of her nose. 'I'll see myself out, then. Take care.'

'You, too.'

When he left, Laura lay back against the sofa, closing her eyes. She hadn't expected it to be quite like this. Mark Beasley was – to say the least – attractive. And he knew all that there was to know about stroking and kissing. No way could she have taught him anything. She smiled wryly. She almost envied Shelley the next part of the programme. And as for the part that Ruth would eventually play . . .

She sighed, stood up, and headed upstairs to run herself a long, sybaritic bath.

Ruth smiled as she recognized her friend's voice. 'Hello, Laura. How did it go?'

'OK. Do you want to come over for coffee tonight, and talk about it?'

'I could do, yes. Hang on a minute.' She put her hand over the mouthpiece, and called out to Aidan. 'Do you mind if I go over to Laura's tonight, for a girly chat?'

'I'll give you a lift, if you like – I'm playing squash, so I'll prop the bar up for a bit and pick you up later.'

'Thanks.' She turned back to the phone. 'Somewhere between seven and seven-thirty all right with you?'

'Fine.'

'Do you want me to call Shelley?'

Laura laughed. 'Already done, sweetheart. She'll be here at seven.'

'See you later, then.' Ruth smiled. 'And I want to know *everything* . . .'

At twenty past seven, Ruth rang Laura's doorbell. Laura opened the door and greeted Ruth with a hug. 'Hi. All right?'

'Fine.' She handed Laura a bottle. 'This is for you.'

Laura unwrapped the blue tissue paper. 'Mm. Penfolds. Aidan's so civilized.'

'And how do you know it was his choice?' Ruth asked, laughing.

'Because he told Nicholas about it, and we've got a case in the cellar,' was the immediate retort.

Ruth hung her coat over the banister. 'Where is he tonight, then?'

'Working late.' Laura wrinkled her nose. 'Which makes me feel even more guilty for lolling around here all day.'

'Oh, come on, Laura. You've put in enough hours lately to deserve having a whole week off – let alone one measly day.' Ruth followed Laura into the sitting room; Shelley stood up, and hugged her. 'Hi. How are you?'

'Fine, thanks. And you?'

'Mm. Just dying to hear what Laura has to tell us!'

'Snap.' Ruth sat down beside her friend, and accepted

the glass of wine from Laura with a smile.

'Help yourself to nibbles,' Laura directed them both.

Ruth took a handful of honey-roast cashews. 'Mm. My favourites.' She gave Laura a sidelong glance. 'So, have I missed anything?'

'No. I wanted the details when I arrived, but she's been keeping me waiting until you turned up,' Shelley informed her.

'Right.' Ruth's eyes danced. 'So, you said that Mark was OK. Was he really just "OK", or was it an understatement?'

'Well . . .' Laura spread her hands. 'What do you think?'

'Musicians usually have sensitive hands,' Shelley said. 'So I'd guess that he was pretty good.'

'He was. And it was a nice touch, the fact that he turned up with flowers and chocolates. My favourites,' Laura confirmed.

'Good.' Ruth sipped her wine. 'I liked him, when I met him. He seemed a genuinely nice guy.'

'He is,' Laura said. 'A bit shy, at first – but I think anyone would be, in the circumstances.'

'Maybe.' Ruth bit her lip. 'The thing is, we need him to be confident, but not cocky.'

Shelley coughed. 'Would you care to rephrase that? I thought the whole idea behind Interlover was to deliver an orgasm!'

Ruth grinned. 'You know what I mean. Confident, but not arrogant.'

'Don't forget, he was here to be "trained",' Laura said. 'Which makes it more awkward than if he was here on a proper assignment.' She grinned. 'Like you say, he's a nice guy. Would you believe, he calls his car "Roach"?'

'Roach?' Ruth was mystified.

'Because it's a rusty orange Beetle,' Laura supplied, laughing. 'He has half-shares in it with his kid sister, who's an actress.'

'You certainly found out a lot about him,' Shelley said.

Laura shrugged. 'Well, I could hardly say to him, "Just shut up and do what you're here for", could I?'

Ruth nodded. 'Precisely. Our target market isn't that sort.'

Shelley's lips twitched. 'We know his conversational skills are up to scratch, then. What about the training? How did it go?'

'To be honest,' Laura said, 'I don't think that I could have taught him anything he didn't already know.'

Shelley groaned. 'You know exactly what I meant. Tell us what happened.'

'Voyeuse,' Laura teased.

'Seriously, Ruth needs to know, because she's masterminding the project. And I need to know, to prepare myself for the next stage,' Shelley reminded her.

'OK, OK. He arrived with flowers and chocolates. I made him a coffee, we chatted for a bit, and then . . .' Unconsciously, she moistened her lower lip with her tongue. 'Then he kissed me. He started undressing me and stroking me. Before I knew it, I was lying on the sofa in just my underwear – and that was all over the place – with his hand between my legs. He kissed me nearly all over, and . . .' She sighed. 'God, when I came.' She swallowed. 'It was fantastic. And he was nice, afterwards, holding me and offering to run me a bath.'

'And did he?' Ruth asked.

Laura shook her head. 'He was also sensitive enough to know that I wanted to be on my own. And he let me choose what I wanted him to do.'

Ruth smiled. 'Good. It sounds like we picked the perfect man, then. Marks out of ten?'

'Ruth.' Laura winced. 'That makes it sound so tacky. Do I have to?'

Ruth produced a pen and a sheet of paper, with a neat matrix on it, and passed them over to her. 'Marks out of ten, for kissing and stroking. Remember, I need to know where his weak areas are. I'll ask everyone the same thing.'

'Nine and a half,' Laura said, writing on the sheet and passing it back to Ruth.

Shelley grinned. 'Is that so he can come back again to earn the other half, by any chance?'

Laura laughed. 'That, I'm not telling!'

'Right,' Ruth said wryly, returning the sheet of paper to her handbag and picking up her glass.

Shelley frowned. 'Ruthie – is it my imagination, or is there something on your left hand?'

'Hm?' Ruth glanced down at her hand. 'Oh, that.'

'What?' Laura came to sit on the arm of the sofa, and took Ruth's left hand. 'Bloody hell. Either I'm hallucinating, or that's an engagement ring. What do you think, Shelley?'

'Same as you. We're hallucinating,' Shelley replied promptly. 'Either that, or Ruth's finally come to her senses.'

'Ha, ha.' Ruth rolled her eyes. 'Yes, it's what you think it is.'

'But – when?'

'Last week.' She sighed. 'After I got back from interviewing Mark. Aidan was a bit twitchy, to say the least, so I thought I'd better reassure him.'

'You mean, you proposed to him?' Laura's eyes widened.

'Yes.' Ruth grinned. 'Well, you didn't think I'd do it the conventional way, did you?'

'Well – no.' Shelley hugged her. 'I don't know what to say. I'm so pleased for you. And it's about bloody time, too.'

'Hear, hear,' Laura said. 'Well, I think this calls for something a bit better than Chardonnay.'

Ruth groaned. 'I just *knew* that you two would go over the top about it. Look, it's no big deal.'

'Oh, so you get engaged every day?' Laura asked. 'Don't tell me. You do it twice on Sundays. And you alternate Kenneth Branagh with Jon Bon Jovi and Keanu Reeves. Sometimes it's all three of them together...'

Ruth laughed. 'Oh, Laura! Don't be ridiculous. You know exactly what I mean.'

'Yeah. Me, too.' Shelley looked at her. 'So does this mean that you've changed your mind about Interlover?'

Ruth shook her head. 'No way. I'm still going ahead with it. And you're next on the list, remember.'

'Right.' Shelley took a sip of wine. 'So. What are you planning next?'

'I did tell you. Can't you remember?'

'Er – no.' Shelley flushed. 'I remember having to persuade Carlo that it was OK, but then I forgot what you asked me to do.'

Ruth grinned. 'Well, I seem to recall one evening when you got very drunk. We'd had a dinner party, and you announced in the middle of the pudding that you liked a man with a good tongue.'

Shelley's flush deepened. 'Oh, Christ. Yes, I remember.'

'Luckily it was before Carlo's time,' Laura said drily. 'Otherwise I think he might have dragged you off to the bathroom or something, for a quick demo!'

'So when does it all happen?'

'When are you free?'

Shelley thought about it. 'Wednesday afternoon.'

'That's it, then. Your place?'

She nodded. 'I'll make sure that Carlo's on location somewhere.'

'Good.' Ruth raised her glass. 'Well. Here's to Interlover.'

'To Interlover,' the others echoed.

FOUR

Meg frowned. 'You what?'

'It's a delivery service with a difference. Pure pleasure, and no strings,' Ruth said.

Meg's eyes narrowed. 'So just where do I fit into this?'

'Because, Meg, you're my perfect target market,' Ruth told her. 'You're single, you're wedded to your career, and you don't get a chance to meet any nice men.'

Meg snorted, tossing her dark hair back from her eyes. 'Oh, come on. I meet a lot of nice men, Ruth.'

'They're all attached, though – married, living with someone, or going through a messy divorce. And the ones that are single – they're either about ninety and past giving you a decent orgasm, middle-aged and patronizing, or the sort that you wouldn't trust enough to do business with them, let alone go to bed with them.'

Meg sighed. 'I suppose you have a point. So what do you want me to do, then?'

'Help us to train our pilot Interlover. You can choose the location, what you want him to do – everything.'

Meg drummed her fingers against her knee. 'I don't know, Ruth. It seems a bit – well, sordid, meeting a bloke just to bonk him. It's too one night stand-ish.'

'It's not sordid, and it'll be *much* better than a one night stand. You wouldn't regret it in the morning – it wouldn't be one of those occasions where you wake up, look at the bloke lying beside you, and wonder just how much you had to drink at that party the previous night. Mark's a lovely guy, Meg. Really, genuinely, absolutely nice.'

Meg's grey eyes sparkled with mischief. 'You mean, you fancy him, Ruthie?'

'I didn't say that.' Ruth pursed her lips. 'Though, yes, he's quite attractive.'

'*Quite* attractive?' Meg prompted.

Ruth rolled her eyes. 'OK, so he's drop-dead gorgeous. Tall, blond, blue eyes.'

'And big nose?' Meg teased.

Ruth grinned. 'That's what Laura and Shelley said, too. Yes. Though they helped to choose him, so it wasn't all me!'

'Have you asked them to do what you're asking me to do?'

Ruth nodded. 'They're in on it, as well.'

'And Nicholas and Carlo don't mind?'

'We have their blessing.'

Meg paused. 'What about Aidan?'

'He wasn't too chuffed about the idea, at first – but he's come round to my way of thinking.'

'Right.'

'Meg, there's no risk. Good sex, with no strings, with a gorgeous man who'll do everything to please you. And you'll get good conversation as well. The whole idea of the Interlover men is that they're more than just a himbo, all cock and no brain.'

Meg sighed. 'I don't know, Ruth. For a start, if he's that gorgeous, and a really nice bloke as well, why is he still single?'

'Because he's been concentrating on his career – like you.' Ruth bit her lip. 'Look, you wouldn't turn down a business opportunity without considering it first, would you?'

'No.'

'Well, then. What I'm offering you is a chance to enjoy yourself. Good conversation, a pleasant evening, and making love with an attractive man who knows what he's doing and is more concerned with your pleasure than his.'

Meg thought about it, 'What's the catch, then?'

'There isn't one.'

Meg raised an eyebrow. 'In business, there's always a catch.'

'I suppose, then, the only catch is that it's a one-off. It's not a permanent relationship. Though if you both like each other enough, it might end up being that. Who can tell?' Ruth spread her hands in mute appeal. 'Meg, I'm only asking people I really trust. Close friends, ones whose other halves won't make a big deal out of it, or ones who are happily wedded to their careers or don't have an other half who'd be upset.'

Meg thought about it for a moment, and finally nodded. 'All right, Ruthie. You can count me in. Just tell me when and where, and what you want me to do.'

Ruth hugged her friend. 'Thanks, Meg. I do appreciate it.'

'Yeah. You owe me one now,' Meg said wryly.

Ruth smiled to herself. Once Meg had met Mark, maybe she'd think that it was the other way round . . .

Mark tried to remember what he knew about Shelley. She liked good white wine, Ruth had said – which was why he had bought Chablis – and she adored soft fruits out of season. Raspberries fitted the bill, there. She was a music teacher, playing the piano and the violin, so they'd have something in common: something to talk about. She was married to a photographer who was half-Italian. She had red hair, and she was either quiet or bubbly, depending on her mood.

And she was going to train him in the arts of oral sex.

His cock twitched at the thought. If she was anywhere near as attractive as Laura or Ruth it was going to be an intensely pleasurable experience. He smiled to himself. If anyone had told him that the ad he'd answered was going to lead to this, he would have laughed, saying that it was ridiculous. Delivering a slightly different service – and being trained for it, in the nicest possible way. It was too far-fetched to be true. And yet here he was, driving to Islington, part-way through his 'training programme'.

He knew the road where Shelley lived; he found a parking space, and walked up the path to her flat. It wasn't quite as sumptuous as Laura's place, but it had a certain sense of style: he wasn't sure if that was due to Shelley, or to her photographer husband.

He rang the buzzer, and waited for the intercom to kick in.

'Hallo?'

'Shelley Mitchell?' he asked quietly.

'Yes.'

'It's Mark Beasley.'

'Come up. We're on the top floor.'

There was a pause, another buzz, and he opened the door. It didn't take him long to cover the three flights of stairs; he rapped on the door, and Shelley opened it.

She wasn't anything like Ruth, or Laura: she was petite, about five foot two, he guessed, with red curly hair that flowed over her shoulders, and green eyes that hinted at mischief. She was dressed more casually than Laura, in a pair of black leggings and an oversized black sweater, with a brightly-patterned chiffon scarf tied loosely round her neck. Her feet were bare, and her toenails were painted blue: he wasn't sure whether to be more surprised or amused.

'Hi,' she said. 'Come in.'

'Thanks.' He smiled at her, and handed her the neatly wrapped bottle of wine and a brown paper bag.

'Pressies? How nice.' She unwrapped the wine. 'Chablis. My favourite. Thank you.' She tipped her head to one side. 'Don't tell me – Ruth gave you a dossier on me?'

'Something like that.' It had been a phone call, which had left him achingly frustrated at the sound of Ruth's voice. And yet he knew that he couldn't push it and demand to meet her: he was terrified that she'd call the whole thing off. If he played it her way, maybe she'd relax enough to see him again.

Shelley opened the paper bag, and laughed. 'She definitely gave you a dossier. Otherwise you would have brought strawberries.'

He smiled at her. 'Actually, it was a lucky guess.'

'A good one, then.' She smiled back. 'I think we should open this, don't you?'

'It's up to you. I'm driving,' he warned.

'I'm not – and one glass won't put you over the limit.' She gave him an impish grin. 'So, how's Roach?'

He laughed. 'Noisy, but she got me here. Laura gave you all the details, then?'

'A bit sketchy, but enough.' Shelley led him into the kitchen, and rummaged in a drawer for a corkscrew. She opened the bottle, then opened a cupboard, and stood on tiptoe to reach the glasses. 'Bloody Carlo,' she said. 'He always puts things away just out of my reach!'

'Let me.' Mark retrieved two glasses for her. 'Carlo's a photographer, isn't he?'

'Mm. He's a good one, too.' She poured the wine, and handed him a glass. 'Come through. I'll show you some of his work.'

He followed her into the lounge, and his eyes widened in appreciation as he saw the framed photographs on the wall. 'Wow. You're right – he's very good.'

The photographs were moody black-and-white shots: a forest in the snow, and a funerary angel wreathed in ivy. 'Walthamstow cemetery,' Shelley told him, catching his gaze. 'Carlo used to live near there.'

'Right.' The rest of the room was far more arty and bohemian than Laura's house. The floor was covered in a pale carpet, with rag rugs scattered across it; pale throws covered the overstuffed sofa and armchairs. There was a piano at one side of the room, with pewter candlesticks on the top; a stereo system nestled in an alcove on the other, with speakers in all four corners. 'I should have guessed that a music teacher would insist on surround sound,' he said, smiling.

'Definitely. You're a musician yourself, so you know how important good sound is.' She sat down on the sofa, curling her legs under her, and patted the seat next to her. 'Don't be shy, Mark. Come and sit down with me.'

He grinned. 'Ruth told me that you were quiet.'

'Sometimes.' She laughed. 'I don't think that we can be shy and quiet with each other, in the circumstances – do you?'

'No.' He sat down next to her. 'So what made you agree to help Ruth?'

'The same as Laura. Ruth's our best friend. It all stems back from university – we had rooms on the same corridor, and the three of us just got on really well. I know they usually say that three's a crowd, but it wasn't like that with us. We were doing different subjects, and came from different backgrounds – but we had so much in common. We got on really well, and we've stayed close ever since, especially as we all ended up staying in London.' Shelley spread her hands. 'I have to admit, I was a bit surprised when Ruthie told us about Interlover. I didn't think she was serious, at first – I thought she was just upset over losing her job.'

'What did she do – before she was made redundant, I mean?'

'She was the marketing manager for a publisher. A dream job, for an English graduate – especially a bookworm like our Ruthie. It specialized in very literary fiction, and she loved it.' Shelley sighed. 'Anyway, when she put the ad in the paper, we realized that she really meant it. She needed our support – so we were there for her.'

'Laura said that her husband was broad-minded. What about yours?'

Shelley grinned. 'He's a photographer.'

'That isn't what I asked.'

'Maybe I should show you something.' She uncurled, and stood up. 'Come with me. And bring your glass.'

She stopped off in the kitchen to retrieve the raspberries and the bottle of wine, and led him into the bedroom.

It was, Mark thought, the most romantic bedroom he'd ever seen. The floorboards were stripped and polished, the walls were white, and the whole room was dominated by a king-size wrought-iron four-poster bed, which was draped in white chiffon. There was a white antique lace throw draped over the duvet, and the curtains at the small window were also white.

It was a room completely geared to the sensual. Instead of a bedside lamp on the antique pine chest next to the bed, there was a candle-light projector: a frosted white vase containing a tea-light candle and a black metal tube with cut-out stars. There was an antique pine cheval mirror opposite the bed and, on the wall opposite the window, a black and white photograph of Shelley, framed in perspex.

She was lying on the bed, naked, her pale skin mottled with a post-orgasmic flush; her lips were swollen and darkened, and her erect nipples were clearly visible. Her legs were parted, and her quim was glistening: with the juices of her own arousal, or of Carlo's, Mark wasn't sure.

He swallowed hard.

'See what I mean?' Shelley asked softly.

'Yes.'

'There are others.' She placed her glass, the bottle of wine and the raspberries on the pine chest, and sat on the bed. She opened the bottom drawer, and brought out a photograph album. 'Here.'

Mark placed his glass next to hers, and sat down beside her on the bed. The album was a professional one, with tissue paper between the leaves, and proper mountings; as with the other pictures, they were black-and-white arty shots.

The first was a close-up shot of one of Shelley's breasts. Her nipple was a hard peak, slightly elongated by the forefinger and thumb which pulled at it. The darkness of the areola testified to her arousal; Mark couldn't help a sideways glance at Shelley.

Her sweater concealed her body too well: he couldn't tell if showing these pictures to him were arousing her or not, but he could imagine only too well the things that the photograph left out. Her scent: light and floral, and incredibly seductive. How she'd feel: warm and soft, the skin of her areola puckered and slightly rough against his tongue. And how she'd taste . . .

With a shiver, he turned to the next picture. It was her face – but the look on her face was obviously caused by an extreme of pleasure. Her teeth were bared, her head thrown back, her eyes squeezed tightly shut. What had Carlo done to make his wife look like that? Had he trained the lens on her face, then thrust deep inside her, taking her to the limits of pleasure, before using a remote tripping device to take the picture? Or had Shelley masturbated in front of him, sliding her finger deep inside her and rubbing her clitoris with her thumb in the way she liked best? Or had she used something else to pleasure herself – a vibrator, a dildo?

The next picture told him exactly what had happened. The woman lying on the bed was completely oblivious to the camera, her eyes tightly shut and her body arched in pleasure. Her hand was slightly blurred, betraying the movement of the object in and out of her quim: the smooth handle of an old-fashioned hairbrush.

Mark turned the page, shifting slightly to ease his sudden erection. The next shot was a close up: Shelley's quim flexing as she withdrew the hairbrush. The smooth wooden handle glistened in the light, and Mark swallowed, his mouth watering. He could imagine how she tasted – and that was the whole point of the afternoon. To make the imagination reality.

He turned the page swiftly. Another, of a man's head buried

between those ivory thighs. Mark guessed, from the darker tone of the man's skin, that this was Carlo. Another, in close-up: a clitoris, teased out of its hood, the tip of the man's tongue probing gently against the erect nub of flesh.

'See what I mean?' Shelley asked softly, placing her hand over his. 'Carlo's very broad-minded. He took these shots.'

'And he's in them with you, isn't he?'

She nodded. 'Though that isn't the point. What I'm trying to say is that Carlo knows about this afternoon, and he doesn't mind.'

'I don't think I'd be too happy, if you were my wife.'

She smiled. 'It isn't a betrayal. We're simply helping out a friend who needs a favour. Something —' she paused '—well, something rather unusual.'

'Right.' He reached over to the bedside cabinet, picking up his glass and taking a gulp from it. Shelley took the glass from him, and deliberately drank from the same place.

'So,' she said, putting the glass down again. 'Did you like what you saw?'

He swallowed hard. 'What do you think?'

'From the way you were fidgeting – yes, I think you did. I think that they turned you on as much as they always turn me on.' She stroked his face; her long sensitive fingers sent a shiver through him. He could so easily imagine them wrapped round his cock. Or easing him into her. Or running down his back, cupping his buttocks as he thrust into her...

'Wake up,' she said softly.

'Mm.' He shivered. 'Shelley.'

'I'm all yours, lover.' Her eyes sparkled with a mixture of amusement and attraction. 'Show me what you can do.'

Mark cupped her face in his hands. She was so delicate, so fine-boned. And yet that was purely physical: she didn't have over-delicate sensibilities. To masturbate with a hairbrush for her husband, and let him photograph her doing it... this was a woman who was in tune with the sensual side of her nature, and didn't try to button it down.

He brought his mouth down to hers, his lips gentle. She opened her mouth, and the kiss deepened: he could taste the wine, mingled with the sweetness of her mouth, and it made him want more.

He loosened her chiffon scarf, dropping it on the floor, then let his hands slide under her sweater. Instead of the softness of her skin, which he'd been expecting, his fingertips encountered lace.

'Take it off,' she urged gently, and Mark tugged at the hem of her sweater. She lifted her arms, and he drew it over her head. He sucked his breath in sharply as he saw what she was wearing: a stretch-lace teddy. The black material contrasted with her pale ivory skin and the rich red sheen of her hair; to his pleasure, it didn't hide her body at all. Her dark nipples were erect and thrown into relief by the clinging garment.

'God, you're so beautiful,' he said.

She smiled. 'Don't think that it's going to be all one-way.' She took the hem of his own sweater, peeling it over his head. 'Mm. Nice. *Very* nice.' She rolled her r's, almost in an Italianate way.

She ran her fingertips over his pectoral muscles, then let her hands drift lower, over his midriff. Mark felt an immediate kick in his loins, and shivered as she lingered over the button of his jeans, deliberately taking an age to undo it.

'I thought I was supposed to be—'

'Pleasuring me?' she finished. 'You are. But I like being skin to skin. Having you completely clothed, while I'm completely naked – well, it'd be like being in a cheap soft-porn movie. Tacky. I want to see as much of you as you'll see of me.'

'Right.' He let her unzip his fly, then lifted himself slightly so that she could push the soft faded denims down.

His underpants clung to his erection. 'Very nice,' she said approvingly, curling her fingers over the bulge.

'Shelley.' He removed his jeans, kicking off his shoes and removing his socks. 'I think you're wearing too much.'

'Very true.' She stood in front of him. 'Excuse me a moment, won't you?'

She walked over to the window, drawing the curtains, then stooped to light the candle. Star-shaped patterns danced around the frosted glass bowl, refracted into the room. She looked over her shoulder to smile at him, then rolled down her leggings, bending over to remove them properly.

The gusset of the teddy clung to her quim; although the material was dark, Mark could see a faint wet patch, betraying her arousal. Part of him itched to tear the garment off her body; part of him held back, knowing that he was still being tested.

In the end, he compromised, getting off the bed and standing behind her, wrapping his arms round her and gently straightening her again. He cupped her breasts, his thumbs rubbing her nipples through the lace of her teddy, and kissed the curve of her neck.

Shelley rested back against him, closing her eyes. Laura hadn't told her that Mark kissed that well. She'd thought straightaway that Mark had a sensitive mouth: the fact that he knew how to use it was something else. Particularly considering just where he was going to use his mouth on her...

Mark turned her round to face him, and slid the narrow ribbon straps of the teddy off her shoulders. He stooped to lick the hollows of her collar-bones, making her shiver, and slowly peeled the teddy downwards, revealing her breasts and licking every inch of skin as he uncovered it.

Her breasts were every bit as beautiful as they'd been in the photographs: but they were better, Mark thought, because he could touch them, feel their weight and their softness. He played with her breasts, pushing them together and upwards, then pulled gently on her nipples, elongating the hard peaks of flesh.

Shelley gave a soft murmur, and Mark buried his face in her cleavage, closing his eyes and breathing in her scent. He stayed there for a moment, motionless; then he moved his head slightly to take one nipple into his mouth. The texture of her skin was exquisite against his tongue, and he made a noise of pure pleasure at the back of his throat.

She arched against him, and he smiled against her skin. If she was this responsive when her breasts were touched, how much more responsive would she be when he touched her more intimately? He pulled away slightly, so that he could continue to roll the teddy downwards. Light from the candle flickered across her skin, turning patches of it from ivory to gold; he nuzzled her midriff, licking the places where the candlelight glowed on her skin.

He dropped to his knees and eased the thin material over her hips, slowly tugging it down her thighs. She widened her stance, resting her hands on his shoulders for balance as she lifted first one leg, then the other, while he peeled the teddy from her body.

'God, Shelley, you're lovely,' he said softly. 'Like an ivory statue of a Greek goddess – except you're warm and soft.'

She chuckled. 'That's very sweet of you.'

'No, I mean it.' He licked her thigh experimentally, and she shivered. Only a few more inches, and his tongue would be licking her somewhere much more sensitive – somewhere much more pleasurable. She pushed her pubis towards him, and he laughed. 'Don't be so impatient.'

She tangled her fingers in her hair. 'Mark. You're teasing me.'

'Am I?' He breathed on her quim.

Her eyes narrowed. 'You know you are.'

'All right. I'm sorry.' He stood up again, and kissed her lightly, before turning round to pull back the bedclothes. Then he scooped Shelley into his arms, lifted her up, and laid her gently on the bed.

She smiled at him, holding one hand up as he was about to climb onto the bed.

'What?' he asked.

She pointed at his underpants, and he grinned. 'OK. I get the message. Skin to skin, you said.'

'It's the nicest way.'

'Right.' He stripped off his underpants, letting them fall onto the floor with the rest of their tangled clothes, then climbed onto the bed to kneel between her ankles.

Shelley drew in her breath. Completely naked, he was beautiful. The fluid lines of his body were the sort that she would love to photograph, if she were as skilled as Carlo behind the lens. The perfect symmetry of his limbs, the beautiful swelling of his cock ... they made her shiver.

Mark mistook the shiver. 'Are you cold?' he asked solicitously.

She shook her head. 'Just anticipating something that I know I'm going to enjoy, very much.'

He grinned. 'Patience is a virtue, you know. I'm sure you tell that to your students, when they want to play Chopin or something and they haven't even mastered *Chopsticks*.'

'This is different,' Shelley retorted, laughing.

'Perhaps.' He picked up one foot. 'Blue nail-varnish,' he said, caressing her toes. 'I bet the kids in your class don't know about this.'

'No. It's my weird streak, as Laura calls it,' Shelley told him with a smile.

'Unusual, anyway.' He massaged the sole of her foot. 'Nice ankles.' He bent his head, licking the hollows of her ankles. 'Nice calves, too.' He stroked them, letting his fingers drift up to caress the sensitive skin at the back of her knee. 'And nice thighs.' He kissed upwards, stopping at a point just short of the apex of her thighs.

Shelley wriggled against him, and he grinned, lowering her leg and starting the same routine on the other one.

'You bloody tease,' she said, half laughing, half scowling.

'Indeed.' A sudden thought struck him. 'Shelley. You don't have a video camera hidden in your bedroom, do you?'

She caught his train of thought, and laughed. 'No. Carlo only does stills, not video. And if you're worried that I've got a trip lead somewhere, don't be. The pictures I showed you are for mine and Carlo's pleasure, no one else's.'

'Right.' He smiled ruefully. 'Sorry. I shouldn't have asked, really.'

'It's OK.' Shelley smiled at him. 'I won't tell Ruth.'

His eyes widened. Had Shelley guessed how he felt about Ruth? God, he had to take her mind off the subject. And quickly. He bent his head again, dropping a trail of tiny kisses along her thighs; he slid his hands along her inner thighs, gently pushing them apart, and she bent her knees to give him easier access.

He could smell her arousal, a heady mixture of spice and musk; unable to resist it, he drew his tongue along the length of her satiny furrow. Shelley moaned, and he repeated the motion, a long smooth stroke from the top to the bottom. He repeated it again and again, gently speeding up the pace, until Shelley was writhing beneath him, tipping her pelvis up and pushing her quim towards him.

Then he made his tongue into a sharp point, flicking it rapidly across her clitoris. Shelley moaned, and reached up to hold the wrought-iron bedstead, her knuckles whitening as the pressure of her grip increased. Mark continued to lap at her, alternately licking the full length of her quim and concentrating on her clitoris, bringing her to another peak of pleasure. She squeezed her eyes tightly shut, able to think only about the sudden surge of her climax, the way it uncoiled from the pit of her stomach and seemed to spread through her entire body.

Some minutes later, she became aware that Mark had shifted up to lie beside her, his arm curved round her waist, and had pulled the duvet over them both to stop them getting cold.

'OK?' he asked softly.

'Yes.' She smiled at him, curling her fingers through his. 'Obviously Ruth didn't give you that thorough an interview.'

'How do you mean?'

'Because if she had, she would have known that you don't need training. Not in this,' was the quiet reply.

'I'm very flattered.' He dropped a kiss on her cheek.

'I meant it.' She sat up, taking the nearest glass and sipping from it. She handed it to Mark, who also took a sip, then replaced it on the bedside cabinet. She eyed the raspberries, then Mark, then grinned. 'I don't know about you, but I'm hungry.'

'Raspberry juice stains,' he said laconically.

She laughed. 'And who says I was intending to crush them over your body and lick them off? Or for you to do that to me?' She took a couple of raspberries, popping one into her mouth and one into his.

'Hm,' he said when he'd swallowed the fruit. 'That could make a very pleasurable afternoon for both of us.'

'It could indeed.'

'Such a shame that it would ruin your sheet.'

Shelley's lips twitched. 'We could always do it without the fruit.'

'We could indeed,' he said, catching the look in her eye and interpreting it correctly. 'Starting now...'

Carlo was sprawled on the sofa, with his wife lying across his lap.

'Ring her now,' he coaxed.

'I'm supposed to tell Ruth and Laura together,' Shelley protested.

'You can tell Laura another time.' His hand slid under the hem of her bathrobe, and he began to stroke the soft skin of her thighs. 'Tell Ruthie now, when I can hear what you tell her.'

'You're a – a – oh, whatever the listening equivalent of a voyeur is,' she said crossly, unable to think of the word.

'Écouteur, probably,' he said.

'Trust you to know it.' Her eyes narrowed. 'Don't be so bloody smug.'

'I'm not.' His hand drifted higher, cupping her mons veneris. 'Just ring Ruth, and tell her what happened this afternoon.'

'With you listening in?'

'Well, it would save you telling the tale twice.'

'If I tell Laura separately,' Shelley pointed out, 'then I'm telling it twice.'

Carlo laughed, and kissed her, hard. When he broke the kiss, she sighed. 'All right. I give in. I'll ring her.'

'Good.' He reached over to the phone, bringing it over to her.

Shelley dialled Ruth's number, and waited. The answerphone cut in; she pulled a triumphant face at Carlo as the beep went. 'Hi, Ruth. This is Shelley. I was ringing to give you my report on our—'

'Hi,' Ruth said, picking up the phone.

Shelley flushed. 'Shit. I forgot that you might be call-screening. Were you doing anything important?'

'Yes. Watching old videos of *The X Files* and eating black grapes,' was the laughing response. 'Don't you want to meet up with Laura before you tell me?'

'Er.' Shelley squirmed. 'I thought I'd tell you now, while it was fresh in my mind. Laura's out somewhere tonight – some office do or other.'

'Right.' Ruth paused. 'So – how was he?'

'Good. He brought me Chablis and raspberries. I showed him some of Carlo's photos, and we chatted for a bit.' She paused. 'Then I took him into our bedroom, lit a candle, and closed the curtains.'

'Seduction by candlelight, in the afternoon. Dead romantic,' Ruth said.

'Mm. I don't think he needed training in that respect, Ruthie. He took my clothes off, kissing my skin as he uncovered it. Then, when I was naked, he picked me up and carried me over to the bed.'

'He'd get a hernia, if he tried that with me. Or with Laura.'

'I dunno, Ruth. He's got muscles in all the right places.' She shivered as Carlo slid one finger along her quim, exploring her more intimate topography. 'Anyway, he kissed his way up my legs then he started licking me.'

'Was he good?' Ruth grinned. 'Your man with the nice long tongue?'

'Yes. Nearly as good as Carlo. I couldn't fault him.' She paused. 'He's got a good body, Ruth. A bigger than average cock. I know I was supposed to just let him bring me to orgasm, but . . .'

'Did he?'

'Yes. He made me come, very pleasurably. He knew just what to do with my clitoris. He was very precise.' She shivered again as Carlo, hearing her words, began to rub her clitoris, the movements of his fingers echoing the way Mark had tongued her earlier.

'Marks out of ten?'

'Nine.'

'Because only Carlo gets ten?' Ruth guessed.

'Something like that.' Shelley swallowed, feeling her insides melt as Carlo continued to pleasure her.

'So then you sent him home?'

'Er – no.'

Ruth groaned. 'You were supposed to be training him in oral sex, not bonking him silly!'

'I know. But I like things to be mutual.'

'So what happened?'

'After he'd made me climax, he cuddled into me. We had another glass of wine between us, and some of the raspberries. I would have liked to crush them against his body and eat them off him, but he said it'd ruin the sheets.' Shelley coughed to cover a moan of pleasure as Carlo tugged her robe completely open and played with her breasts with his free hand. 'I suppose he was right, so we just ate the raspberries. Then I said maybe we could use my original suggestion – without the raspberries.'

'Indeed.'

Carlo nibbled at the nape of her neck.

'He had a gorgeous, cock, Ruth. Thick and long, the sort you'd want to photograph from every angle and then taste it. So I kissed my way down his body. God, Ruth, the texture of his skin! It's so fine and soft. By the time I got to his cock, there was a tiny drop of moisture on the tip. I licked it, and then worked my mouth down over his shaft. He tasted clean and spicy.'

'You sound like you're coming, just at the memory of it,' Ruth remarked, hearing the huskiness in her friend's voice.

'Something like that.' Something very like that, Shelley thought, writhing under her husband's ministrations. 'Anyway, I fellated him for a while; he lifted himself slightly so that he could stroke my back, my buttocks. I moved towards him, so he could touch me more easily, and he moved me so that I was lying on top of him, straddling his chest.'

Ruth, who could picture the scene very easily – and picture herself in Shelley's position – closed her eyes. 'And?'

'He started licking me again, using the same rhythm as I was using on his shaft. We came together, within seconds. It was so good.' She stiffened, trying to fight her climax; then gave in and let it flow through her, her body convulsing around Carlo's fingers.

'He's good, Ruth,' she said huskily. 'Very good. I think he's going to make Interlover a real success.'

'Good.'

'I'll talk to you later, OK?'

'OK.'

Shelley hung up, and turned to Carlo. 'That was mean. Making me come while I was talking to Ruth.'

'Anything Loverboy can do, I can do better,' her husband retorted with a grin. 'Which includes making you come.'

'Right.'

He rubbed his nose affectionately against hers. 'I wish I could have seen you. You actually showed him that album?'

'Mm. He was being shy with me.'

Carlo grinned. 'And the album was kill or cure, hm?'

'Something like that,' Shelley said, grinning back.

He rolled her off the sofa, then stood up, picking her up in his arms.

'Carlo, what are you doing?'

'What I've been dying to do while you were yakking to Ruth. Taking you to bed.'

She laughed. 'Considering that you were the one who wanted me to ring her, in the first place . . .'

'Who said anything about being consistent?' Chuckling, Carlo kicked open the sitting-room door and carried his wife off to their bedroom.

FIVE

'You're doing *what*?'

Ruth grinned. Helen's reaction was exactly the same as Meg's had been. Shock, surprise and disbelief, all rolled into one. 'I'm setting up my own business. It's a kind of delivery service – a very intimate and special one.'

Helen rubbed her jaw. 'It sounds illegal to me.'

'Laura knows all about it, and she's given it the OK.' Ruth spread her hands. 'So there's nothing to worry about.'

Helen sighed. 'You're completely mad, you know.' She topped up their glasses. 'So who's going to buy your services?'

'Lots of women. Women who just don't have the time for a relationship, but still need their carnal urges satisfied and want more than the latest toy from Ann Summers or whoever. Women who have just split up from someone, and need cheering up. Sex is a great healer, you know – and the sort of men I'll have as the Interlovers are perfect. They're all going to be articulate, nice – not in love with themselves – and dead sexy.'

Helen thought about it. 'In principle, it's a nice idea.'

'Well.' Ruth looked slightly diffident. 'I have this friend who's recently split up with her long-term lover. He cheated on her, and brought her self-esteem to an all-time low. I'd like to cheer her up.'

'You could start with chocolate and wine, and a shoulder to cry on,' Helen said.

'I've tried that. Anyway, she seems pretty together, but . . .' Ruth shrugged.

'But what?'

'She's still carrying a torch for her ex. A delivery from Interlover might help her to forget him – at least, physically.'

'And this friend wouldn't happen to be a painter, by any chance? One who's also been affected by the demise of Romulus because she did a few book jackets for them?' Helen raked a hand through her short blonde curls.

'Funny you should say that,' Ruth said, smiling. 'Yes, she is.'

Helen shook her head. 'Nice try, Ruthie, but no, thanks. I don't need this Interlover of yours. I don't need anyone.'

'So what are you going to do? Mope around after Stu, for the rest of your life?'

'No, of course not.'

'Just for the next few months,' Ruth supplied.

Helen sighed. 'I don't want another relationship, right now. I just don't need the added complication to my life.'

'Exactly. And bearing in mind that sex – good sex – is about the best thing to take your mind off your problems, and there are absolutely no strings attached . . .' Ruth spread her hands. 'Think about it, Helen. It's the answer to your dreams.'

'All right, I'll think about it – but I'm not promising anything,' Helen warned. 'So don't expect me to say yes.'

'OK.' Ruth sipped her wine. 'Let's change the subject. How's that commission coming on?'

'Pretty well. Do you want to have a look at the preliminary sketches?'

'Yes, I'd love to.' Ruth followed her friend into the studio, smiling to herself. Helen was stubborn. She liked to think that things were her idea, her decision. All she needed was a little time, and she'd come round to the idea of seeing Mark. And if Mark arrived with champagne, Belgian truffles and some white roses, Helen would enjoy the evening even more . . .

INTERLOVER

*

Swallow Hills Country Club. Mark smiled to himself. There wasn't a swallow – or a hill – in sight. Just a few golfers, who were too obviously talking business as they went over the links; and probably some bored executive housewives having various beauty treatments inside.

He wondered why Meg had chosen this place to meet him. Ruth's note had said that Meg was an antiques dealer who lived in Islington. She liked art, music and good wine; but, at a country club, no doubt it would be frowned upon to bring a bottle of wine with you. In the end, he'd settled upon having some freesias delivered to Meg, that morning, with a note: *See you at half-past two. Mark.*

He glanced at his watch. Twenty-five minutes past. Perfect timing. Thank God that Roach hadn't decided to play up, he thought wryly. That would have ruined everything. He flexed his shoulders, then left the car, locking it and grinning to himself. As if anyone would steal an ancient and battered Beetle, when the car park was filled with shiny new executive BMWs and Saabs.

He walked into the reception area; a confident-looking woman, her dark hair swept back in a chignon, was sitting reading a magazine. Unless she was late, this had to be Meg. He went over to her. 'Excuse me, please. Would you be Meg Stannard?' he asked diffidently.

She looked up, and smiled. 'I would indeed.' She placed the magazine on the table next to her. 'And you must be Mark.'

'Yes.'

She smiled again, and stood up, proffering her hand. 'Thanks for the freesias. They were lovely.'

He couldn't help smiling back. 'Pleasure.'

'And it's nice to meet you, at last.'

He took her hand, shaking it, and was pleased to find that

her grip was firm. 'You, too.' It wasn't just a pleasantry, either. His gut reaction was to like Meg.

'Well. Shall we go in?'

He frowned. 'Where?'

'Didn't Ruth tell you? This place isn't just for golfers. There's a pretty good spa here.'

'Right.' He winced. 'I'm afraid that I didn't bring any swimming trunks or whatever with me.'

'No problem. I'm sure that Reception can find you something – anyway, I have to sign you in.'

His eyes widened. 'You mean, you're a member of this place?'

'Yes.' Meg smiled at him. 'It's a good place for doing business.'

'Over a round of golf, you mean?'

Meg shook her head, laughing. 'I hacked out so many divots, they banned me from playing! No, I tend to do business in the relaxing side. In the jacuzzi, the sauna, or over a massage. It's a good place to bring clients: we can relax, enjoy ourselves, then discuss exactly what they're looking for and in what sort of price range.'

'Mm. Though I think that the membership fees of this place might be a little out of my reach,' he said wryly.

'They're tax deductible – just talk to your accountant,' Meg told him, with a broad wink. 'Come on. Let's get you sorted out.'

A couple of minutes later, he'd been signed in as her guest, and Reception had found him a pair of brief black trunks. They'd been given thick towelling robes and bathsheets; Meg gestured to the changing rooms. 'See you outside here in five minutes?'

'OK.'

Mark stripped ruminatively. Meg Stannard was a beautiful woman. She was a little shorter than Ruth, a little less curvy: but she had a fine bone-structure, and her creamy skin threw her dark hair into sharp relief. Her grey eyes were lively; though, at the same time, he could imagine her being coldly businesslike, when necessary. Meg had that certain air of efficiency about her. She had a beautiful mouth, too, almost a perfect rosebud; it made him itch to kiss her.

He hadn't noticed a ring on her left hand, though he knew that that didn't mean anything. Ruth hadn't worn a ring when he'd met her for his first interview, but she was involved with Aidan. Maybe Meg fell under Ruth's category of women married to their careers.

He pulled on the trunks. They were close-fitting, betraying every line of his body; he grinned. They were a little blatant for his taste, but that was Meg's fault — and Ruth's — for not giving him proper details about his assignment. He wrapped the robe round himself, slung the towel over his arm, and went to meet Meg.

She was already waiting for him. 'OK?' she asked him.

'Yes.'

'Follow me.'

He was surprised to see that the spa pool was empty. He'd been expecting to see at least one or two other people there. Meg smiled at him. 'It's off-peak,' she explained. 'And Wednesday afternoons are nearly always empty — which, considering it's early-closing day for half of us, is surprising. But bloody nice.'

'Right.'

She stripped off her robe, dropping it at the edge of the spa pool, with her towel. Mark followed suit, surreptitiously eyeing her; her legs were long and shapely, and although her breasts were minimized by her demurely-cut navy costume, they still held the promise of lushness.

Meg climbed into the pool and lay with her head resting against the side, her eyes closed. Mark followed suit.

'So how did you get involved in Interlover?' he asked.

Meg pulled a face. 'Ruth talked me into it. I'm not sure who's doing whom the favour, though.'

'Right.' He smiled. 'Have you known Ruth very long?'

Meg nodded. 'We met at an auction, ages ago. I was just starting to set up my shop, and I was bidding for a few choice items. She was standing next to me, and bid against me for one lot I really wanted – some antique brass candlesticks. When the auction was over, we started chatting, and had a coffee together. I suppose our friendship started from there.' She grinned. 'Not that she'll ever sell me those bloody candlesticks – and that's after years of trying to persuade her.'

'Stubborn, hm?'

'Yeah. Mind you, I'm pretty much the same. We share the same star sign – Gemini.'

'I'm a Libran,' Mark told her.

'That's probably why she took to you. Air signs attracting, and all that.'

Though Ruth hadn't shown any signs of being attracted to him. Not since their first meeting – their *only* meeting. She'd barely even spoken to him on the phone, since then. Mark had the distinct impression that she was avoiding him – but why? 'Does she have the split personality to go with it?' he asked

'Not as much as Shelley. You never know whether Shelley's going to be quiet and sweet, or wild and outrageous!'

He was surprised. 'You know Laura and Shelley, then?'

'Oh, yes. We've met at parties, and the odd girly evening at Ruth's. Carlo buys the occasional prop from me, if he's doing a particular type of shoot, and Laura collects Spode – which I can obviously find for her at a more reasonable price than she'd get through the rest of the dealer network.' She grinned. 'And, yes, I did ask them all about you. I wasn't taking just Ruth's word for it. I thought at first that she was trying to fix me up with someone – she isn't above matchmaking, if she meets some nice young man she thinks would suit one of her friends.'

'But you'd rather be wedded to your career?'

'Yes. I've had my fingers burned, a couple of times – men who couldn't understand that I needed to spend time on my business to get it off the ground, and told me to choose between my work and them. The choice was obvious – and I don't regret it. It's a much easier life. I can do what I want, when I want. Selfish, maybe; but I suppose I'm getting more set in my ways as I get older.' She opened her eyes, looking at him. 'So how did you get involved? The others didn't tell me a lot about you.'

'I answered an ad in the paper, for a broad-minded person to look at an exciting new business venture. I figured that it wasn't going to be sales – that it would be something a lot more interesting – and I need a second job.'

'Your first one is in the music business, isn't it?'

He nodded. 'I play in a band. We do the pubs-and-clubs circuit. Mainly bluesy stuff and soft rock.'

Meg grinned. 'The garage band, moved one step on, hm?'

'Yeah. Though I don't think we're ever going to make the big time. It's more . . . well, pleasure. We all enjoy playing, but none of us has any ambition to be much more than what we are.' He smiled. 'We're lucky enough to do what we love, but without the pressures that fame would give us.'

'Right.' She smiled. 'You're pretty much how Ruth described you.'

Mark stiffened. 'Which is?' He was careful to keep his voice neutral.

'A genuinely nice guy.'

He raised one eyebrow. 'That's almost as damning as "pleasant".'

'Hey, don't take it personally! She didn't mean it in that way.' Meg lifted a hand to stroke his face.

'Then what did she mean?'

'That I'd like you. That I'd find you attractive. The way Ruthie put it is that we'd have good conversation, a nice time together, and—' her lips curved '—I'd make love with a man who knew exactly what he was doing, and would be as concerned about my pleasure as he was about his own.'

Mark smiled wryly. That was what he was supposed to do. The thing was, Ruth didn't know from personal experience. It bothered him. He wanted to prove to her personally that he could deliver up to her expectations – not just have it reported back to her by satisfied 'customers'.

She traced his lower lip with the tip of her finger. 'I wasn't convinced about her Interlover idea, when she first told me about it. But . . . I think I might be, now.'

He drew her fingertip into his mouth, sucking it; she closed her eyes, tipping her head back and giving herself up to pleasure. He did the same to each of her other fingers, drawing them into his mouth and sucking erotically on them, one by one, in the same way that he would have liked to feel her mouth working on his cock. The same way that Shelley had worked on him, while he licked her until she came, again and again, flooding his mouth with her sweet nectar.

Gently, he curved his hand round the nape of her neck, stroking the sensitive skin until Meg arched her back; then he let his hand drift up to her hair, loosening its fastenings so that it fell down around her face.

'Mm. You look like a water nymph,' he told her. 'One of those ones in that Waterhouse painting.'

'*Hylas and the Nymphs*, you mean?'

'Yeah, that's the one.' He smiled. 'Except that the nymphs weren't wearing bathing costumes. Especially ones like this.' He hooked his finger under one shoulder-strap, drawing it down; when Meg made no protest, he did the same with the other strap, pushing the navy lycra down until he'd bared her breasts.

They were as soft and round as he'd expected – maybe not quite as lush and generous as he imagined Ruth's to be, but still beautiful. He traced the curves of her breasts with the tip of his middle finger, and her nipples began to harden; he smiled, and let his finger drift over to trace her areolae. She shivered, and he caught the hard peak of flesh between his thumb and forefinger, rolling it gently and tugging on it until Meg groaned, tipping her head back and pushing her breasts towards him.

Then he dipped his head, taking one nipple into his mouth while he played with its twin. Meg slid her fingers into his hair, the pressure of her fingertips against his scalp urging him on. He transferred his mouth to her other breast, licking her skin and tasting the salt of the spa water, then closing his lips over her nipple again.

Meg groaned, and he lifted his head to kiss her. Her mouth opened under his, her tongue sliding against his as she kissed him back, hard. Mark eased one hand between her thighs, cupping her mound of Venus; she pushed against him, and he eased his finger under the edge of her swimming costume, sliding his finger along her quim until he found her clitoris.

She gave a gasp of pleasure as he began to rub her, his touch sure and steady; she rocked gently against him, increasing the friction between his fingers and the sensitive nub of flesh. Mark suddenly longed to be inside her: he nuzzled her cheek. 'Meg.'

'Mm?' Her voice was husky with arousal.

'I'd like to make love to you. Properly.'

'That's the best idea I've heard all week,' she informed him.

He grinned and lifted her slightly, removing her swimming costume completely and throwing it over the edge of the spa pool. He stripped off his borrowed swimming trunks, glad to free his erection from the clinging material, and sat down again, manoeuvring Meg so that she was facing him and straddling his thighs.

'Are you sure about this?' he asked, idly stroking her breasts.

'Yes. Oh, God, yes,' she said, curling her fingers round his cock and lifting herself slightly so that she could guide it to her entrance.

At last, he felt her sliding down over him, her quim like warm wet velvet wrapped around his cock; he gave a sigh of satisfaction. 'You feel so good, Meg.'

'You don't feel so bad yourself,' was the reply, accompanied with a lazy grin.

He laughed, and cupped her face, kissing her hard. She began to move over him, lifting and lowering herself on his rigid cock, and rubbing her own nipples, pulling at them so that they were distended. Her rhythm changed, her movements becoming faster as her arousal grew. Mark eased his hand between their bodies, rubbing her clitoris as she pushed down on him. He felt her shudder, and then her quim rippled round him, pushing him into his own climax.

She buried her head in his shoulder for a moment, until the aftershocks of her orgasm died away; then she lifted her head again, smiling at him.

'OK?' he asked softly.

'Very OK.' She stroked his face. 'To be honest, I wasn't expecting you to be that good.'

'Thank you. I'll take that as a straight compliment, rather than a backhanded one.' He smiled back at her.

'That's how I meant it. Anyway, I think we ought to get out of here, before we both turn into prunes,' Meg said.

'And then what?'

'Shower, change ... Then how about a walk? It's lovely, round here – we could go for a stroll, talk a bit, then go back to my place for coffee?'

'Sounds good to me.' He kissed her lightly on the mouth. 'Or maybe we could go back to mine, and I could cook you dinner. Though it won't be anything spectacular,' he warned. 'Just pasta and sauce. And it's a shared house.'

'Which will remind me of my student days, and I can pretend to be in my early twenties again, instead of being too near to thirty-five,' she replied with a grin. 'You're on.'

*

The phone shrilled; Mark leaned his guitar against the bookcase, and went to answer it. 'Hallo. Mark Beasley speaking.'

'Hallo, Mark.'

He smiled as he recognized the voice on the other end of the phone. 'Hi, Ruth. How are you?'

'Fine, thanks.'

'What can I do for you?'

'Well, I have another training assignment for you.'

His eyes widened. Ruth had been careful not to see him – or even to phone him – since their 'interview'. She'd simply sent him some short but sweet notes, telling him where to go and who to meet. He hadn't had the courage to ring her, not wanting to push it. Maybe his patience was paying off, at last. 'Oh?' He was careful to keep his voice light. 'Where's that?'

'Walthamstow – not far from you, in fact. Helen's a friend of mine who used to do cover illustrations for me, when I was at Romulus.'

'Right. Where does she live?' He scribbled down the address as she spoke. 'What else do I need to know?'

'She likes champagne, smoked salmon or Belgian truffles, and white roses.'

'And the subject?'

'Just general. She's had a rough time, lately, so she could do with cheering up.'

'Right.' He paused. 'So how do you feel it's going, then?'

'The pilot? Well, the feedback I've had so far is good.' She coughed. Meg had been extremely complimentary, and she'd felt a small twinge of jealousy when her friend had described the way Mark had made love to her in the spa pool, then taken her back to his house for dinner. Although Meg hadn't said that they'd be seeing each other again, Ruth had a feeling that they probably would. 'How about you? Are you happy with the way it's going?'

'It's OK.' Ask her, his body urged. *Ask her.* At the worst, she can only say no; you've got nothing to lose. He swallowed. 'Maybe we could discuss it over a drink, or something?'

'I'm a bit busy,' she hedged.

'Look – my band's playing pretty near you, tomorrow night. Why don't you come and see us, and have a drink with me afterwards?'

She paused, then asked quietly, 'Is Aidan included in the invitation?'

He squeezed his eyes shut. Christ. He'd forgotten that Ruth was involved with someone else. Well, he hadn't forgotten, exactly – more like deliberately blanked it from his mind. If he said no, Ruth wouldn't come. If he said yes . . . he'd have to put up with seeing them together. He plumped for the lesser of two evils. Seeing her was better than not seeing her. 'Yes, if you like.'

'Right.' Ruth paused. 'I'll ask him. If we're free, we'll be there. Where and what time?'

He named the pub. 'Our set finishes at about half-past nine.'

'OK. I might see you tomorrow night, then.'

'I'll look forward to it. See you.'

'See you.'

Mark sighed as he replaced the receiver, and walked back to his guitar. He began strumming chords, singing almost under his breath, then strumming more and more loudly as his frustration grew. Christ, he was being an idiot. The woman was involved with someone else. What was the point of hoping that there could ever be anything between them? It was obvious that she wasn't going to leave Aidan for him. Why would any woman leave a rich and successful financier for a man who still lived like he was a student, when he was over thirty?

He jumped as a female hand patted his shoulder.

'Bloody hell, Lou! Don't sneak up on me like that,' he snarled.

'I wasn't sneaking anywhere. You were banging hell out of that guitar – that's why you didn't hear me.' His sister smiled sweetly at him, and threw herself into a chair. 'So. What's the matter, then, Markie?'

He scowled at the hated diminutive. 'Why should anything be the matter?'

'Because you're playing depressing stuff – more depressing than the usual blues crap you play, that is – and you look like the whole world's worries are on your shoulders.' She grinned, playing with the ends of her shoulder-length fair hair. 'Even Leonard Cohen sounds happier than you do!'

He sighed. 'Thanks for asking, but I'm OK, Lou.'

Lou's blue eyes narrowed. 'It's her, isn't it?'

'I don't know what you mean.'

'The woman setting up this Interlover stuff.'

'Ruth?'

'Yes.' She rubbed her chin. 'I think you've fallen for her, big time.'

'No, I haven't.'

'Don't lie, Mark. I might be merely your kid sister, but I can read you like a book.' She drew her knees up, linking her hands over her ankles. 'Why don't you just ask her out for a drink, or something, and see if you can find out how she feels about you?'

'I just did. I asked her to come and see the band.' He sighed. 'She's bringing someone with her.'

' "Someone" being male, and her other half?' Lou guessed. 'Trust you to go for the complicated option.'

'Huh.'

'What about Meg? I liked her. Why don't you see her, instead?'

'Because she's firmly wedded to her career. We can enjoy each other's company—' he ignored his sister's amused snort of 'Sex, more like!' '—but otherwise, it's a relationship that's going nowhere.'

She looked thoughtful. 'Well, Ruth obviously finds you attractive.'

Mark frowned. 'And how do you work that one out, Miss Marple?'

'It's obvious, Mark. Blindingly obvious. She picked you, out of all the other people who replied to that ad. And she gets her friends to train you, rather than doing it herself – which means she doesn't trust herself not to get involved with you. *Ergo*, she fancies you.'

Mark rolled his eyes. 'It's more like she thinks that I'm right for her business, but not right for her. Or doesn't find me attractive.'

'Suit yourself. But don't underestimate the power of feminine intuition.'

'You've not even met her!'

'I don't need to,' Lou retorted sweetly, uncurling and standing up. 'Well, I've got lines to learn, and I need some coffee. Want some?'

'Yeah. Please.'

She ruffled his hair as she walked past. 'Courage, bruv. Faint heart never won fair lady.'

He sighed. 'If I rush her, she'll back off.'

Lou grinned. 'Try the other tack, then. Softly, softly, catchee monkey. Or, in your case, catchee fuckee.'

Part of Mark wanted to slap his sister for being so flippant and coarse. The other part of him knew that she was right. If he wanted to make love with Ruth, he'd have to take it slowly and make sure that it was all on her terms.

In the end, Aidan was playing squash, so Ruth went to see the band on her own. She sat quietly in a corner, out of view of the stage; the support band wasn't to her taste, but Mark's band was something else. Soft, bluesy rock, the sort of music which always made her want to make love – and Mark's voice was enough to make her knees weak and her sex liquefy. His voice had turned her on when he'd just spoken to her; his singing made her feel even hotter.

She nearly walked out before the end of the set, not wanting to face Mark on her own. On the other hand, she reminded herself, they were in a crowded pub. Nothing could happen. So she waited; when Mark's band had finished their set, she walked over to the stage.

His eyes lit up as he saw her. 'Ruth! I didn't think that you were coming.'

'Well, I was free – though Aidan's playing squash, so he couldn't make it.'

Even better, he thought. Even bloody better. Just the two of us.

She smiled at him. 'Can I buy you a drink?'

'Thanks. A pint would be nice.' He named some beer she'd never heard of; she assumed that it was some kind of real ale.

'Right. See you in a minute, then.' She smiled again, and headed for the bar. God, he was even nicer than she remembered. Not just the sexy voice: it was the smile, the look in his eyes. She smiled wryly. And the fact that he was the typical Ruth Finn type: tall, blond, blue eyes, good body.

It had been a real mistake to do this, she thought. If only Aidan had been with her. On the other hand, Aidan would have been able to tell straightaway how much she fancied Mark, and it would have caused even more problems between them. Things were difficult enough as it was, without making it worse. Best to keep them well apart.

She reappeared with the said pint of beer, and a mineral water for herself.

'Let's sit down,' he said, leading her to a table in the corner and draping his jacket on the back of his chair.

She followed suit, and sat down. 'Well – cheers,' she said, lifting her glass. 'Here's to the success of your band.'

'And to Interlover.' He lifted his own glass, then took a sip. 'So. What did you think?'

'I wasn't too keen on the support band – but I liked yours.'

He smiled. 'I thought you were an opera fan. That's what Laura said, anyway. That, and chamber music.'

She nodded. 'I am. Though I like driving to the sort of stuff you play.' Among other things – but it was dangerous to think of those sort of things, with Mark around. Making love. Masturbating, in the bath . . . Her skin heated, and she coughed. 'I believe you got on pretty well with Meg.'

'Yes.' He grinned. 'I don't suppose you want to sell any candlesticks, do you?'

She threw her head back, laughing, suddenly at ease with him again. 'No. And you can tell Meg that she can find herself another pair!'

God, she was beautiful when she laughed. The curve of her throat – he wanted to stroke it, to kiss it. And then to undo her shirt, kiss every inch of skin as he revealed it. The very idea made him shiver.

Ruth caught the intense gaze in his eyes and groaned inwardly. Hell. Laura and Shelley had both warned her that he'd asked a lot of questions about her. It looked like he felt the same way that she did. Had it not been for Aidan, it would have been the perfect opportunity. She sighed inwardly. But because of Aidan, she had to keep this on a businesslike footing.

'Laura and Shelley liked you, by the way.'

'It was mutual.'

Ruth remembered her telephone call with Shelley, and flushed. The idea of Mark licking his way down her body in the same way, kissing her most intimate places, was almost too much for her.

Mark noticed how her eyes had dilated; he couldn't resist taking her hand, kissing the palm, and curling her fingers over it. He held her hand cupped in his. 'Ruth.'

She squeezed her eyes shut. 'Mark, this is business. Just business.'

'I know.' His thumb stroked her inner wrist, brushing against her rapidly-beating pulse.

She snatched her hand back. 'We're here to talk about your training program, and how you think it's going. How it could be improved.'

It could be improved, Mark thought, if I simply lifted you up and carried you out of this bloody pub and into my bed. Yet he knew there would be no point in telling her that. It would only scare her away. He had to take this slowly. 'Well, I don't know. I've never done this sort of thing before, so I've got no idea if I'm doing it right, or not.'

'Your trainers certainly think you are.'

Then why don't you find out for yourself? he asked her silently.

She finished her mineral water, and pushed back her chair.

'Would you like another?' he asked. He would have bought her gallons of the stuff, to make her stay with him a little longer.

She shook her head. 'I'd better be going, really. It's late.'

'I'll walk you home.'

'Thanks, but there's no need. I'll be fine.'

'Look, it's no trouble. I'd be happier knowing that you're back home, safe and sound rather than worrying all evening in case you've been mugged.'

'London isn't *that* dangerous. Anyway, I got here without any problems, didn't I?'

'That's the sort of thing that Lou says. My sister,' he explained. 'But I think she's a bit more streetwise than you are.'

'I've probably read the same books, or heard the same theories. You hold your head up, look positive, and march along as if you know where you're going – even if you don't,' Ruth told him.

'Just humour me?' Mark asked.

She sighed. 'OK, I give in.'

As she stood up and put on her jacket, he suddenly realized

what had been bugging him ever since he'd seen her, that evening: what it was that was different about her. The diamond solitaire sitting on the ring finger of her left hand. He made no comment, but drained his glass and shrugged on his jacket. 'Right, then. Let's go.'

They walked down the road together in virtual silence. Mark was brooding too much on the fact that she'd got engaged to Aidan — and hadn't told him — to speak; and Ruth was too preoccupied with fighting her attraction to him to start up a conversation.

Eventually, they reached the gate of her house; she stopped, and smiled at him. 'Well. Thanks for walking me home.'

'Pleasure,' he responded politely.

'I'll be in touch, then. After your assignment with Helen.'

She licked her lower lip, feeling awkward and nervous; the action drew his attention to her mouth, and it was suddenly too much for him. He cupped her face, and brought his mouth down on hers, needing to kiss her.

She resisted him for a moment: then she kissed him back, opening her mouth under his and letting him have the access he wanted. He put his arm round her, resting his hand in the curve of her back: he could have stayed there, kissing her, all night.

Except that it was in front of her house, and her fiancé could appear at any moment. Regretfully, he broke the kiss. 'Goodnight, Ruth,' he said, his voice cracking, and turned to walk away.

Ruth watched him walk away, her fingers pressed to her mouth. Her legs felt like jelly and the worst thing was knowing that she'd wanted Mark to do much more than kiss her. Much more.

'Get a grip, Finn. He's off limits. Way off limits,' she told herself roughly, and marched up to her front door.

SIX

'So, what's this fantastic new idea of yours?' Selena asked. 'You wouldn't tell me anything on the phone.'

'Well,' Ruth said. 'I don't know if there's a tactful way to put this. Meg and Helen didn't quite believe that I was telling them the truth.'

'Come on, then.' Selena topped up their glasses.

'Imagine, then,' Ruth said. 'What would be the best present you could have, if you'd had a really bad day – you know, one of those days when just about everything you've touched has gone wrong and you feel like hell?'

Selena thought about it, twirling the ends of her long straight hair round her fingers. 'Dinner out, maybe, with some good friends who'd laugh me out of my bad mood.'

'I meant something a bit more than that.'

Selena shrugged. 'I don't know. You tell me – what would *you* want?'

'I'd just want to go home. Then I'd run a nice, long, relaxing bath, pour myself a glass of Chardonnay or something like that, put some music on the stereo, light a scented candle and get Aidan to give me a back rub.'

'Well, if you're offering me Aidan for the night, thank you.' Selena grinned, her grey-blue eyes crinkling at the corners. 'I might just take you up on that some time, Ruthie!'

'Not Aidan himself.' Ruth smiled at her. 'How about someone even nicer?'

Selena grimaced. 'Apart from the fact that I know damn well that Aidan's the only man in your life – the only man you have eyes for – if you're trying to matchmake, forget it. I know I'm not with anyone at the moment, but I'm happy that way. I just don't have time for relationships.'

'That's what Meg said – and Helen.'

'Meg and Helen? You've tried this on them, too?' Selena eyed her friend curiously. 'So just what are you up to, Ruth?'

'Interlover. It's a sort of delivery service. Except as well as delivering a good evening, the delivery "boys" will also give you an orgasm – if you want one, that is. If you'd rather have a chaste goodnight kiss, they'll deliver that on your doorstep, see you in, and leave.'

Selena laughed. 'I don't quite believe you said that, Ruth! A delivery service – orgasms on your doorstep?'

Ruth coughed. 'I'm being serious.'

'You mean, you're just going to find a bloke on the street and pay him to make love to me?'

'No, it's not just any bloke – there's a tight selection process. If we like the answer to the ad—'

'We? Ad?' Selena asked.

'Laura, Shelley and me. I put an ad in one of the papers, asking for broad-minded individuals . . . Anyway, Mark is one of the men who answered my ad. We all liked him. He's been through a training programme, courtesy of Shelley, Laura and Meg; and he's really very nice.'

Selena frowned. 'So this is what you're going to do, then? Become a female Pandarus?'

'Now you're making it sound sordid. I mean it to be something to cheer up people who've had a bloody lousy time and could just do with something *nice* happening in their lives, for once. Anyway, you don't have to order it yourself. Someone can order it for you. A bit like someone sending you flowers – you don't send them to yourself, do you?'

'No,' Selena admitted, 'but I can buy myself expensive chocolate, in large quantities. That's just as good.'

Ruth grinned. 'It's hardly in the same league, though. Even if you buy one of your little toys to go with it.'

Selena grinned back. 'My little toys, as you put them, are a damn sight more reliable than the last few men I've been with. At least they're always guaranteed to please me. Ruthie, I think you've gone mad.'

'I'm perfectly sane, Selena.'

'What about your marketing career? You worked bloody hard for those exams. Now you're throwing them away.'

'Not at all – I'm using them in Interlover. I've seen a need in the market, and I'm providing a service that will meet those needs.'

Selena ignored her. 'You've done really well in your career. You've made a good name for yourself in the publishing world. If you want to work for yourself, why don't you set up your own publishing company? A small press, or something? It wouldn't cost that much to set it up. You could even – oh, I dunno, set up a management buyout of Romulus, or something.'

Ruth shook her head. 'I want to do something different.'

'Then why not combine the two?' Selena suggested. 'You can run this Interlover thing at the same time. Bearing in mind the sort of clients you'd go for – the sort of people you mix with – you could get the Interlovers to deliver one of your latest books and the catalogue, as well as everything else.'

'Yes, I like it,' Ruth said, smiling. 'It could be a refinement for the future – an early refinement.' She coughed. 'Actually, I have had a couple of job offers. It's leaked out on the grapevine that I'm officially unemployed.'

'And?'

'I don't think anything's going to match up to Romulus, to be honest, so I've turned them down,' Ruth said. 'Anyway, I quite like the idea of being my own boss. Being the one in control – not having to listen to other people's accountants and their common sense saying that your idea won't work, when you have a gut feeling that it will.'

Selena grinned. 'That's rich, considering that you live with an accountant.' She suddenly noticed the ring on Ruth's finger. 'And not only live with him, by the looks of that rock.'

'Ah, yes. That.' Ruth glanced at the ring, and coughed. 'I know I said I'd never do it, but it's a small price to pay to make sure that Aidan doesn't start feeling insecure about Interlover.'

Selena's eyes narrowed. 'In other words, there's something you're not telling me.'

'I don't know what you mean.'

'Oh, come on. I've known you since we did that course together, years ago; and Aidan isn't exactly the paranoid type. He's the most well-adjusted bloke I've ever met. There must be a reason why he'd suddenly start to feel insecure.'

Ruth sighed. 'OK. If you must know, Mark – our pilot Interlover – is probably one of the most attractive men I've ever met. I'd like to go to bed with him, but I can't. It wouldn't be fair to Aidan. And you shouldn't sleep with your staff: it's the first rule of business.'

'Perhaps it would do you good, to get it out of your system,' Selena suggested.

'Maybe, but I don't know if I could live with the guilt, afterwards.'

'You never know till you try.'

Ruth grinned. 'Anyone would think you were trying to set me up with the guy! So – are you up for it, then, or not?'

'I'm not sure.'

'I need to know if it's a viable proposition.' Ruth tipped her head on one side. 'Meg and Helen both agreed.'

'*Helen* agreed?' Selena was surprised.

'Mm. I had an ulterior motive in asking her – I thought that Mark might help her get over Stu.'

'I hope he does.' She spread her hands. 'Well, all right. If they're in, so am I. Though I think you've been incredibly sneaky, talking to us all individually and persuading us that we'll be the only ones not to help out.'

'Now, would I do something like that?'

'It goes with the marketing training.'

'Yeah.' Ruth grinned. 'Like I said, it's called meeting customer needs.'

Selena grinned back. 'Delivering your fantasies, gift-wrapped. A sexy, broad-minded man whose aim is to give you pleasure – and lots of it. Actually, the more I think about it, the more I like the idea.'

Ruth smiled. 'I thought you would. Out of all of my friends, I thought you would . . .'

The buzzer rang; Helen put down her brush and frowned. Who the hell was coming to visit her at this sort of time? She wasn't expecting anyone – unless it was Stu, come round to apologize for hurting her, tell her that it was all over between him and the latest bimbo, and talk her into trying again. Her face hardened. If it was him, he could bloody well go away again. She wasn't taking him back, this time. As far as she was concerned, it was all over between them. History.

Then she suddenly remembered. Mark, the man that Ruth was sending round to see her – the trainee Interlover. She rubbed a hand across her face, not realizing that she'd managed to smudge blue paint on her nose, and went to answer the door.

Mark stood there, smiling. 'Hi. You must be Helen.'

'And you must be Mark.'

He frowned. 'Weren't you expecting me?'

Helen smiled ruefully. 'Actually, I'd forgotten the time. I was working. Come in, anyway. Would you like a coffee?'

'Look, I can always come back another time, if it would be more convenient.'

'No. It'll probably do me good to have a break, anyway.' She flexed her shoulders. 'I should have stopped an hour or so ago. I get stiff, if I paint for too long.'

'I know what you mean – if I spend the afternoon strumming on the guitar, hunched up on the sofa, I suffer for it afterwards. Well, these are for you.' He handed her a carefully-wrapped bunch of white roses, and a carrier bag printed with the name of the local off-licence.

'Thank you.' She buried her face in the roses, inhaling the bouquet. 'These are gorgeous. I'd better put them in some water. Come in.'

He followed her into the kitchen. She reminded him a bit of Ruth: the same hazel eyes, which would grow dark if she was upset about something, and turn almost gold when she came. He squeezed his eyes shut. Hell. He had to stop thinking about Ruth. Besides, he was here for a purpose – not to moon about a woman who was out of his reach.

He studied Helen's rear view. She was wearing a loose cotton shirt and a pair of old faded leggings, which obscured her figure: he guessed that it was generous, judging by her pretty but slightly plump face. She was shorter than Ruth, though a little taller than Shelley, and her mop of golden-blonde curls gave her the look of a Botticelli angel.

She turned round and gestured to him to sit down at the small bistro-style table, while she put the flowers in a vase and made the coffee.

'Ruth tells me you're a painter,' he said. 'I hate to admit it, but I'm not exactly familiar with your work.'

'It's mainly commercial stuff,' Helen replied, 'so you've probably seen it – you just haven't known that it's mine. I do illustrations for book jackets and CDs, that sort of thing.'

'If we ever put out a demo, maybe you could do a cover for us,' he suggested.

'Sure. Just lend me a copy of the tape, and I'll work out something to suit the music.'

'Cheers.' He paused. 'Book jackets, too. So that's how you know Ruth? Through your work?'

She nodded. 'It's a real shame about Romulus folding. Not just because of the money – being freelance, I can find work somewhere else – but for Ruth. She loved that job.'

'It does seem to have hit her quite hard.' He shrugged. 'Still, I imagine she'll cope. She's engaged to this Aidan chap, so I suppose he gives her all the support she needs.'

'You've not met him, then?'

Mark shook his head. 'What's he like?'

'A nice guy. He and Ruth have been together for a long while.' She tipped her head on one side. 'Does Ruth know how you feel about her?'

Mark kicked himself mentally. How stupid could he be? Mooning around after Ruth was bad enough, but telling her friends that he was half in love with her... He decided to bluff his way out of it. 'Sorry, I'm not with you.'

'Oh, come on. It's pretty obvious that you're carrying a torch for her. The way you said Aidan's name – as if he were some kind of enemy, rather than just someone you hadn't met.'

Mark sighed. Hell. He had to come clean, now. 'Yeah. I answered her ad as a bit of fun. I was intrigued, wanted to know more: plus I need another job anyway, to supplement my income from the band. I wanted to do something a bit more interesting than working in a hamburger place, this time, and the ad seemed to fit the bill. Then, when I met her and she offered me the job...' He shrugged. 'I discovered that she was my ideal woman. But – she's attached, and she's sort of my boss, so that means she's off limits.'

'She is indeed,' Helen said drily. 'Mind you, in a way, I was surprised that she'd agreed to marry Aidan. He's wanted to make more of a commitment for ages, but Ruth's very independent. She's always resisted the idea.'

'I gathered that. I wonder why she changed her mind?'

Helen shrugged. 'Maybe she realized that it was what she wanted, after all.'

'Right.' Mark paused. 'So what's he really like? I know you said he's a nice guy, but . . .'

Helen whistled. 'You really have got it bad, haven't you?'

Mark flushed. 'Sorry. Just forget I asked.'

'No, it's OK.' Helen had felt the same sort of thing, the desperate need to know more about her rival. 'Well, he's an accountant. I suppose he's about the same age as us, in his early thirties. He's about the same height as you: blond hair, blue eyes, broad shoulders. He looks a bit like you, actually.' She grinned. 'I probably shouldn't say this, but you're the typical Finn type. Ruth always goes for tall blonds with blue eyes, a nice bum and a big nose.'

'A big nose?' His eyes widened.

She grinned. 'Meant in the nicest possible sense.'

Mark felt his loins kick. 'So there's some hope?'

'To be honest, I doubt it. Ruth and Aidan go back quite a while, and she fell for him the first day they met. They like the same sort of things – the theatre, books, music, art galleries – and, although they don't live in each other's pockets, they're close enough virtually to read each other's mind. To talk to him, you'd never think that he was a boring accountant. You'd think he was the arts editor for some highbrow magazine, or something like that.' She smiled. 'Like I said, he's a nice guy. In other circumstances, the two of you would get on really well.'

'In other circumstances,' Mark agreed. He couldn't imagine himself ever getting on well with Ruth's lover. *Fiancé*, he reminded himself harshly. He bit his lips. 'Helen, I don't want to make a mess of things. You won't say anything to her, will you?'

'Of course not.' She handed him a mug of coffee. 'Milk or sugar?'

He shook his head. 'Neither, thanks.' He took a sip. 'Mm. This is good.'

'Blue Mountain. Ruth's influence – she was the one who discovered it, and once I'd tried it, I loved it, too.'

'Mm.' Mark nodded. 'So how did you get involved in Interlover?'

'The same as the rest of us, I suppose. Ruth told me about the idea. Anyway, I've recently split up with Stu – we'd been together for about six years, in between his affairs with other women.' Her eyes darkened with sudden pain. 'The last affair was a bit more serious – she wanted to marry him. Though he always told me that he wasn't the marrying type, and a bit of paper didn't make any difference to his feelings, this time something seemed different. I think he wanted to marry her, too.' She shrugged. 'So, I thought it was best for both of us if he left.'

'But you're still carrying a torch for him?'

'If I'm being honest – yes. Like I said, we'd been together for six years. Though I'm trying to persuade myself that my feelings for him are more habit than anything else. When Ruth told me about her idea, I wasn't convinced, at first. But the more I thought about it, the more I thought that she was probably right. Seeing someone else, no strings attached, might be good for me.'

'You mean,' Mark said, 'having a damn good fuck with someone who won't hurt you or demand things you can't give?'

'Exactly. Ruth has this theory that sex is a good healer. So maybe we can help each other, in that respect.'

'Maybe.' He smiled at her. 'Did you know that you have paint all over your face?'

She grinned. 'It wouldn't surprise me.'

'So what were you working on?' he asked.

'A book jacket. They wanted something blue.' She winced again as the muscles in her shoulders twinged.

Mark put his mug down. 'I might be a bit presumptuous here, but would you like that neck massage?'

'Actually, yes, I would,' she admitted. 'Ruth didn't tell me that you were an expert masseur.'

'Among other things. Lou taught me.'

'Your girlfriend?' she guessed.

'No, my sister. She's an actress. She gets tense before interviews, and one of her tutors suggested that she had a massage. So she learned how to do it, and taught me.' He grinned. 'You could say that I indulge my kid sister a bit too much.'

Helen was secretly impressed. Not many brothers would act like that. 'So you see a lot of her, then?'

'You could say that! We share a house, with a few mutual friends. There are six of us. We also have half-shares in a car.'

'Ah, yes – the famous Roach.'

He grinned. 'News travels fast. Unlike my poor Roach.'

Helen eased her shoulders again. 'Should we go somewhere more comfortable for this massage?'

'I can do you while you're sitting up.' He nodded to the carrier bag. 'That might help, too.'

Helen looked inside, and grinned as she retrieved the bottle. 'Champagne. Lovely.'

'And it's already chilled,' Mark said. 'The off-licence round the corner had a chiller cabinet.'

She smiled at him. 'Here's the deal. You open the bottle – I'll get the glasses.'

He nodded and swiftly uncorked the champagne, without spilling a drop. He poured it into the two glasses; Helen lifted hers. 'Here's to us – and an uncomplicated relationship.'

Mark echoed the toast, and drank to it. He turned her chair to face his. 'You might find it more comfortable if you rest your arms on the back of the chair, and put your head forward.'

Helen did as he asked, sitting with her back to him. 'Do you want me to take my shirt off?' she asked.

'Please.'

She unbuttoned it, discarding it on the floor.

'Do you have any massage oil?'

'Only bath oil.'

'Not quite the same thing. How about olive oil? At least your skin wouldn't drag then.'

'There's some in the cupboard.' She indicated one of the cupboards; Mark retrieved the oil, and anointed his hands. Helen closed her eyes and rested her head on her arms; Mark began to rub the tension out of her shoulders.

He had nice hands, she thought. Firm, and yet sensitive. She remembered that he was a musician; and all musicians had sensitive hands.

Mark was doing something she'd always wanted Stu to do for her – but Stu, being the selfish bastard he was, had never done so. No doubt he had given his bimbos a back massage, though. Using sensual oil, as a prelude to love-making. It was one of the reasons that Helen had never bought any proper massage oil. If Stu had borrowed it to use on one of his women, it would have been too much for her to bear.

She forced herself to stop thinking about Stu and let herself relax as Mark continued to ease her shoulders, his fingers digging into the knots of tension and loosening them. It would be so easy for his hands to dip down slightly, she thought, to curve across her ribcage and touch her breasts.

Almost as if she'd spoken aloud, she felt him undo the clasp of her bra, and slide the garment off her shoulders. He paused, waiting for her to protest; when she said nothing, and arched her back slightly to indicate her consent, he continued rubbing her skin, his hands sliding down her spine. Eventually, his hands curved over her ribcage to touch the underside of her breasts, and she made a small sound of pleasure.

He continued to caress and stroke her skin, cupping her breasts and pushing them up and together slightly; she tipped her head back, arching her body to give him easier access. His fingers splayed over her breasts, letting her nipples peep out between his middle and ring fingers; then he squeezed his fingers together again, gently pinching her nipples.

At the same time, he kissed the curve between her neck and shoulders, making her shiver with arousal. His lips travelled up the side of her neck, concentrating on the sensitive spot just below her ear. He nipped gently at her earlobe, and she shivered again. Her nipples were hard and taut, needing release: she wanted him to kiss them, to lick them and suck them. She wanted him to lick her in more intimate places, too – to use his mouth on her until she came, her eyes wild and her hair mussed, her sex flexing under his tongue.

'Mark,' she said, her voice a hoarse whisper. 'I think I need this as much as you do. Let's go to bed.'

He nodded, releasing his hands from her body, and she stood up, unconcerned by her semi-naked state. He took her hand, bringing it to his lips, and kissed her fingers, one by one.

She licked her lower lip. 'When Antonio Banderas did that to Tom Hanks in *Philadelphia*, I thought it was one of the most erotic things I've ever seen.'

'Me, too,' he said. 'And you have beautiful hands – which makes it even more of a turn-on.'

He let her lead him out of the kitchen into her bedroom. She unbuttoned his shirt, sliding her hands underneath the soft cotton. He felt good, and Helen acknowledged wryly that Ruth had been right. Mark *was* going to be very good for her. But what Ruth didn't know, she thought, was that Helen was going to be equally as good for Mark, easing the ache he felt at not having Ruth. She slid the soft cotton from his shoulders, letting his shirt drop to the floor.

He smiled, then, and cupped her face, kissing her lightly on the lips. 'Helen,' he said softly, 'I have a feeling that we're both going to enjoy this.'

'So have I.' She smiled back. 'Though about that champagne – if we leave it for too long, it'll go flat.'

'Hint taken,' he said with a grin.

He went into the kitchen to retrieve the wine and their glasses; while he was gone, Helen removed her old faded leggings, and the remaining wisps of her underwear. When he returned, she had just pushed the duvet from the bed.

'Do you want me to close the curtains?' he asked.

She shook her head. 'We're not overlooked; besides, I want to see you.'

He nodded, and placed the champagne by the bed, peeling off his faded denims, followed by the rest of his underwear.

Helen's eyes widened. Ruth hadn't told her just how good Mark looked naked: maybe because she didn't actually know. 'I'd like to paint you,' she said.

'What, now?' He smiled at her.

'Some other time. Maybe later.' Later, when he was asleep . . . She shivered inside at the delicious possibilities.

He climbed onto the bed beside her, running the flat of his hands lightly across her midriff, then stroking down towards her thighs. 'You have beautiful skin,' he said, 'soft and smooth.' Just as he imagined Ruth to be, warm and soft and inviting.

She flushed, unused to compliments. Stu had never noticed things like that – or, at least, he'd never commented. 'Thank you.'

He rubbed his nose against hers. 'And I love your scent.'

'It's probably paint,' she said, laughing.

'No, there's a deeper note. I can't place it, but it's gorgeous.'

'Soap?' she hazarded.

He laughed, kissing her lightly on the mouth; then his lips began to track downwards over her throat. She closed her eyes, tipping her head back into the pillow to give him better access. Mark smiled, and took a mouthful of champagne; keeping the wine in his mouth, he stooped to kiss one nipple, swooshing the bubbly liquid over her skin.

She wriggled at the unfamiliar sensation, and opened her eyes. 'What the hell . . . ?'

Mark swallowed the wine, and smiled at her. 'Just trying out something I read in a book. Some erotic novel that Lou or one of the others had left lying around – I picked it up, and the first thing I read about was a champagne blowjob. So, I thought, what's sauce for the goose . . . And here we are, with a bottle of champagne. It's too good an opportunity to miss.'

She chuckled. 'Yeah.'

He picked up the bottle and poured a tiny amount of the wine in the vee between her breasts, pressing his tongue against it to make the bubbles burst over her skin.

Helen was surprised, shocked and pleased, all at the same time. She hadn't expected him to have such a virtuoso style. When he poured more champagne over her midriff, nuzzling her skin as he licked it clean, she arched up towards him. Gradually, he moved southwards, towards her mound of Venus, and stopped.

'Don't worry,' he said softly. 'I wasn't intending to use champagne on you here.' He ran his fingers along her labia. 'You'd be too sensitive, and it'd sting. Now, if we had ice cubes, or strawberries, it'd be a little different. I'd like to slide an ice cube over you, then warm you up with my mouth. Or push a strawberry into you, and suck it out again, tasting your sweetness mingled with the sweetness of the fruit.' He stroked her thighs apart, and drew his tongue down her satiny cleft. 'Mm. On second thoughts, I think I'd rather have you as you are. Honey and musk and spice.'

He began lapping at her in earnest; at last, Helen felt the tiny shivers of her climax approaching. To her mingled surprise and disappointment, he stopped; she frowned, opening her eyes.

'Shh, it's all right,' he said, shifting to kneel between her thighs. 'I just wanted to be inside you when you came. To feel your body clinging to mine.' As he spoke, the tip of his cock butted against the entrance of her sex; she pushed up, and he slid deep inside her. As he entered her, she came, her flesh convulsing sharply round the hard rod of his penis; he began to thrust, long, slow, deep strokes which made her orgasm last longer, a thousand tiny ripples round him.

He didn't stop, but continued pushing into her. She felt the wave of another climax rushing through her and curved her hands round his buttocks, her fingers digging in slightly to urge him on. He changed his rhythm, his cock moving deeper and harder inside her; Helen felt as though she were drowning in pleasure, and cried out as a second orgasm bubbled through her. She heard his answering cry, and felt his body surge against hers, his cock throbbing in tune with the beat of his heart.

He buried his head in her shoulder; she slid her hands up to caress his back. They lay there in silence for a while; at last, Mark withdrew from her, rolling onto his back and tucking her into the curve of his body, keeping his arms protectively round her.

It was strangely comforting, Helen thought. Breathing in the scent of his skin, a clean and musky male smell which aroused her and relaxed her at the same time. And the way he was holding her – Stu had rarely, if ever, done that. He'd been more concerned about his own comforts than hers. Whereas Mark . . .

Eventually, she fell asleep, her breathing becoming deep and regular. Mark lay awake, thinking. He'd enjoyed what he'd just done with Helen – so had she, by the look in her eyes – but it wasn't the same as making love with the woman of his dreams. Ruth Finn. If only it had been Ruth in his arms, instead . . .

He knew that Ruth was attracted to him. She'd kissed him back, that time, and Helen had admitted that he was Ruth's 'type'. Maybe it would have worked between them – but she was engaged to Aidan. They were the perfect couple, by all accounts: it wouldn't be fair to break it up, cause her so much pain. And yet his body yearned for her. He sighed. Hell. Maybe it would work out. But just now, he couldn't quite see how.

At last, he drifted off to sleep; he woke, later, when he turned over to cuddle Helen and realized that the bed was empty. He came to with a jerk and sat up, feeling disoriented and wondering where the hell he was. Then he saw Helen sitting in a chair by the bed, sketching with a piece of charcoal.

'What are you doing?' he said.

'I told you – I want to paint you. But I need a preliminary sketch. I've nearly finished.'

'Can I see it?'

'Sure.' She handed the pad to him.

His eyes widened. 'Wow! It's a very good likeness.'

'I should hope so. I'm a professional artist, remember,' she said, smiling to take the sting from her words.

'Yes. And a good one.' He smiled at her. 'Because the two don't necessarily go together.' He handed the pad back to her. 'Could I have a copy of it, please?'

'Sure. On one condition.'

'What's that? I mean, I'm happy to pay you.'

'I don't want payment.' She grinned. 'But I could really do with a coffee, at the moment . . .'

He laughed, and climbed off the bed. 'Coming right up,' he said.

'You're looking pleased with yourself.' Aidan came to sit beside Ruth.

'I am. It's a good book,' Ruth said, slipping a bookmark between the pages and putting the book on the floor so that she could curl into Aidan's arms.

'It takes more than a book to put that sort of look on your face.'

'All right. I had a call from Helen, and she said that she felt a lot brighter. I think my delivery to her helped her forget about Stu, for a while.'

'Ah, yes. The famous Mark Beasley.'

There was a slightly bitter twinge to Aidan's voice, and Ruth sighed. 'Look, Aidan – I wish you'd stop fretting about it. I told you, it's purely business.' Even though, a small voice in her head reminded her, she would have liked it to be more than that. A lot more than that. 'Anyway, don't forget I have my slave badge on now.'

He frowned. 'What slave badge?'

She lifted her left hand, letting the diamond sparkle in the light. 'This.'

'A bloody expensive slave badge, actually,' he said, rubbing his nose against hers. 'But before you say it – yes, it was worth every penny.'

'Good.'

He lifted her hand to his lips, drawing her fingertips into his mouth and sucking gently on them. Ruth shivered. God, after all this time, he could still arouse her with the simplest action. All thoughts of Mark went straight out of her head as Aidan began to kiss his way up her arm, licking the skin in the crook of her elbow.

'Aidan,' she said softly.

'Mm, I know.' He slid his hands under her T-shirt. 'I love you – you know that, don't you?'

She nodded. 'Same here.'

'You mean, you love you, too?' he teased, wriggling his fingers under the edge of her bra.

She laughed. 'No. You know exactly what I meant!'

'Yeah.' His fingers curved over her breast. 'Mm. You feel good. In fact . . .' He removed his hand, leaving her bra awry, and urged her forward slightly so that he could remove her T-shirt. 'And you look as good as you feel.' He teased the hard peaks of her nipples. 'I wonder if . . .' He bent forward, taking one nipple into his mouth, and drew gently on it.

Ruth made a small sound of pleasure and closed her eyes, sliding her hands into his hair and urging him on. Aidan slid his hands round her back, smoothing them down her spine, and undid her bra, removing it deftly and then stroking her breasts. His hand slid down to span her waist; he began to push at the waistband of her leggings, rolling them down. Ruth lifted her bottom to let him remove them completely, and he smiled.

'What?'

'This is just how I like you,' he said softly. 'Lewd and wanton.'

'Oh, yes?'

He slid one finger under the gusset of her knickers. She was already warm and wet, and he grinned. 'I see. That sort of book, was it?'

'What?'

'One of Selena's? Or Shelley's?'

She sighed. 'Would you believe me if I told you it was something literary?'

He shook his head. 'You don't get that turned on, that quickly, without reading something that sparks off your imagination. And no way can Dickens be arousing!'

'Hardy can, though. And Eliot. I've always fancied Will Ladislaw.'

'That's since you, Shelley and Laura watched the TV adaptation of *Middlemarch* and decided that you all fancied the actor who played him,' was the swift retort.

Ruth grinned. 'OK. So I was reading smut. It's literary, though – ancient Chinese porn, called *Chin P'ing Mei.*'

'Indeed.'

'Selena's, as you so rightly guessed. She said I'd enjoy it.' She gave him a sidelong glance. 'So would you, actually.'

'Then you can read me some, later.' He smiled at her. 'But first . . .' He moved her so that she was sitting on the very edge of the sofa, her legs spread wide, and knelt on the floor in front of her. He undid his fly, and eased his swollen cock out. As he pressed its tip to Ruth's sex, she curved her legs round his waist, pushing her heels onto his buttocks; he slid deep inside her.

'God, you feel so good,' he breathed, and began to thrust, tilting his hips to penetrate her more deeply. She slid her hands round his neck and kissed him, hard; he rested his hands on the sofa and quickened the rhythm, pushing in hard and pulling out slowly.

At last, he felt the familiar pressure of orgasm at the base of his loins; as he came, he felt her internal muscles flex sharply round his cock. He cried out her name, burying his face in her shoulder; she stroked his hair.

'Rampant beast,' she teased softly.

'Sorry. You looked so gorgeous, I couldn't wait to take you to bed.' He smiled at her, rubbing his nose against hers. 'Though, since you've raised the subject . . . Let's take your book with us.'

Ruth grinned. her lover was back to normal. 'I thought you'd never ask . . .'

SEVEN

Ruth looked at the sketch. It was the nearest she'd ever come to seeing Mark naked. His body was beautiful: she could see why Helen had itched to capture the clean lines. There was a kind of vulnerability about his mouth as he slept, which made her stomach clench with longing,

'Oh, what a tangled web,' Helen said, catching the look on her friend's face.

'I don't know what you mean.'

Helen coughed. 'The two of you. It's fairly obvious that you've got the hots for him, but you don't know what to do about it, because you don't want to hurt Aidan – and, at the same time, you can't help wondering what it would be like to make love with Mark.'

'Yeah. Aidan's understanding about a lot of things, but I don't think that he'd appreciate this, somehow,' Ruth said.

'Is that why you're avoiding the poor guy? It's hardly fair.'

'How do you mean?'

'You take Mark on to train him for the Interlover job – then you ignore him.'

'I'm not ignoring him. I've talked to him on the phone. I saw his band play at the pub, the other night.'

'And?'

Ruth sighed. 'He walked me home, and then he kissed me on the doorstep. I'm not sure which of us broke the kiss, but I panicked a bit afterwards.' She sighed again. 'Part of me wishes that I'd never even thought of this bloody Interlover thing. Maybe I ought to be sensible, like Aidan says, and get myself a proper job again.'

'Is that what you really want?' Helen asked.

'No. I was upset when Romulus folded – we all were – but now that I'm actually out of the rat race, I've discovered that I rather like the freedom. I'm not in any hurry to go back to stuffy Tube journeys, and working from ten till six every weekday, bringing stuff home in the evenings and at weekends.'

'Fair enough.' Helen paused. 'So what are you going to do about Mark?'

'I don't know.' Unconsciously, Ruth's fingertips moved across the charcoal, caressing the sketch of Mark's body. 'At the moment, I just don't know.'

'It's just as well that I put some fixative on that, isn't it?' Helen asked drily.

Ruth looked down, shocked, as she realized what she'd just been doing. 'Oh, God.'

'You're going to have to do something about it, Ruth. For all your sakes.'

'I know.' Ruth sighed. 'The question is – what?'

Mark strolled along the street. He'd taken the Tube to Holborn; Lou had offered him a lift in Roach, but he'd waved her away with a smile. He'd wanted a walk, to clear his head. He'd lived in Holborn, once, and liked the place: the second-hand bookshops, the street-traders selling 'papyrus' and Egyptian mementoes, the antiques and curio shops. It had a certain atmosphere which set it apart from the rest of London.

He stole a swift look at the piece of paper in his hand. He was on the right street: he glanced at the number on the door. Half a dozen places more, and he'd be at Selena's flat. He wondered what she was like. Ruth hadn't given him much information on the phone: merely that Selena was a translator, lived in Holborn, and liked good red wine.

He smiled to himself. Maybe she was like Juliet Stevenson in *Truly, Madly, Deeply*, with an interesting and unconventionally pretty face, a tip-tilted nose, and blonde hair that curled round her face. As his fantasies grew, his smile turned into a wry grin. He was hardly the Alan Rickman type. He had the wrong hair colour, for a start: and he was a guitarist, not a cellist. Anyway, for all he knew, Selena could be tall, with dark hair and hazel eyes. An accessible version of Ruth.

The thought sobered him. Ruth. She'd spent the bare minimum of time on the phone to him, and her voice had been faintly clipped. Maybe she was still angry at him for kissing her.

And yet she'd kissed him back. For that one brief moment, she'd wanted him as much as he wanted her. It was enough to sustain him; he lifted his head, and found Selena's flat, above a bookshop. He leaned on the bell; he heard an answering buzz, and opened the door.

Selena was waiting for him at the top of the stairs. His eyes widened as he looked at her: she was a little shorter than Ruth, with long straight hair the colour of winter wheat in the sunlight. She wore it tied back with a silk scarf; as he neared her, he realized that her eyes were a deep grey-blue, and she did indeed have the slightly tip-tilted nose he'd thought about.

'Hello, Selena,' he said softly, taking her hand and kissing it.

'Hello, Mark.' She smiled back at him. 'Come in. Can I get you a coffee?'

'Thanks. That'd be nice.'

'How do you take it?'

'Black, no sugar, please.'

'Right.' She closed the door behind him, ushering him in.

'For you,' he said, handing her a neatly-wrapped bottle, and a bunch of white irises.

She smiled, and Mark's heart turned over. Smiling completely altered her face: instead of looking slightly severe, she looked suddenly warm and slightly vulnerable. 'Thank you,' she said quietly; her eyes lit when she unwrapped the bottle and discovered a bottle of Margaux. 'Did Ruth prime you, or was it a lucky guess?'

'Lucky guess. I tend to drink more red than white,' Mark said. 'I just hoped that you'd like the same sort of stuff as I do.'

'Very much so.' She tipped her head on one side. 'So are you driving?'

He shook his head. 'I caught the Tube.'

'Perhaps you'd like to share this with me, then?'

'Thanks, I'd love to.'

'Good. Then you can open it and give it time to breathe while I sort out the coffee.' She led him through to the kitchen, rummaged in a drawer, and produced a corkscrew. While Mark opened the Margaux, she switched on the kettle, added coffee to the cafétière, and put the irises in a jug of water.

'Ruth tells me you're a translator.' He paused. 'Did you meet her through work?'

'No. We were at an evening class together, actually. It must have been five or six years ago.'

'What subject?'

'Film studies. We joined for the same reason, actually: we both enjoyed films, but wanted to be able to appreciate them a bit more. Anyway, I ended up sitting next to Ruth in class. Our first session was about *film noir*, and we did the opening scene of *Don't Look Now* – which was one of Ruth's favourite films ever. It's one of mine, too: so we went for a drink after the class, got chatting, and discovered how much we liked each other.' She grinned. 'And Ruth quite fancied Orson Welles, too – when he was young, that is.'

'The early part of *Citizen Kane*, you mean?'

Selena nodded. 'Don't tell me that you're a film buff, too!'

'A bit,' he admitted. 'I like all the old James Stewart films. Especially *Harvey*.'

She smiled. 'Softie.'

'Yeah.' He grinned. 'I also like *Truly, Madly, Deeply*.'

She groaned. 'No. Why did I know you were going to say that?'

'Because I imagine everyone says the same thing, when they first meet you.'

'Yeah. And how they were half-expecting me to be Juliet Stevenson.'

'Mm.' He spread his hands. 'But your hair's lighter, and you look much more organized than the character she played.'

'And I don't play the piano.'

'I don't play the cello, so that makes us about quits.'

Her lips twitched. 'The thing is, can you sing Joni Mitchell songs out of tune?'

He warbled a couple of bars of 'Case of You' in an off-key falsetto, and they both started laughing.

She handed him a mug of coffee, and added sugar to her own. 'Let's go and sit down,' she suggested. 'By the time we've drunk this, the wine should have breathed enough.'

'Sounds good to me.' He followed her through to the lounge. Her flat was light and airy, with pale walls hung with perspex-framed Dufy prints. The alcoves around the fireplace were filled with open pine shelving that was crammed with a selection of videos of classic films, well-thumbed paperbacks, and a collection of CDs.

Like Shelley, she had throws draped over her sofas; there was a large cotton Turkish rug in blues, purples and greens in the centre of the room, and the original fireplace was filled with dried flowers.

'It's a nice room,' he said.

'Thanks.'

'Would you mind if I . . . ?'

She grinned. 'I'm just as nosy, when it comes to other people's shelves. Be my guest.'

'Thanks.' He placed his mug carefully on the floor, and walked over to the shelves. The paperbacks turned out to be novels and collections of poetry in a variety of languages – French, German, Italian and Spanish, as well as English. His eyes widened as he realised that some of them were decidedly erotic. '*Justine* – is that in the original?'

'Have a look,' was the dry response.

He took the well-thumbed book from the shelves; as he'd half-expected, it was in French. With a wry smile, he returned it to its place. 'I suppose at least your *Perfumed Garden* won't be in the original, though!'

'No.'

Mark turned to look at her. She really was attractive, sitting there with her legs curled under her, sipping from a mug of coffee and looking at him through her lashes, her eyes amused. He suddenly wanted to take the scarf from her hair and see her hair streaming over her shoulders: a shiver went through him.

'Selena.'

'Yes?'

'Do I take it that you approve of Ruth's idea? Interlover?'

Selena smiled. 'Because of my reading habits, you mean?'

He nodded.

'That's exactly what she thought. Actually, I'm cross with her for wasting her talent. All those exams, all that studying – and she's turned down a couple of job offers. Good ones, too.'

Mark frowned. 'So you don't approve, then?'

Selena smiled. 'Yes and no. I love the idea – just wish it was someone other than Ruth doing it.'

'Because it'll affect her relationship with Aidan?'

Selena shook her head. 'I don't think so. He was probably a bit fed up to start with, but now he's used to the idea . . . Well, he trusts her, and she won't betray that trust.'

Another oblique warning, Mark thought. All Ruth's friends had seen through his pathetic attempts to find out more about her – and about Aidan – and they'd all told him the same thing. Hands off.

He went to sit beside Selena, taking the coffee from her hand and placing it on the floor. Wordlessly, he reached over to remove the scarf from her hair. He wasn't sure which was softer: the thin black silk scarf that bound her hair, or her hair itself. He tossed the scarf to the floor, and her hair fell loosely over her shoulders. He ran his hands through it, spreading it out.

It was the sort of hair that made a man want to bury his face in it. He couldn't resist the temptation, gathering the soft silky tresses in his hands, and drawing them up to his face. Her hair was clean and fragrant; he couldn't quite place the scent, but it was somewhere between vanilla and apricots, and it aroused him. He could feel his cock hardening and pushing uncomfortably against his jeans.

Almost reluctantly, he lifted his face again, letting her hair fall down again, and cupped her chin. 'Selena,' he said softly.

Her eyes had darkened nearly to the colour of steel. Yet they weren't hard and cold – more warm and inviting. Like the depths of a winter sea, drawing him in and drowning him. Her mouth was slightly parted; she drew her tongue along her lower lip and he was lost.

He bent his head to hers, kissing her hard. Her mouth tasted of sweet coffee, and he wanted to know what the rest of her tasted like. He broke the kiss, sliding his mouth down the side of her throat, licking the sensitive spot in a way that made her shiver and arch against him. He slid his hands under the bottom of her loose sweater, spanning her narrow waist.

'Selena,' he murmured against her skin, 'I want you. I want you so badly. I want to kiss you and taste you. I want to lick you until you come.' He wanted a whole host of other things, too. For her to read de Sade to him, in French, or maybe some erotic Italian poetry. He knew that he wouldn't be able to understand the words – his French was rusty O-level, and the rest of his languages were nonexistent – but he could guess them from the cadences of her voice, and then live out some of them with her.

This was a woman he would woo with poetry. He smiled. Of course. There was that poem that Lou liked, that she'd declaimed once when they'd had friends round for dinner. He could barely remember it, but even so . . . He stroked her face. 'I could kiss your honey-sweet eyes all day . . . and still feel hungry to begin again.'

Selena looked at him, surprised. 'Catullus, isn't it?'

'You know it?' He was equally surprised.

'Mm. I did Latin at school. I suppose, really, that was when I started getting into languages.' She grinned. 'My father had a very battered old book in his study – the poems of Catullus. It was in Latin, and he thought that I couldn't translate it. Unfortunately for him, I could.' Her grin broadened. 'Some of them are really obscene.'

'Are you going to enlighten me?'

She shook her head. 'I think I'll take you up on your other idea instead.'

'What's that?'

'Going somewhere more comfortable.' Gently, she removed his hands from her waist, kissed his fingertips, then curved her fingers over his before standing up.

Mark watched her appreciatively. Selena was all elegance, clean lines and beautiful limbs. And he wanted her, very badly. He stood up, and let her lead him to her bedroom.

Selena's bedroom turned out to be almost as dramatic as Shelley's. She, too, had a wrought-iron bedstead, although hers wasn't a four-poster; and the floorboards were stained and polished, with a couple of rugs similar to the one in the living room.

'I bought them in Turkey,' she said, following his gaze. 'On holiday.' Her lips curved. 'I'll always remember that holiday. I went to Ephesus. It was a sticky, hot day; the cold water I'd brought with me was warm by the time I'd walked from one end of the ruins to the other. The guide showed us some ancient graffiti – directions to the nearest brothel. He borrowed my water to sprinkle over the stones, so we could see the graffiti properly, these little brown scratchings on the pavement. There was something in his eyes – and I just couldn't resist him.'

Her eyes sparkled at the memory. 'He was gorgeous. While the others were looking round, we went behind some fallen columns, and he started kissing me. He slid his hand under my T-shirt – I wasn't wearing a bra – and started rubbing my nipples. He slid his other hand between my thighs, rubbing the hard base of his thumb against my quim in a way that made me want to rip my clothes off and screw him there and then. It was crazy – anyone could have caught us, and he'd probably have lost his job if we'd been caught together like that – but I would have done it. I wanted him to fuck me under the hot Turkish sun.

'I think he came to his senses first, and we stopped. He put his fingers on my lips, and said, "Later." I knew what he meant – that we'd spend the night together, do it properly. Somehow, we managed to keep our hands off each other on the rest of the tour. We didn't sit near each other on the bus; but then, when we stopped for some food, he sat opposite me. I felt his foot brush against mine, then caress my calves, and move slowly upwards . . .' She shivered. 'By the time he'd reached my thighs, my quim was soaking. I wanted him so much. But we had to wait.

'We went to a carpet factory. I fell in love with some of the carpets, but I couldn't afford any of them. I was only a student

– I didn't have much money, not even enough to buy one of the cheap wool ones, let alone a silk one. He whispered in my ear that he knew I wasn't a rich tourist, and he knew where I could buy something cheaper, but still very nice.

'We arranged to meet later, and he took me round the bazaars. We found these, and he bargained for them to save me the hassle.' Her lips twitched. 'The fact that I'd bothered to learn a little Turkish was probably why he picked me, out of all the hundreds of other women. *Mil se chok*. That's "thanks".' She smiled. 'Every time I think of Turkey, I think of sweet apple tea, and that rug.' She nodded to the one beside the bed. 'We christened it, that night, in my apartment. I don't think I've ever had a night like it, before or since – we just kept going and going and going. My stomach muscles ached for weeks afterwards, he made me come so much – when his cock was tired, he used his hands and his mouth, and then his cock again. He was the most virile man I've ever met, and the most versatile.' She smiled. 'It's made me think about going to China or India to find myself a Tantric scholar – just to repeat the experience. Or even enhance it.'

Mark smiled at her. 'You're nothing like you seem, are you?'

'How do you mean?'

'When I first met you, I thought you were very graceful, very beautiful – and very much on the formal side. Untouchable, almost.'

Selena spread her hands, smiling. 'You must have had quite a shock when you looked over my books, then! Didn't Ruth tell you much about me?'

He shook his head. 'No.' She hadn't said a lot to him at all. Not since he'd kissed her. He sighed inwardly. One day, Ruth Finn, he thought. One day... And, in the meantime, I'll get your clients to sing my praises, so you know exactly what you're missing.

Selena closed the curtains, and he walked over to her, sliding his hands under her loose cream sweater again. 'Selena.' He breathed in the scent of her hair. This time, there was a slightly different note in the fragrance. The warm, spicy aroma of a woman's arousal, her anticipation of what was about to happen between them.

He turned her round to face him, and kissed her. Her mouth was so soft, so sweet. Gently, he coaxed her arms up above her head; he took the hem of her sweater, and removed the garment in one go. She was thinner than Ruth: tall and willowy. Yet her breasts, pushed together and upwards by her underwired cream lace bra, were promisingly lush.

Mark drew her back into his arms, kissing her again, then slowly let his mouth track down, licking the hollows of her throat. He stooped as he kissed her, unclasping her bra so that he could stroke the length of her back. She had a beautiful back, he found; her spine almost rippled under his questing fingers.

She closed her eyes and tipped her head back; Mark pulled off her lacy bra entirely, dropping it to the floor. Her breasts were beautiful, creamy and rosy-tipped. As he looked at her, her nipples hardened, the skin of her areolae darkening and puckering.

He dropped to his knees in front of her, cupping her breasts and gently drawing one nipple into his mouth. Again, he could smell the scent of apricots and vanilla; he wondered idly what she bathed in. Probably something of her own concoction, or something French. Whatever, she tasted as good as she smelled, clean and fresh. He sucked on one breast for a moment, then transferred his attention to its twin, rubbing her other nipple with his thumb and forefinger. Her breathing quickened, became more ragged, and he smiled. Bestowing one last kiss on each nipple, he moved down, licking her midriff.

She was wearing a pair of well-cut crinkled silk trousers; he hooked his thumb into the waistband, and drew them gently over her hips. He eased the material down her thighs; she leaned on his shoulder for balance as she lifted first one foot and then the other, letting him free her from the clinging garment.

He noticed with pleasure that her knickers matched her bra, cream silk trimmed with lace. Selena really was the sort of woman who had everything perfect, right down to the last detail. He rested his forehead against her midriff for a moment, his mouth watering with anticipation; then he hooked his thumbs into the waistband of her knickers, dealing with them as rapidly as he had dealt with her trousers.

He licked his way back up her thighs; she widened her stance, giving him better access. He paused for a moment, offering silent thanks to whatever god had given him the chance of Interlover, then drew his tongue along her silky cleft. He began a leisurely exploration of her more intimate topography; his tongue slid across her labia to seek out every fold and crevice, though he deliberately avoided her clitoris, so as to tease her.

Eventually she lost patience and thrust her pelvis towards him, wanting him to pleasure her more. Mark smiled against her skin, and drew her clitoris into his mouth, sucking gently on the hard bud of flesh. She gasped, and he began to use his tongue in earnest, flicking it rapidly over her clitoris in a figure-of-eight motion, until she cried out.

He felt her internal muscles flex hard as she came, filling his mouth with a sweet musky nectar. He dropped a kiss on each thigh, and then stood up. Selena's eyes were very wide, her pupils dilated. 'OK?' he asked softly, stroking her face.

Her hand came up to cover his. 'OK,' she confirmed, with a smile. 'Very OK.'

There was a pause. 'So, what now?' he asked.

'Well,' she said, 'the whole point of an Interlover is to help you live out your fantasies.'

Mark felt a slight flicker of apprehension. This was a woman who read de Sade in the original. The titles of the modern erotic novels on her shelves had implied that the contents were fairly violent. Just what did she have in mind?'

His alarm must have shown on her face, because she smiled. 'Nothing *too* kinky, I promise you. Not this time, anyway.' She spread her hands. 'I think you might even enjoy this.'

She unbuttoned his shirt and pushed the soft cotton from his shoulders, her fingers skating lightly over his skin. He shivered with pleasure, liking her touch, and she smiled, misreading his shiver. 'Mark, there's nothing to be scared about. I promise you.'

Her hands drifted down to the button of his jeans. Mark felt his sex swelling as she slowly unzipped his denims, not touching him intimately. He had half-expected her to curl her fingers round his cock, feel its length and breadth and decide whether she was satisfied with it. But no: she merely held his gaze, and drew her tongue over her lip in a deliberately lascivious way.

She eased the soft material over his hips; he stepped out of them, removing his socks at the same time. 'Turn round,' she said softly. 'I want to see you properly.'

He did so, and she laughed softly. 'I bet Helen painted you, didn't she?'

He flushed. 'Well, actually – yes, she did.'

'I thought so.' She smiled. 'If I had half her talent with a brush, I'd do the same. As it is . . .' She let the words trail off, and pushed the duvet from her bed. 'Let's make ourselves more comfortable.'

He sat down on the bed; she sat down beside him and kissed him hard, pushing him back and manoeuvring him so that he was lying full-length on the sheet. She knelt beside him. 'Close your eyes,' she said softly.

'Why?'

'Just humour me, will you? I won't do anything that you won't like.'

'All right,' he said eventually, closing his eyes.

'And put your hands above your head.'

He smiled to himself, suddenly knowing what she was going to do. Selena was the sophisticated sort, and she obviously appreciated a little light bondage. He would lay bets that she'd use a black silk scarf, too, like the one she'd worn in her hair earlier.

True to his expectations, he felt something being tied very gently round his wrists. There was a slight jerk as she tied him to the bedstead, then tugged experimentally at his bonds. 'That'll do,' she said.

He opened his eyes. 'I really don't know why you told me to close my eyes. I knew you were going to do that.'

'Did you, now?' She sat beside him, and opened the drawer of her bedside cabinet. Mark's eyes widened as he saw the large vibrator in there.

Selena caught his gaze, and smiled. 'Don't worry,' she said, 'I'm not planning to use it on you. It's my personal favourite toy when I've had a hard day at work and just want to forget everything. Particularly translations of French legal documents.' She rolled her eyes. 'Which is what I've had to deal with, all this week.'

'So you want something to take your mind off it, do you?' Mark asked, making his cock nod at her.

She grinned. 'Yes, indeedy.' She brought out a small packet of condoms. 'Would you prefer that we use these?'

'I don't mind,' Mark said. 'Originally, I told Ruth that I'd only be interested if we used standard protection, but—'

Selena nodded. 'Mm. You never get quite as much sensation, do you?'

'No.' He looked at her, smiling. All of Ruth's friends seemed like any other professional woman: slightly formal, with a kind nature. It was only when you looked below the surface that you discovered just how deeply sensual they were – and how at home they were with their sensuality. Pictures flashed into his mind: Laura, half-naked and rumpled on her sofa. Shelley, and those beautiful photographs. Meg, in the jacuzzi. Helen, with her beautiful hands and generous mouth. And now Selena, sophisticated and all woman.

Selena put the box of condoms back into the drawer. 'Now we know that we're not using these, it's quite safe to use something else...'

His eyes narrowed. 'Such as?'

'This.' She knelt between his thighs, bowing her head. Her hair fell against his skin, tickling him slightly, and he wriggled. She smiled, and then wrapped the ends of her long hair around his cock, rubbing it gently. The friction was amazing; Mark almost cried out in pleasure. She smiled then, and uncoiled her hair from his cock.

He waited in an agony of anticipation. Was she going to do what he so badly wanted her to do? Was she going to take his cock into her beautiful mouth, licking the seeping moisture from the top and then working her way down the shaft?

To his intense pleasure, that was precisely what she did.

This was something that Selena had done quite often, he thought. That, or she was just naturally brilliant. The way she knew exactly when to put pressure on, to suck harder or to let her tongue swirl against his glans. The way she made her tongue into a sharp point to tease his frenum. The way her lips moved over his skin...

Within minutes, he was writhing beneath her, tugging at his bonds and desperately wanting to bring his hands down so that he could touch her, stroke her, let her know how much pleasure she was giving him and how he appreciated it. And yet he couldn't: his movements were completely controlled by her. He closed his eyes, tipping his pelvis upwards. 'Selena, if you don't stop,' he said huskily, 'I'm going to come.'

She stopped for a moment. 'That,' she said, her voice filled with laughter, 'is the whole idea.' She bent her head again, taking the tip of his cock into her mouth and teasing him. He felt his orgasm boil up, his cock stiffening and an almost unbearable pressure in his groin: then, at last, he came, his cock throbbing. Selena swallowed every drop of the warm salty liquid, and Mark groaned.

He twisted his head on the pillow, his damp face relaxing against the cool crisp cotton. As his orgasm died away, Selena came up to lie beside him. She kissed him hard, so that he could taste himself on her. 'OK?' she asked.

'Mm.' His smile was rueful. It would have been even better if he'd been able to touch her.

She knelt beside him, and kissed down his body again. Mark looked at her. 'Are you going to untie me?'

She shook her head. 'Not just yet.'

'My arms ache,' he complained.

'As the saying goes,' she retorted, a mischievous glint in her eyes, 'hang on in there!'

He groaned. 'That's probably the worst pun I've ever heard.'

'In that case . . .' She began to tickle him mercilessly.

Mark writhed underneath her, laughing helplessly, until tears came to his eyes. 'Selena, no, please stop!'

She noticed with pleasure that his cock was rigid again. 'Why – do you have something better in mind?'

'I might have.'

'Such as?'

He grinned. 'You've already shown me that you've got one hell of an imagination. Why don't you use it?'

She smiled then, and straddled him, her long legs brushing against his. She lowered herself gently until her quim was just resting on his cock. He could feel the moist heat of her sex against his and it drove him mad, wanting more. Had his hands not been tied, he would have eased them between their bodies, raised her up slightly, and then fitted the tip of his cock to her quim, letting her slide down onto him. As it was, he had to wait until she was ready.

She moved down onto all fours, deliberately pushing her quim along his cock so that its head rubbed against her clitoris. She sighed with pleasure, placing her hands by his shoulders and lowering her upper body so that the hard tips of her breasts brushed his chest.

Mark groaned, and pushed his pelvis up against hers. 'Selena, please.'

'What do you want to do?' she asked.

He saw the teasing light in her eyes and realized that what *she* wanted *him* to do was to tell her everything, in graphic detail. 'I want to feel you slide your hands around my cock. I want to feel you fit it to your sex and then slide down very slowly onto it, so it feels like warm wet silk wrapping round me. I want you to use your internal muscles to flex against me. And because you've got me tied like this, so I can't do it myself, I'd like to see you rub your nipples and your clitoris. I want to see you arouse yourself, so that you're as turned on as I am. I want to see you come, your eyes all wild and your hair flying.'

She tipped her head on one side, as if considering his request. 'Well,' she said, 'I think that seems clear enough.' Then she proceeded to follow his fantasy to the letter. She curled her hand round his cock, feeling its weight and thickness and length; then she lifted herself slightly, shifting so that the tip of his cock was pushed hard against her sex. Very slowly, she sank down onto him, flexing her internal muscles so that he felt as though she were rippling round him: tightening and loosening, tightening and loosening.

She sat up straight, leaning back slightly to increase the angle of his penetration; then she began to move, lifting herself off his cock and sliding back down again. She slid one hand between her legs, rubbing at her clitoris; he could feel her fingers touching his cock as she raised herself.

Noticing his parted lips, she smiled and brought her hand up to his mouth, rubbing her glistening finger along his lower lip. He licked it, loving the taste of her arousal. She laughed throatily and let him suck her fingertips, one by one, and then returned to rubbing her clitoris.

Her other hand was massaging her breasts, pulling at one nipple and then the other, distending them. When she drew her hand from between her legs again and anointed her nipples so that they, too, glistened, Mark thought that he would die in bliss.

Again, had he not been tied, he would have lifted his lower body so that he could kiss her breasts, having the twin delight of tasting the richness of her sex and feeling the hardness of her nipples against his tongue.

Her movements grew more and more rapid as her arousal increased; at last, he saw a tell-tale rosy flush spread over her throat and her breasts. She gave a cry, and then she came, her sex contracting powerfully round him. It was enough to tip him into his own climax.

She lowered herself onto him again, resting her cheek against his. He kissed her ear. 'Selena,' he said softly, 'untie me. Please.'

She nodded, dealing swiftly with his bonds; he wrapped his arms round her, holding her against him and stroking her hair. 'You're one hell of a woman,' he said. 'I can't understand why you're single.'

'It suits me that way,' she replied shortly.

Realising that he'd strayed onto forbidden ground, he fell silent, hoping that the movements of his fingers against her skin would make her realize that he hadn't intended to hurt her.

Eventually, she lifted herself off him. 'I think the wine's had more than a chance to breathe now – don't you?'

'Do you still want me to stay and share it?'

'Yes.' She gave him a sideways look. 'Are you any good in the kitchen?'

'If you like Chinese and Italian food, yes.'

'Then what I'd really like is to have a nice long bath, then wrap myself in a dressing gown, eat with you, and then watch a film.'

'You've just described my idea of a perfect evening.' He smiled. 'And as I don't have a gig booked for tonight, I'd like to take you up on that.'

She smiled at him, stroking his face. 'I think you're the best idea Ruth has had in a long, long while.'

Maybe, Mark thought silently. But she doesn't know that. And with Aidan around, I don't think she ever will.

EIGHT

'So what did Selena think of Mark, then?' Shelley asked.

'She liked him,' Ruth replied shortly. 'I think he's about ready for his first proper assignment.'

'Really?' Laura looked at her. 'How can you say that?'

'Selena liked him, Helen liked him, Meg liked him, and you both liked him.' Ruth ticked off their names on her fingers. 'So I think we're just about there.'

'What about you?' Shelley asked.

Ruth shrugged. 'What about me?'

'Well, *you* don't know what Mark's like.'

'I can take your word for it.'

'There's no substitute for personal experience,' Laura added, her eyes sparkling. 'Come on, Ruth, you said yourself that it was going to be part of his training programme: that you were going to be the last person to, shall we say, test the service?'

'What about Aidan?' Ruth asked.

'I thought you'd discussed it with him? That he wasn't wonderfully happy about it, but he accepted that you had to do it, for the business?' Shelley asked.

'Even so, I feel guilty.' Ruth pulled a face. 'Things are different now. I'm engaged to Aidan.'

'You'll feel worse if you don't do it,' Laura said. 'You've got the hots for Mark – even if *you* don't admit it, *we*'ve known you long enough to know the signs, and he's just your type.'

'There *is* such a thing as self-control,' Ruth reminded her waspishly.

'Yes, I know. But, Ruth, I think you need to get it out of your system. I think *he* needs to, as well. Otherwise it's just going to fester . . . and when it does happen, it'll be hell instead of being completely pleasurable.'

Ruth's eyes narrowed as she stared at her friend. 'How do you mean, out of *his* system, as well?'

Laura smiled. 'Put it this way, Meg dropped over the other night, with a piece of Spode for me. We started talking, and – er—' she flushed '—the subject of Mark came up.'

Ruth sighed, staring at the floor. In other words, they'd had a girly gossip about Mark and herself. 'I see.'

'When I talked to him, I thought that, too,' Shelley said. 'He was asking so many questions about you. It was more than just the curiosity of an employee about his boss, too. It was – oh, I dunno. Like a lover trying to find out more, so he could surprise his partner with a favourite fantasy that they'd not yet shared. That sort of thing.'

Ruth remembered the look in his eyes when he'd walked her home, just before he'd kissed her, and shivered. Her friends were right: she knew that. She and Mark *were* attracted to each other. And yet she wasn't free to act on that attraction. 'If I bed him, I'll feel bad about Aidan. If I don't . . . I'll just keep thinking about it, and wondering what it would be like.' She sighed. 'It's a hell of a dilemma,' she said. 'And I feel like a bitch.'

'Not really. Just think of it as a business transaction,' Laura said. 'That's how you told us to think about it.'

'Yeah. You have a point.' Ruth shrugged. 'OK. I'll ring him, and I'll talk to him.'

'Good.' Shelley and Laura exchanged a glance. This, they thought, would do Ruth a lot of good. And, once it was out of her system, maybe things would go back to normal for her.

'So, once Mark starts working for us, what happens then?' Shelley asked.

'We'll need to train more Interlovers.' Ruth's eyes narrowed. 'Though I should add that I will *not* be training any of them.'

'I have to admit,' Laura said, 'I don't think that Nicholas would be too happy if I continued to train the Interlovers for you.'

Shelley grinned. 'Neither would Carlo – unless he could film it, of course, and use the shots in an exhibition...'

The three women burst out laughing, and Laura topped up their glasses. 'Well,' she said, 'maybe you can persuade Helen, Meg and Selena to do it for you.'

'Maybe,' Ruth agreed. 'We'll see how it goes.' She smiled at them. 'I would suggest that we started looking at the files to pick the next trainees, but the papers are all at home.' She lifted her glass. 'Anyway, to Interlover.'

'To Interlover,' the others echoed.

'Mark, it's for you,' Lou called.

'Who is it?'

She shrugged. 'I don't know. Some woman.'

His heart started racing. Was it Ruth? He shook his head, cross with himself. He was being stupid. Of course it wouldn't be Ruth. She'd studiously avoided him since he'd kissed her. He picked up the receiver. 'Hallo?'

'Hallo, Mark.'

It *was* her. 'Ruth!' His voice came out almost as a squeak, and he kicked himself mentally. God, when would he learn not to overreact to her? 'How are you?' he asked.

'I'm fine, thanks. And you?'

'Fine, thanks. So – what can I do for you, then? Another assignment?'

'Yes,' she said. 'Selena was the last one on your training programme – well, almost the last.'

'How do you mean?'

She paused. 'As the saying goes, I can't really sell a product that I, um, haven't tried myself.'

Mark leaned back against the wall, steadying himself. 'What does that mean, precisely?' he asked carefully.

'It means,' Ruth said, 'that we need to meet. Discuss a few things, and . . .' Her voice trailed off, but it was obvious what she meant. Have sex together. Make love. Explore each other's bodies, and all the sensual possibilities. She felt guilty, excited, ashamed of herself and wildly reckless, all at the same time. 'I don't think that we should meet at my house, though,' she added.

'No.' He still couldn't quite take it in. Ruth was actually going to let him make love to her, after all the agony of wishing and waiting and hoping? 'You could come here, maybe,' he suggested. 'What sort of time's best for you?'

'An afternoon.'

'Make it lunch,' he said. 'I'll cook something for you.'

'You don't have to do that. Though Selena says you're good with pasta.'

And a lot of other things, where you're concerned, he thought. 'I'd like to. I'd be making myself something in any case, and it's just as easy to cook for two as it is for one.' Shit, he thought, I'm gabbling. Why am I acting like a stupid teenager? I've coped with her most sophisticated friends, acquitted myself pretty well – but the thought of Ruth herself makes me go haywire. The thought of Ruth, letting herself melt into my arms . . . He closed his eyes, forcing himself to sound light and neutral. 'So, just say when.'

'When are you free?'

Damn, he thought, she's putting it back into my court. He wanted to say 'Tomorrow', but knew that it would be the wrong thing. 'How about Wednesday?' Five days' time.

'Sounds good to me. See you Wednesday, then.'

'You know how to get here?'

'Yes.' She grinned. 'Officially, you should be coming to me, as an Interlover, but in the circumstances . . .'

'Mm,' he agreed wryly. Part of him itched to see her house, how she lived, all the little intimate things she kept by her: but the last thing he wanted was to see photographs of Aidan or whatever around the place.

'Wednesday afternoon it is, then. I'll see you later.'

'Yes.' Mark replaced the receiver, feeling dazed, and walked slowly back into the living room.

Lou was sitting there, her nose in a book. She looked up as her brother entered.

'What's up?' she asked.

'I need a favour,' he said.

'Such as?'

'Um, to help me tidy the house.'

Her eyes narrowed. 'Tidy the house? You?'

'Well,' he coughed. 'Somebody's coming to see me, on Wednesday.'

Lou's eyes flashed with understanding. 'You mean *her*? Ruth, isn't it?'

'Yes.'

She grinned. 'Right, you're on. I'll mobilize the troops, and we'll make sure that the place is spotless. Though you can clean your own room,' she warned. 'And I'll also make sure that we all make ourselves scarce on Wednesday.'

'Thanks, Lou.' He hugged his younger sister. 'I owe you one.'

'That's easy. I get Roach to myself, for the whole week.'

'Yeah. For the month, even.'

'You *have* got it bad.' She smiled at him. 'Don't worry, bruv. I'm sure things'll turn out all right.'

'I think,' he said, smiling back, 'that they just have.'

*

The following Wednesday saw Ruth walking through Walthamstow. She discovered that Mark lived in a large Victorian terrace house, with bay windows and a black-and-red chequered path. The garden was bare, but tidy; she walked down the path to the front door. She smiled as she saw the door knocker: polished brass, shaped like a pre-Raphaelite nymph with long flowing hair. Flexing her shoulders, she knocked on the door.

A few moments later it opened, and Mark stood there. She'd almost forgotten how attractive he was, and the way he was dressed made it so much worse. Casual – but the sort of casual that could be rumpled within moments, betraying his sensuality. A tight pair of soft faded denims, a white T-shirt, and an open faded rust-coloured cotton shirt flung over the top, the sleeves rolled up halfway between his wrists and his elbows. He looked good enough to eat, she thought, feeling a kick in her loins.

'Hi. Come in.' He gazed at her. She was dressed casually, like the last time he'd met her, in leggings and a loose sweater. She was wearing a brown leather jacket and matching ankle-boots; she wore very little make-up, just a touch of mascara to widen her dark eyes, and the thinnest coat of lipstick.

'Can I take your coat?' he asked.

'Thanks.' She shrugged it off, and handed it to him; he hung it on the bentwood hatstand in the hall. 'Should I take these off?' she asked, noticing that he wasn't wearing shoes.

'Only if you want to.'

'Right.' She removed them quickly, bending over; Mark felt a surge of lust at the curve of her buttocks, and only just managed to restrain himself from touching her. She straightened up again, and he forced his face back into a polite mask.

'These are for you.' She handed him a bunch of flowers.

He grinned. 'Shouldn't that be me giving you flowers, not the other way round?'

'Yeah, well. In the circumstances...' She smiled back.

'And what's sauce for the goose, as they say.'

'Thanks.' He sniffed them: deep crimson carnations, mixed with white gypsophilia. 'They're lovely. I'll put them in water.'

She grinned. 'And I believe that's my line . . .'

The awkwardness between them was suddenly dispelled; he ushered her through to the sitting room. 'What can I get you to drink? Coffee? Fresh orange? Mineral water?' His eyes held hers for a moment. 'Though I trust that you'll indulge me in wine, over lunch?'

'Yes, though I did say not to go to any trouble,' she warned him.

'No trouble at all.'

'In that case, I'd love a coffee, please.'

He nodded. 'I'll be back in a minute, then,' he said, and left the room. He'd bought some Blue Mountain especially, knowing that she adored it. At least that was one thing he'd get right.

Ruth watched him go. The room was large and comfortable, with a couple of large overstuffed sofas dominating it. There was a television and video on one side of the room, and a hi-fi in the other. The alcoves by the fireplace were filled with bookshelves, housing a mixture of CDs, video tapes and battered paperbacks.

She couldn't resist glancing through them. A lot of the tapes were home recordings, filled with arty productions of plays and drama series. The books were mainly old classics and biographies of actors – Laurence Olivier, Orson Welles, Marilyn Monroe. Then she remembered that Mark's younger sister was an actress. No doubt half the books were hers. There was also a collection of gothic novels – mainly vampire – and a couple of modern erotic novels for women. Also his sister's, she thought.

The CDs were a mixture of blues-rock with the odd compilation of classical tracks from the movies.

'They're not all mine,' he said, coming in with two mugs of coffee.

'Yes – you live with your sister, an actress, don't you?'

'Plus a couple from the band, and some of Lou's friends.' He grinned. 'And before you ask, the film soundtracks are mine.'

'Selena mentioned that you were quite a film buff.'

'Mm.'

She smiled at him. 'I don't know if I dare ask what your favourite film is!'

'Two, actually. I can't choose between *It's a Wonderful Life* and *Blade Runner*.'

She grinned. 'Quite a contrast!'

'That's what life's about, contrast,' he replied lightly. 'Yours is *Don't Look Now*, isn't it?'

She nodded. 'One of them. It's just so brilliantly done. That, and *Citizen Kane*.' She went over to one of the sofas, and sat down; Mark sat beside her.

'Funny,' he said, 'all these training sessions have been more awkward, in a way, than the real thing will be.'

'Don't worry, you've already had good reports; the others all really liked you.'

He couldn't help asking, 'What about you?'

She sighed. 'I hardly know you, really.'

'And that's what this afternoon is about?' he asked. 'To get to know me?'

'Sort of.' Ruth's stomach was churning. She wanted him so much. All she had to do was move her hand a couple of inches, to touch him. And yet, at the same time, she couldn't help thinking of Aidan and feeling guilty. She really shouldn't be doing this. It wasn't fair to any of them.

'Hell is other people,' he quoted softly, catching her off guard.

'What?' She stared at him.

'Sartre.'

She smiled wryly. 'You're beginning to remind me of Selena.'

He grinned. 'Though she would have been able to quote it in the original.'

'*L'enfer, c'est les autres*,' Ruth supplied. 'You don't speak French, then?'

'Not since school, which is too many years ago for me to want to remember.'

'I know the feeling. I did A-level French, but it's pretty rusty. Selena occasionally makes me talk to her in French, but I'm usually too lazy to keep it up for long.'

'Ruth . . .' He put his mug on the floor and took her mug from her, putting it down next to his. He took her hand, his thumb stroking her palm. 'Ruth.' His eyes glittered. 'Today, it's – it's not like the others. I like your friends – they're all very sweet, very attractive, lovely women. But they're not you.' He coughed. 'I'm probably going to ruin this, by telling you that this isn't all routine for me. But it isn't. This is special.' He brought his hand up to his mouth, sucking her fingertips one by one.

She shivered. 'Very *Philadelphia*.'

'Mm.' He smiled wryly. 'Apart from the fact that I fancy you more than I'd fancy Tom Hanks or Antonio Banderas.'

'That's not what Shelley would say,' Ruth said, striving to keep her feelings under control.

'But I'm not Shelley.' He kissed her palm, his lips gentle against her skin, and gradually moved up to kiss the skin at her wrist, pressing his tongue against it. Her pulse was beating rapidly, and he smiled to himself. Well, Ruth, he thought, you're not quite as immune to me as you'd like to think you are. You feel the same way that I do, if the truth be known.

She was wearing a loose sweater; he pushed the sleeve up, and began to kiss along her arm. He paused at the crook of her elbow, nipping gently at the skin in a way that made her shiver. When he lifted his head to meet her eyes, he saw that her pupils had expanded and the rims of her irises were almost pure gold. 'Ruth,' he said, 'I think you need this almost as much as I do.'

She nodded, and he drew her to her feet. He didn't dare

kiss her, knowing that it would snap the last remnants of his control and he'd make love to her there and then in the middle of the sitting room – not caring who was passing the window and could see inside. It wouldn't be fair to either of them, particularly if one of the others in the household forgot that Lou had asked them to stay out for the day and came back to catch Ruth and him *in flagrante delicto*. He knew that this would only happen once, and he wanted to make the most of it.

He led her upstairs, still not speaking. When they reached his room, he paused. 'There's something I want to do,' he said. 'I hope you'll humour me, and not take this the wrong way.'

She frowned at him, not understanding, and he picked her up, walking into the room with her in his arms and kicking the door shut behind them. He laid her gently on the large double bed. 'I've fantasized about doing this for a long time,' he said. 'Carrying you to my bed.'

'It's terribly macho,' Ruth said, trying to sound reproving; and yet the action had thrilled her.

'When I saw you,' he said, 'I thought that you were the most beautiful woman I'd ever met. I think I even said it aloud – that I wanted to kiss you all over – because you're a dark-haired version of Marilyn Monroe, my all-time dream woman, and I want you very badly.'

'I remember,' she said softly, taking his hand.

He caressed her fingers. 'Everything about you turns me on. The way you smile, the way you tip your head on one side when you're thinking, the way your body curves – I want to kiss you, touch you, and then some.' He cupped her face, splaying his fingers along her cheek; her skin was soft, and he tingled where he touched her.

He sat down on the bed beside her and lowered his face to hers, closing his eyes as his lips touched hers. He kissed her gently at first, nibbling softly at her lower lip until she opened her mouth, giving him the access he needed. He slid his tongue inside her mouth, exploring her; she kissed him back, sliding her hands round his neck. Her kiss held all the fierceness he'd longed for, dreamed about, and he felt his erection throb uncomfortably.

Mark burrowed under the edge of her sweater, his hands gliding over her midriff, and then, at last, he touched her breasts, rubbing her hardening nipples through the lace and silk of her bra. She arched against him, and his control snapped entirely. He pulled off her sweater, and realized to his delight that she was helping him, as eager as he was to feel his body against hers, skin to skin.

He unclasped her bra, dropping the garment on the floor and caressing her breasts. They were as beautiful as he'd dreamed, soft and warm and lush and ripe. 'God, you're beautiful, Ruth,' he said huskily, 'so very, very beautiful.' He could have stared at her all day: but he could smell her perfume, a rich warm chypre, and he had to taste her. He kissed her throat, loving the softness of her curves, and began a trail of kisses down to her breasts. He took one nipple into his mouth; he drew fiercely on the hard peak of flesh as she responded, arching her back and pushing against him.

Gently, he pushed her back against the bed, lifting her slightly so that he could remove her leggings and her knickers in one go. She closed her eyes, tipping her head back; her mouth was slightly parted, and her tongue moistened her lower lip. He parted her legs, gently bending them and moving her so that her feet were flat on the mattress. He looked at her for a moment. Her quim was utterly beautiful, her labia puffed and glistening with her arousal. All the colours of red, from vermilion through to deep crimson . . . He could hardly wait to touch her, taste her.

He drew one finger along the fringed slit; her flesh was warm and soft and slippery to touch. He pushed one finger deep inside her, and was gratified to find how wet she was, how her quim flexed round him, sucking against his finger. She wanted this as much as he did. Well, Ruth, he thought, I'm going to make this something that neither of us is going to forget in a hurry.

He rested the heel of his palm against her mound of Venus, and began to rub her rhythmically, his finger travelling the length of her slit and dipping into her quim, spreading her musky juices across her skin. He sought out her clitoris, teasing the hard bud of flesh from its hood. Ruth moaned softly as he began to rub her with a gentle rocking rhythm at first, and then harder, faster, until, finally, her sex convulsed and she cried out.

Not stopping, he knelt between her thighs, dipping his head and letting his lips traverse her skin. He made his tongue into a sharp point, letting it drift along her musky slit and tasting the evidence of her recent climax. Honey and seashore and vanilla, he thought. His tongue probed her deeply, delving into her quim and then exploring her soft folds and crevices. His tongue skated over her clitoris, making her jump; he did it again and again, until she tipped her pelvis towards him. Then he took the hard bud of flesh into his mouth and sucked on it.

Her hands came down to tangle in his hair. 'Oh, yesss,' she murmured, her voice throaty. 'Yes, Mark, yes, yes. I need this.'

So do I, he thought. And even better than that would be if she slid her mouth over his cock, too, bringing him to a climax at the same moment as his tongue brought her to orgasm.

Almost as if she'd read his mind, he felt her tug gently at his hair. He lifted his head. 'What's the matter, Ruth?' he asked.

'I need you, too,' she said softly. 'I need to taste you as well, the same way that you're tasting me.'

'There's only one problem, then,' he said, smiling at her, his eyes sparkling.

'What's that?'

He gestured to himself. 'I'm still fully dressed.'

'Then do something about it. Strip for me,' she invited huskily.

He did so with pleasure, standing up and shrugging off his shirt.

Ruth began to whistle the tune for 'The Stripper', off-key; he laughed. 'I've got a better idea,' he said, and began singing the old Bon Jovi standard, 'Bed of Roses'.

Ruth thrilled to hear his voice. This was what she had half-imagined when she'd seen his band play at the local pub. The singer, focusing on his audience of one, and singing his intentions to her. The fact that he'd chosen one of her favourite songs, one she played in the car in traffic jams, fantasizing that the singer was singing only for her and that she could do whatever she liked with him afterwards, made it even better. And the idea of making love on a carpet of rose-petals... She shivered.

Mark removed his T-shirt, throwing it onto the floor, and swayed his hips as he unbuttoned his jeans.

'Better than the Chippendales,' she informed him as he slid the soft denims over his hips. Had they been leather jeans, she thought, she'd have removed them for him, sliding her fingers over the soft hide and then stroking his skin until he shivered, wanting her to touch him more intimately. As she was going to, now. 'But I want to do this.'

She sat up, then, and hooked her thumbs into the waistband of his underpants, easing them down to free his cock. Her eyes widened in anticipation. He was even nicer than the sketch she'd seen of him at Helen's flat. His cock was long and thick, and there was a small bead of clear moisture at the top. She couldn't resist dipping her head, touching the tip of her tongue to the eye of his cock, lapping at the pungent fluid.

Mark groaned. 'If you do that much more,' he said, 'I'll...'

'I know,' she said softly, sitting up straight again. 'Though

I believe there is a way round this.' She pushed the duvet off his bed, and patted the mattress beside her.

Suddenly realizing her intention, he smiled and lay prone, tipping his head back against the pillows. She shifted and, with an almost balletic movement, arched one leg over him, kneeling by his shoulders. She kissed her way down his body; as she stretched out, Mark lifted up, so that he could draw his tongue along her musky slit again.

If he could die at that moment, he thought, he would be supremely happy. Kissing her intimately, like that, and feeling her mouth wrapped round his cock and her breasts brushing against his belly, the nipples hard peaks. Her tongue, licking delicately at his frenum; and the gentle rhythmic sucking of her mouth, drawing him nearer and nearer to ecstasy. Just as, in turn, he lapped at her quim, every stroke of his tongue bringing her to her own climax.

He felt the familiar pressure of orgasm bubble through him; he tried holding back, but it was too much for him. The proximity of Ruth, and what they were doing, after he had waited for so long ... He pushed his pelvis up, as though he were trying to pour his whole body into her; he came, shivering. Almost at the same moment, he felt her sex flexing under his tongue, and she came, too, her sex liquefying over his mouth.

They stayed still for a moment, neither of them wanting to move – just wanting to fix the moment into their minds. Then she shifted to lie beside him, and he pulled her into his arms, holding her close and stroking her hair, raining a hundred tiny kisses on her face. He couldn't stop touching her, stroking the curve of her hips and waist. His fingers rested along the line of her buttocks; she was perfect, he thought. All woman, lush and curvy: a body to drown in.

He rolled her over onto her back and turned onto his side, smoothing his hands over her midriff and her breasts; he wanted to learn her body intimately, to sustain him when she'd gone.

Every curve, every scent, from the designer perfume she wore to the more intimate aroma of her body's arousal. The way her skin tasted. The way her nipples jutted out, the way they felt when he rolled them on his tongue . . . Everything.

She felt his renewed erection pressing against her and curled her fingers round it. 'Mark,' she said softly. 'Let's make it the ultimate. Let's go all the way.'

He smiled, then, shifting to kneel between her thighs. Her sex was still soft and liquid from her recent orgasm; it quivered slightly as he pushed the tip of his cock against it. He wanted this to last forever – the first and only time his cock would slide into her gorgeous quim. He moved slowly, achingly slowly: her body seemed to draw his into it, and at last he was inside her, up to the hilt, his balls rubbing gently against her quim.

'God, Ruth, you feel so good,' he said. The way her flesh clung to him, hot and wet and tight: he'd remember this for the rest of his life. He rubbed his nose affectionately against hers. 'So very good,' he breathed. His voice cracked slightly. 'I need this so much.'

He lowered his mouth onto hers, kissing her hard; she brought her legs up, wrapping them round his waist. As he thrust into her, she urged him on with the slight pressure of her heels against his buttocks. His tongue pressed against hers, echoing the action of his loins; she began to move rhythmically under him, increasing the pace of his thrusts by pushing up towards him and pulling back again.

Mark felt that he was drowning in bliss: wrapped in Ruth's arms, her hands caressing his back, while his cock was buried deep inside her. And then, at last, he felt her quim ripple around his cock, her muscles clutching at him and hastening his own orgasm. He cried out her name as he climaxed, his seed pumping hotly into her, and buried his face in the side of her neck.

They lay there together in silence, neither of them willing to part; Ruth stroked his hair, holding him close and keeping her legs wrapped round him. Eventually, he slipped out of her and rolled over onto his side. He kissed her lightly on the lips. 'Thank you,' he said softly.

'Pleasure,' she said. Her irises were still ringed with gold, and her lower lip was full and swollen; Mark thought he'd never seen her look more desirable. He couldn't help kissing her again: then he suddenly remembered that she was supposed to be meeting him for lunch, and broke the kiss.

He rubbed his nose against hers. 'Are you hungry?'

She smiled at him. 'A little bit,' she admitted.

'Tell you what – why don't you go and freshen up? I'll bring lunch up to us.' He stood up gracefully, walking over to the door and removing his navy towelling robe from the hook. She stood up, and went to join him; gently, he helped her into the robe. 'The bathroom's just down there, on the right.'

'Thanks.'

He bent his head and licked her earlobe. 'I would escort you – but if I washed your back in the bath, or saw you get into the shower, you definitely wouldn't get any lunch.'

She shivered at the pictures his words had conjured up: Mark climbing into the bath behind her, washing her back and then urging her gently to her knees, taking her from behind. Mark in the shower with her, lifting her and supporting her against the tiled wall, driving his cock inside her while the jets of water rained down on them...

'Off you go,' he said huskily, opening the door and tapping her lightly on the bottom.

He pulled on his jeans and padded downstairs to the kitchen. When he returned, Ruth was sitting on his bed, still wearing his robe; her hair was still slightly damp from the shower, as was her skin. She smelled of his favourite shower gel, although the Armani perfume she favoured still lingered.

Her eyes widened as she saw the tray. 'Wow. I feel spoiled.'

He smiled at her. 'You said not to go to too much trouble, so I just did something for snacks.'

'Snacks.' Ruth eyed the selection of tiny rounds of ciabatta bread, topped with smoked salmon and mozzarella. There was a slab of rich creamy brie, with the tiny water biscuits she adored, and a large bunch of black grapes. A bottle of chilled champagne and two glasses stood next to the food; she smiled at him. 'Champagne, in the middle of the day?'

'Well,' he said, 'I think that this is a special occasion.' He paused. 'Did you drive over?'

She shook her head. 'It's a nice day, so I took the Tube, and walked the rest of the way.'

'Good.' He smiled. 'So here's to the proper launch of Interlover.' He uncorked the bottle deftly, not spilling a drop, and poured two glasses. He handed one to her and chinked his own against it. 'To Interlover,' he said softly. 'And may it be a huge success.'

'For both of us,' she added, sipping the wine.

He couldn't resist kissing her again. 'This is a one-off,' he said, 'so I'm going to take advantage of it.' He smiled at her. 'In fact . . .'

'What?' She tipped her head on one side.

'Will you humour me?' He put his glass on the floor, stripped off his jeans, and sat next to her on the bed, completely unselfconscious. He picked up a smoked salmon canapé and popped it into her mouth. She ate it, surprised and delighted. 'I want to treasure you,' he said softly, moving to sit behind her and drawing her to lean against his chest. His hands cupped her breasts. 'I want to cherish you, in the short time we have together.'

Her eyes crinkled at the corners. 'If you say that to all our customers, we're going to be in huge demand.' She ran the backs of her fingers down his arm. 'And I mean huge.'

'Mm.' He buried his face in her hair. Just let the world end now, God, while she's smiling and resting in my arms, he said silently. Now.

NINE

'So how did you get on, then?' Shelley asked, her eyes twinkling.

Ruth smiled. 'Fine.'

'Oh, come on, Ruth, you can't do this to us!' Laura took a sip of wine and glowered at her friend. 'Considering that we told you everything about what happened when we were training him . . . I think you ought to tell us everything, too – don't you?'

'OK, OK.' Ruth spread her hands. 'I went to his house in Walthamstow. It was a nice place, actually – a Victorian terrace. Late Victorian, I'd say. Beautiful mouldings around the door – the plasterwork was very Arts-and-Crafts. And there was stained glass above the—'

'Ruth,' Laura cut in warningly.

Ruth grinned. 'All right, I'll cut the architectural details. Anyway, I took him a bunch of carnations.'

Shelley laughed. 'Hang on, since when does a woman buy a man flowers?'

'Well, why *shouldn't* a woman buy a man flowers? It's all part of the Interlover service. Anyway, he made me a cup of coffee, and we talked for a bit. He's a nice guy, as I told you before.'

'We already know that,' Shelley said impatiently. 'Come on, tell us what happened!'

Ruth's dark eyes sparkled. 'Well, I'll admit it now. I did have a bit of a thing about him. He's very, very attractive – as you both know. Anyway, then we started kissing, and he led me upstairs to his bedroom. We spent the rest of the afternoon making love.'

'And this is the woman who made me tell her *all* the details over the phone,' Shelley said. 'I don't think this is good enough – do you, Laura?'

'No, I don't!' Laura agreed, laughing.

Ruth coughed. 'OK. He stroked my skin, kissed me all over, and brought me to orgasm. He sang to me – 'Bed of Roses'.'

Laura groaned. 'Oh, hell. He's given her the Bon Jovi fantasy. She'll be high on this one for *weeks*.'

'But, unlike Aidan, Mark can actually sing,' Ruth said with a grin. 'He stripped off for me, while he was singing – my God, what a body! I itched to taste him. So I did.'

Shelley smiled. 'Yeah. He had that effect on me, too.'

'He brought me to orgasm at the same time. Then he held me; and I could feel his erection pressing against me. So we made love properly.'

'And?' Laura asked.

She nodded. 'I loved every second of it. Though it wasn't like making love with Aidan – I had the hots for Mark, and I admit it, but there wasn't that extra-special chemistry between us. So I'm not about to run off with him, or anything like that.' She smiled. 'Then he made us a picnic lunch – and fed me every single morsel.'

'*Nine and a half weeks*, eat your heart out!' Laura quipped.

'It was incredibly erotic, and I loved every minute of it. I might try it out on Aidan, some time. Smoked salmon and mozzarella canapés, brie and water biscuits, black grapes. Champagne.' A blissful expression crossed her face.

'All your favourites,' Shelley remarked with a grin.

'Yes.' Ruth folded her arms, and stared sternly at her friends. 'Now I come to think of it, it's a bit of a coincidence, isn't it? That he'd guess them all?'

Laura had the grace to blush. 'OK, OK, I'll come clean. He rang me and asked what sort of things you liked to eat. So I told him.'

Ruth smiled wryly. 'I should have guessed that one of you two would be behind that.'

'Don't forget, that's the point of Interlover. They're briefed to know all the little things which make the service more special, aren't they?' Laura countered, laughing. 'So he had to know what you liked.'

'Yes, I suppose so.'

'So what do you think of him?' Shelley asked.

'He's good,' Ruth admitted, flushing. 'Very good. Though things have been a bit difficult between Aidan and me since it happened.'

'Why?'

She sighed. 'My meeting with Mark was when Aidan was away on business. Anyway, when he got back, I think he realized that I'd finalized Mark's training programme. I didn't tell him any details, because it would have made it seem – oh, I dunno, sordid – and he's been sulking, ever since.'

'Typical man,' Shelley said. 'Cook him something nice for dinner, give him a back rub in the bath, and let things go from there. It always works for Carlo, if he's in a bad mood.'

'Yeah.' Ruth fiddled with her engagement ring. 'The thing is, I thought he'd be OK about it. I warned him beforehand, and – well, I'm engaged to him, for God's sake. I'm going to marry him. Doesn't that mean anything to him?'

'Calm down, Ruthie.' Laura patted her hand. 'It's probably a temporary thing. Male pride, and whatever. He'll sulk for a bit longer – then, when it suits him, he'll be back to normal.'

'I hope so.'

'Trust me.' Laura gave her friend a searching look. 'Unless you've really fallen for Mark?'

Ruth shook her head. 'Like I said, he's a lovely guy, and I

find him really attractive – but he's not the one for me. It's made me realize what I really want from life.'

'Any regrets?' Shelley asked, catching the tone of her friend's voice.

Ruth thought about it for a moment. 'No. Actually, I'm glad we did it. It's got the lust thing out of both of our systems, like you said, so we're going to get along much better now. I think we can both cope with having a relationship on a purely business-cum-platonic basis.' She sighed. 'The problem's Aidan. I think he wants me to have a proper job.'

'And what do you want to do?' Laura asked quietly.

'This. I'm enjoying the freedom. When I get fed up with this and want to be in a more structured environment, then maybe I'll look for another job. At the moment, I'm perfectly happy with the Interlover project.' She took a sip of wine. 'Talking of which, I ought to start finding Mark his first proper assignment. I'd rather that we were recommended to people by word of mouth – advertising a service like this would make it seem too tacky.'

Laura looked thoughtful. 'Actually, I think I might know someone. Marie – she's in commercial conveyancing. She's a bit of a powerhouse – more of a workaholic than Nicholas, which is saying something – and I think she's had a rough time lately.'

'Right.' Ruth rubbed her jaw. 'Do you think she'd go for the idea?'

Laura nodded. 'She's very nice, actually. And, under the power suit, I think she's quite broad-minded.' She smiled. 'Just leave it to me.' She paused. 'So what does Mark need to know about her?'

'Her favourite fantasy, so he can act it out for her. The sort of things she likes – food, drink, flowers, whatever.'

Laura smiled. 'No problem.'

*

Mark smiled as he recognized the voice at the other end of the line. 'Hi, Ruth, how are you?'

'Fine, fine,' she said.

He smiled. Since they'd made love, things were much easier between them. He thought that, at last, he could cope with her being just his employer, not the woman of his dreams. It had been good, making love with her – very good – but they both knew that it was a one-off.

'I've got an assignment for you,' she said. 'Her name's Marie, and she's a friend of Laura's. They work together, though Marie's in commercial rather than private litigation.'

'Right.' Mark nodded. 'So what's the story?'

'She's about the same age as us – in her early thirties – and she's worked hard to get where she has. She's spent so much time with her career that she's had no time for a social life. The way she looks at it, all the men in our age group are either attached, going through a messy divorce, or losers.'

He whistled. 'I'm not attached, and I'm not divorced – so I guess that puts me in my place, doesn't it?'

Ruth chuckled. 'You know damn well you're not a loser. It's just that Marie doesn't get a chance to meet many people outside work. Nice, available men, that is. They're either married, looking for a bit on the side, wanting a shoulder to cry on, or looking for a rich sugar mommy. What she needs is – well, Interlover."

'And you want me – as her Interlover for the night – to help her live out her fantasy.' He paused. 'So what is it?'

'A very sweet one. Right down your street, in fact. She wants to come home to an attractive man who has the dinner ready and will pamper her, when she's had a hard day. So we're talking about dinner, maybe a back rub, making love . . . That sort of thing.'

'Fair enough. When?'

'Does tomorrow night suit you?'

'We don't have a gig, so yes, that's fine. Where does she live?'

She gave him Marie's address. 'I think Laura can get a key for you, so you can have access to her flat in the afternoon, to get everything ready.'

'I'll ring Laura tonight, and sort it out,' Mark promised.

'Well, good luck – just give me a ring afterwards, and let me know how it went.'

'Will do, boss.'

Just as she replaced the receiver, Aidan came into the hall. 'Who was that?' he asked.

'Mark,' she said shortly. 'It's to do with Interlover.'

'I see.' Aidan appraised her darkly. She seemed to have changed, recently. There was something about her – he couldn't quite define it, but it unsettled him. He loved her, but he didn't seem to *know* her any more. The thing that worried him was that if she changed much more, she might not want to be with him. She was wearing his ring, he knew, but what difference did that make, if she'd fallen out of love with him? He couldn't bear losing her. Especially to Mark bloody Beasley. He had to do something – and fast.

'I was thinking, maybe we could go out to dinner tonight,' he said. 'There's a good film on at St Martin's. An old one – but a good one. *Diva*.'

'I'd love to,' she said warmly. 'I'll go and get my glad rags on, shall I?'

'You do that.'

She grinned. 'And don't follow me upstairs, either. If you come and wash my back in the shower, we'll end up not going out at all – and I love that film.'

As long as you still love me, he thought, I'll play it any way you want. 'Sure. Come and get me when you're ready.'

'I will.' She reached up to kiss him lightly, and went back upstairs.

*

Marie was slightly nervous as she walked back from the Tube station. She began to wonder whether she was doing the right thing. It had seemed such a good idea at the time, when Laura had suggested it over lunch: the idea of coming home after a hard day, to find a nice-looking, kind, funny and considerate man – not that she believed that one really existed – in the kitchen, cooking dinner for her, making a fuss of her as soon as she walked in the door.

It had seemed like a great idea, in fact. She'd been having such a lousy time at work; recent negotiations in the case she was dealing with had become decidedly sticky. She'd been in the same frame of mind when Laura had asked her for her spare door key, to give to the Interlover. And now... reality hit her.

She'd been stupid. Completely and utterly *stupid*. Supposing that this man turned out to be a maniac? Supposing that he'd had her key copied, during the day? It meant that he could walk into her flat any time he chose, and burgle her. Or sell her key to some low-life, someone who'd rape or murder her or...

She caught her thoughts, and smiled wryly. There was no way that Laura would be involved with anyone who behaved like that. Not only was Laura too nice to know that sort of person, she was also too shrewd a judge of character to be taken in by someone like that. Mark Beasley was probably just what Laura had said he was: nice-looking, considerate, sweet-tempered, and a good cook to boot.

Marie opened her front door, and sniffed appreciatively. Something smelled absolutely wonderful. She walked into the kitchen to find a man standing there, doing something complicated with vegetables; her eyes widened. Laura hadn't said that Mark would be this good-looking. Tall, with blond curly hair that was slightly overlong for her taste, but which gave him an attractively roguish air. Deep blue eyes that crinkled at the corners, as though he laughed a lot. A very handsome face – not to mention a gloriously mobile mouth that she could imagine doing all sorts of pleasurable things to her, and then some.

He smiled at her as she walked in, and put down the kitchen knife. 'Hello, Marie.' He came over and kissed her on the cheek. 'How was your day?'

'Lousy, actually,' she said. 'But dinner smells nice.'

'Well,' he said, 'I thought I'd do something that I could just leave to cook itself, so I could spend some time with you instead of faffing around in the kitchen and leaving you to your own devices. It's *coq au vin*, jacket potatoes, and vegetables.'

'Sounds lovely,' she replied.

'Come and sit down and tell me about your day.' He poured her a glass of red wine and ushered her through into the sitting room. He switched on the CD player, and the soft strains of a Haydn cello concerto – borrowed from Laura, on Nicholas's advice – filled the room.

'So,' he said softly. 'What was so bad about today?'

'Just one of those cases where I have to deal with someone I don't like very much.' She flexed her shoulders. 'I have to watch every word I say, because he's waiting for me to make the tiniest slip . . . and it just leaves me drained.'

'Maybe I can do something about that,' he told her, his eyes glittering.

'Oh yes?'

'Just lean forward a bit.' He came to sit next to her on the sofa; he took the glass from her hand, placing it on the low coffee table.

She did as he directed, closing her eyes, and he began to massage her neck, finding the tense knots of muscles and digging the pads of his thumbs into them to loosen them.

'Oh, that's very good,' she said gratefully.

'I have an even better idea,' he told her, his voice low and husky. 'Come with me.' He stood up and drew her to her feet, leading her into the bathroom. He ran a bath, adding liberal quantities of liquid from an unfamiliar bottle.

'It's aromatherapy oil,' he said, catching her glance. 'An energizing one. My sister uses it a lot.'

Marie smiled at him. 'Don't tell me you pinched it from her!'

'No. She'd have my guts for garters if I did that.' He smiled back. 'But I do know where she buys it. So I went shopping this morning.'

A citrus-and-ginger scent filled the air. Marie sniffed. 'It smells gorgeous.'

'I know.' He slipped her formal navy jacket from her shoulders and began unbuttoning her white silk shirt. Now that she was relaxing with him, and smiling, she was almost pretty, he thought. Before, she'd seemed like the distant professional woman everyone probably thought her at work, her brow creased in a workaholic's concentrated frown.

She had beautiful eyes, he thought, an unusual aqua grey; and glossy dark hair that was trained into a sleek bob. She was smaller than Ruth: petite, like Shelley, with the same fragility in her face. He eased her shirt out of the waistband of her skirt, then turned her round, unzipping the short tailored skirt and removing it. He hung the garment neatly over the pine towel-rail, making her smile, and pulled her into his arms, kissing her lightly on the lips.

Marie's legs turned to jelly. God, the man knew how to kiss, she thought. The way he took tiny nibbles from her lower lip, soothing the sting by running his tongue over it. And the way that he slid his tongue into her mouth, a foretaste of the way that his cock would slide into her . . . She felt her sex begin to pool.

Her skirt had been lined, so she wasn't wearing a half-slip;

Mark ran his hands lightly down her sides, moulding the shape of her curves. She had an hour-glass figure, a slim waist and soft hips; he let his fingers run over her buttocks, squeezing gently.

She shivered, closing her eyes and tipping her head back slightly. He took advantage of her position to slide his fingers underneath the cups of her bra, tugging the white lacy material down so that her breasts were exposed: they were pushed up and slightly together by the way he'd arranged her bra, and looked ripe and luscious, her skin creamy and her nipples dark.

He nuzzled her throat, making her shiver again, and slowly tracked down to her breasts. He buried his face in them for a moment, inhaling her scent, and then licked her areolae in a way which had her nipples stiffening instantly.

He chuckled. 'I'm sorry. I just couldn't resist that.'

'No, please. I enjoyed it.' She opened her eyes again and he noticed with pleasure that her pupils were dilated. She was enjoying this as much as he was.

He undid her bra, dropping the garment to the floor, and peeled off her knickers. She was wearing lace-topped hold-up stockings; he smiled. 'I bet if half the men you work with knew what you were wearing under that neat and professional suit . . .'

'Yes?' she said, tipping her head to one side and giving him an appealingly impish grin.

'If they knew about this, most of them would be in exactly the sort of state I'm in now. And they'd want to do what I'm about to do with you . . .' He took her hand, guiding it down to his erect cock; she flushed, half embarrassed, half excited. He smiled at her, lifting the same hand to his lips and kissing it, then dropped her hand, turning the taps off and testing the bath water. 'A bit too hot, I think,' he said, adding cold water. When he was satisfied with the temperature, he turned off the tap, then shifted to face her.

He rolled her stockings down, stooping to stroke her thighs

as he did so; the pulse between Marie's legs began to beat hard. Was he going to do what she hoped he'd do? She was faintly disappointed when, instead of touching his mouth to her sex, he merely lifted her up and placed her in the bath.

He rolled up the sleeves of his shirt. 'Lean forward,' he said, kneeling down beside her and lathering his hands.

Marie closed her eyes, revelling in the way that he soaped her back and then sluiced the suds from her skin. His hands were very gentle, very sure; by the time that he'd finished her back, she was feeling more relaxed than she had in months.

'Better?' he asked.

She looked up at him and smiled. 'Yes, I think so.'

To her mingled surprise and amusement, he dabbed a small amount of foam on her nose, and grinned. 'You look just like a little girl.'

'Not so little – and I'm a woman, not a girl.'

'Definitely,' he agreed, ignoring the slightly waspish tone to her voice. He soaped his hands again, paying attention to her breasts. '*All* woman, I would say. Beautiful and lush and ripe. I can barely keep my hands off you.'

The huskiness in his tone thrilled her. Where had Laura found such a gorgeous man? Did she have some kind of secret supply of them? Did her husband know about all this?

He saw the questions in her face, and smiled. 'Wondering how I know Laura, are you?'

'Are you telepathic, as well?' she asked, shocked at how easily he'd read her face.

He laughed. 'No, it was just an obvious question. I know her through a mutual fiiend.'

'Anyone I know?'

'Maybe, maybe not.' He didn't enlighten her, but continued to soap her, washing her feet carefully and gradually working his way up her legs, massaging her calves and the sensitive spot at the back of her knees.

Marie closed her eyes and relaxed. He had a sure touch, gentle and yet firm. She ached to feel him touch her sex, his fingers sliding over her labia and then finally pushing deep inside her, relieving the nagging ache.

Almost as if he could read her mind, he parted her thighs; she shivered as he washed her sex, his fingers playing lightly over her intimate flesh. He leaned over to kiss her lightly on the mouth. 'Right, then, let's be having you.' He finished washing the soap from her skin and pulled the plug. As she stood up, he wrapped a towel round her and lifted her out of the bath. He dried her carefully, paying attention to every inch of skin; by the time he'd finished, Marie was tingling all over, and longing for him to finish what he'd started in the bath.

'What now?' she said.

'It's up to you. Either you can dress up for dinner with me, or . . .' He let the sentence hang in the air.

'Or what?'

'Well – as the saying goes, slip into something more comfortable.' His eyes glittered. 'And maybe then I can claim my reward for dinner.'

'What if you're a lousy chef?' she parried.

He nodded. 'It's a possibility. But I did check with Laura whether you'd like the menu.'

'Then we'll go for the comfortable option.'

'I'm glad you said that.' He smiled at her, wrapped another towel round her, and led her to the bedroom.

Her eyes widened as she saw the box on the bed. 'What's that?'

'Something I hope you'll like.'

She opened it, to find a bright scarlet silk robe. 'Thank you. It's beautiful.'

'I have to admit, I did ask my sister's advice. I knew your colouring and your size, from Laura, and my sister has impeccable taste . . . so it was easy, really.'

Marie fingered the soft material. 'It's absolutely beautiful, Mark. I don't think anyone's ever bought me such a gorgeous present.' Or such an unexpected one. Laura had said that Mark would make a fuss of her, but presents hadn't even been on the agenda. She'd half expected flowers or some chocolates, but this . . .

He tugged at the edge of her towel, spinning her round and dropping the material to the floor. 'Try it on.'

She nodded, and put it on, twirling round and giving him a curtsey. He smiled, and ruffled her hair. 'It suits you. You should wear red more often.'

Her eyes widened. 'At work?'

'Mm. Give them a surprise. Be a scarlet woman in a scarlet suit.'

She laughed. 'That's terrible! I knew that you had to have a flaw.'

'Which is?' he asked, laughing back.

'A terrible taste in puns.'

'I'll ignore that.' He took her hand, and led her through to the dining room. 'I think the first course is just about ready.' He rescued her wine, then lit the candle and went into the kitchen, returning with two plates of mushrooms in a cream and garlic sauce. He topped up her glass and filled up his own, lifting it in a toast. 'Here's to a very pleasant evening,' he said.

She echoed the toast, and took a mouthful of the mushrooms. She was surprised at just how good the meal was: most men of her acquaintance couldn't – or wouldn't – cook. The *coq au vin* was just as good. 'You could be a professional chef,' she said.

He shook his head. 'Apart from anything else, the hours would clash with my job.'

'Which is?'

'A musician, in a pub band. I play a bit of guitar, and also do the lead vocals.'

'I'd like to come and see you play, some time.'

'That would be nice.' He smiled at her. 'I'll let you know when our next gig is.'

Dessert was, as Mark admitted, a complete cheat. He'd bought the tiramisu from a local delicatessen.

Marie finished her pudding with a sigh. 'That was absolutely lovely. Thank you. I can't remember when I've been so spoiled.'

'Pleasure.' Mark smiled at her. 'I'll even do the washing up, later, so you don't have to worry about that, either.'

'Let's go and sit down,' she suggested.

He followed her into the sitting room and sat next to her on the sofa. He slid his arm round her and she curled into him, resting her hand on his waist and her cheek on his shoulder. He stroked her hair. 'How do you feel?' he asked quietly.

'A hell of a lot better.'

'Good.' He bent his head so that he could kiss her, rubbing his nose affectionately against hers. Her mouth opened beneath his and he deepened the kiss, exploring her mouth. His hands drifted down to the belt of her robe, and he untied it, pushing the robe open to reveal her body. As he began to stroke her midriff, Marie slid her hands round his neck, the pads of her fingers digging into his skin, and urged him on.

He broke the kiss, his lips travelling down to the sensitive spot at the side of her neck. She gave a small gasp of pleasure as he stroked her breasts, his fingers idly tracing the areolae and then pinching the hard peaks of her nipples, rolling them between his thumb and forefinger.

'Marie,' he said softly. 'Do you want to continue this somewhere more comfortable? I know it's a cliché, but I'd rather make love to you in the comfort of your bed than on the sofa.'

She nodded, and they stood up. He walked with her to the bedroom; she reached up to stroke his face. 'Thank you,' she said softly, 'for making tonight so good for me.'

'I haven't finished yet,' he replied, equally softly. He kissed the tip of her nose, and began to undo his shirt. Her hands came over the top of his, and he let her continue undressing him, pushing his silk shirt off his shoulders and undoing his dark trousers. He kicked the material aside, deftly removing his socks.

Marie's eyes widened as she looked at him, clad only in his underpants. The thick, rigid line of his cock was clearly visible; if the way he made love was anywhere near as good as the way he massaged or the way he cooked, she thought, she was in for one hell of a good night. At least then the dark shadows under her eyes would be caused by something far more pleasurable than working on awkward legal contracts.

'Touch me, Marie,' he invited huskily.

Almost shyly, she tugged at the waistband of his underpants, easing the material down over his cock. Fully naked, he looked even better. This was a man, she thought, who could turn her on with a look.

He curled his fingers over hers, drawing her hands down to his cock and placing them against his flesh. 'Touch me,' he said again.

He felt as good as he looked; she began to rub him, pulling his foreskin back. He was in perfect proportion, she thought, long and thick.

'Marie,' he said again, bending his head to kiss her hard. Hearing the note of urgency in his voice, she let her hand drop; he picked her up, laying her on the bed. He knelt beside her, kissing a trail down her body. He paused to kiss her nipples, drawing them gently between his lips and using his teeth just hard enough to make her arch her back in pleasure. His trail continued over her midriff; he made her laugh by licking round her navel, then paused between her thighs.

The mixture of the citrussy bath oil and her own arousal was very heady; he drew his tongue along her slit, hearing her little 'Oh' of pleasure as his tongue skated over her clitoris.

He began to lap in earnest, working on her clitoris until she writhed beneath him.

'Mark, make love to me properly. Please,' she said, her voice cracking.

'I'd better get something, first.' He went over to his trousers, taking a small square of foil from the pocket. This was something that Laura had told him when he'd gone to her office to pick up Marie's door-key, and he smiled.

'There's something I've always wanted to do,' Marie said, sitting up.

He knew exactly what she meant, thanks to Laura; he handed her the little foil square, and she opened it, laughing with pleasure when she saw that the condom was blue.

'It goes with the eyes,' he said laconically.

She giggled, and put the little rubber disc in her mouth. He knelt on the bed next to her and she put the condom over his cock, using her mouth. Mark shivered as her hair brushed over his midriff.

'Lie down,' she requested softly. He did so, smiling up at her. She straddled his thighs.

'You look so beautiful,' he said.

She flushed. 'Thank you.'

'No, I mean it.' He lifted his torso so that he could kiss her breasts; she eased her hand between their bodies, guiding his cock to the entrance of her sex, and slowly slid down onto him. She raised and lowered herself over him; he edged his hand between their pubic regions, rubbing her clitoris as she moved over him.

She shivered and leaned back slightly, changing the angle of his penetration to give them both more pleasure. 'Touch yourself,' he urged. She nodded, and began to massage her breasts, stroking the soft undersides and squeezing her nipples, distending them. He thrust into her, quickening the rhythm. He felt her go rigid for a moment; she gave a little cry, and suddenly her body relaxed, quivering round his.

He sat up, wrapping his arms round her and burying his face in her breasts. She rested her forehead against his hair, shaking.

'My God,' she said quietly. 'That was so good.'

He lifted his head and smiled at her. 'That's just for starters. I believe we still have the main course, dessert, and a couple of sorbets to go . . .'

Marie smiled to herself. This was one service she was certainly going to recommend to her friends. And one she herself would certainly use again.

'Ruth,' Aidan said softly.

'Mm?' She looked up from her book, the tiny frown of concentration on her face disappearing as she met his eyes.

His heart melted. He loved her so much: he couldn't start a row over Mark Beasley. Not now. 'Do you want a coffee?' he asked, half cross with himself for not asking the question he really wanted to ask, but not wanting to fight with her, either.

'Thanks. That'd be nice.' She placed a bookmark between the pages, and uncurled. 'Though I think I ought to make it. After all, I'm the one who's slobbing around the house all day.'

'I've never accused you of that,' he said, hurt.

'Figure of speech,' she said lightly, going over to him and cupping his face. She kissed the tip of his nose. 'Actually, I'm self-employed, not unemployed.'

'Right.' His face tightened. Interlover. God, how he hated the name. He hated everything about it.

'I've found a couple more trainees. One's an aspiring actor, and one's a research student. Specializing in Metaphysical poetry.' She grinned. 'So we ended up talking more about Donne than about Interlover, when I interviewed him this morning.'

Aidan's eyes darkened. 'So you're planning to train more of them?'

'Not personally.' She smiled. 'I have a few people lined up for that little task.'

'Right.'

'Relax, Aidan.' She slid her hands round his waist. 'There's only one man in my life, and that's you.'

'Yeah.' Why couldn't he believe her? 'I think I'll go and make that coffee.'

Ruth's heart sank as he left the room. It was going to be another bad evening. For a moment, she almost wished that she'd never thought of Interlover. She sighed. Aidan would come round, in the end. It would just take a bit more time – and a bit more effort. Maybe if she took him out to dinner, or something . . .

TEN

Ruth wasn't at home when Aidan walked in the door. His face tightened. No doubt she was off somewhere, interviewing one of her bloody Interlovers. If only she would just go back to doing a normal job. Or if she preferred working for herself, couldn't she just pick something a bit less extreme?

He left his briefcase in the hall, kicked off his shoes, and walked into the kitchen. As he switched on the kettle, he noticed the folded piece of paper on one of the worktops and picked it up. Seeing Ruth's name at the top, he put it down again: they didn't read each other's mail without being asked.

Then he realized that the name on the headed paper had been that of a publisher. He frowned. Maybe that was why Ruth had been so quiet lately. Maybe she had indeed been applying for jobs back in her old profession: but perhaps she'd been unsuccessful, and hadn't wanted to talk about it. But why on earth would a publisher turn down someone as good at the job as Ruth was?

He picked up the letter again, and read it swiftly; his frown deepened. On the contrary: they hadn't turned Ruth down. She had turned *them* down. She hadn't even wanted an interview – though they'd asked her to get in touch, if she ever changed her mind. He swallowed. How many more letters like this had Ruth had? How many other things had she not bothered sharing with him? And, more to the point, just what was her relationship with this bloody Mark Beasley? He knew that she'd made love to him – as part of his 'training programme' – but had it been just the once? And had it been more than just business?

He made himself a cup of coffee, stomped into the sitting room, and put on a CD, turning up the volume so that the room was flooded with music. The drama of the Rachmaninov piano concerto suited his mood. Had Ruth been standing in front of him, he could have been very tempted to strangle her. He could understand, now, why some men were driven to murder their lovers . . .

As the music continued, he became calmer; then, finally, introspective. This business of Interlover was taking up so much of Ruth's time. She'd told him that she still loved him but, at the same time, he knew that their relationship was going downhill, fast. If he didn't do something about it, he'd lose her. The question was, what *could* he do about it?

A smile spread across his face. Of course. The answer was fairly drastic, but it was the right solution. The only possible solution.

Ruth picked up her mail, and smiled to herself. Her Interlover ad was receiving a very good response indeed, and she was surprised at the variety of people who had answered. Everybody from bored insurance professionals who had the steady job but needed some excitement in their lives, through to those who led exciting lives but needed something more steady: part-time musicians and actors.

She went home, and began to sift through the day's batch of replies, sorting them out into 'definitely nots', who'd receive her standard letter thanking them for their letter but advising that they weren't quite what she was looking for; 'possibles', whose details she'd keep on file; and 'absolute definites' – usually the smallest pile.

This time, there was only one 'absolute definite'. Stretching, she began to study the application. Robin Deptford. He was in his early thirties, a painter who adored Donne, Bach, the cinema, and eating out. He'd added in a postscript that he enjoyed cooking, too, and his idea of a perfect evening was cooking a meal for his partner, having a long leisurely bath together, then spending the whole night making love in a four-poster brass bed – one with a thick feather mattress and lots of pillows.

She was disappointed to find that he hadn't sent a photograph; still, at least he'd given her a phone number. She walked over to the phone and dialled his number; the phone rang twice, and then an answerphone cut in. 'Hi, this is Robin Deptford. I'm sorry, I can't take your call right now, but if you leave your name and number, I'll call you back as soon as I can.'

He had a nice voice, she thought, well-spoken without being too plummy. Something nagged in the back of her mind: his voice reminded her of someone she knew, something familiar. She shrugged. Voices and faces played tricks on you. You often thought you saw or heard something familiar about a stranger.

After the tone, she took a deep breath. 'Hello, Robin. This is Ruth Finn. Thanks for replying to my ad – for Interlover – and I'm sorry that I've missed you. I'd like to meet you and discuss your application further. How about Thursday, at half-past twelve?' She named her favourite wine bar. 'If you can't make it, let me know, and maybe we can arrange something else. I look forward to meeting you. Bye.'

Robin. She wondered what he'd be like. It was an unusual name – one which conjured up a picture of a very arty, upper-class family. Public school and an Oxbridge education, no doubt; but he was probably the younger child, not forced into one of the professions or the family firm like the eldest son would be. Being an artist, he'd have long, sensitive hands; maybe he'd also be a bit of a rebel, with long hair which he'd wear in a ponytail.

She caught herself fantasizing, and smiled. Robin Deptford might turn out to have no personality at all, or he might be so intense that he'd make her clients nervous. Even so, Thursday seemed a long way away. She was itching to meet him, to find out if he was as promising as his application seemed.

The next two days passed surprisingly quickly. Ruth found herself dithering, for once, over what to wear. Part of her thought that she should look businesslike and wear a sharply tailored business suit. Then again, the man was an artist. If she looked too formal, it might put him off. Maybe she should wear something casual – leggings and a baggy sweater.

In the end, she decided on a compromise: a dark green ankle-length pleated skirt, a cream lambswool sweater, and a black jacket. Teamed with black stockings and flat black leather court-shoes, it looked smart without being overpowering.

When she walked into the wine bar, she scanned the room swiftly. She didn't actually know who she was looking for, but nobody seemed to be waiting, watching the doorway. She glanced at her watch: she was ten minutes early. Sighing, she went over to the bar, and ordered herself a glass of Chardonnay. 'Has anyone called Robin Deptford asked for Ruth Finn?' she asked the barman.

He shook his head, smiling at her. 'I'm afraid not.'

'Well, if he does – I'll be sitting over there, in the corner,' she said.

As usual, she had a paperback in her pocket: a collection of fairly literary short stories that she'd been meaning to read for a long time. She'd lost herself in the pages when there was a polite cough beside her.

She looked up, expecting to see Robin Deptford, and her face drained of colour as she recognized the man standing next to her. 'Aidan! What the hell are you doing here?'

'Meeting you, as your answerphone message requested,' he told her with a smile. 'Here, at half-past twelve.' He glanced at his watch. 'And I'm exactly on time.'

'*What?*' She stared at him. 'I don't understand.'

He smiled. 'Robin Deptford, at your service, madam.' He gave her a small bow, and slid into the seat opposite her. He refilled her glass with the bottle he'd brought over.

Ruth scowled as she saw the label. 'How did you know I was drinking that?'

'Because, my love, I asked the barman.' He grinned at her. 'You look as if you've lost a shilling and found a sixpence, as the saying goes.'

'Aidan, I . . . I . . . Bloody hell, I was expecting to meet someone to interview!'

'I know that, and you are,' he reminded her. 'You're interviewing me.'

'You mean, you're Robin Deptford?'

'Yep. I wrote the letter. Though I didn't send a photograph, for obvious reasons. Anyway, shall we proceed to the interview?'

She shook her head. 'No way. Aidan, you are *not* going to be one of my Interlovers!'

'Why's that? Where do I fall down?' He tipped his head on one side. 'Some women would describe me as passably attractive.'

She glowered at him. He was extremely attractive, not just passable.

'I'm a professional man; I have good conversational skills; I have a wide variety of interests, from sport to the arts; I get on well with people.' He leaned over to whisper in her ear. 'And a certain person not too far from here used to say that I was pretty good at making love.' He straightened up again. 'So why shouldn't I be one of your Interlovers? I think I fit your requirements.'

'Because,' Ruth reminded him stiffly, 'you happen to be my fiancé.'

'So you're turning me down, then?' His eyes glittered.

'Yes, I bloody well am.' She ground her teeth. 'It's really unfair of you, Aidan.'

'What, to answer your ad?' He took a sip of his own wine. 'Maybe, but you've been so busy with Interlover that – well, things just haven't been right between us, lately. I thought that this might be the way to get you to notice me again.' He took her hand, stroking her palm. 'Don't be angry with me, Ruth. I'm not doing this to mock you, or to wreck your business – I just wanted to spend some time with you. I wanted things to be OK between us again. More than OK, in fact: I want things to be back to how they were.' He sighed. 'It seemed like a good idea at the time, to apply to be one of your Interlovers.'

'So whose phone did you borrow?' she asked tightly.

'Jake's, at work. I had it diverted to an extension in the office.'

She frowned. 'That was risky. Supposing a client had phoned you direct? Or supposing I had?'

He shook his head. 'My extension was switched through to my secretary. I told her that I was plotting a surprise for you, so I wanted her to take all my calls for a couple of days.'

'So who else knew about this set-up of yours, then?'

'Only Jake,' he reassured her. 'He was a bit doubtful about it, but it was the only way I could think of to make you talk to me.'

'Hm.' She was unimpressed; she sipped her wine, and refused to meet his eyes.

'Ruth,' he said softly, 'will you take me through the Interlover training, anyway? Maybe I can tell you if you're missing anything out.'

She looked at him. 'I don't do the training personally.'

'Don't you?' His face tightened as he thought of Mark Beasley. He knew that Ruth had made love with him.

She shook her head. 'If you're referring to Mark, he was the pilot Interlover, so I suppose I had to make sure that I knew what sort of service I'm offering. But I'm not training anyone else – I'm leaving that to Meg, Helen and Selena.'

'What about Laura and Shelley?'

'Ah.' She coughed. 'They were in with me, but that was only for our pilot. Nicholas and Carlo agreed to it. But, like me, they won't be doing it in future.'

'I see.' His eyes sparkled. 'Well, why don't you break your own rules and show me, anyway?'

Her eyes narrowed. 'Aren't you supposed to be at work, Aidan?'

'No. I took the afternoon off. I said I was working at home.' He grinned. 'Which I am. But it's not working on my business – it's working on yours. I thought I could spend the afternoon, very pleasurably, with a certain very beautiful woman.'

'Such as?' She deliberately kept her voice cold.

'Well, Robin Deptford's an artist. I'm sure he'd like to spend the afternoon wandering round the Tate with you. Then he could take you out for a meal at some nice little Italian restaurant—'

'His letter said that he enjoyed cooking,' she interrupted.

'He does, but he also likes eating out,' was the swift response. 'And then he can take you home, and . . .' He spread his hands. 'Let's rediscover each other, Ruth. Unless there's something else you'd rather do? Go to Hampstead Heath for a walk, stroll around the British Museum? I'm happy to fit in with whatever you like. But spend the afternoon with me. Just you and me.'

She looked at him. 'All right. The Tate it is. Though we might as well finish this, first.' She nodded at the wine.

He refilled their glasses. 'So how's it going, anyway? Did you find anyone else, apart from Robin?'

She smiled reluctantly. 'Not in that batch of mail. Though I think you knew the right buttons to press, didn't you?'

'I hope so.' He grinned. 'I had a fair idea, but Shelley just happened to tell me what sort of men you were looking for.'

'You asked *Shelley*? You mean, she knew about this as well?'

'Not exactly. I did my jealous fiancé act on her, and she said that I had nothing to worry about. She said that most of the men you picked were like me, but slightly different physically. With the exception of a certain Mr Beasley, who looks very much like me.' Aidan folded his arms. 'The typical Finn type, as she put it. Blond hair, blue eyes, big nose, nice bum.'

Ruth groaned. 'Good old Shelley. Diplomat to the last.'

'Well, I did ask her. I deserved to hear what she told me.' He took another sip of wine. 'Though I was bloody upset, afterwards. The thought of you in his arms, instead of mine . . . I tried looking at it as a perverse kind of compliment – that you'd chosen someone like me – but it didn't help much. I thought about murdering you, actually.'

'Seriously?'

'For a while, yes.' He took her hand. 'Though I'd never lay a finger on you. You know that.'

She tipped her head on one side. 'You're not still jealous of Mark, are you?'

'A bit,' he admitted.

'Well, don't be. There isn't anything going on between us. Yes, I did sleep with him, but I warned you about it beforehand. It was purely business, and it only happened the once. It won't be repeated.'

'Really?'

'Really. I promise.' She sighed. 'I haven't thrown your engagement ring back at you and said I don't want to marry you, have I?'

'Actually,' he said, 'seeing as *you* asked *me* to marry you, maybe you should have bought me a ring, so that I could have thrown it back at you.'

Ruth was shocked. 'Would you have done that?'

He thought about it. 'If you'd caught me in one of my worse moods, yes. I've been very tempted, over the last couple of weeks.'

'Have I been that awkward to live with?'

'You've just driven me mad with this bloody Mark Beasley, that's all.'

'I keep telling you, there's nothing to worry about. What else do I have to do to prove it to you? Apart from give up Interlover, and I'm not prepared to do that.'

'I know.' He smiled at her. 'So, supposing that I am your latest trainee . . . I'll meet you outside the Tate, in half an hour.'

'I'm not going to call you "Robin" all afternoon.'

'Why not?' He eyed her hands. 'And, seeing as we're doing this properly – an engaged woman is hardly likely to need the services of Interlover. Put your ring on your other hand.'

'What?'

'Let's make it seem illicit. Exciting. Maybe it's what we both need – to bring some spice back in to our relationship,' he said with a grin. He brought her hand to his lips and kissed the tips of her fingers; then he left the wine bar.

Ruth stared after him for a moment. Aidan had used pretty drastic measures to get her attention: he must have been worried about their relationship. Really worried. Well, maybe she could finally prove to him that there was nothing to worry about. She finished her wine, then left the wine bar and headed for the Tate.

The tall, blond man was loitering in the entrance of the Tate; he walked over to the dark-haired woman as she reached the top of the steps, and smiled. 'Would you be Ruth Finn, by any chance?'

'Yes. And you must be Aidan—'

'Robin Deptford,' he cut in with a smile. 'Pleased to meet you, Ruth.'

She couldn't help smiling back. This was faintly ridiculous, pretending that the man she'd lived with for three years or so was a complete stranger – but if this was what it took to prove to him that he had nothing to worry about, this was how it would have to be. 'And you, Robin.'

He took her hand, kissing the inside of her wrist; the look in his eyes made a shiver of desire run down her spine. 'I'm so glad that you agreed to come here with me,' he said softly. 'Shall we go in?'

'I'd like that,' Ruth said. 'I haven't been to the Tate for a long while.'

'Neither have I, though it used to be one of my favourite places.'

She tipped her head on one side. 'Though I'm afraid that I don't appreciate modern art, Mr Deptford.'

'Robin, please.'

'Robin.' Her voice was warm and caressing. 'I prefer Victorian art.'

'That's a coincidence. So do I,' he said, smiling.

They wandered through the gallery, looking at the paintings and chatting lightly. Eventually, they reached the end of their favourite rooms; Aidan looked at his watch. 'I've had such a nice time, I don't want it to end yet. Would you have dinner with me, Ruth?'

'I'd love to,' she said warmly.

'What sort of food do you like?'

'Anything, really. French, Chinese, Italian . . .' She shrugged. 'I'm not fussy.'

'I know a nice little Italian in the middle of town. Do you have to rush back?'

She shook her head. 'No. The whole evening's free.'

'Right.' He paused. 'Well, we could either see a film and then eat, or . . .'

She laughed. 'I think I've had enough culture for today! Let's just eat.'

'OK.'

He slid his arm round her shoulders as they sat on the Tube; Ruth, seeing their reflections in the glass, shivered. It was almost like her first date with Aidan, all over again: except, this time, she didn't have to wonder what the good-looking man beside her was like in bed. She already knew.

A *frisson* of anticipation ran down her spine as they left the Tube and walked to the restaurant, his arm still lightly round her shoulders. Was he going to hold her at arm's length at the end of the evening, and tell her that he respected her too much to sleep with her on their first meeting? Or was he going to act the part of one of her Interlovers, and spend the whole night making love with her?

She wished that she'd been wearing more erotic lingerie: a lace teddy or a basque, instead of her rather plain and workman-like white undies.

Aidan looked at her as they went into the restaurant. 'Would you prefer to order for yourself, or may I surprise you?'

'Surprise me,' she said with a smile. Aidan knew her taste well enough to pick something that she'd adore.

She was right. He ordered mushrooms in a creamy cheese and spinach sauce, followed by steak with dolcelatte, a crisp green salad, and ciabatta bread, with out-of-season strawberries for pudding.

Ruth enjoyed every mouthful – and the Chianti he'd ordered. 'I must say, Robin Deptford,' she smiled, 'that you have incredibly good taste.'

He laughed. 'Thank you very much. Or are you saying that because it's so similar to your own?'

'Hm.' Her eyes crinkled at the corners. 'Supposing I tell you that I would have preferred fish, this evening?'

'Well,' he said, 'you should have told me, when you agreed to let me order for you!' He took her hand as the waiter brought their espressos. She leaned across the table, and he fed her the tiny amaretti biscuits. 'You're one hell of a beautiful woman, Ruth Finn,' he said softly. 'I don't think I've ever met anyone with such a gorgeous bone structure, such beautiful eyes, and a mouth that's ripe to be kissed.' He swallowed hard. 'I'd like to undress you, very slowly.'

'In the middle of the restaurant?' she asked, pretending to be shocked.

'Anywhere,' he said, his voice growing husky. 'I prefer not to have an audience – but I'm not sure how long my control will last, with you. I'd like to peel every layer from your skin, and lick every inch of your skin as I uncover it. I want to make your eyes turn pure gold with passion, and make your body quiver in response to me.'

'Then,' she said softly, 'let's go back to my place. Now.'

'What a good idea,' he told her quietly. He called the waiter over and paid the bill – ignoring Ruth's protests that she wanted to pay her share – and went back to the house in silence. He waited politely at the door for her; Ruth almost reminded him that he had a set of keys, too, but then remembered that he was her Interlover for the night, so of course he wouldn't have a key.

The moment that they were inside the door, Aidan took her into his arms and kissed her, his mouth moving gently against hers and then becoming more insistent as her lips opened under his. Gently, he removed her jacket, walking her over to the hatstand so that he could hang up the garment without having to take his arms from her.

She helped him remove his own jacket, hanging it over the banister. 'God, Ruth, I want you so much.' He kissed her throat. 'I adore you.' He kissed her again, and picked her up.

Ruth giggled. 'Put me down, Aidan!'

'Robin,' he reminded her.

'Robin.'

'No. I want to carry you to your bed.' He walked up the stairs, still carrying her; then paused as he reached the top. 'Where now?'

'First on the right,' she said, her eyes sparkling. He was playing his part perfectly. He'd be perfect for her business –

though she couldn't bear to share him with anyone else. Which was, she thought wryly, exactly how he felt about her. In his position, she'd have been ragingly jealous of Mark, too...

He nudged the door open, then kicked it closed behind them, setting her back on her feet.

She let him peel off her sweater; he gave a sharp intake of breath as he looked at her. 'You're so beautiful. Your skin's so soft.' He nuzzled her shoulders, nosing the straps of her bra downwards.

As he stooped, his hands came behind her back, unfastening her bra and letting it drop to the floor. He cupped her breasts, his thumbs rubbing the soft undersides, and drew the tip of his nose down along the curve of her throat, down through the deep vee of her cleavage. She shivered, and he took one hardening nipple into his mouth, sucking gently on it and tracing the dark areola with the tip of his tongue.

She gave a small moan of pleasure, and he transferred his attentions to her other breast, drawing the pad of his thumb over her glistening nipple. Ruth arched her back, and Aidan's hands came down to span her waist.

Gently, he pushed at the waistband of her skirt, easing the material over her hips. She wriggled slightly, helping him push the material to the floor, and stepped out of it. Her half-slip followed suit; Aidan sat back on his heels, looking up at her.

She looked totally beautiful, and totally unselfconscious, standing there in white lace-trimmed knickers and a pair of plain black hold-up stockings. 'I'd like to see you in black underwear,' he said softly. 'Black lace, to show off the colour of your skin and the way it gleams in the light.'

She smiled back at him. 'Is that the painter in you talking?'

'Oh, I can do better than that.'

'Such as?' she challenged.

'You'll find out, in a moment.' He smiled at her, and began a trail of kisses over her midriff. He tugged at the waistband of her knickers with his teeth, making her giggle; finally, he gave up. 'So much for trying to be sophisticated . . .' He hooked his thumbs into the waistband of her knickers and eased them down. Gently, he rolled her stockings down, stroking her skin as he did so. By the time that he'd finished, Ruth was shivering with expectation.

'Undress me,' he invited softly.

She loosened his tie, dropping it to the floor, then unbuttoned his soft cotton shirt. He had a thing about pure cotton shirts, she knew, preferring the feel of them against his skin; but at least he ironed them himself, not making her do it. She smiled at him, running her fingers over his skin. It felt good, the way his muscles moved beneath her hands. Mark had been good — but Aidan was something else. Something she knew that she didn't want to lose.

She pushed the shirt from his shoulders, then drew her nails lightly down his back, making him shiver. Her hands came to the waistband of his trousers, undoing them and then sliding down over his zip. She could feel his cock swelling hard against her hands, and smiled to herself. He felt so good: long, thick and hard. The fact that he was going to slide it deep inside her made it even better.

When she'd finished undressing him, she dropped to her knees and drew the tip of her nose along his shaft. He groaned, willing her to take the hard muscle into her mouth. She breathed on him, teasing him, and he gave a small moan, betraying his need. She eased her mouth over the head of his cock, licking the small bead of clear moisture from its eye; then took as much of him into her mouth as she could.

Aidan cried out, sliding his hands into her hair and massaging her scalp. 'Oh, God, Ruth. If you do this much more, my control's going to snap. I want to make tonight good for you.'

She released him then, gently untangling his fingers from her hair and standing up. Aidan picked her up and laid her on the bed, kissing her gently – and then harder, as she pushed up towards him.

'Close your eyes,' he commanded softly.

'Why?'

'Remember I told you I could do better than paint you?'

'Ye-es.'

'Well, as your Interlover, I've brought a little treat for you.' He leaned over, and rummaged in the top drawer of his bedside cabinet.

'What are you doing?'

'Keep your eyes closed,' he warned. 'Just humour me, Ruth.'

'OK.' She shivered with delight. Aidan had a very inventive mind, she knew: just what was he planning?

She soon found out, when something warm and wet dropped on her skin. She opened her eyes, lifting herself slightly so that she could see what he was doing. 'What's that?'

'I said, keep your eyes closed,' he informed her, smiling and kissing the tip of her nose. 'Now, are you going to do as I ask, or do I have to blindfold you?'

'Blindfold me?'

'That's what you expect from an Interlover, isn't it? Someone who'll fulfil your kinkiest fantasies – along with your not-so-kinky ones, and the ones you didn't even know you had?'

'True,' she agreed.

'If you don't like this,' he said, 'just tell me to stop. But keep your eyes closed.'

She felt something brushing across her midriff, and suddenly realized what he was doing. Brushing the oil into her skin. Vanilla-scented oil, she realized, as the warmth of her skin made the perfume blossom in the air.

The teasing brush played across her nipples, oiling the hard peaks of flesh, then dipping down in between them, back over her midriff. She wriggled slightly, laughing. 'That tickles!'

'That might, but this won't.' Gently, he parted her legs, and began to use the brush up and down her satiny cleft.

Ruth stiffened for a moment. 'Have you been reading Anaïs Nin?'

'Yes, but I'm not going to shave you,' he replied with a grin. He widened the gap between her thighs, and knelt between them so that he could see her. 'She was right. The way your sex blossoms, it's like a flower.' He continued to brush her with long, slow strokes up and down her musky divide, tracing every fold and curve. He teased her clitoris out of its hood with the brush, circling it and flicking rapidly over the hard bud of flesh until Ruth was writhing beneath him, her sex flexing with the need to feel his cock inside her, filling her.

Almost as if Aidan had read her mind, she felt something press against her, and sighed in relief. He was pushing a finger deep inside her to ease the ache. Then she realized that whatever was inside her was a little too smooth to be his finger. He was using the shaft of the brush on her.

The shock of knowledge was enough to make her come, and she cried out, her sex flexing sharply round the smooth shaft of the brush. When the aftershocks of her orgasm had died down, Aidan removed the brush from her. 'Sit up,' he said softly. 'Open your eyes.'

She did so, and saw him lick every drop of the gleaming moisture from the handle of the brush. She shivered. 'That's the lewdest thing you've ever done to me.'

'I know.' His eyes glittered. 'I love watching you come, Ruth. I love the way your lips go red and puffy, your mouth opens, your throat arches and your breasts swell. I love those soft little cries that you can't quite suppress. The way your body quivers: and I love it even more when it does it round me.'

'Then,' Ruth said huskily, 'what are we waiting for?'

She took the bottle of oil from him, pouring some into one

palm and rubbing her hands together. She smoothed the oil over the muscles in his shoulders, then down over his chest, her fingertips working the liquid into his skin.

'We really ought to be doing this by candle-light,' she said, loving the way his skin glistened as she stroked it.

'Maybe tomorrow night,' he suggested. 'Because, right now, there's no way I want to leave this bed.'

She ran her hands over his midriff, and oiled his cock. 'And miss this, you mean?' she teased, rubbing his foreskin back and forth.

He leaned back, resting his hands behind him and tipping his head back. 'Oh yes,' he moaned softly. Ruth continued to masturbate him, the movements of her hand becoming harder and faster as his arousal grew. Finally, his body jerked and he came, the salty white liquid spraying over her skin.

'Quits, I think,' she said quietly.

'Yeah.' He leaned forward, and licked every trace of the silky fluid from her body; then he kissed her hard, so that she could taste him in his mouth.

Desire shot through her, and she pushed him back against the bed. He uncurled his legs so that he was lying supine and she crawled up his body, straddling him, placing her hands either side of his shoulders and resting her quim against his cock. He cupped the soft globes of her breasts, loving their weight and shape and texture; his fingers manipulated her nipples in a way which made her groan.

'God, Aidan, I need you so much,' she said, her voice husky.

She felt his cock stiffening against her flesh, and lifted herself slightly, easing her hand between their bodies so that she could fit the head of his cock to her sex. Slowly, she lowered herself onto him. He gave a gasp of pleasure. 'Ruthie, you feel so good. Warm, wet and tight.'

'You don't feel so bad yourself,' she quipped. She straightened up, leaning backwards to increase the angle of his penetration; he stroked her thighs, then pressed his thumb over her clitoris, rubbing it softly as she raised and lowered herself over him.

The scent of vanilla, combined with the memory of what they'd just done and the way he felt inside her, was too much for Ruth. She groaned, and her whole body quivered with the strength of her orgasm, her internal muscles contracting hard around his cock. The movement was enough to tip Aidan into his own orgasm and he cried out, lifting his upper body so that he could wrap his arms round Ruth and hold her close, resting his head against her shoulder.

They remained locked together for a while, unwilling to part; then, eventually, Aidan slipped from her. They shifted so that they were lying back against the pillows, Ruth in Aidan's arms. She curved one arm over his midriff.

'So what do you think?' he asked softly. 'Do I pass muster as one of your Interlovers?'

'No,' she said.

'No?' He was shocked. What the hell had Mark Beasley done to her that he hadn't been able to do?

She smiled. 'What I mean is that you're far too good. There's no way I'm letting you loose on any of my clients. I want you all to myself.'

He grinned. 'You bloody tease. I thought . . .' He let the words trail off.

'Yeah, I know.' She rubbed her nose against his, then kissed him softly on the mouth. 'Interlover isn't a threat to you, Aidan. Which reminds me.' She shifted so that she could remove the solitaire from her right hand, and held it up to him. 'I think you need to put this back in its proper place, don't you?'

He smiled, taking it and sliding it back onto the ring finger of her left hand. 'As long as you're sure about this.'

'Oh, I'm very sure,' she said. 'And, in future, I'll involve you more in Interlover. In fact . . .'

He groaned. 'Why do I get the feeling that I'm going to wish I'd never started this?'

She grinned. 'On the contrary. I think that you're going to enjoy this...'

ELEVEN

Aidan sat on the sofa with Ruth curled up in his arms. 'So you're going for quite a small launch party, then?'

She nodded. 'The usual big media event doesn't seem – well, appropriate, really. We're talking about a very personal and intimate service – so I think I'll launch it in a very personal and intimate way.'

He stiffened. 'Such as?'

'A dinner party, here. I'm inviting four potential clients – that's Meg, Selena, Marie and Helen – and four of the Interlovers.'

'Plus us.' He relaxed again. 'Mm, ten's manageable enough for a dinner party. But won't Laura and Shelley feel a bit left out?'

'No. I talked it over with them, and they're fine about it.' Ruth grinned. 'We've already celebrated the launch of Interlover, in our own way!'

Aidan stroked her hair. 'I take it you could do with a hand with the catering, then?

'Yes, please. And with the table plan.'

'Just as long as I'm not sitting anywhere near Mark Beasley...'

Ruth stroked his thigh. 'You're not still hung up about him, are you?'

Aidan thought about it. 'Yes and no. I know you've told me there's nothing to worry about, but... Oh, I don't know. I suppose it's just the standard jealous fiancé reaction.'

'In other circumstances,' Ruth said, 'you'd get on very well. You'd really like each other.'

'Maybe.' He paused. 'So have you thought about how you're going to pair everyone off at the end of the evening?'

'Yes, but I haven't decided yet. In some ways, I feel I ought to plan in it advance; in other ways, it'd be more fun to leave it till the end.'

Aidan stroked her hair. 'I've been thinking. You don't have to have crackers just at Christmas time, do you?'

'I suppose not.' Ruth was intrigued. 'What do you have in mind?'

'We could make our own. Instead of the silly hat, the joke and the plastic heart-shaped key-ring, we could put whatever we wanted in them. The women would have a cracker with a condom and someone's name on, and the men would have a cracker with a little treat for their partner, later that evening.'

Ruth beamed at him. 'Aidan, you're brilliant! That's a great idea.' She paused. 'Though what about us? Are we part of the same set-up?'

Aidan smiled at her. 'Of course we are. The deal is, whoever's name is on the condom in your cracker, you go with that person at the end of the evening.'

'Are you sure about that?' Ruth asked.

'Positive.'

She reached up to kiss him. 'Aidan Shaw, you're one of the world's unacknowledged geniuses.'

He smiled at her. 'Flattery, my love, will get you just about anywhere.'

'So what's this all about, then, Aidan?' Shelley asked, sipping the mineral water he'd brought her.

'I need your help,' he said. 'Both of you.'

Laura looked at him. 'But why don't you want us to say anything to Ruth?'

'Because I want it to be a surprise for her,' he explained. 'It's to do with Interlover – the launch party.'

'The famous dinner party, you mean?' Laura said.

'Mm.' Aidan cracked his knuckles, feeling uncomfortable. 'I know you two, Nicholas and Carlo should be there, too, but fourteen's going to be too big to get the right effect. Ruth wants it cosy and intimate.'

Shelley laughed. 'Don't worry about it, Aidan. We've already helped Ruth celebrate the launch of Interlover, in our own way.'

'Your dinner party should be for the clients, not us,' Laura agreed. 'And that's what I told Ruth, when she originally invited us.'

Aidan smiled at them, relieved. 'So you promise you won't say a word to Ruth about this?'

'Of course we promise.' Shelley tipped her head on one side. 'Now, will you stop tormenting us and tell us what you're plotting? I'm dying to know!'

'Like I said, it's for the dinner party. We're going to have crackers on the table. The women's crackers contain a condom and someone's name; the men's crackers contain a nice little treat to share with their partner.'

'That's a brilliant idea,' Laura said. 'Inspired.'

'I know. Ruth says I'm one of the world's unacknowledged geniuses.' He breathed on his nails, polishing them on his sweater and making them both laugh. 'But the thing is, I'm stuck for ideas.'

Shelley was surprised. 'Ruth always gave me the impression that you were rather – er – inv—' Her voice trailed off as she remembered who was sitting opposite her. She coughed, and sipped her water, to cover her embarrassment.

'Inv what?' Aidan asked.

Shelley winced. 'Inventive.'

He flushed as he realized what she meant. 'Do women talk about – you know?'

'Our sex lives? Yes, of course we do. When we're in all-female company, and fuelled with good wine.' Shelley waved her hand impatiently. 'Don't get paranoid about it, though. It's nothing personal.'

He grinned. 'That's funny, I always thought that sex was *very* personal!'

She rolled her eyes. 'You know what I mean. It's standard girl-talk – sex and shopping.'

'Yeah.' He sighed. 'Anyway, as I was saying, Interlover's all about fulfilling women's fantasies – which aren't necessarily what men think they are. So I need a woman's help to make sure I get it right. I can't ask Ruth, because I want it to be a surprise for her, too – so that's why I'm asking you.'

'I see.' Laura's eyes crinkled at the corners. 'Because you think we'd 'ave some 'ot fantasies, babe?' She adopted a mock East End accent.

He laughed back, realizing that she was teasing him. 'A posh bird like you? Yeah, course ya would, darlin'!'

'Well, where do we start?' Shelley asked. 'What sort of thing did you have in mind, Aidan?'

'I don't know.' He spread his hands. 'What sort of things do you fantasize about? And are they the same sort of things that Ruth fantasizes about?'

Shelley and Laura exchanged a glance. 'Probably.'

'Then I'm in your hands.' He tipped his head on one side, looking appealingly at them.

'Well, I suppose there's the standard massage fantasy. You could put a little bottle of oil in a cracker,' Laura suggested. 'Get a sensuous oil. There are enough aromatherapy places around that will blend something specially for you. Something with ylang-ylang – not sandalwood, though, as it's a bit intense. Something floral. Jasmine and rose.'

Aidan nodded, and quickly tapped the details into his electronic organizer. He looked up as he became aware that Shelley and Laura were grinning at him. 'What's so funny?' he asked, frowning.

'You and your gadgets,' Laura said with a smile.

'Actually, Ruth bought this for me.'

'Yes, but I bet you pointed it out to her in the first place.'

He grinned. 'Mm, you're right – I did. Anyway, that's one fantasy. Four more to go.'

'How about honey?' Shelley suggested.

'Honey?' He was surprised.

'For smearing over each other. You can have a lot of fun, doing that,' Shelley told him.

Aidan grinned. 'I don't know whether I dare ask you if it's just fantasy, or whether you've actually done it.'

Shelley winked. 'That's for me to know, and you to guess. Anyway, you can get one of those little tiny trial-size pots, so it'll fit into the cracker.'

'Massage oil and honey.' Aidan nodded. 'What else?'

Shelley sipped her water thoughtfully. 'How about a bottle of champagne? It doesn't have to be vintage. Sparkling wine would do, actually.'

Aidan frowned. 'I don't think the cracker would be big enough, even if I bought one of those mini-bottles.'

'Then why don't you put a piece of paper in the cracker, saying that the champagne's in the fridge?' Laura suggested.

He grinned. 'I knew I was right to ask you two! So that's three. Two more to go.'

'There's the old standby of a black silk scarf,' Laura said thoughtfully.

Shelley suddenly remembered what Mark had brought her. 'And a pot of raspberries.'

'Raspberries?'

'For crushing into your skin. Strawberries, if you prefer.

You can treat them like the champagne – a note in the cracker and the goodies in the fridge.' Shelley smiled at him. 'So that's your five treats.'

'Right.' He nodded.

'What sort of condoms are you going to get?' Laura asked. 'You're not going to buy a pack of boring ordinary ones, are you?'

'Well – what do you suggest?' Aidan asked.

'Coloured ones, flavoured ones, the ones with little twiddly bits on. Something different. Something fun.'

Aidan smiled at them. 'OK. And thanks very much for your help. I think it's going to be an evening to remember.'

'It certainly sounds like it,' Laura agreed. 'Though I still think that you're inventive enough to have thought them up on your own.'

'Maybe. But, like I said, I want to get it right. For Ruthie. It means a lot to her.'

Shelley eyed him curiously. 'Is Mark going to be there?'

'Yes.' He sighed. 'To be honest, I'm not looking forward to meeting him.'

'Honestly, you'll really like him. Forget everything that's happened – just pretend you've never heard of him, that you know nothing about him. The two of you will get on fine,' Laura said.

'Mm, I don't think Ruth would appreciate the jealous fiancé act, especially on the launch night,' Shelley added. 'Considering how long it's taken you to get the woman to agree to marry you – it'd be best to play this one cool, Aidan.'

'Yes, you have a point.' He smiled. 'Well, I'd better go shopping. And I owe you both chocolates for this.'

'I'll hold you to that, definitely!' Shelley said. 'Belgian ones. In large quantity.'

He grinned. 'And I'll leave it to you two to explain to Ruth just why I'm pandering to your whims . . .'

*

The following Saturday night saw Ruth pacing nervously up and down the kitchen. Aidan poured her a glass of wine, shoving it into her hand. 'For God's sake, Ruth, calm down. Everyone's going to turn up, they're going to be on time, and they're all going to like each other.'

'But—' she began.

'But nothing,' he told her. 'Selena, Helen and Meg know each other from way back, and they get on well. Marie's a friend of Laura's, so she's obviously the same sort of person so there's no problem there. You picked the Interlovers personally, so they're the sort of people you want.' He spread his hands. 'So what is there to worry about? Absolutely nothing!'

'I suppose so.' Ruth wasn't convinced.

The doorbell rang and she jumped. Aidan smiled at her. 'Go and sit down. I'll answer it.' He came back into the sitting room, a few moments later, with Meg and Selena, both of them brandishing bottles of Chardonnay.

'We weren't sure whether it was red or white tonight,' Meg said, 'but I know this goes with nearly anything.'

'Actually, white's perfect, thanks,' Ruth said.

'Definitely,' Aidan agreed, pouring the women a glass of wine.

'Oh – and I'm sure that these will go nicely with coffee.' Meg handed her friend a box of white chocolate mints. 'I discovered these, the other week, and they're absolutely addictive. Even more so than those chocolate-covered coffee beans.'

'I'll put them in the fridge, out of temptation's way,' Aidan said, taking their coats as well. 'I'm really glad you're here, you know.'

'Because of our beauty, wit and charm?' Selena teased.

'But of course, my lady.' He gave them a deep bow. 'And because you'll calm Madam down a bit. She's panicking.'

'Why?' Meg asked, mystified. Ruth wasn't the panicky sort.

'She thinks that no one's going to turn up,' Aidan supplied.

Meg laughed. 'You must be joking. None of us would want to miss the big night!' She exchanged a glance with Selena. 'Dare I ask who's going to be here tonight, Ruth?'

'Helen and Marie.'

'I meant *men*,' Meg said.

'Right. First, there's Mark – you've both met him. Then there's Niall: he's an actor. He's about twenty-five. Tall, dark hair, blue eyes – your Charlie Sheen fantasy, Selena.'

'Sounds good to me,' Selena said.

'Then there's Jed – he's an artist, in his mid-thirties. I think he'll get on well with Helen. He's another tall, dark and handsome one.'

'All your men are the same – tall and gorgeous. What about having some short, ugly men?' Meg asked mischievously.

Ruth grinned back. 'Find me a woman who fantasizes about short, balding, fat and obnoxious men, and I'll find you a man to suit! Just – not tonight.'

'What about the last one, Ruth?' Selena asked.

'Tim. I'm afraid he's another tall, dark and handsome one. Dark eyes, too: very intense and soulful. He's a researcher – he's doing his post-grad in English at UCL. He's the youngest; he's twenty-three.' Ruth tipped her head on one side. 'He's writing his thesis on John Donne, would you believe?'

Meg groaned. 'No. Please. Don't start capping quotes with each other over dinner, will you?'

Aidan, returning to hear the last few words, laughed. 'If she does, Meg, you and I can talk antiques, or something!'

'Sounds good to me,' Meg said with a smile. 'Perhaps we can have those candlesticks as a forfeit . . .'

Ruth burst out laughing. 'I know you're dying to get your mitts on them, but no!'

Helen and Marie arrived separately, a few minutes later; when Aidan had taken their coats and given them a glass of wine, he glanced at Ruth. 'I think maybe you ought to answer the door from now on. I'd hate to put off any of your Interlovers!'

She nodded. 'No problem.'

Mark was the first to arrive. Ruth had been dreading the moment for some time – the moment when Mark and Aidan finally met. She smiled her thanks at the bottle of wine he thrust into her hands, and kissed him on the cheek.

'You look lovely tonight, Ruth,' he said, smiling at her.

'Thanks.' She'd taken extra care with her appearance, wearing a formal black dress and high heels, plus the obligatory make-up; Aidan, too, had complimented her on the way she looked, holding her close and whispering in her ear that she was the most desirable woman he'd ever met, and he was half-tempted to cancel the dinner party and take her to bed instead.

And yet she still felt tied in knots, inside, convinced that it was all going to go horribly wrong. 'Come through. I'll introduce you to everyone.' She swallowed nervously as she ushered him into the sitting room. Mark knew the women, and greeted them all with a kiss; finally, he came to Aidan, who was sitting, unsmiling, on the sofa.

'Aidan, this is Mark Beasley, our pilot Interlover. Mark, this is Aidan Shaw, my fiancé,' she said quietly.

To her relief, they both behaved impeccably. Mark held out his hand. 'Nice to meet you at last, Aidan. Ruth's said a lot about you.'

Aidan stood up, shook his hand, and gave him a grin. 'You, too – and I can see now why Ruth picked you! Would you rather have a beer, or a glass of wine?'

'Beer, please.'

Aidan nodded. 'Well, come and have a look in the fridge, and see what you fancy. If you're a lager man, I'm sure I can find something.'

'Thanks.' Mark smiled. 'Though I'm more of a real-ale man.'

Aidan's face lit up. 'In that case, you'll definitely like the contents of our fridge. Come through – we'll leave this lot to yak about girly stuff. And we can have a decent chat about beer.'

Ruth raised her eyebrows as the two men left the room, chatting companionably. 'I wasn't expecting that,' she said quietly.

Helen smiled at her. 'Come on. Aidan's far too nice to pick a fight with anyone. Anyway, there isn't any need. We all know how things stand, don't we?'

'Yeah. I suppose so.'

Ruth was saved from further introspection by the arrival of Niall, Jed and Tim. When she'd finished making introductions and topping up everyone's drinks, Aidan touched her lightly on the arm. 'Time to eat, I think,' he said softly.

She nodded. 'Right – well, if everyone's ready, shall we go through to eat?'

Aidan had written out place cards; Meg's eyes widened in appreciation as she sat down and looked at the plate in front of her. 'Wow. Is this what I think it is?'

'Smoked salmon, stuffed with mozzarella and dill. Aidan's latest speciality,' Ruth confirmed.

'Gorgeous,' Selena added as she tasted it.

'What about these crackers?' Mark asked, spotting the discreet dark green tubes by the side plates.

'Another of Aidan's ideas,' Ruth said. 'It's a slightly different way of finding out who you'll be spending the evening with, later. The women's crackers all have condoms in, with a man's name on.'

'So are you two included in this?' Selena asked.

'Yes, we are,' Ruth affirmed.

'What about the men's crackers?' Tim asked.

'That's the interesting bit. They contain a little pressie – something nice to share,' Aidan told him with a grin.

'And you can blame it all on him – he stuffed the crackers,

and I don't have a clue what's in them,' Ruth said. 'He wouldn't let me in the room while he was doing them, and he locked them in his briefcase so I couldn't peep at them. I don't know why he doesn't trust me.'

Aidan laughed. 'Think about Christmas. Every present you get, you rattle it and prod it until you've worked out what it is. So nothing's a surprise on Christmas morning unless I hide it from you!'

She laughed back. 'Just because you're so disciplined and wait until after breakfast on Christmas morning before opening yours!'

'So do we pull the crackers now, or later?' Marie asked.

'Later – just after coffee might be a good time,' Aidan suggested.

'Sounds good to me.' Helen smiled at him. 'So are there any party hats or silly jokes in them, then?'

Ruth groaned. 'Knowing Aidan, I hate to think.'

Helen laughed. 'It's a bit like that episode of *The Good Life* – do you remember, when they made their own crackers from the insides of loo rolls and bits of holly, and had paper hats made from newspapers?'

'I promise you,' Aidan laughed back, 'that there aren't any loo rolls or newspaper hats in mine . . .'

'How about candlesticks?' Meg asked hopefully.

Ruth groaned. 'You're never going to let me forget that, are you?'

'No. Even though I have found three identical pairs since,' Meg said, laughing back.

'What's the story about the candlesticks?' Tim asked.

'It's how I met Ruth,' Meg explained. 'I was at an auction, and I wanted these candlesticks. But Ruth beat me to it.'

'The ones in the middle of the table,' Ruth said. 'And since then, she's been trying to get me to sell them to her.'

'Unsuccessfully,' Meg said with a sigh.

'So is antiques a hobby, or your business?' Tim asked.

'Both,' Meg said. 'I'm lucky enough to be in a business I love.'

'Me, too,' he said. 'Though being a research student doesn't pay quite as well as having your own antiques business.'

'Your thesis is on Donne, isn't it?' Selena asked.

He nodded. 'My passion.'

'Ruth's, too. So please don't start her off!' Helen said, smiling.

They chatted through the first course; then Ruth and Aidan cleared the table, bringing through tureens of buttered new potatoes, mangetout, button mushrooms and baby corn.

'Tarragon chicken,' Jed said appreciatively as he tasted his main course. 'And this is even better than Marks and Spencer's!'

'And how do you know that there aren't five empty packets lurking in their bin?' Meg teased.

'I can vouch for it,' Aidan said, 'because Ruth made me skin the chicken breasts.' He grimaced. 'Which has to be the worst job ever.'

'Apart from taking giblets out of turkeys,' Selena said, with a shudder. 'Which is definitely a man's job!'

'So what do you do, Jed?' Marie asked.

'I paint. I do portraits of people's pet poodles,' he said, 'though I prefer doing non-commercial stuff. My own compositions.'

'Helen paints, too,' Selena said. 'I've got some of her paintings on my walls.'

'But, like you, I do commercial stuff for bread-and-butter work,' Helen said. 'Book jackets, that sort of thing.'

'What about you, Niall?' Meg asked.

'I'm an actor, in rep,' he said.

Ruth smiled at him. 'What are you playing at the moment?'

'*Hamlet*. Well, I'm Laertes. We're doing the full four-hour production, so it's pretty gruelling – luckily, tonight's my night off,' he said, smiling back at her. 'I drew the short straw for tomorrow, though. It's the school matinée run.'

'Wasn't there an actor who stopped a production of *Hamlet*, and said that every time the kids interrupted him, he'd go right back to the beginning, and do that every time until they shut up?' Selena asked, laughing. 'I'm sure I heard it on the radio, the other day.'

'Believe me, I sometimes feel like that!' Niall said, laughing back. 'So what do you do, Selena?'

'I'm a translator. Mainly French legal documents, though Ruth sometimes used to give me Italian poetry. It was a bit more fun to work with.'

'What about you, Marie?' Jed asked.

'I'm just a boring lawyer,' she said lightly. 'Commercial property.'

'That's not as boring as being an accountant, though,' Aidan said with a grin.

Ruth's eyes met his. 'Stop fishing! I don't think anyone who knows you would make that mistake.'

He raised his glass to her. 'Thank you.'

When Mark said what he did for a living, the talk turned to music. 'I'd love to play the guitar,' Aidan said.

'Yeah, but my nerves won't stand it, because you're tone deaf!' Ruth said.

Aidan pulled a face at her. 'I *do* appreciate music.'

'There's a huge difference between appreciating something and doing it. I love Helen's work, but I can't do it myself.'

'True.' He grinned at her. 'Everyone has a talent.'

'And I think the men in this room share one in particular,' Meg said wryly.

'They'd better!' Ruth said. 'And I'll drink to that. To Interlover.'

'To Interlover,' they echoed.

The pudding – crème brûlée – was a success, with Selena

begging Aidan for the recipe. Ruth served coffee and the white chocolate mints Meg had brought, then sat down. 'Mm. I feel lazy, now.'

'Me, too,' Selena said.

'It's the sort of time when you just want to loll around, listening to music,' Meg said. 'Mark – why don't you sing something for us?'

'What – now?'

Aidan smiled at him. 'Trust a woman to put you on the spot! You don't have to, if you don't want to.'

'No, it's OK.' He smiled back. 'I didn't bring a guitar with me, though.'

'*A capella* will do nicely,' Selena said. 'How about something nice and sensual?'

Mark spread his hands. 'I'm open to requests, as long as they're not too obscure!'

'What about Chris de Burgh – one of the old ones?' Helen suggested. 'Something like 'Satin Green Shutters'?'

'OK.' Mark took a sip of his coffee, then began to sing. The others listened, spellbound: Ruth suddenly wished that she'd broken her own rules and sat next to Aidan. The haunting quality of Mark's voice made her want to touch her lover, be close to him.

Mark followed it with Paul Weller's 'You Do Something To Me', and then brought everything up-tempo again with 'All Right Now'. 'I think I've earned my supper now,' he quipped when he'd finished.

Aidan clapped. 'You certainly have. Tell me when your band's playing next – Ruth and I will come and see you.'

Mark looked at him, and smiled. 'Yeah. I'd like that.' Despite what Laura and Shelley had told him, he had expected not to like Aidan. He was pleased to discover that he was wrong.

'I suppose it's time for the reckoning, then,' Ruth said softly. 'Who's going first?'

'It has to be ladies first,' Aidan added.

'In that case, Meg,' Selena said with a grin.

'Right.' Meg handed the other end of her cracker to Mark. 'Pull!'

There was a crack, and Mark handed the larger half of the cracker back to Meg – who deliberately took a long while to open the small parcel inside.

'Oh, come on, Meg, don't keep us waiting!' Helen said, her smile taking the sting out of her impatience.

'OK.' Meg grinned as she looked at the small packet. 'I bet you had a good time shopping for this, Aidan – a blueberry-flavour condom! Wherever did you find it?'

'My sources are secret, I'm afraid.' He spread his hands. 'I just wanted to find something a bit original.'

'Who are you sharing it with, Meg?' Mark asked.

'Niall.' Meg smiled warmly at the young actor; he blew her a kiss. 'And I reckon you should be next, Helen.'

'OK.' Helen pulled her cracker with Aidan, and laughed aloud as she opened the contents. 'Well, Mark. You get the kinky black ribbed condom.' She smiled at Marie. 'You next, Marie?'

Marie turned to Jed, who smiled at her and pulled the other end of her cracker. 'Tim,' she said quietly. 'With a green condom.'

'That's green in colour, not as in recyclable,' Aidan said, making them all laugh. 'Selena?'

Selena pulled her cracker with Tim. 'Wow,' she said. 'This one's champagne-flavoured.'

'Who's sharing it?' Meg asked.

'Jed.'

Ruth looked at Aidan. 'Well, I don't exactly need to pull mine, do I?'

'Hey, it was a random choice. For all I know, you could have shuffled the crackers round,' Aidan protested, laughing.

'Or the place cards. I've known you do that before.'

'Except this time, I didn't.' She turned to Niall. 'Well, I'd hate to be a party pooper, so . . .' She pulled the cracker with him. 'Oh, gosh, what a surprise,' she drawled. 'Mine has Aidan's name on it.'

'But what is it?' Marie asked.

Ruth looked, and burst out laughing. 'Would you believe, gold?'

'So now we know who – and what sort of condom,' Helen said. 'The question is – what other little treats are in store for us?'

Mark pulled his cracker with Ruth. 'A pot of honey.' He tipped his head on one side as he looked at Helen. 'I think I could be quite inventive with that.'

'If you're not, I will be,' she said softly.

Marie and Niall were next. Niall opened the folded piece of paper, and grinned.

'What?' Meg asked.

'It's a punnet of strawberries – which are in the fridge,' he said, smiling.

'Well, I didn't want them to go all squashy; besides, they didn't quite fit into a cracker,' Aidan explained with a grin.

Jed pulled his cracker with Helen to discover a small bottle of massage oil. Selena flexed her shoulders. 'I'm not sure if I'm looking forward more to using it or having it used on me!' she said, smiling.

Tim pulled his cracker with Meg to discover another of the folded pieces of paper: 'Champagne,' he said, raising his eyebrows. 'Also in the fridge, for obvious reasons.'

'Which leaves you,' Mark said, gesturing to Aidan. 'I know that you know what's in it, but the rest of us don't!'

'True.' Aidan pulled his cracker with Selena, and handed it to her. 'Selena, would you do the honours for me?'

'A black silk scarf,' she said, unwrapping the small parcel.

'Now, *there's* a possibility, if ever I saw one!'

'Hm.' Ruth looked at her lover, who had the grace to blush. 'I'm almost tempted to make everyone swap again, to make it properly random.'

Mark took her hand, squeezing it. 'Don't be a spoilsport. If I'd been Aidan, I would have done the same – fixed it, so I ended up with you. Wouldn't you, Jed?'

'Yes,' the painter agreed.

'Me, too,' Niall added.

'And me,' Tim said.

'Thanks for the vote of confidence, guys,' Aidan said, smiling at them.

'You get our vote, too,' Selena said. 'So you're stuck with it, Ruth!'

'Yeah. Well, who's for more coffee?' she asked.

'Please,' Mark said.

Ruth went to get a fresh pot of coffee; when she returned, the others were laughing and chatting.

She leaned on Aidan's shoulder as she poured his coffee. 'You fixed it,' she said quietly in his ear, 'and I'll make you admit it, later.'

He turned his face to kiss her lightly. 'Maybe. Mm. You still make better coffee than anyone I know, except Laura.'

'Flattery isn't going to get you out of it,' she warned, but her eyes were filled with amusement.

Eventually, Niall stretched. 'I hate to be a party pooper, but it's getting late.'

'Laertes doesn't need his beauty sleep that much,' Selena teased. 'He follows the primrose path of dalliance.'

'Or he certainly will this evening,' Meg said, smiling and standing up.

Aidan went to fetch their coats and the punnet of strawberries.

'Thanks for a nice evening,' Meg said, hugging Ruth and kissing Aidan. 'I've really enjoyed it.'

'Yes, it's been very nice,' Niall agreed, shaking Aidan's hand and kissing Ruth on the cheek.

'We'd better be going, too,' Tim said, standing up and walking over to Marie.

Mark, Helen, Jed and Selena also left; finally, Ruth closed the door behind them.

'Just you and me again, then,' she said to Aidan.

'Yes.' He kissed her lightly. 'Just you and me.'

Mark took Helen's hand as they left the house. 'Your place or mine?' he asked softly.

'I don't mind,' Helen said. 'It's up to you.'

'We could go back to mine, but we wouldn't be on our own. Someone's bound to be in, hogging the kitchen or the bathroom or the sitting room.'

'Better make it my flat, then,' Helen said. She smiled at him. 'A pot of honey. I wonder what made Aidan think of that?'

'Maybe it's something he does with Ruth,' Mark suggested.

Helen tipped her head to one side. 'So what did you think of Aidan, then?'

'He seemed a nice guy,' Mark admitted. 'In a way, I still feel a bit jealous of him – he's got Ruth – but he obviously loves her a hell of a lot.' He shrugged. 'Things aren't quite so bad now. Ruth's lovely, but she and I probably aren't meant for each other.'

'Sometimes dreams are best kept as dreams,' Helen said.

'How are things with you? Still thinking about Stu?'

She shook her head. 'Actually, no. You helped me a lot there.'

'I'm glad,' he said softly.

They caught the Tube back to Helen's flat. Mark smiled at her as he followed her through the front door. 'Shall I make us both a coffee?'

She shook her head. 'I don't know about you, but I'm a bit tired.'

TWELVE

Marie smiled at Tim as they left the house. Although she'd found Mark very, very attractive, she'd always preferred dark-haired men. Tim's intense dark eyes and good looks appealed to her immensely.

'Tell me more about your PhD,' she said. 'John Donne, isn't it? I don't really know anything about him.'

'He's the greatest poet who ever lived — as far as I'm concerned, anyway,' Tim told her. 'He's a Metaphysical poet, which means he used really unusual imagery — it's all very clever stuff. He lived around the time of Shakespeare.' He paused. 'And he wrote some of the most erotic poems I've ever read.'

'Perhaps you could quote me some.' He had a nice voice: Marie could imagine him reading pornography to her, and she liked the idea.

Tim smiled. 'Not in the middle of the street! Maybe later.'

Marie tipped her head on one side. 'That raunchy, is it?'

'Not so much the words themselves — more the effect they have on me,' he said softly. 'There's one particular one. It's an elegy, on his mistress going to bed. He doesn't even mention her naked body, but the way he talks about undressing her, and touching her... It's a real turn-on. Some of my female friends have said the same — that a man reading that poem to them would have them wanting to make love with him all night.' He shivered. 'I've often wondered who inspired that particular poem. I'm sure it couldn't have been written for the money, like most poems were in those days.'

'So what will you do, when you've finished studying?'

Tim sighed. 'That all depends on what sort of jobs are around at the time. I'd like to stay in London, but I might have to move to get a decent lecturing post. Something to do with Renaissance poetry, anyway.' He smiled at her. 'What about you? You said that you're a lawyer.'

'It's commercial law. Property, mainly, so it's not particularly exciting. No Mafia trials, or anything like that,' she said.

'Do you enjoy it?'

'I used to,' Marie said, 'but just lately, I haven't. It seems such a rat race. I really admire Ruth – the way she's decided not to go back to it but to set up Interlover instead.'

Tim's curiosity was roused. 'So how did you get to hear of Interlover?'

'I work with one of Ruth's best friends, Laura. In fact, I was the first "proper" assignment for Mark.'

He smiled wryly. 'It looks like I have a lot to live up to, then.'

Marie laughed. 'Don't get hung up about it, Tim. Mark's a lovely guy, but Ruth's chosen you all for particular qualities. You're someone I can talk to, as well as . . .' She shrugged. 'As well as enjoying the physical side with you, I suppose.'

He grinned, and took her hand. 'Right.'

'Let's get a taxi,' Marie said. 'I really can't be bothered with the Tube tonight.'

'We'll go Dutch on it.'

'No, we won't.' Marie squeezed his hand. 'You're a student – so you don't have much money. I work, so I can afford it. I'll pick up the cab fare.'

'Thanks.' Tim smiled at her. 'I must say, I liked the idea of those crackers.'

'So did I.' Marie smiled back. 'And our particular prize.

It'll be a nice way to round off the evening, drinking champagne.'

'Yes.' He looked at her. 'Tell me – how big is your bath?'

'My bath?' Marie was surprised. 'I suppose it's a bit bigger than average.'

'Good. Do you have any candles?'

'Ye-es.'

'Then how do you fancy,' he asked, 'drinking champagne by candlelight, in the bath?'

Suddenly remembering the way Mark had aroused her in the bath, Marie shivered. 'It sounds good to me,' she said quietly.

They hailed a cab; when they climbed into the back, Tim slid his arm round Marie's shoulders. She stiffened at first; then relaxed.

He nuzzled her cheek. 'I was watching you all evening, you know.'

'Really?'

'Mm. Your eyes are such an unusual colour. Aqua grey, like the sea on a stormy winter's day.' He grinned. 'As you can tell, I study poetry – but I'm not a poet.'

'Neither am I, so that makes us quits,' Marie said, smiling back.

'I meant it, though. I really do think you're beautiful.' He looked at her, his eyes intense. 'I'd like to kiss you.'

'In front of the taxi driver?'

'He's probably seen far more than people just kissing.' Tim leaned over, touching his lips very gently to hers. Marie found herself responding to his gentleness, and kissed him back, pushing her tongue against his. Tim broke the kiss, shaking. 'Marie,' he said huskily, 'I think I'd better stop there. Otherwise I might embarrass you.'

Marie flushed. 'Right.'

He nuzzled her cheek. 'Kissing you makes me think of all the other things I want to do with you. I want to touch you, stroke you, kiss you all over,' he whispered. 'Everywhere, from the soles of your feet to your breasts, to . . .' He let the sentence trail off, and Marie felt the pulse between her legs begin to beat hard as she realized what he meant. Her sex. Licking her, his tongue moving in long slow strokes from the top to the bottom of her quim, until she came . . .

At last, the taxi pulled up outside her flat. She paid the driver; Tim followed her up the path to the front door, and she let them both into the flat.

As soon as she'd closed the door, Tim took her in his arms, spinning her round to face him. He cupped her face in his hands. 'I meant it,' he said. 'You really are a beautiful woman. All the things I've been looking for – clever, witty, sophisticated. And with a body that turns me on without trying.' He kissed her again, letting his hands slide down her body, moulding to her curves. Marie found her hands automatically rising to tangle in the hair at the back of his neck, urging him on.

This time, when he broke the kiss, he rubbed his nose affectionately against hers. 'What we need is a candle – and a glass. Then we can drink champagne by candlelight.' He kissed her again. 'In the bath.'

Marie led him into the kitchen. 'Only one glass?' she asked. 'There are two of us.'

'I know.' He nodded. 'But I think it'd be more romantic to share it.'

'Right.'

While she reached up into one of the cabinets for a glass, Tim stroked the curve of her buttocks. 'God, I can't keep my hands off you,' he murmured.

A shiver of pleasure ran down her spine. 'I'm glad to hear that,' she said, equally softly.

She fetched a wrought-iron candelabrum from the sitting room, and a small box of matches; then they went into the bathroom.

He sniffed appreciatively as she lit the candles. 'Scented, aren't they?'

'French vanilla,' she confirmed.

'Beautiful.' He smiled at her. 'In some ways, it's a shame that we didn't have the massage oil. I would have liked the excuse to touch you, to oil your body all over.'

'You don't need an excuse,' she told him, her voice growing husky.

'I'm glad to hear it.' He stroked her cheek, then put the plug in the bath and began running the water. 'Do you have any bubble bath?'

'Bubbles, rather than oil?'

'Definitely.'

She smiled, and picked up the bottle of aromatherapy foam bath that Mark had brought her the previous week. She tipped some into the water, and the scent of citrus and ginger flooded the air.

'This is gorgeous,' Tim said.

'Mm. A friend bought it for me.'

He caught the look on her face. 'You mean, Mark did.'

She coughed. 'Yes.'

'I think I could learn a lot from him,' Tim said. 'But then again . . .' He placed the lighted candles on the windowsill and turned off the overhead light, so that the room was bathed in a soft, sensuous glow. 'Perfect,' he said quietly. He uncorked the champagne, not spilling a drop, and filled the glass. Placing both the bottle and the glass on the windowsill, he turned to Marie. 'Now.' His eyes lit up. 'That poem I was telling you about, earlier . . .' He unzipped her dress, sliding the material off her shoulders. ' "Your gown going off, such beauteous state reveals, As when from flowery meads, the hill's shadow steals." '

Marie shivered. 'That's lovely.'

'There's a lot more. He talks to his mistress about going to bed with her, but he doesn't describe her body at all. He just describes her taking off her clothes...' He stroked Marie's shoulders, pushing her dress down to her waist. 'You feel gorgeous. Soft and smooth and warm.' He pulled her back into his arms again, kissing her hard, and undid her lacy bra, letting it fall to the floor. He cupped her breasts, pushing them together slightly, and spreading his fingers so that her dark nipples peeped out between them.

'You're beautiful,' he said softly, stooping to nuzzle her breasts. He smoothed his hands over her hips, pushing the dress completely from her. ' "Licence my roving hands, and let them go Before, behind, between, above, below," ' he quoted.

Marie's tongue moistened her lower lip. 'My God, the picture that conjures up!' she said huskily.

'Exactly.' Tim's dark eyes glittered. 'That's what I want to do. I want to touch you everywhere, with my hands and my mouth and my cock.'

'Licence granted,' she said softly.

He smiled to himself. Ruth hadn't told him that much about the people who'd been invited to the dinner party. At the time, he'd said that it was unfair – how was he supposed to know what they wanted? – but Ruth had smiled and said that he'd know, because the woman he was with would tell him exactly what she wanted. He had a feeling that Marie, once she'd overcome her initial reserve, would have some very interesting ideas indeed.

He continued undressing her, dropping to his knees so that he could peel down her stockings. He stroked her skin as he revealed it, and Marie's sex flexed. She itched for him to touch her properly, to slide his fingers along her quim and then push one deep inside her.

Almost as though he'd read her mind, he removed her knickers, then gently stroked the length of her musky furrow, his fingertips skating against her moist flesh. ' "O my America, my new found land, My kingdom, safliest when with one man manned, My mine of precious stones, my empery, How blessed am I in this discovering thee!" ' He continued to stroke her sex. ' "Then, where my hand is set, my seal shall be." '

Marie frowned at him. 'Sorry, I don't follow that.'

'Donne liked double meanings. First, that he'd signed a compact between him and his lover, and he'd make it legally binding with his seal.' His eyes glittered. 'And then there's the other meaning. Where his hand is, he'll consummate their love, later.'

'And that's what you're proposing to do, right now?'

'Well, I wouldn't have been at Ruth and Aidan's place tonight if I didn't intend to do something like that.'

'That's true.' She helped him to his feet. 'Though you're wearing too much, at the moment.'

'Also true.' He went over to the bath, and turned off the taps. He stripped swiftly; Marie watched every movement, spellbound. Tim really was nice-looking. He wasn't quite as tall or as broad-shouldered as Mark, and his skin was paler – because he spent so much time studying in dusty libraries, she assumed. Even so, she found what she saw attractive.

She reached out to touch him, letting her hand drift down over his chest; his hair felt slightly rough against her fingertips. He wasn't a gorilla but, at the same time, he was no smooth-chested boy.

'In Renaissance times, the term was "beardless boys",' Tim said with a grin.

Marie coloured instantly. 'I'm sorry. I didn't realize that I'd spoken aloud.'

'No problem.' He stroked her face. 'I'm only glad that you like what you see.'

'Very much so.' She helped him remove his dark trousers, and was gratified to find that his cock was every bit as large as Mark's, showing thick and rigid through the thin cotton of his underpants.

His look invited her to touch him further, more intimately; she curled her fingers round his cock, through his underpants, and rubbed it slightly. His mouth opened, and he made a small sound of pleasure. She smiled at him, and removed his underpants completely. 'So, what now?'

'This,' he said. He picked her up, putting her in the bath, and handed her the glass of champagne. Then he climbed into the bath, sitting in front of her.

Marie smiled, noticing that he'd taken the tap end. 'Very gentlemanly of you.'

'Basic courtesy.' He smiled back. 'Well, cheers. Here's to us.'

She took a sip of champagne, then handed him the glass. 'To us,' she repeated.

He turned the glass round so that he could drink from the same place her lips had touched.

'Don't tell me – inspired by another Donne poem?' she suggested.

He shook his head. 'Afraid not. Just me being corny.' He set the glass on the side of the bath and picked up the soap. He lathered his hands and soaped her breasts. Her nipples hardened as he stroked her skin. She tipped her head back, a ripple of pleasure coursing down her spine. 'God, that feels so good.'

'I've hardly started yet,' he said softly. He lathered his hands again, and picked up her left leg, washing her foot and stroking its sole.

Marie's sex pooled. He had to be ten years younger than her, at least. Twenty-three, twenty-four? But he was gorgeous, she thought. And he knew exactly how to seduce a woman.

His fingers moved across the hollows over her ankle, over her calves to the soft skin behind her knees. She couldn't help a small moan of anticipation as he washed her thighs.

'Don't be so impatient,' he admonished, sluicing the suds from her skin and then picking up her other foot and starting all over again.

By the time that he reached her thigh, Marie was almost begging him to touch her. She needed to feel him inside her. 'Tim,' she said softly, 'don't tease me.'

'Who said anything about teasing?' He took another sip of champagne, handing the glass to her. She copied his actions, turning the glass round and drinking from the same place as he had.

' "Drink to me only with thine eyes And I will pledge with mine. Or leave a kiss but in the cup And I'll not look for wine," ' he quoted, his voice low and husky.

'That's lovely,' she said. 'I know that from somewhere.'

'Ben Jonson – *To Celia*. He's one of Donne's contemporaries,' Tim supplied.

'Very pretty words.'

'Mm.' He nodded. 'And I promise you, my deeds will match them.'

She took the soap from him and began to wash him, her fingers playing over his muscles and delighting in the feel of him. His sex reared up as she slid her hands over his midriff, she couldn't resist soaping it, too, rubbing it back and forth.

'Now who's teasing?' he asked.

'Do something about it, then.'

'With pleasure.' He narrowed his eyes as he looked at the bath.

'What?' she asked, catching his gaze.

'I was just wondering . . . I think it will be more comfortable for both of us if you turn round,' he said softly.

'How do you mean?'

'Because, otherwise, I'll have to get you out of this bath – and I don't think I can wait to dry you before carrying you off to bed. I'm sure you don't want your sheets ruined, but . . .' He swallowed. 'I want you now, Marie. I want to slide my cock deep inside you, right up to the hilt, and feel your flesh closing round mine, warm and wet and tight.'

She nodded: her need was as urgent as his. She stood up, turned round, and knelt in the bath again, her back to him. His hands travelled the length of her spine, curving over her buttocks, and he gently manoeuvred her so that she was leaning forward, her sex exposed to him and her hands gripping the edge of the bath.

He knelt behind her; unable to resist it, he bent his head and drew his tongue along her sex. She felt him probe the soft folds and contours, and her body quivered as his tongue flicked over her clitoris. He drew the hard bud of flesh into his mouth, sucking gently; then he dropped a kiss on her quim, trailing his mouth up over her buttocks to her lower back.

Marie wriggled. 'Tim,' she said huskily. 'Don't tease.'

He traced the contour of her spine with the tip of his nose, finally kissing the nape of her neck. 'I haven't washed your back yet.'

Marie made a soft murmur of protest; Tim smiled and lathered his hands. He soaped her shoulders, his fingers working along her muscles and loosening them. He worked down her spine, playing along the vertebrae and letting his fingers splay across her back. Each movement up or down her back brought his fingers closer to her breasts: but never quite touching there. He remained tantalizingly close, with the intention of arousing her to fever pitch before working on her erogenous zones again.

The movement of his fingers made her feel deliciously languorous; at the same time, she wanted a more intimate caress. Eventually she straightened up, leaning back against him, and took his hands, placing the heels of his palms on her ribcage and his fingers on her breasts. Tim took the hint, and began to stroke the soft undersides of her breasts, his fingers tugging gently at her nipples.

He buried his mouth in the corner between her neck and shoulder, taking tiny nibbles at the skin which made her shiver. She could feel the hardness of his cock thrusting between her thighs, the muscle engorged and erect, and she longed to feel it pushing inside her, blindly exploring her.

She reached one hand between them, caressing his cock. 'Tim . . .'

'Mm?' He licked her shoulder.

She flushed. 'Please. Don't make me beg. I know you want this as much as I do.' She grasped the edge of the bath, pushing her bottom back towards him; at last, Tim moved so that he was poised at her most intimate portal.

She felt his glans butting against her sex then, and flexed her internal muscles. He slid into her, up to the hilt. 'Oh, God,' she said softly. 'You feel so good.'

'So do you,' he said, his voice shaking. He slid one hand round her midriff so that he could continue to play with her breasts, his fingers pulling at her nipples in a way that made her gasp with pleasure and tip her head back. Then he began to thrust, the movements of his body causing little waves in the bath.

His other hand trailed down between her thighs, his fingers seeking and finding the hard button of her clitoris. He murmured happily into her ear and caressed the little nub of flesh, his fingers setting up the same rhythm as his cock.

She pushed back against him, flexing her internal muscles as he entered her and then squeezing them round him as he pulled out, increasing the friction between them. The heady scents in the air, the vanilla of the candle mingling with the citrus and ginger notes of the bath oil, combined with the sensuousness of the candlelight and the taste of the champagne, were too much for her. Orgasm surged through her veins, and she cried out. A moment later, he gave an answering cry, and she felt his cock throb inside her, his seed pumping into her.

He stayed there for a moment, unwilling to leave her body; at last, he slipped from her. He climbed out of the bath, then lifted her up, washing her sex clean again. Then he lifted her out of the bath, wrapping her in a towel and drying her tenderly. He rubbed his nose against hers. 'You're irresistible – do you know that?'

She smiled. 'And I'm beginning to think that you could be addictive.'

'How about we take the rest of the champagne to bed?' he suggested.

She grinned. 'Yes. And I have a few ideas about how we could use it . . .'

Jed looked at Selena. 'I don't know what the form is here – whether I should be coming back to your place?'

'Do you have any other ideas?' she asked.

'Yes. My studio.' He looked at her. 'It's at the top of the house – the light's wonderful, and we're not overlooked.' He smiled at her. 'I'd like to paint you.'

She grinned. 'I bet you say that to all the girls!'

'Not all of them.' He shrugged. 'Actually, I've recently split up with someone. I don't need any commitments, right now. I love the company of women, but I don't want to go round the usual meat-markets: discos, clubs, whatever.' He grinned. 'Mind you, I'm too old for discos.'

'Thirty-four, thirty-five?' she guessed.

'Yes.'

'That's only three years older than me.'

'What about you?' he asked. 'Why are you involved with Interlover?'

She wrinkled her nose. 'I'm too busy for commitments. I love my career.'

'So we know where we both stand. Good.' To her surprise, he took her hand, turning it over and placing a kiss on her palm. 'Let's go back to my place, then.'

She nodded. 'OK.'

They caught the Tube to Pimlico; Jed stopped outside a

Georgian three-storey terrace. 'It's a converted house. Because I have the top floor, it means I get the attic, as well – and I've made it into my studio.' He opened the front door, then ushered her up the stairs through to his flat. 'I suppose the studio's big enough for me to live in, but I wanted to keep work and home separate.'

Selena looked at him. 'This wouldn't have something to do with your ex, by any chance?'

'Yeah.' Jed smiled wryly. 'She had a point – I'll give her that much. If I slept in my studio, I'd end up working myself to death. At least this way, I'm physically removed from my painting.' He led her into the kitchen. 'What can I get you? Coffee? Wine? Fruit juice?'

'I don't mind.'

'Right.' He opened the fridge. 'There happens to be a bottle of white wine in here. Nicely chilled.' He brought out a bottle of Chardonnay, and Selena chuckled.

'Anyone would have thought that you had this all planned.'

'Actually, it's been there for about three weeks. I forgot about it,' Jed told her, laughing.

'So what do you paint? You said that it was commercial.'

'Unfortunately, yes. Mainly portrait work – kids and animals – though I've done brochure work as well.'

'What do you paint for you?'

'I might show you, later.'

Selena wondered why he was being so secretive about it, but decided not to labour the point.

Jed opened the wine, and took two glasses from a cupboard. He inspected the glasses closely. 'Just to check that they're clean,' he said with a grin. 'Housework isn't my strong point.' He led her through to the living room. 'If you'd prefer to sit here,' he said, 'that's fine – but I really would like to take you up to my studio.'

'Then lead the way.'

He ushered her up some narrow stairs, and she found herself in a very large room. There were no curtains at the sloping windows, and the floorboards were bare – apart from a large Turkish rug in the middle of the floor. It was very like the one she had in her bedroom: memories of her Turkish lover flashed into her mind, and a thrill rippled through her. She could imagine making love with Jed on his rug, in the same way.

'Don't worry,' Jed said, seeing her eyes widening and misinterpreting the cause. 'We're not overlooked.'

She looked at him, seeing the desire in his eyes, and a *frisson* of pleasure ran down her spine. This man was a sensualist. Whatever he had in mind, it was going to be very, very pleasurable indeed. He was good-looking in the conventional way, but there was something else about him: a sensual curve to his mouth, and eyes which crinkled slightly at the corners.

His eyes were green and very intense; his dark curly hair was pushed back from his forehead, giving him a rumpled look, as though he didn't care how he looked. He was the arty, bohemian type that Selena had always found attractive: she found herself wondering what he looked like underneath his silk shirt and formal dark trousers.

'So,' she said. 'Are you going to show me your paintings? The ones you paint for pleasure, I mean?'

'It depends,' he said slowly, 'on how broad-minded you are.'

'Does owning a large collection of European pornography, some of it in the original texts, make me broad-minded?'

He grinned. 'I should say so!' He tipped his head on one side. 'So my studio meets with your approval, then?'

She nodded. 'I like the rug, in particular. I've got one like it at home.'

'Similar tastes, then.'

'Do you think we were paired up deliberately?'

He shrugged. 'I thought it was meant to be random.'

'Apart from Aidan and Ruth, that is.' She nodded. 'Maybe.'

'I think it's going to work out just fine, though.' The huskiness in his voice told her that he was just as aroused as she was — and just as careful, waiting to see who made the first move.

There was a large table by one of the windows, with a drawing-board perched on it and a sofa covered with cushions just in front of it. There was also an easel, and several paintings were stacked against the wall. Selena looked at them, then at Jed. 'Do you mind if I look?'

'Be my guest,' he said laconically. 'My private collection is the one furthest from the desk.' He topped up their glasses and sat cross-legged on the Turkish rug, watching her.

She flicked through the paintings and swallowed hard. God, the man really was a sensualist. The paintings were all very erotic. There was a picture of a naked woman standing by the window, her back to the artist; her face was in profile, and she looked on the point of orgasm. Selena's gaze travelled down the canvas, and she saw why: the woman was masturbating, one hand between her legs and the other touching her breasts.

There were several more in the same vein, all with the same model: Selena guessed that she was Jed's ex. And there was also a picture of a naked man. He was lying on the bed, stroking his rigid cock; Selena unconsciously licked her lips as she recognized the man. Jed. If his self-portrait was accurate, he was a very beautiful man indeed, with a perfectly contoured body.

'What do you think?' he asked eventually.

She turned to face him. 'I like them.' She paused. 'When you said that you wanted to paint me, earlier — was this what you had in mind?'

'Yes.'

Without another word, she reached behind her to undo her dress, letting the black material slip from her shoulders. She was wearing a black underwired push-up bra: that received the same treatment, dropping to the floor with her dress.

She kicked the clothing aside, and stood with her hands on her hips, wearing nothing but a pair of black lacy knickers which revealed as much as they concealed, and a pair of black hold-up stockings. She was about to peel down her knickers when a movement from Jed stopped her.

'In some ways,' he said, watching her closely, 'I know I should have taken you to my bed. The sofa here isn't particularly comfortable. But that's deliberate.'

She didn't follow him. 'Why?'

'Because otherwise, I'd have clucking mothers looking over my shoulder all the time. I hate people watching me paint. So I put them on the sofa – within half an hour, they've had enough of sliding off the sofa and they leave me to it.'

He went over to the sofa, taking one of the cushions from it and placing it on the carpet. 'Come here,' he said softly. She did as he asked and lay on the floor, her head supported by the cushion.

'Is there any particular pose you'd like me to adopt?' she asked as he fetched his sketchpad and pencil.

He smiled. 'Yes.' He came over to sit beside her, and she suddenly realized that he wasn't just carrying a sketchpad and pencil. He was also holding what looked like a large black dildo. Her eyes widened. 'You're going to use this on me?'

'For starters.' He stroked her face. 'You're very lovely, Selena. Your skin's so fine, so clear. You'll make a beautiful subject.'

Again, she made as if to remove her knickers and he shook his head, closing his fingers over hers. 'Not yet.' His touch was light, yet firm and masterful; Selena shivered. She had a feeling that she was in an expert's hands.

Although he hadn't touched her, she felt her nipples hardening. She looked up at him in mute appeal, willing him to touch her and bring her pleasure. He smiled, and took the small bottle of massage oil from his pocket. 'I believe,' he said softly, 'that we were supposed to be using this.' He ran his tongue over his lips. 'I think it might make things a little easier, too.' He poured some oil into his palm, rubbing his hands together to warm the oil, then gently smoothing it over her body.

She gave a gasp as he touched her, his fingers firm and sure as he kneaded the hard peaks of flesh. She couldn't help tipping her pelvis up to him, and he smiled. He stroked her thighs, gently rolling down her stockings, and she quivered. He let his hand drift over the gusset of her knickers. 'Like a furnace,' he said softly.

'Then why don't you do something about it?'

'With pleasure.' He hooked his thumbs into the waistband of her knickers, gradually drawing them down. Selena closed her eyes, her quim flexing in anticipation. She was surprised to realize that although he'd pulled her knickers down, he hadn't actually removed him. He'd left them lying around her ankles.

She wondered where he'd learned a trick like that. Did he share her taste in bedtime reading? Gently, he stroked her thighs again; she tried to widen the gap between them, giving him access, but he wouldn't let her bend her knees. She lay there, frustrated and almost hating him.

'Shh. I haven't finished yet.' She opened her eyes, and he bent to kiss her lightly. 'Half the pleasure's in waiting,' he said softly.

Selena wasn't convinced, but there was nothing she could do about it. Jed continued to oil her until her skin was gleaming, then sat back on his haunches to admire his handiwork. 'Perfect,' he said. 'Open your eyes. See how beautiful you look: the way the texture of your skin's changed with the oil, the way the light reflects off you.'

She shivered at the huskiness in his voice. He was as turned on as she was, by the sound of him. She opened her eyes, and involuntarily glanced at his groin: she could see his erection pressing through his trousers. She reached up to touch him, but he shook his head. 'Not yet. I want to pleasure you first. I want to watch you come.'

He picked up the dildo, smoothing oil onto it. Selena wondered if the oil was really necessary: her quim felt soaking, and she was longing to feel the dildo inside her, to ease the ache. He leaned over to kiss her lightly. 'Trust me. You're going to enjoy this. And remember, half the pleasure's in waiting.'

He gently eased the phallus between her thighs, so that the tip of it touched her sex. Selena's eyes widened. It was certainly bigger than any of her own favourite toys. He slid it slowly into her, still keeping her thighs pressed together. She felt it stretch her, and closed her eyes in pleasure.

'And now,' he said quietly, 'I'm going to sketch you.'

'What?' She'd been expecting him to move the phallus in and out of her.

He stroked her face. 'I know what you want, and I know you're dying to touch yourself – but don't. Just wait – wait and see what happens.'

'You've done this before, haven't you?'

He nodded. 'Several times. Just close your eyes and relax.'

She did as he said, closing her eyes tightly shut. It was almost silent in the room: she could hear the soft scratching of his pencil against the paper, but that was all. She could imagine what she looked like, lying there on the rug: her hair mussed and wild around her shoulders, her eyes closed and her head tipped back, her mouth parted in pleasure, her knickers pulled around her ankles, and the large black phallus protruding lewdly from her quim.

The idea of it made her sex moisten, and she suddenly realized what he was doing. He was leaving her imagination to do all the work. She flexed her internal muscles experimentally, feeling the phallus inside her. She could imagine what it would feel like if Jed used it on her properly. Maybe he'd take one end of it in his mouth, pushing it back and forth and smelling her arousal as he pushed it into her.

Or maybe he'd lie beside her, licking her breasts and sucking on her nipples as he pushed the dildo inside her. Then he'd pull it out, very, very slowly, so that she could feel the bulbous head squeezing past the narrowest part of her. Then he'd plunge it back in, hard, making her body jerk with pleasure.

Or he'd have her legs as wide apart as possible, kneeling between her thighs so that he could see the way the phallus slid into her, the way she opened for it, the smooth black plastic glistening with her juices. Or maybe he'd hold her as she was now, her ankles bound by her knickers, so that she'd feel every movement of the phallus stimulating her clitoris, arousing her beyond the peak.

She felt the familiar rush of pleasure in her veins, and cried out in surprise as she came. 'Christ, I didn't even know that could happen!' she said.

He grinned, putting the sketchpad down. 'I told you, anticipation is half the fun. Now, open your eyes.'

She did, and he gently drew the phallus from her, holding it in front of her so that she could see just how wet and shiny it was, her own musky juices covering it. Her eyes widened as he proceeded to lick every single drop of it from the phallus. 'Beautiful,' he said. 'The finest wine known to mankind.'

She flushed. 'What about your picture?'

'Here.' He came to kneel beside her and she sat up, taking the pad from him. It was a clean line drawing, and very obviously her. It excited and appalled her at the same time, to see herself looking so abandoned. 'My God,' she breathed.

'It's a preliminary sketch. I'll paint you later.' He handed her a glass of wine, then stood up and stripped swiftly. Selena watched him, liking the clean lines of his body. His picture hadn't done him justice, she thought. He was utterly beautiful – perfectly contoured. Not skinny, but not overdeveloped, either.

Simply perfect. If she'd been able to sculpt, she would have chosen him as her model.

His cock was well-shaped, too, and gratifyingly large. It was too much for her to resist: she smiled, picked up the bottle of oil, and tipped some in her palm, rubbing her hands together to warm it. 'I might not be able to paint,' she told him quietly, 'but I can do other things . . .'

THIRTEEN

'A blueberry-flavoured condom,' Meg said, chuckling. 'I wonder where the hell Aidan managed to find that?'

'Somewhere in Soho, I should think.' Niall smiled at her. 'But teaming it with strawberries – now, that's what I call inspired. There's a café, near the theatre, that sells health food – they do strawberry and blueberry "healthy shakes", based on yoghurt, bananas, orange juice and whatever fruit you fancy. They're gorgeous.'

'They sound it; it's a nice mixture,' Meg said. She looked at him. 'Do you really have to go home early, Niall?'

He grinned. 'I think that should be my line! No. I do have to be at the theatre for one o'clock tomorrow, but the rest of my time's all yours, Meg.'

'Right.' She suddenly noticed that there was something that looked like a script, stuffed into his jacket pocket. 'What's that?' she asked.

He glanced down, and smiled. 'Oh, they're just my lines for the next production. I was reading them on the way to Ruth's. We're doing *The Cherry Orchard* next month, and I'm playing Trofimov, the eternal student.' His lips twitched. 'I say things like "We are above love", when I'm really dying to make love to the woman of my dreams. But she's in a social class above me, so I can't have her.'

'Mm, I remember reading it at A-level,' she said. 'The stage directions used to make me shiver – something about a string breaking. Very symbolic, and there's something horrible about it.'

'I know what you mean. It's a bit sobering,' he agreed. 'So, what now? Would you like to go for a drink somewhere? Or back to my place?' He winced. 'Actually, I should warn you that I share it with three other actors, and we all hate housework, so it's a complete tip. If we could afford it, we'd get a cleaner, but I think we'd have to pay one danger money...'

Meg laughed. 'And we won't get the chance to enjoy our strawberries on our own, hm?'

'Exactly.' He smiled ruefully. 'Don't you believe all the tales you hear about actors going to luvvie parties and staying up all night. Half of us supplement our earnings by working as waiters, and by the time you've got home after a shift at the restaurant, you're too knackered to do anything else but slob in front of the television with a drink.'

'Let's go to my place, then.' They caught the Tube, and chatted easily on the way back to Islington.

'So do you want to work in film, or television?' Meg asked.

'Not really, no. I like having a live audience.' His blue eyes were earnest. 'I know I was moaning about the school matinée audience, earlier tonight, but even those can be good. If you can bring home the magic of Shakespeare or whatever to just one kid, it's worth it. You can see it on their faces, and it's a real thrill. You don't get that with films or television – the audience is too far removed.' He shrugged. 'And you don't get their undivided attention. As well as watching the television, and flicking through the channels, they're probably having an argument, or reading a book, or doing a crossword.'

'Or making love,' Meg added, 'while eating expensive ice-cream...'

He smiled. 'Something like that.'

'So it's the roar of the crowd and the glitter of the greasepaint that you love, then?'

'Yes. Though there is one film I wouldn't mind acting out. One scene from it, anyway – seeing as we have a punnet of strawberries.'

'Oh yes?' Meg was intrigued.

'Mm. Do you happen to have any spray cream?'

She laughed. 'No. But I think I can rustle up something.'

Niall's eyes widened when they reached Islington High Street, and stopped outside Meg's shop. 'When you said that you had your own business, I don't know what I expected, really – though it wasn't a posh antique shop in Islington High Street!'

'Just call me Lovejoy,' Meg quipped.

He tipped his head on one side. 'Actually, I can see you in a leather jacket. You'd look rather nice.' His blue eyes sparkled. 'Particularly if it was nothing *but* a leather jacket. Just you, all curves, and opening your jacket to reveal how beautiful your breasts are.' He shivered. 'Mm. I could really go for that. A butter-soft hide jacket, and you . . .'

Meg smiled at him. 'It's an idea, certainly! Sadly, I don't have a leather jacket, or I would act it out for you. Anyway, come in.' She unlocked the door, and they walked up the stairs to her flat. She kicked off her shoes and hung her coat on the bentwood hatstand; Niall shrugged off his jacket, hanging it next to her coat.

He handed her the punnet of strawberries; she stretched, flexing the muscles in her back, and smiled. 'Cream. Well, come through to the kitchen,' she said. 'I'll see what I can find.'

Niall followed her to the doorway, and eyed the terracotta flooring in dismay. 'That looks a bit cold for what I had in mind.'

'You'd be surprised,' she said. 'Take your shoes off, and come in.'

He did so, and his eyes widened in surprise. 'It's warm!'

'Yep. The pipes for the central heating system go through

here, so it's never as cold as it looks.' She put the strawberries on the worktop.

Niall removed the small foil square from his pocket, and handed it to her. 'I think this is supposed to go with it.'

'Mm.' She looked at him. 'Would you like a drink?'

He shook his head. 'I'm fine, thanks.'

'Me, too.'

'In that case . . .' He walked over to her, placing his hands on her shoulders, and brought his mouth down gently on hers. He nibbled at her lower lip, and her mouth opened; he kissed her properly, his tongue moving against hers and probing the contours of her mouth.

Meg's hands slid down his back, curving over his buttocks. She pressed her pubis against his, and was pleased to find the beginnings of a promisingly large erection.

He broke the kiss, holding her gaze. 'It's the first dinner party I've been to in a long while,' he said, 'where I've actually had to dress up. With most of my friends, if you eat at their place, it's more casual.'

Meg fingered his green silk shirt. 'I take it you're a bit uncomfortable in this, then?'

He nodded.

'Then let's do something about it.' Slowly, she unbuttoned his shirt, letting her fingers slide over his chest. He felt good: obviously, working in the theatre kept his muscles well-toned. She removed his shirt, letting it drop to the floor, and stroked over his midriff. He had a typical younger man's flat stomach. She smiled to herself. It might be nice to have a toyboy. Although Ruth had always said that none of the Interlovers would be himbos or virgins – they'd all be experienced, and would be able to hold a decent conversation as well as make love – it didn't mean that they all had to be over thirty.

Niall, Meg thought, was just about perfect. He had a good body, well-toned and muscular, teamed with Celtic good looks:

most of the women in the audience would go home and fantasize about the good-looking male lead, she thought. His blue eyes were fringed by unfairly long lashes, and he had a generous mouth. She hated thin-lipped men: they were usually mean-spirited. Niall's mouth was very promising indeed.

He kissed her again as she undid the button of his formal dark trousers. She slid the zip down, feeling his erection pressing hard against her fingers, and eased the material over his hips. He was wearing silk boxer shorts, and the navy blue material set off the fairness of his skin. His cock was clearly visible through the soft material. She curled her fingers round it. 'Mm, nice.'

'My turn, now,' he said softly. He unzipped her black dress, his fingers tracing the curve of her spine; Meg arched against him, and he smiled, sliding the dress from her. To his delight, he discovered that she was wearing a black stretch lace basque underneath it, with matching knickers and black stockings.

'You look so good in that, it almost seems a shame to take it off.'

'Don't, then,' she said with a grin. It would be interesting to find out if he was unconventional as well.

Her nipples protruded sharply through the thin material. He drew his thumbs across the hard points of flesh, rubbing them gently through the lace, and Meg made a small sound of pleasure, tipping her head back and offering her throat to him.

'Meg,' he said softly. 'Tell me – do you mind getting a bit messy?'

She frowned. 'What exactly do you have in mind?'

He grinned. 'You started it, talking about strawberries and blueberries. I was thinking about fruit salad – and fruit salad always has cream. So either a tin of spray cream, or some ordinary cream and a whisk.'

'I know I don't have spray cream,' she said. 'I hate the stuff. But . . .' She opened the fridge door, and grinned. 'You're in luck,' she said. 'One of my bad habits is liqueur coffee. Ruth came over the other night, and there's half a pot of double cream left.' She peered at the lid. 'And it's still within the sell-by date.'

'Good.' He grinned. 'This is going to be very, very messy. Gloriously so.' He stretched. 'Mickey Rourke, eat your heart out,' he quipped.

Meg, catching his reference, laughed. 'I don't have any chillies in my fridge, either. Or maple syrup.'

'The cream will do just nicely, ma'am.'

She handed the pot to him. 'I don't know if I dare ask what you're planning!'

He grinned. 'Trust me, Meg. I think you're going to like this.' He tipped his head on one side, giving her an appealing look. 'Do you have a whisk and a bowl, please?'

'Yes.' She tipped her head to one side. 'Does a glass of wine fit in with your plans?'

He considered it for a moment. 'Yes, it could do.'

'Red or white?'

'White, I think. It's usually white wine with strawberries, isn't it?'

'Right. But it'll be dry – I don't have any dessert wine chilling.'

'Dry will be lovely, thanks.'

Meg rummaged in one of the drawers, extracting a whisk and a corkscrew. She reached into a cupboard to get a bowl and two glasses, then handed him the whisk and the bowl. While she took a bottle of wine from the fridge and opened it, Niall whipped the cream, the tip of his tongue protruding slightly as he concentrated on what he was doing. Meg watched him, a sudden surge of lust shooting through her as she wondered what it would feel like when he used his mouth properly on her.

She dropped her gaze as he suddenly looked up. 'Meg,' he said softly.

'Mm?'

He smiled at her.

'We're ready, I think. All we need now is some music.'

'Anything in particular?'

He thought about it. 'If you've got *Don Giovanni*, that'd be good – it's really sensual. Or Mozart's *Requiem* – I love the *Confutatis*, it's so passionate. Otherwise, whatever you fancy.' He shrugged. 'No, you choose something you like, something you enjoy.'

'I'm not an opera buff, I'm afraid – Ruthie's tried, and failed, to convert me. I play *The Four Seasons* and stuff like that in the shop, but that's because my customers expect it. I'm afraid the culture doesn't go any deeper than my love of antiques!' She went over to the tape deck in her kitchen, and skimmed through the rack of tapes next to it. She smiled, choosing one and sliding it into the machine. 'How about this?'

He smiled as the first bars of 'Telegraph Road' flooded through the kitchen. 'Yuppie rock.' She was about to turn it off, when he walked over to her and slid his arms round her waist, kissing the side of her neck. 'And I like this very, very much. It's probably my favourite Dire Straits one ever.'

'Are you old enough to remember this coming out, young man?' she teased.

'Yeah, I was about thirteen and I wanted to be a guitarist.' He chuckled. 'If I couldn't make it as an actor, that is.'

She turned round, kissing him, and he waltzed her over to the other side of the kitchen.

'Mm,' he said. 'I'm looking forward to this.' He curved his fingers over her buttocks. 'I love the way you feel.'

She slid her hands down his back. 'You're not so bad yourself,' she said softly. She handed him a glass of wine.

'To us,' he said, lifting his glass.

'To us,' she echoed.

'Now.' He set his glass on the worktop above the fridge and

took her glass from her fingers, setting it next to his. 'Meg.' He cupped her face, kissing her lightly; she pressed against him.

'I seem to remember that Mickey Rourke was wearing a lot more than you are,' she quipped.

'But this is the Niall Hamilton version of the scene,' he retorted. 'Which means that I get as messy as you do – and you can see everything that's going on.' He opened her fridge door, then switched off the overhead light.

'Niall,' she protested, laughing, 'isn't this going to be cold?'

'You assured me that your floor was warm.' He dropped the whisk in the sink, and stooped to put the bowl of cream in the fridge. He took Meg in his arms again, kissing her; she slid her hands down his back, liking the feel of his skin.

He moulded her to his body, so that she could feel his erection; she shivered. 'Niall. I want to see you. Properly.' He nodded and stepped back, letting her remove his boxer shorts. She shivered as she saw his cock rising from the cloud of dark hair at his groin, long and thick and rigid; she couldn't help touching the tip of her tongue to her lower lip. Tonight, she thought, was going to be good. Very good.

Gently, he drew her down to the floor and adjusted their positions so that they were sitting facing each other, her thighs draped over his.

'One last adjustment, I think,' he said, hooking his thumbs into the waistband of her knickers and pulling the material down. Meg placed her hands flat on the floor, lifting herself momentarily so that he could remove her knickers properly. 'Beautiful,' he said, drawing the tip of his finger down her glistening quim. He brought his finger to his lips, licking off the moisture. 'Mm. And you taste as good as you look.'

'By fridge-light.'

He grinned. 'A bit more original than candles, hm?'

'You can say that again,' she said drily.

'Well.' He tipped his head on one side. 'You're lovely, Meg. Looking at you just isn't enough. It makes me want to touch you, taste you, feel your body react to mine.' He slid one finger under the edge of her basque, pulling the material down to expose one breast. 'Beautiful,' he breathed unsteadily, doing the same to her other breast.

Meg shivered at the lewdness of her position. She was sitting on her kitchen floor, wearing just her basque and a pair of stockings, her legs sprawled over his in a way that exposed her quim to his gaze, and her breasts displayed wantonly.

'Utterly beautiful,' he said, reaching into the fridge and loading one finger with whipped cream. He smeared the mixture over her nipples, and Meg gasped.

'That's cold!'

'*This* isn't.' He leaned forward, licking the cream from her skin and then taking one nipple into his mouth, sucking gently and warming it.

Meg gave a small moan of pleasure and tipped her head back, arching her back. He repeated the action with her other nipple, arousing her even more; she closed her eyes, feeling her quim flex and grow even wetter. God, she wanted him so much!

He felt her shiver, and smiled against her skin. She was beautifully responsive: and he had a feeling that his fantasy tallied neatly with her own. He lifted his head. 'Meg,' he said softly.

'Mm?' She opened her eyes; again, he was struck by their beauty.

'You're still wearing too much. Would you mind if I . . . ?' He drew his finger down her back, pausing at the top of her basque.

She nodded, running her tongue along her lower lip, and he smiled, swiftly undoing the fastenings of her basque. He eased the garment from her, throwing it aside, and reached up to the strawberries on the worktop. He crushed one between her breasts, letting the red juices trickle down her creamy skin, then licked her skin clean again, savouring the taste of the fruit against the clean fresh taste of her skin.

He crushed two more strawberries between his fingers, then rubbed the squashy fruit over her nipples, smearing it over her areolae. Meg gave a small moan as he proceeded to suck the fruit from her breasts, and tangled her fingers in his hair. 'Niall. Please,' she said softly, tilting her pelvis towards him.

'With pleasure,' he whispered, his voice husky with desire. Meg closed her eyes, willing him to touch her more intimately, to slide one finger deep inside her, then add another and another, to piston his hand back and forth until she came wildly, her internal muscles convulsing and her voice hoarse as she cried out.

She shuddered as she felt him part her labia; then she opened her eyes in shock. It definitely hadn't been his fingers pushing inside her. 'What the—'

He placed one finger on her lips, silencing her. 'Shh, it's all right. I promise you, Meg, you're going to enjoy this.' He stroked her arms, placing her hands on the floor and urging her back slightly; he moved so that he was kneeling between her spread thighs, and dipped his head to touch his mouth to her sex.

Meg shivered as he sucked the strawberry out of her, then ate the fruit lasciviously. He pushed another one inside her and sucked it out again; she could feel the rough texture of the fruit against her skin, and it thrilled her. She flexed her muscles experimentally, and felt the fruit crushing slightly, its juices flowing from it and mingling with her own wetness.

Niall ate the strawberry. 'Mm. You taste good,' he said softly, pushing another strawberry into her. He drew it out with his fingertips this time. 'Close your eyes,' he said softly.

Meg did so.

'And open your mouth.'

She was shocked when he slid the strawberry into her mouth; it was slightly warm from being inside her, and the sharpness of the fruit was softened by the taste of her own juices. She ate it; then Niall kissed her, hard, and pushed another strawberry into her. As he used his mouth on her, sucking the fruit out again, she felt her orgasm boil over; she cried out, and her sex convulsed madly. 'See? I told you that you'd like it,' he said, licking the mixture of fruit juice and her own arousal from her skin.

Meg's pupils had expanded so that her eyes were almost black. 'Bloody hell. No one's ever done anything like that to me before!'

'There's always a first time.' Niall gave her a wicked grin. 'And, believe me, it always gets better...'

She nodded. 'And what's sauce for the goose, I suppose...' She reached up to take the little packet of foil from the worktop, opened it, and brought out the little rubber disc. 'So I can make a fruit salad of you, too!'

Niall smiled, and sat on the floor, leaning back against the wall. 'I'm in your hands entirely.'

'Good.' She eased the condom over his cock, then reached up to load her finger with cream. 'My favourite ice-cream is blueberries and cream,' she told him, smearing the cream over the condom. 'So it follows that I'm going to like this...'

He shuddered as she bent her head, licking the cream from him and then sliding her mouth over his cock. She drew her head back a couple of moments later, laughing. 'Sadly, Aidan was conned. It doesn't taste a bit like blueberries! It's more like one of those cheap and nasty imitation fruit lollies.'

'That's a shame. I was beginning to enjoy what you were doing,' Niall said huskily.

She grinned. 'I think I've got a better idea.' She swiftly removed the condom, discarding it carelessly on the floor, and crushed a strawberry, smearing it over his cock and then adding cream. 'A rather special sundae.'

He glanced at his watch. 'Actually, you're twenty-three hours out. It's nearly one o'clock on Saturday morning.'

She groaned. 'That's terrible.'

'Well.' He smiled. 'Now you know why I'm an actor, not a comic!'

'Yeah.' She dipped her head, and began to lick the fruit and cream from his skin. Niall closed his eyes, giving a soft murmur of pleasure as Meg finished cleaning his glans and started working on his frenum, making her tongue into a sharp point and probing the delicate tissues.

'Oh, God,' he moaned, and she began to work on him properly, ringing the base of his shaft with her thumb and forefinger and squeezing gently as she ran her mouth up and down his cock, sucking and nibbling.

He stroked her hair, the pads of his fingertips urging her on, and cried out as she took him deep into her mouth, so that the tip of his cock almost touched her soft palate. Pressure built up in his loins, and he gasped. 'Meg. Meg, I'm going to come, if you don't stop!'

She lifted her head just long enough to say, 'That's the whole idea,' and then set to work on him again. He cried out her name; she felt his cock twitch in her mouth, and then her mouth was filled with warm salty fluid. She swallowed every last drop, then lifted her head. 'Better, now?'

'Much better,' he agreed huskily, bending down to kiss her. 'Though the night has only just started . . .'

Tim switched on the light, and smiled. He'd been hoping that Marie didn't sleep in a cramped single bed. But this was even better than a double: it was king-size.

He took her hand and squeezed it. 'OK?' he asked softly.

'Mm.' She went over to the bed, pushing back the duvet

and sitting down. She put the champagne and the glass on the bedside cabinet, turned on the bedside lamp, and patted the bed beside her; he smiled, switching off the overhead light, and vaulted lightly onto the bed.

'Cheers,' she said, raising the glass and taking a sip, then handing it to him.

'Cheers,' he echoed, taking a sip and leaning across her to replace the glass on the bedside cabinet.

'That was deliberate,' she accused, laughing, as he nuzzled her breasts.

'A feeble excuse to touch you,' he agreed, smiling against her skin.

She stroked his hair. 'Tell me, Tim – why is a man as attractive, intelligent and sensual as you still single?'

He licked her nipples to acknowledge the compliment. 'Because I've been busy studying.'

'Really?' There was something in his tone that didn't quite ring true.

He sighed. 'All right. There *was* someone, last year, but she decided that she was sick of being with a penniless student who couldn't afford to take her out to expensive restaurants and whose idea of a nice day out is to go for a walk on Hampstead Heath, rather than go shopping for baubles. And she found herself someone who could give her what she wanted. It's just a shame that I decided to work from home rather than in the British Library one afternoon, and caught them together in our bed.'

She winced at the bitterness in his voice. 'I'm sorry.'

'I'm not. Better to find out now than in another five years, when there might have been children involved or whatever.'

'I suppose there is that to it. And that's why you answered Ruth's ad?'

He nodded, sitting up so that he could look her straight in the eyes. 'I figured that "broad-minded" meant something interesting. I was right.' He traced the outline of her jaw. 'It meant "no strings", and that suits me fine. I give Ruth's clients what they want, and I get my fix of affection and good sex in return, without having to worry about my studies being affected.'

'That's bitter,' Marie said softly.

'Just realistic, I think.' He leaned forward to kiss her lightly on the lips. 'And you're the same, Marie. With Interlover, you get the good things out of a relationship – the warmth, the companionship, and the good sex – without someone putting pressure on you to make his career, rather than your own, the focus of your life. It's the best of all worlds, really.'

'Mm.' She slid her hands round his neck. 'I admit, it's nice to sleep with someone, from time to time – to wake up in someone's arms. But I like having my own space.'

'I, too.'

She grinned, noting his pristine grammar. 'So you're a pedant, as well?'

He grinned back. 'Just practising for when I get my doctorate. And in thirty years' time, I'll be Dr Chambers, crusty professor of Renaissance literature, who puts the fear of God into his students.'

'With his long shaggy greying beard, little round glasses, and his baggy green cardigan,' she teased.

'And his tweed jacket with leather patches on the elbows, and the *de rigueur* beige cords which are old and shiny,' he added.

They both laughed, and Tim pushed her back against the pillows, sliding his hand across her body. 'Mm. You feel so good.' He rubbed his nose against hers, then slowly began a trail of kisses down her body. He licked the soft undersides of her breasts, and she shivered, arching up towards him. He nuzzled her midriff, breathing in her scent, then parted her thighs and shifted to kneel between them. 'Marie.'

'Yes?'

'I've just remembered. Aren't we supposed to be using that green condom?'

She laughed. 'I won't tell, if you won't!'

'Deal,' he said softly. He licked his way up her thighs, making her shiver, then breathed softly on her quim. Marie gave a small moan of pleasure, and he smiled. She was wet enough not to need any lubrication — but what the hell. He loved the taste of a woman's arousal, and most of the women he'd made love to enjoyed a man using his mouth on them.

He made his tongue into a sharp point, drawing it very slowly down her quim, tracing every fold and crevice. Marie's hands tangled in his hair, and she tipped her pelvis up slightly, giving him easier access. He continued to lick her, his tongue skating over her clitoris, until he felt her breathing begin to quicken; then he lifted his head.

'Much as I'd like to feel you come in my mouth, I think we both need something else first,' he said softly.

'Yes.' Her voice was slightly ragged with arousal.

He shifted so that the tip of his cock was pressed against the entrance to her sex. Bearing his weight on his hands and knees, he pushed very gently, so that he slid into her millimetre by millimetre. Marie flexed her internal muscles, trying to draw him into her more quickly, but he resisted; by the time that he was in her to the hilt, she was almost coming.

Then he began to thrust, his hips moving in small circles; her legs came up to grip his waist. Gently, he stroked her thighs, making her relax, and unclasped her legs from him: he held her knees wide apart, sliding his hands down to her ankles, and began to thrust hard, pumping into her.

Marie shuddered with pleasure. She'd had lovers before who'd had a good technique, but this was something else. The way he held her open, changing the angle of his penetration to give her the most pleasure, was enough to make her come. The feel of his balls slapping against her quim, and the way he moved so that the root of his cock rubbed against her clitoris, made it even better.

He held himself slightly apart from her; she looked down between her widely-parted thighs, and the sight made her sex even more liquid. Tim's large cock slowly emerged from her, wet and glistening with her juices, until the head was almost out of her: then he slammed back in hard, the thick rigid muscle pushing deep into her.

Tim saw the look on her face, and glanced down; he smiled. 'Yeah, I'd like to film that, too. Then I'd project it onto the ceiling, when I was alone, and watch myself sliding into you: just the look of it would make me remember how you feel.'

She licked her lower lip. 'And what else would you do, while you were watching us?'

He chuckled. 'What do you think?'

'I think,' she said slowly, 'you'd do what I'd do, if I were a man. I'd lie there, one hand fondling my balls, and the other stroking my hard cock. I'd rub my foreskin back and forth, the pressure light at first, and then harder, my hips pushing up as I watched myself come inside you – and then I'd come, myself. Is that what you'd do?'

He bent to kiss her, his tongue pushing against hers. 'Yes,' he said as he lifted his head again. 'Though even better than that, I think I'd ring you up, tell you what I was watching and what I was doing. And I'd like you to tell me what you were doing, too.'

'And what would I be doing?'

'Well, I think you—'

She reached up to place her forefinger on his lips. 'No. Tell me what I'd be doing, as if you were me.'

He grinned. 'Are you sure you want to hear this?'

Her voice was husky. 'Yes, I'm sure.'

'I'm lying on the bed, the phone cradled between my neck and shoulder. I'm naked, because I always sleep naked, and you've just phoned, a few minutes after I've gone to bed. I've been reading, but as soon as you started talking, I put my book down.'

He swallowed. 'When you tell me what you're watching, I start imagining it, remembering what it was like between us. As you speak to me, my hand slides down my body; my nipples are already hardening, so I stroke them. They feel tight, and I need something more; I lick my fingers, and pull harder on them, but it's not enough. So I let my hand drift down between my legs. I'm already wet – just because of what you're telling me – so my finger slides easily along my cunt. I push one finger into me – the middle finger, because I need something to fill me as deep as possible – and rub my clitoris with my thumb. I'm warm and wet, and my cunt seems to suck my finger into it; the lightest touch is all it needs to pleasure my clitoris.

'But it's not enough. I need something more to fill me. I just happen to keep a vibrator in the top drawer of my bedside cabinet; I reach over, and take it out. I switch it on – making sure that you can hear what I've done – and slide the tip of it against my sex. It feels good, so good: not quite as good as you, but it'll do, for now. I push it into me, and begin using it: all the time you tell me what you're doing to me, on the film, I do exactly the same, in my bed, stirring the vibrator in me.

'I can hear how turned-on you are; the tone of your voice, and the way you have trouble talking, tells me that you're going to come. And then I come, too, with the vibrator deep inside me.'

Marie groaned, imagining the scene: it was enough to tip her over the edge into orgasm, and she climaxed hard. A split-second later, Tim came, too; she felt him stiffen, and then his cock throbbed inside her.

He lowered his body onto hers, still supporting his own weight. 'Oh God, Marie,' he said softly. 'That was so good.'

'Mm.' She stroked his hair away from his face; his skin was damp. 'That was incredible. And how did you know that when I masturbate it's like that?'

'Hazarded a guess.' He flushed. 'A combination of how you feel when I touch you, and what I know of previous girlfriends.'

'You mean, they let you watch them masturbate?'

He kissed her gently. 'Yes.'

She shivered. It took a hell of a lot of trust, letting a man see you in such an intimate position. More than just simple fucking. It was something she'd never done – but she felt that, with Tim, it was a distinct possibility.

'That's what I thought,' he said softly, and her eyes widened as she realized that she'd spoken aloud. 'And if Interlover brings us together again . . .'

Her lips curved. 'When, not if. Yes, I think I'd like that.'

He rubbed his nose against hers. 'And I'll leave you deliciously obscene messages on your answerphone, between now and then . . . so you can play them back and masturbate to the sound of my voice.'

'Better than that. Ring me.'

'Telephone sex.' He nipped at her earlobe. 'Mm. I like that. Are you on electronic mail, at work?'

'Yes.'

He grinned. 'Then maybe we can have the odd obscene conversation, during work.'

She grinned back. 'And I can imagine my secretary's face, when she reads through my mail and discovers one of yours!'

'Now, there's an idea . . .'

FOURTEEN

Selena removed the constriction of her knickers from her ankles and knelt up, sliding her hands over Jed's midriff. Then she bent her head to his cock, licking delicately at his glans. He closed his eyes and rested his hands on her shoulders, tangling one in her hair. She began to suck him in earnest, savouring his clean male taste, her head moving back and forth with increasing speed. He groaned, and she stroked his perineum, letting her finger drift further and further towards his anus.

She pushed her middle finger against the puckered rosy entrance; he groaned as her oiled finger slipped easily into him, and she began to massage him, pushing her finger back and forth in the same way that she'd imagined him pushing the dildo inside her. She increased the rhythm, pushing hard into him and massaging his prostate gland.

Jed cried out, writhing under her ministrations; she continued sucking him, working her mouth over his glans in a way calculated to give him the most pleasure. The combination of her mouth and her finger massaging him was too much for him: his body stiffened, and she felt his cock throb. Then her mouth was filled with silky warm fluid.

She waited until the last aftershocks of his orgasm had died away; then she swallowed the liquid in her mouth and released his cock, sitting back on her haunches to look up at him. He knelt down and kissed her. 'Thank you,' he said. 'That was fantastic.'

'Pleasure.' She smiled. 'I think I enjoyed it as much as you did.' It always thrilled her, that feeling of being in absolute control, and knowing that she could make him come or stall him for a little longer, by a slight change of pressure.

He stroked her face. 'I'm looking forward to painting you, Selena. Your skin's so pale, so soft. I'll paint your hair the colour of winter wheat, and your eyes the colour of a river under a stormy November sky.' His hands drifted down to her breasts. 'And here, I'll paint you pale cream, with delicate tracings of blue.' He touched the mole between her breasts. 'And here, sepia. The same colour as your nipples.' He stroked the hardening peaks of flesh. 'Sepia, but this time shading into a flushed rose.' He cupped her mons veneris. 'And here again, cream and winter wheat – because your hair colour's natural, not out of a bottle.'

She grinned. 'You noticed, then?'

He laughed, liking her dry sense of humour. Selena was someone he'd like to get to know a lot better, he thought. He had a feeling that she'd be abandoned enough to be a really good model for him – a woman who wouldn't mind how lewd her position was, as long as he rewarded her for her patience afterwards.

He parted her legs, and knelt between them. 'And here,' he said, 'I can almost taste the way you look. Vanilla and roses. Here, where your blood runs hottest, you're every shade of red from vermilion through to crimson through to plum.'

His words thrilled her, and she shivered. She could imagine him painting her, spreading her legs so that he had a good view of her quim. Perhaps he'd paint her with glycerine, to make her skin shine as though it were aroused – she'd read a similar scene in an erotic novel once, of a photographer doing that to a model, and the idea had made her masturbate for the rest of the afternoon.

'If we'd had the pot of honey, instead of the massage oil,'

he said, 'I'd have painted your quim with honey, using the softest, thinnest brush, until your skin was soaked with it. And then I'd have licked it from you, until your own honey had replaced it.'

Selena's tongue moistened her lower lip. God, the way he spoke, she could almost feel it. And honey would be nicer than glycerine, more viscous and dragging slightly on her aroused sex-flesh, the slight pressure adding to her pleasure.

'In fact . . .' He dipped his head. 'I know I've already tasted you once tonight, but once isn't enough.' He drew his tongue along her musky furrow, and worked her with his mouth until she was writhing beneath him.

Then he kissed her thighs, nuzzling her skin. 'Selena,' he said. 'Moon goddess. That's what I'm going to call my painting of you: *Moon Goddess*.'

She opened her eyes, disappointed that he'd stopped, and he smiled at her. 'As I said, anticipation is half the fun.'

'Though too much anticipation causes an anti-climax,' she reminded him.

'I have no intention of letting there be any "anti", tonight,' he told her. 'Just a climax. Or a series of them.'

Her eyes darkened. A series of them. Yes, she could imagine that Jed had the staying power to bring her to climax after climax. And he'd enjoy doing it, too, taking as much pleasure from it as she did.

He knelt, looking at Selena. 'You're so lovely,' he breathed. 'I love the way you look, the way you feel. I don't think I can wait much longer to slide my cock inside you.'

She shivered at his words. She wanted it, too. Having Jed's large black dildo inside her had been one thing, but having the real thing was entirely different. At the moment, it was what she wanted most in the world: to feel his cock inside her.

'Selena.' He drew his hands down her sides, stroking her; he loved the way her body curved. He wanted to paint her and fuck her in equal measures. Painting would normally have won but, just then, the lure of her body was too much for him.

She shivered, tipping her head back and exposing her throat to him. He dipped his head so that he could kiss her, licking the hollows of her collarbones. His cock reared up from the cloud of hair at his groin, its head dark and glossy. There was a clear bead of moisture at its tip; Selena touched her finger to it and then transferred it to her mouth, savouring its pungent taste.

Gently, Jed lifted her up, bringing her closer to him so that she was straddling his thighs. His cock butted against her quim; she shifted so that its head pressed against the entrance of her sex, and then lowered herself very slowly onto him.

Jed's dildo had been big, she thought, but his cock was even bigger. She delighted in the way that it stretched her, filling her completely. She rested her hands on his shoulders and brought her mouth down to his, kissing him fiercely; her tongue probed his mouth, pressing against his own tongue. Jed seemed to enjoy the fact that she was taking control, and was happy to let her guide his movements, to give them both the most pleasure.

She began to lift and lower herself over his cock. The position meant that her thighs were spread more widely than usual, and the angle made his cock penetrate her more deeply. She flexed her muscles round him, loving the feel of him inside her.

He drew one finger down her spine, making her arch her back and thrust her breasts towards him. Her nipples were hard and prominent, and he pulled on them, his fingertips brushing her areolae. Selena gasped, and he touched her more roughly, stopping just short of the edge of pain.

Her movements grew more frenzied; she rocked over him, and he slid his hand down from her breast, caressing her midriff and then curling his fingers round her mons veneris. She was very wet; his fingertip skated easily over her clitoris, the light contact enough to make her cry out. He repeated the action again and again, one very light movement.

She gasped, and he felt her internal muscles contract sharply round him. The tiny movements were enough to bring him to his own climax. She leaned against him, her skin damp; he buried his head in her hair, drinking in her scent. They remained locked together for a while, until Jed's cock finally slipped from her.

He stroked her face, lifting her chin so that she met his eyes, and kissed her lightly on the mouth. 'Much as I'd like to stay here all night with you,' he said, 'I think that the floor's a bit hard. Come to bed with me, Selena.'

She nodded, and climbed off him. He stood up, taking her hand, and led her out of the studio. Neither of them bothered to pick up the tangled heap of clothes; they could wait until morning.

He led her into his bedroom. Like the other rooms she'd seen in the flat, it was furnished in a minimalist way. The floorboards were bare, without even a rag rug to break up the expanse of polished wooden flooring. There was a narrow-slatted Venetian blind at the window, rather than billowing drapes, and the low chest of drawers next to the mattress on the floor had nothing but a lamp, charcoal and paper on the top.

The walls were pale, and there were several charcoal drawings hung in perspex frames, all of them erotic. There was a haunting quality to them that attracted Selena. She wondered for a moment why Jed's ex-lover had left him. He was good company, a talented artist, physically attractive, and very good in bed. Why would a woman give up someone like that?

Maybe he was secretly psychotic, she thought, possessive and quick-tempered. But she had a good instinct, and she didn't think that Jed was like that. Maybe, she thought to herself, the woman had just been too straight-laced and hadn't appreciated the more sensual part of Jed's nature. Jed struck her as the sort of man who enjoyed experimenting.

He came to stand behind her, putting his hands round her waist and resting his chin on her shoulder. 'What are you thinking?' he asked softly.

'Just how lovely she was. Your ex.' Selena nodded to the charcoal drawings.

'Mm.' He sighed. 'Go on, you might as well ask. You want to know why we split up, don't you?'

She was surprised by his perception. 'Am I that obvious?'

'No. It's just the question I suppose anyone would ask, in your position.' He kissed the curve of her neck. 'The problem was, I had another mistress.'

Selena's eyes widened. 'You were unfaithful?' Though he didn't seem the type.

He laughed shortly. 'No. The "other mistress" was my work. She couldn't understand my need to paint. For me, it's like breathing – if I don't do it, I'm not alive. In the end, she made me choose between them.'

'And you chose your work.'

'Exactly.'

'Do you miss her?'

Jed shook his head. 'I did, at first; but I've grown used to living on my own, and I like it. I'm selfish, at heart, and I like to do what I want to do, when I want to do it.' He licked her earlobe. 'Though I do miss waking in the morning with the woman I love in my arms.'

'Maybe you could do a Pygmalion, and make one of your paintings come to life.'

He chuckled. 'That's something else I miss. Fencing intellectually with my lover. That's what's so good about Ruth's idea: all her clients want someone who'll talk to them.'

Selena grinned. 'As well as being hung like a donkey?'

Jed laughed back, knowing that he was being teased. 'If you must put it that way, yes!'

She glanced at his bed. 'You really are a minimalist, aren't you?'

'How do you mean?'

'Not even a proper base for your mattress – let alone a headboard.'

'It does me.' Jed nuzzled her shoulder. 'Anyway, I don't need a headboard.'

She drew him down onto the mattress with her. 'It depends on what sort of games you like playing.'

He grinned. 'Like I said, I don't need a headboard – or a base for my bed.' He looked at her. 'I've always thought that if you play games, you should play them professionally.'

Her eyes narrowed. 'Meaning?'

'Meaning that if you like the same games that I do, there are some very effective rings sewn into the sides of the mattress. Much easier than fiddling around with the headboard.' He sat back on his haunches. 'Why don't you open the top drawer of the cabinet?'

Selena did so, and her eyes widened. 'What a treasure-trove,' she said softly, fingering the contents.

'I thought you might see it that way, somehow.'

She took out one of the long black silk scarves. 'I think I'd like to use this on you, first.'

'Be my guest.' He sprawled on the bed. 'Tell me – were you planning to stake me out?'

Selena thought about it. 'In boring old bordello style?'

'Well, if you have any better ideas . . .'

She grinned. 'I have. But I'll tie you the lazy way, for now.'

Jed lay back on the bed, stretching his arms out; he reminded Selena of the da Vinci drawing, the man stretched out in the circle. She smiled at him, and gently tied one of the long silk scarves to his wrist, fastening the other end to one of the rings she found sewn into the side of the mattress. She did the same with his other wrist, and then with both ankles. 'How's that?' she asked.

He tugged at his bonds. 'Fine. Not too tight – but good enough to hold me.' He ran his tongue along his lower lip. 'So, what now?'

She smiled and knelt astride him, leaning forward so that her breasts swung freely, just above his face. He closed his eyes, taking in a deep breath of her scent, and she smiled. She turned round, backing up his body, and pressed her quim to his mouth; Jed shuddered with delight, and drew his tongue along her musky flesh, kissing her deeply. She bent her head to kiss the tip of his stiffened cock, pushing the foreskin back with her lips; she felt his body jerk beneath hers as she worked him, sliding her mouth up and down his shaft. His balls began to lift and tighten; when she judged that he was fully aroused, she climbed off him. She was tempted to stay, to let him lick her into another glorious orgasm – but she had other things she wanted to do first.

'I think you're going to enjoy this,' she said softly, standing beside him so that he had a perfect view of her. Then she widened her stance, tipping her head back, and slowly began to stroke the soft undersides of her breasts. Jed groaned appreciatively as she began to caress her nipples, licking her fingers and then pulling on the hard peaks of flesh. She saw the muscles in his jaw tighten as she slid one hand between her legs and slowly began to rub herself, still working on her nipples with her other hand.

The middle finger of her right hand slipped into the old familiar position, and she masturbated slowly, drawing out the maximum pleasure from her movements. Jed swallowed hard as she slid a second finger into herself, and a third; she was very wet, and he could hear as well as see her fingers sliding into her. She was near enough so that he could smell the pungent scent of her arousal, too; he yearned to taste her again, to break from his bonds and lick her, slide his cock into her and fuck her to orgasm.

By the time that she came, her internal muscles spasming round her fingers, he was shaking, tugging against his bonds and mouthing obscenities at her for tormenting him, not letting him join in. Selena merely smiled, and put her hand over his mouth so that he could smell and taste her arousal. He sucked her fingers, loving the taste of her.

Then she sat next to him on the bed, curling her hand round his cock. The rigid muscle leaped towards her, and her grin broadened. 'Like I said,' she repeated softly, 'I think you're going to enjoy this.' She moved her hand back and forth, each movement quick – but with a second's pause in between each stroke.

Jed began to pull against his bonds again, struggling helplessly; Selena took pity on him after the twentieth stroke, giving him ten quick rubs in succession – then resumed her slow and deliberate masturbation of him. Again and again she repeated the routine – twenty slow strokes, ten fast – until Jed was crying out, his voice husky and his groans sounding as though they were ripped from him.

She leaned over to kiss him, her tongue invading his mouth; he strained up to meet her, and she broke the kiss, smiling. 'Now, now. Take your time, Jed.'

He groaned as she resumed the slow masturbation. 'You bloody tease. You're driving me crazy!'

'That's the whole idea, lover.' Her lips quirked. 'Or are you used to being in control all the time?'

Jed was too near the edge to reply; he merely groaned and then, at last, he came, the white silky fluid fountaining in the air and splattering his skin. She rubbed it into his skin, then licked him clean, before kissing him hard.

He relaxed, his muscles growing limp, and she untied him, rubbing his wrists and ankles where the bonds had been. 'OK?' she asked softly.

He nodded, taking her back into his arms and pulling the

duvet over them. 'You're one hell of a woman, Selena. One after my own heart, I think.'

She stroked his face. 'Yeah. I reckon we could enjoy each other's company – on a part-time basis, that is. So it doesn't interfere with your work, or mine.'

'Though if you pull any more tricks like that on me . . .' He let the warning trail off, unspoken.

'What will you do?' She looked up at him, her eyes teasing.

'Put it this way,' he said, kissing her lightly, 'I'll have to get my own back on you. Don't forget, whatever you do to me, I can do something very similar to you.'

She grinned. 'That sounds much more like a promise than a threat.'

He grinned back. 'Believe me, it is . . .'

Meg lay curled in Niall's arms, at peace with herself and the world. After their gloriously messy love-making session in the kitchen, they'd had a shower, washed each other thoroughly, and gone to bed, leaving their clothes all over Meg's flat and not caring about the mess.

It was good, Meg thought, just to be held close like this. Niall was a good lover – and she didn't think that their night was over yet – but it was nice just to relax with him.

Niall stroked her hair. 'OK?'

'Mm.' She turned her face to kiss his chest. 'You?'

'Yes. I was just wondering . . .'

'What?'

He adopted the accent of a Swiss psychotherapist. 'Zo tell me about your favourite fantasy, Miss Stannard.'

Meg giggled. 'Shouldn't I be lying on a couch while you sit beside me, listening and making notes?'

'This will do me nicely. Skin to skin. Just how fantasies should be shared.' He stroked the curve of her buttocks. 'Seriously, Meg. I'd like to know your favourite fantasy.'

'So you can act it out with me?'

'It depends on what it is.' He kissed the top of her head. 'If I can, yes – after all, you indulged me in the whipped cream.'

'Well.' She wrinkled her nose. 'It sounds a bit stupid, actually.'

'I won't laugh, I promise. Tell me.'

'All right.' She sighed. 'It's something I thought about, years ago: something I read in a friend's sex manual, when I was at college. Anyway, this book reckoned that the best sex – for a woman – is on a swing. It's all to do with g-force and pressure in the pelvis. I laughed at the time, thinking that it sounded bloody dangerous, more than anything else; but the image stayed with me.' She smiled ruefully. 'I've used it, in the past, if I've been in bed with someone and needed to spice things up a bit.'

'Hm.' He rubbed his nose against hers. 'Remind me never to bore you in bed.'

She chuckled. 'I think you'd find that difficult! I just think it's kinder to fantasize and turn yourself on than to lie there like a sack of potatoes and let your lover know how useless you think he is.'

'Plus it's more fun for you, I imagine, than lying there and wishing that he'd hurry up and finish.' He stroked her breast. 'Tell me more about your swing, then.'

'It's a hot sunny day. I'm in a walled garden, filled with damask roses and apple trees, and there's a swing hanging from the biggest tree – a fairly simple one, made with thick rope and a smooth plank of wood. Anyway, I'm in Edwardian dress – a white linen dress, down to my ankles. I'm wearing white stockings, white silk knickers, and a white lace camisole; my hat's big and floppy and also white, covered with roses.

'I'm sitting on the swing, pushing myself, and I think I'm all alone in the garden. I'm a guest – I don't know where everyone else is, but I've been left to my own devices for the afternoon, so I decided to come and play on the swing. I'm probably too old for it, but I don't care. It's strong enough to hold me.

'All I can hear is the birds singing. The sun's warm on my face, and I'm really enjoying myself. I'm soaring, higher and higher – and then I see him, standing by the entrance to the walled garden. He's just leaning against the wall, watching me. I have a feeling that he can see up my skirt – even though it's a long dress – and I'm not sure whether it makes me more nervous or excited.'

'Who is he?' Niall asked softly.

Meg shook her head. 'I don't know. He's the proverbial tall, dark, handsome stranger. He might be the son of the owner of the house I'm visiting, or he might be a cousin, another visiting friend – I don't know. But he's very attractive. Dark hair, and very blue eyes – the same colour as the sky. He's wearing a striped blazer, a white shirt, Oxford bags, and a straw hat. I think he's a bit older than me – I'm about eighteen, in the fantasy – and he might be on vacation from university.'

Niall continued to stroke her breasts, rolling her nipples in turn between his forefinger and thumb. 'And he's just watching you?'

Meg nodded. 'He's watching me. I show off, a bit, swinging dangerously high; I know that it means he can see more of my legs, because my dress is riding up from the force of the swing. I swing, and swing . . . Then he walks towards me, and I slow down.

'I stop, and he takes hold of the ropes, one in each hand. I know that he's going to kiss me – and he's very good. The way his lips touch mine, oh so gently, encouraging me to open my mouth: I can't help responding, pulling his hat off so I can tangle my hands in his hair, and he pushes his tongue against mine. It makes my toes curl, he's so exciting. Like no man I've met before.

'The next thing I know, I'm on my feet, in his arms. He's undone all the buttons on my dress and pushed it off me, so I'm standing there, dressed only in my camisole, knickers and stockings. My hat's on the ground, by my dress, and I'm barefoot. My nipples are hard, and obviously visible through the thin silk; he touches them through the material, and it makes me want to feel his mouth on my skin. I'm very excited, and there's a pulse beating between my thighs; he seems to know that, because he touches me there, too. Again, it's through the material of my knickers – not skin to skin – but it's so intoxicating. I think I'm going to come, there and then, just from him touching me lightly like that.

'He undresses, too. It doesn't take him long; his body is pale, because he obviously spends a lot of time indoors, but he's not at all weedy. I think he must do a lot of punting at Cambridge or Oxford, wherever he is, because his arms are so strong. My gaze travels downwards, and I blush – like the good little Edwardian girl I am – when I see his cock rearing up from the cloud of hair at his groin. He looks so big, I'm half scared that I won't be able to accommodate him.

'I think he's going to take off my stockings – but he doesn't. What he does is even more exciting than that. He takes the top of my camisole between his fingers and thumbs, and he rips it open – the little pearl buttons go everywhere. I ought to be angry with him, but he smiles at me, and says he'll buy me a new one – and that my body's too beautiful to be covered up.

'My knickers get the same treatment – being silk, they tear easily, and he literally rips them off me. Though he's not forcing me to do this – I could have said no, right at the start. I want this as much as he does. I want him to be—' she paused '— not violent with me, not hurting me, but just forceful.

'So I'm standing there, my ruined knickers on the ground, and my camisole hanging in rags on my shoulders; only my stockings are intact. He leaves those, though. He smiles then, and sits me back on the swing, pushing my legs wide apart so that he can look at me. I feel so hot, so wet – I want to feel him touch me. I want him to fuck me. I want him to talk dirty, and I want to talk dirty back. I feel like a whore – and it's so different from my usual demure behaviour that it excites me even more.

'He kneels down in front of me, and takes one nipple into his mouth. It feels so good, the way he sucks my flesh! Little tiny nips, not hurting me – just making me more and more aroused. I can feel his teeth grazing me, and his tongue soothing my skin; where he's licked me, my skin seems to tingle.

'I close my eyes, tipping my head back, and his mouth slowly travels down over my stomach. I swallow hard, wondering what he's going to do next – is he going to touch me, where I ache most for it? Is he going to use his mouth on me? I wait for what seems like years; then, at last, he puts his hand over my quim. He cups it so that his fingers rest against my slit.'

'Like this?' Niall whispered, cupping her mons veneris.

Meg gave a sigh of pleasure. 'Exactly like that. Then he draws up his middle finger, and lets it lie flat again, stroking me as he does so.'

'Like this?' Niall repeated the action she'd just described, loving the way her flesh felt beneath his fingertips, warm and wet.

'Yes. Oh, yes.' Meg took a shuddering intake of breath as Niall began to rub her. 'And then he keeps doing it, over and over, until I'm writhing beneath him. I feel like a furnace, and he's stoking me – every time he touches my clitoris, it makes me hotter and wetter, but he doesn't stop, doesn't push a finger into me. Not yet. He just keeps stroking me until I come so hard that I'm scared I've wet myself

'I haven't, though. He's just turned me on so much, I'm really wet. And then he pushes a finger into me.' Niall followed her instructions to the letter, pushing a finger into her. 'God, it feels good!'

He wasn't sure whether she was talking about her fantasy or what he was doing to her; it didn't matter. 'Keep talking. Tell me what he's doing to you,' he muttered.

Meg's voice grew huskier. 'Just as I think it can't get much better, he dips his head and starts tonguing my clitoris. Back and forth, back and forth – and then in a figure of eight, faster and faster and faster. Then he takes my clitoris into his mouth, sucking gently on it. I think I'm going to scream, it feels so good – but he seems to sense what I want to do in the way my body stiffens, and he withdraws the hand from my quim, placing it over my mouth to silence me. I can taste my own arousal on his fingers, and I know that I ought to be shocked – but I love what he's doing to me, the way he's pushing his tongue deep into me and lapping at me; and all the time, I'm sucking his fingers, tasting myself. I come again and again, in his mouth, but he's not complaining. I think he's enjoying it as much as I am.

'Then he stands up again, drawing me to my feet. I curl my hand round his cock, feeling how thick and long it is. He laughs, and tells me how lewd and wanton I look, with my cunt and my tits bare and my stockings still on.

'I feel lewd and wanton, too. I want to push him as hard as he's just pushed me – to the limits of pleasure. I lick my lips and kneel down in front of him, taking the tip of his cock into my mouth. That takes his breath away – he can't speak, only moan, as I work him with my mouth. I like the way he tastes, clean and fresh and male, and I keep fellating him, sucking hard as I withdraw from him, then sliding back until he's as deep as I can take him.

'His body stiffens; I feel his balls lift and tighten; and then his cock throbs, and my mouth's full of warm salty fluid. I swallow every last drop; then he helps me to my feet and kisses me, hard.'

Niall wanted to kiss her hard, too – but he wanted to hear the rest of the story. He contented himself with inserting another two fingers into Meg's quim, and pistoning hard.

'Then he sits on the swing; he's already hard again, and his cock looks so inviting. It's beautiful, the tip purple fading into maroon. I'd never realized before just how beautiful a naked man looks.

'Anyway, I sit on his lap, facing him – the swing's more than strong enough to take both of us – and he lifts me slightly. The head of his cock presses against me; then he lets me sink back down onto him, until he's in me up to the hilt. The root of his cock presses against my clitoris, and it feels so good; I flex my internal muscles round him, and he chuckles. His eyes are still very blue, though his pupils have expanded; he's got a nice smile, and it's all for me.

'I hold the ropes, balancing both of us, while he strokes my breasts – God, it feels so good, to have him deep inside me and rubbing me at the same time. Then he takes the ropes, and starts to swing us. It's like nothing on earth. I thought he was good, before, but this is way beyond that. I'm in orgasm from the first swoop – and he takes us both higher, higher, until I'm almost blacking out with the intensity of it.'

Niall could stand it no longer; he rolled over onto his back, pulling Meg on top of him, and eased his hand between their bodies, fitting his cock to the entrance of her sex. Meg sank down on him, and began to ride him, very gently; he raised his upper body, resting his weight on his elbows, and kissed her breasts.

Meg adopted the same rhythm as her imaginary swing, long and slow. 'It's good,' she said. 'I love the feel of his cock in me. I love the feeling of being almost weightless – the only bit that's any different is where our bodies are joined. When he comes inside me, it's like stars are flashing in front of my eyes...' She gave a groan, and then her internal muscles contracted sharply round his cock.

It was enough to tip Niall into his own climax; he, too,

groaned and came, pushing up into her. He wrapped his arms round her, holding her close and stroking her hair; Meg let herself relax against him. 'And that's it, doctor,' she whispered mischievously.

'Just find me the swing. I'll get you a costume from the theatre – and we'll do it, in the summer,' he promised.

Meg grinned. 'You know, I might just hold you to that. Because I've not acted it out.'

'Yet,' he added, kissing her. 'Yet.'

FIFTEEN

Ruth turned to face Aidan. 'So, here we are. On our own again.'

'Yes.' He looked at the pile of dirty crockery, and wrinkled his nose. 'Forget this, for now. I'll do it in the morning.'

'We'll do it together,' Ruth said. 'You helped me with dinner. I can't expect you to do all the washing-up as well!'

He took her hand, pulling her into his arms, and kissed her lingeringly. 'I love you.'

'You, too.' She looked at him. 'Do you think that tonight was a success?'

He grinned. 'If for nothing but my cooking...'

She punched him lightly. 'You know what I mean!'

'Yes, I do.' He rubbed his nose against hers. 'And I have to admit, you were right about Mark. I *did* like him. He's a nice guy.'

'And you're not jealous any more?'

'No.'

'Good.' She tipped her head on one side. 'But tell me one thing. Was the cracker selection really random?'

He saw the look in her eyes, and decided to tell the truth. 'Eighty per cent of it was.'

'So you *did* fix it that we'd end up together.'

'There was a twenty per cent chance that we'd end up together... and it wasn't high enough,' he said quietly. 'So yes, I fixed it. Do you mind?'

'Well – no, not really,' she admitted.

'In that case, Ms Finn, let's go to bed.'

She tipped her head on one side. 'Is that under the Interlover terms?'

He grinned. 'But of course!' He fished the little foil packet from his pocket, and waved it at her.

She grinned back. 'A gold condom. I can't believe you did that. It's a bit flash, isn't it?'

'The name's Shaw – Aidan Shaw,' he said, in his best Bond impression.

Ruth laughed. 'So does this make you the Man with the Golden Cock, Gold-condom, or Goldencock?'

He laughed. 'Let's try it out, and you can tell me afterwards.'

'Right.' She paused. 'And then there's the black silk scarf – which means that one of us won't get the full effect of your gold condom.'

He spread his hands. 'Who says that they're going to be used at the same time? Or that I'm going to use the scarf as a blindfold?'

'I suppose you have a point,' she said.

'Ruth.' He rubbed his nose against hers. 'Will you just stop talking and come to bed with me?'

'Bully,' she said, walking upstairs with him, hand in hand.

He closed their bedroom curtains, and switched on the bedside lamp. He undressed her slowly, unzipping her black dress and stroking each inch of skin as he revealed it; Ruth shivered as the dress dropped to the floor. He undid her bra, cupping her breasts in his hands and pushing them together to deepen the vee of her cleavage, then stooped to nuzzle between her breasts, breathing in her scent. 'Mm. I love this perfume on you.'

'So you should. You bought it for me,' she reminded him.

'And I love your breasts, too. I love the way you curve.'

'Supposing I'd been as flat as a pancake?' she tested.

'I would still have loved you.' He grinned. 'Though, luckily for me, you're not one of those skinny androgynous women. You're all curves, all soft and womanly and sexy. Perfect.' He took one nipple into his mouth, sucking gently on it. 'Mm. I love the way you feel. The way you taste.'

He knelt before her, undoing the catches of her suspender belt, then unclasping the hooks at the back, letting the garment fall to the floor. He stroked the soft curves of her buttocks, kneading them gently, and Ruth gave a soft murmur of pleasure. He dropped a trail of kisses over her midriff, and Ruth arched her back, willing him to go lower.

Aidan chuckled, knowing exactly what she wanted. He smoothed his hands over her thighs, gently rolling down one stocking and then the other, making her lift each foot in turn so that he could remove the stockings completely. He stroked the arches of her feet, the delicate bones of her ankles; Ruth closed her eyes, giving herself up to his gentle caresses. Then, at last, he brought his face down to her quim; he breathed in her scent through her knickers, making her shiver. She widened her stance, to give him better access, and he hooked his thumbs into the waistband of her knickers, slowly peeling them over her hips. As he drew them downwards, he stroked her buttocks again, and licked the soft skin of her inner thighs.

She shivered, waiting for him to use his mouth on her properly; instead, he simply helped her step out of her knickers, then stood up.

She looked at him, a mixture of disappointment and hurt written all over her face.

He smiled, knowing exactly what she was thinking. 'Maybe later. Not yet. First . . .' He flexed his shoulders. 'I think I'm wearing too much, don't you?'

'Mm. And you want me to do something about it?'

'Yes, indeedy.' His smile broadened.

Slowly, she undressed him, taking her time and arousing him in the same way that he'd aroused her. The pads of her fingertips skated over his skin; a thrill ran through her as she touched him. She loved the interplay of his muscles under her fingertips, the way he moved when she touched a sensitive spot, the way his mouth opened involuntarily as she caressed his buttocks.

Seeing Aidan in the same room as Mark had crystallized her feelings. She still found Mark attractive, but there was no longer that desperate illicit urge to make love with him. What she felt for Aidan eclipsed everything else. Besides, there was a very good chance that Mark was having the same sort of effect on Helen, making her forget Stu: Ruth rather liked the idea.

When she'd finished undressing Aidan, he drew her over to the bed, and kissed her lightly. 'Humour me for a moment, will you?'

'What?'

'I'll be back in a minute.' He left the room, and Ruth frowned. What was he going to fetch? Did he have some other surprise planned for her?

She was amused when he returned with the brass candlesticks. 'It's more romantic, this way,' he said, lighting them and placing one on each bedside cabinet, then turning off the lamp so that shadows flickered over the bed. 'And candlelight makes your skin look even more beautiful.'

'Thank you,' she said quietly.

'I mean it. I love everything about you,' he said. 'The way you look, the way you feel in my arms, your scent . . .' He laughed. 'Even the way you snore.'

'I do *not* snore.'

'You do, when you have a cold.' He knelt on the bed between her thighs, licking his way up her legs. He paused to lick the hollows of her ankles, then nibbled over her calves to the sensitive skin at the back of her knees.

Ruth shivered, widening the gap between her thighs as his

mouth drifted upwards to her quim. She closed her eyes in anticipation, willing him to draw his tongue along her musky flesh – not to tease her, like he had earlier. He did exactly what she'd hoped he'd do, his tongue moving in long slow strokes from the top to the bottom of her slit. He repeated that one movement again and again, alternating the pressure by using the very tip of his tongue, then his whole mouth, until the tension of her orgasm began to build up to an almost unbearable pitch.

He stopped just before she climaxed. 'I love making you come like this,' he said softly, 'I love the way you taste, sweet and salt at the same time; I love the rich scent of your arousal. But, right now, I want to feel your cunt flex round my cock as you come. I want to feel your flesh ripple over mine, pulling me deeper into you.' He leaned over to remove the little foil square from his abandoned trousers.

'I think I should be doing this,' Ruth said, taking the package from him and opening it to reveal the little rubber disc. She fitted it over the tip of his cock, and expertly pulled the sheath over his erection. She looked up to see him smiling. 'What?' she asked, smiling back.

'I was just thinking. Ten years ago, if you'd have asked me to wear a condom, I'd have run a mile, saying it would be too much of a passion-killer. I hate using them. But because we never do – somehow, it makes this a real turn-on.'

'And more fun. Besides, you were talking about normal boring condoms – this is a gold one.'

'True.' He glanced down at the thin latex sheath, which glittered in the candlelight. 'Put it this way, it's the nearest you're ever going to get to fucking King Midas.'

She laughed. 'Or any of the Greek gods who'd been immortalized in an ivory and bronze statue.'

He grinned. 'Oh, yes. I can just see it, now. One of the women would have brought the offerings to her god, seen the enormous erect penis on the statue, and been unable to resist ripping her clothes off and masturbating in front of it, it made her feel so horny. Maybe she'd have taken the phallus in her mouth, sucking it and imagining what it would be like to fuck the god she dreamed about, feel him filling her mouth when he came. Or she'd have rubbed it between her breasts; and then, finally, it would have been too much for her.' He licked his lips. 'Her sex would have been so hot and wet, the only thing that she could do to give herself relief would be to lower herself onto the statue, feel its hardness stretching the walls of her cunt.'

Ruth grinned back. 'Now, *there's* a male fantasy, if ever I heard one!'

'Yeah.' A lascivious smile crossed his face, and he closed his eyes. 'A beautiful woman riding a statue, massaging her own breasts, her head tipped back and her mouth open. She'd be moaning with joy, completely abandoned to . . .'

'Aidan?'

'Mm?' He opened his eyes again and looked at her.

'Would you just stop talking and fuck me, please?'

'Whatever you say, my love,' he said softly.

He slid his hands down her thighs, curling his hands underneath her and manoeuvring her legs until they were bent and her thighs were spread wide. He sat back and pushed his pelvis forward so that the tip of his cock pushed against her moist and puffy sex; he slid easily inside her, up to the hilt.

Then he began to move, his body pushing into hers with long slow thrusts. Ruth gave a small moan of pleasure as the delicious sensations built up again, closing her eyes and tipping her head back against the pillows. She reached up behind her to grip the rails of their headboard, her knuckles whitening as her pleasure grew.

Aidan thrilled at the sight of his lover abandoning herself to pleasure: though he wasn't finished with her. Not by a long way. He slid his hands down her legs, straightening them again and lifting them up so that her feet hooked over his shoulders. Then he began to move harder and faster, pushing deep inside her.

Ruth cried out his name as the pressure of her orgasm became unbearable. She climaxed, wave upon wave upon wave of pleasure flooding through her. He didn't stop, but continued thrusting, bringing her to a higher peak. And then, at last, the way her quim rippled round his cock brought him to his own climax.

He lowered her legs back down to the bed and sank into her arms, supporting his weight on his knees and elbows. He kissed her lightly. 'OK?'

She stroked his face. 'Yes. Very OK.' She smiled. 'Maybe we should use condoms more often.'

'It took me ages to find gold ones,' he reminded her, and they burst into shared laughter.

Eventually, he slipped from her and rolled over onto his side. 'I'm just going to the bathroom. I won't be a minute.'

'Don't tell me that you're going shy on me!' Ruth teased.

'No.' He shook his head. 'But as the taste and smell of rubber isn't one of your fetishes, I think I ought to have a quick shower.'

'Right.'

He returned a few minutes later, his skin still damp from the shower. Ruth stretched lazily on the bed. 'Mm. I could do that all over again.'

'You will – but without the condom, that's all.' He smiled at her. 'Though we *do* have the black silk scarf.'

'So what are your intentions?' she asked. 'Tying someone up, or blindfolding them? And who's going to have the scarf used on them – you or me?'

'Bondager or bondagee,' he said with a grin. 'Bagsie be bondager – or we could take turns, if you like.'

Ruth shook her head. 'I'm not in the mood for being tied up,' she said. 'I want to touch you.'

Aidan smiled to himself. That fitted in very nicely with his plans. 'Then blindfold it is,' he said, softly.

She wrinkled her nose. 'Why?'

'Because it'll help you to concentrate on the way you feel. If you can't see me, you won't know what I'm going to do to you. Anticipation is—' he smiled '—one of the nicest sources to pleasure.'

'Supposing you don't do what I think you're going to do to me – what I want you to do?'

'Then either you'll be pleasantly surprised . . . or you'll have to tell me what you want, won't you?'

'Hm.' She wasn't convinced, but she sat up; he sat next to her on the bed, and tied the black silk scarf over her eyes.

'Is that OK?' he asked gently against her ear, his breath fanning warm against her skin and sending shivers down her spine.

She nodded.

'It's not too tight?'

'No, it's fine.'

'Open your eyes,' he said. 'Can you see anything?'

'No,' she said truthfully.

'Good.'

She frowned. 'Aidan, what are you up to?'

'Wait and see,' he said infuriatingly. Gently, he lowered her back to the bed.

'I hate to think what you've sneaked upstairs in your bottom drawer,' she murmured.

'It's in my top drawer, actually. I put it there while you were cooking the chicken. And you're going to like it, I promise you,' he said softly. 'In fact, you'll adore it.'

'Convince me.'

He grinned. 'Anything you say.' He kissed her lightly on

the lips. 'What I want you to do is talk to me. Tell me what I'm doing to you.'

Ruth frowned. 'But if I can't see . . .'

'Concentrate on your other senses, instead. Touch and smell and sound.'

'What about taste?'

He grinned. 'Maybe later! Just describe what's happening to you, how you feel.'

Ruth wasn't sure whether to be more nervous or excited. She lay back against the pillows and waited. She could hear a slight squeak as Aidan opened a drawer; then she felt the mattress give as he sat down next to her.

He drew the flat of his hand across her body, and she arched up to meet him; as he caressed her, she relaxed. Aidan watched her, smiling; then he picked up the feather he'd taken from the drawer, and gently traced the outline of her breasts with it. Ruth found herself arching up towards the gentle – literally feather-light – caresses, her skin sensitized where he touched her.

'Talk to me,' he reminded her. 'Tell me what I'm doing.'

'You're touching my breasts. Very lightly.'

'How does it feel?'

'Lovely. It tickles, a bit – then, just when I'm about to wriggle and laugh, you alter the pressure, and it's very arousing. It's making my sex grow warm and very wet; I want to feel you inside me.'

Aidan continued tracing the outline of her breasts for a little longer, watching her nipples harden and stand up; then he let the feather move lower.

Ruth writhed as he teased her, the feather stroking the ticklish spot by her hip-bones. 'That tickles!' she protested, laughing.

'How about this?' he asked, brushing the feather up the inside of her thigh.

Ruth waited in quivering anticipation of what he was going

to do next. She was surprised to feel him kneeling between her thighs; she had expected him to start brushing her quim with whatever he was using on her.

'What do you want?' he asked softly, seeing the yearning look on her face.

'I want you to touch me with – whatever it is. The brush. Arouse me.'

He grinned. 'If you want me to do that, you'll have to ask me properly.'

'Please?' she tried.

'No. Tell me exactly what you want me to do.' He paused. 'Explicitly.'

Ruth smiled, knowing what he wanted. 'I want you to use it on my cunt. I want you to stroke me with it, brush my clitoris until the brush is wet and fragrant with my juices. I want you to make me come with it, bring me right to the edge, again and again.'

His voice grew husky. 'Then your wish is my command.' Though he had something much more exotic in mind than using his hands to guide the feather. He gripped the end of the quill firmly with his teeth, and began to brush her labia with the feather, stroking every crease and fold. His breath was warm against her, a light and equally teasing caress; Ruth wriggled impatiently beneath him, wanting to feel his tongue or his fingers trace the same path, a firmer and more satisfying touch than what he was using on her.

Still he worked at her, the feather gripped in his teeth. She smelled of honey and seashore, and he itched to let the feather go and taste her properly.

Barely resisting the lure of her quim, he moved his head up and down, long slow strokes of the feather running along her labia. The strands grew dark and sticky with her honeyed juices; he felt like a painter, creating a special piece of work for his lover. Something tactile instead of visible, and something that only the woman writhing beneath his ministrations could appreciate.

Diligently, he stroked on, until finally Ruth gave a groan and shuddered; he could feel the throbbing of her sexflesh through the feather.

'Better?' he asked, putting the quill on her bedside table, but not removing her blindfold.

'Mm.' She stretched luxuriously. 'So what were you using? The brush you used on me the other night, or a new one you'd bought?'

'No. Guess again.'

She shook her head. 'I can't.'

'It's a feather. A goose feather.' He grinned. 'The sort they used for quill pens. Though I bet Shakespeare never had so much fun using a quill pen.'

'I wouldn't bet on that,' Ruth said drily. 'I studied the bawdy bits of Shakespeare once, and he knew quite a lot. He got away with a lot, too – one of the characters in *The Taming of the Shrew* talks about putting his tongue in someone's tail.'

'Hm. Now, do you think he meant here—' Aidan bent to draw his tongue down her quim '—or here?' He slid one finger over the crease of her buttocks, pressing lightly at the puckered rosy hole of her anus.

'I'm not sure, to be honest,' Ruth admitted. 'But I bet he used a feather like that on someone.'

'Hm. Feathers.' Aidan grinned.

Ruth heard the laughter in his voice. 'What are you thinking?'

'It's obscene.'

'That doesn't surprise me! Tell.'

'No.'

'Please?' she coaxed.

'Supposing it had been a swan's feather instead of a goose's?'

She caught his reference immediately. 'Just call me Leda,'

she quipped, putting her hands on her hips and pouting at him.

'Doesn't it make you wonder, though? Just how Zeus made love to the beautiful Leda, when he was in the form of a swan?'

Ruth grinned. 'I'd imagine it had more to do with a beak than anything else.'

He chuckled. 'Now *that's* lewd.'

'Mm. I must remember to tell Selena, next time I see her...'

He moved back to the open drawer. 'In the meantime...'

'What?'

'I haven't finished with you yet.' He removed the banana he'd placed there earlier, and peeled it.

'What are you doing?' Ruth asked, straining to hear; whatever Aidan was up to, he was nearly silent, and the sounds she could hear told her nothing.

'Something I think you might like,' he said softly.

'Another of your little surprises, like the feather?'

'Yep.' He grinned. And just how surprising it was going to be... He moved back between her legs, licking his way up her thighs. Ruth sighed, and widened the gap between her thighs to give him easier access. She loved it when he went down on her; she felt slightly selfish about it, letting him give her all the pleasure, but he'd always said that he enjoyed it nearly as much as she did.

Her hands came up to touch her breasts; she rolled her nipples between finger and thumb. Aidan could see exactly what she was doing, and only just managed to suppress a wicked laugh; holding her labia apart with one hand, he began to rub the end of the banana over her clitoris.

Ruth frowned. She'd been expecting to feel his thumb, or his tongue. Instead, it was – what? Not the feather. The texture was different. And not his cock, either.

'Just lie back and enjoy yourself,' Aidan said, seeing the frown.

'What are you—' she began.

He silenced her with a kiss. 'Indulge me, this once? After all, I indulged you, tonight.'

Ruth tugged at her blindfold. 'What about this?'

'That's different,' he informed her, laughing. 'I promise you, Ruth, you're going to enjoy this. A lot.

'OK.'

She settled back against the pillows, spreading her legs more widely apart and bringing her hands up to grip the headboard; Aidan knelt to kiss his way down her body again. Part of him itched to squash the banana against her breasts and massage it into her skin, then eat the sticky mixture off her; but what he had in mind was far more fun. He contented himself with toying with her nipples, his tongue bathing the hard peaks of flesh, then blowing gently on them to make her squirm and push herself up towards him.

He rubbed the tip of his nose round her navel, making her laugh, then slowly moved southwards, alternately licking her skin and blowing on it. By the time that he reached her quim, Ruth was panting, pushing her pelvis up towards him. He drew his tongue very slowly across her labia, then played with her clitoris, flicking his tongue over it in quick bursts with long pauses in between licks, until she writhed underneath him.

'Aidan, don't tease,' she said huskily. 'I need to feel you inside me. Now.'

'Like this?' He slid one finger into her; she was hot and tight, her flesh slippery to the touch. He moved his hand back and forth, until Ruth thrust her hips up again to meet him, the movements of her body increasing the friction; then, with a smile, he held her open, and inserted the banana fully.

'Aidan?' She flexed her internal muscles experimentally. She'd been half-expecting him to insert something other than his cock – but what *was* it? It was too soft to be a dildo or vibrator, even one of the geloid ones; and it wasn't the handle of the brush he'd used on her before. It had a different texture, a different feel.

'Just relax,' Aidan directed, with a grin.

Ruth shook her head. 'Not until you tell me what you're doing.'

'Guess.'

'You've just put something inside me – but what?'

'Guess,' he said tormentingly. 'You've got three chances.'

'And if I get it wrong?'

'You let me do whatever I want to you. Anything at all.'

She groaned. 'You tormenting bastard.'

He leaned over to kiss her. 'Since when have I ever done anything to you that you haven't liked? Now, guess what I'm using in you . . .'

She sighed. 'A dildo, one of those soft geloid ones?'

'No.'

'A vibrator?'

'Nope.'

'I give up.'

'I gave you three guesses,' he reminded her. 'One more.'

She shook her head. 'I dunno. The brush you used on me, the other night?'

'Completely wrong.'

'Then what?'

He gently removed the banana. 'Open your mouth.'

'I beg your pardon?'

'Open your mouth,' he repeated.

She did so, and he rested the banana on her lower lip. 'Take a bite.'

It was the last thing she'd expected him to say; she was slightly shocked. Just what the hell was her lover up to now? He was inventive, she knew that – but he must have borrowed one of Selena's more obscure books to come up with something like this.

'Take a bite,' he urged again.

She took a tiny nibble; then she burst out laughing as she recognized the taste – banana, mixed with her own sweet-salt juices. She swallowed the mouthful, still smiling. 'Oh, honestly! A banana!'

'The oldest trick in the book, my love. Now, can I go back to what I was doing?'

'You're a pervert,' she said, laughing.

'Think of it this way – it makes a change from root vegetables,' he said laconically. 'Now, where was I?' He slid the banana back into her, and kissed his way up her thigh before settling comfortably on his stomach between her legs, and starting to eat the banana.

Ruth wriggled as she realized what he was doing – eating the fruit very slowly, pulling it out of her a couple of millimetres at a time. It was incredibly erotic, the gentle drag of the fruit against the walls of her vagina; she smiled, and flexed her internal muscles, drawing the fruit back slightly as Aidan went to take another bite.

He laughed. 'Tug of war, is it?'

She laughed back. 'Something like that.' She had good muscles, and she knew how to use them. If Aidan wanted to play games – then he'd better not underestimate his opponent, she thought with a grin.

He sucked the fruit back into his mouth, loosening his hold on it as he felt her pull it back, and then relaunching his assault. He took it from her bite by bite, moving the fruit a couple of millimetres each time; as he took the last mouthful, Ruth climaxed, her honeyed juices spilling into his mouth.

'Mm, what a dessert,' he said, shifting up to lie beside her and kissing her deeply.

'And now I know why you wanted to use that blindfold,' she said, laughing. 'You know, I'm almost tempted to make you give training classes for the next crop of Interlovers.'

He laughed back. 'I might just call your bluff, and accept . . .'

SIXTEEN

The next morning, Helen woke and stretched luxuriously. She sniffed, and smiled as she recognized the scents of freshly brewed coffee and toast, and heard some muted clatters. Mark was obviously busy in the kitchen – and trying to be quiet, not waking her. A few moments later, he walked into the bedroom, carrying a tray, with a towel wrapped round his waist. 'Good morning,' he said softly. 'Sorry if I woke you.'

'You didn't.' She yawned. 'I'm wide awake.'

He tipped his head on one side. 'Did you sleep well?'

'Yes.' She smiled at him. She'd fallen asleep in his arms; and although she'd woken once or twice in the night, it had been in his arms, and she'd gone back to sleep almost immediately, lulled by the security of his warm body wrapped round hers. 'So what's all this, then?'

'Breakfast is served, my lady,' he said with a grin, sitting next to her. He handed her a mug of coffee. 'There's orange juice as well; I took the liberty of raiding your fruit bowl, so it's freshly squeezed.'

Helen took a grateful sip of her coffee. 'Mm, that's wonderful.' Stu had never even brought her coffee in bed, let alone made her breakfast. Or such a breakfast as Mark had prepared – the freshly squeezed orange juice, good coffee, and a large plate of toast for them to share. He'd also brought in a box of muesli, two bowls, and a jug of milk. 'I feel thoroughly spoiled. Thank you.'

'Pleasure. Do you want to start with cereals, or toast?'

'Toast, I think. Please.'

He grinned. 'Don't forget the honey.'

She glanced at the plate; when she saw how thinly he'd spread the honey on the toast, she laughed. 'Talk about tight! I like my toast dripping with honey, so I can taste the stuff – not having to imagine that it's there!'

'Ah,' he said, 'but it was only a small pot, and the honey was supposed to be used on your body, not for your breakfast.' He lifted up the tiny pot to show her that it was still half full. 'So I saved some.'

'Very clever of you,' Helen said, grinning.

He fed her a slice of toast, eating one himself at the same time; she arched forward, nibbling at it daintily; Mark smiled to himself. It reminded him of the way he'd fed Ruth, that afternoon; there was something incredibly erotic about feeding your lover, bite by bite. Helen ate delicately, but there was still a smear of honey and butter on her lips when she'd finished; he couldn't resist reaching forward to lick it off.

She tipped her head up, sliding her hands into his hair, and he kissed her, hard, his tongue exploring her mouth. He broke the kiss and took the mug from her hands, putting it back on the tray and placing the tray on the floor. 'Let's have the rest of our breakfast later,' he suggested.

'Come back to bed, Mark,' she said softly, tugging at the fastening of his makeshift loincloth; it fell apart, revealing his erect state, and she gave him a lascivious pout. 'I hope that this was on the menu for breakfast, too,' she said, running her fingertips lightly along the length of his erection.

'What do *you* think?' he smiled back. He dropped the towel on the floor, climbing into bed beside her. He reached down to take the pot of honey from the tray, and dipped one finger into it. He smeared the honey over her nipples, working it gently into her areolae, and she shivered. 'That's sticky.'

'Apparently, it's very good for the skin. Or so my sister tells me.'

Helen chuckled. 'Do you think that your sister does this sort of thing?'

'Knowing Lou – probably, yes. I think she's done things that I've never even dreamed about – not that we've ever really discussed it, though. I've just caught the occasional tail end of a conversation between her and some of her female friends, and they were enough to make me blush!' He smiled at her, and stooped to lick the honey from her skin. His tongue flickered across her areolae; then he sucked gently on her nipples, cleaning her skin. 'Mm. You taste gorgeous – and it isn't just the honey!' He traced the curve of her breasts with the tip of his nose, making her arch her back.

'Anything you can do . . .' she quipped lightly, pushing the duvet off the bed. She took the pot from him and dipped her fingers into the sticky mixture. His cock stood proudly, rearing up from the cloud of hair at his groin; she began to smear honey over its tip, rubbing it in gently. The stickiness of the honey made her fingertips drag slightly over his skin, increasing the friction as she manipulated his foreskin.

He closed his eyes and leaned back, putting his hands behind him and resting his weight on them. 'God, Helen, that feels *so* good.'

'I haven't finished, yet,' Helen told him huskily.

Mark groaned as she dipped her head, her tongue skilfully lapping over his glans. When she'd finished cleaning the honey from his cock, she lifted her head, gave him a mischievous smile, and dipped her head again. He gave a sharp intake of breath as she took his cock deep into her mouth, inching her lips slowly down the shaft and relaxing her palate so that she could take him more deeply. She worked him until he was trembling, then released him so that she could smear more honey on the tip of his cock. She licked the head like a lollipop, her tongue flickering back and forth across his glans and dabbling in the small groove under the head.

He groaned as she took him fully into her mouth again, cupping his sac with one hand and raking his inner thighs lightly with the nails of her other. A shiver went down his spine, and he tipped his head back. She sucked hard, moving her head back and forth rapidly, varying the pace and pressure to increase his pleasure.

To his intense surprise and delight, she dipped her fingers in the honey again, and began to smear it over the soft silky skin of his perineum. She pressed one finger against his anus, as though she were lightly pressing a button, letting the viscous fluid do all the work; although she hadn't penetrated him, he shuddered as sensation coursed through him. 'Christ, that's so good,' he murmured.

Helen lifted her head for just long enough to say, 'Glad you like it,' and then resumed licking his penis, her tongue swirling over its head and cleaning the honey from him. She continued to massage the skin between his balls and his anus, her fingers dabbling very gently along it. Mark felt excitement kick in his loins, and his balls began to lift and tighten. With a sudden unexpected movement, Helen's finger plunged into him; she began to work it back and forth, and he yelled out in pleasure.

She stopped then, fearing that she'd hurt him. 'Are you all right?' she asked anxiously.

'Yes.' He shuddered. 'Christ, yes. Don't stop. Please, Helen, don't stop!'

She bent to her task again, sliding one finger back inside him and massaging him gently; all the while, her mouth worked over his cock, bringing him to the peak. He tangled his hands in her hair, the tips of his fingers massaging her scalp and urging her on; then he felt a sharp kick in his groin, and he came, filling her mouth with warm salty fluid.

'Oh, Helen,' he sighed. 'Beautiful, beautiful Helen.'

She didn't lift her head until his cock had stopped throbbing; then she swallowed, tossed her head back, and licked her lips. She looked up at him, her eyes almost black; Mark's eyes, too, had darkened, his pupils expanding. He caught her to him, kissing her hard. 'God, Helen. That was fantastic. No one's ever done that to me before – smeared me with honey and then sucked me and fucked me till I came.'

'I have to admit,' she said, 'I've never done that before, either.' Stu had always liked his sex extremely straight; Helen, under Mark's influence, was discovering that she had a more inventive and sexually interesting imagination, and she was enjoying using it.

'Let's try it the other way, now,' he said softly.

'Hm?' Helen wasn't quite sure what he meant.

'Spread your legs for me.' It was a request, not a command; Helen did so, willingly, lying back on the bed and bending her knees, putting her feet flat on the mattress.

'It's a shame that you've got short hair,' Mark said ruminatively.

'How do you mean?'

'If your hair was long, you'd probably wear it tied back in a scarf, when you were working. And if you wore the scarf in bed, then I could free your hair, shaking it over your shoulders like a shower of gold.'

She smiled. 'Very fanciful.'

He ruffled her hair. 'You'd look like a pre-Raphaelite model.'

'Hm.' Helen wasn't convinced.

'Anyway, once I'd freed your hair, I'd use that scarf on you.' He stroked her cheek. 'Not painfully – just enough to give your muscles some resistance, something to do – then, when you came, it would be more intense.'

Helen smiled at him. 'Yeah, well. Like you said, it's a shame that my hair is short.'

'So you wouldn't mind if I tied you to the bed?'

She bit her lip. 'It's not something I've ever done, but . . . yes, I think I trust you enough to try it.'

'Maybe next time we're together, I'll do that.' His hand stroked down her legs. 'I'll tie your wrists above your head. Not tightly – just enough to hold you firmly, without hurting you. Then I'll move down to work on your feet.' He gently picked up her feet, placing the soles together and letting her knees fall back against the bed, pushing her feet towards her quim so that she was more exposed to him. 'I'll position you like this, then I'll tie your feet so you look like a ballerina, laces crossing the arches of your feet, supporting your ankles and then crossing up to your calves.'

Helen shivered, imagining it. 'We could always pretend now, if you like.'

Mark shook his head. 'If we did, you'd have to concentrate on keeping yourself still – and I'd much rather that you concentrated on what I want to do to you next.'

'Which is?'

'This,' he said. He knelt beside her, one hand still pinioning her feet together; he dipped the forefinger of his other hand into the pot of honey, and slowly drew it down her quim. Helen's mouth opened in an involuntary 'Oh' of pleasure as he began to rub her clitoris, the extra friction generated by the honey making the movement of his fingers feel even better. The way Mark was holding her feet meant that her muscles tightened when she pushed her pelvis upwards; he smiled, and increased the tempo, rubbing her very quickly.

She groaned, lifting her hands to grip the headboard; Mark dipped his finger in the honey again, and slowed the speed right down, his finger moving in long slow sweeps across her quim. Helen clenched her jaw, and tried to move against him to quicken the rhythm again, but her position made it impossible.

Just as she was about to beg him to stop teasing her and finish her off, he bent down to touch his mouth to her clitoris, lapping at the honey he'd smeared over it: it was enough to tip her into a violent orgasm, and her muscles spasmed wildly. Mark kept hold of her ankles and continued lapping at her, pushing her into a higher peak; she dropped her hands and sagged against the pillows, shaking.

He released her, and shifted up to take her into his arms. 'OK?' he asked, stroking her back.

'Mm.' Helen could barely speak.

He smiled, and cuddled her; they lay in silence until Helen had recovered.

'My God,' she said at last. 'I don't know if I dare ask you where you learned tricks like that!'

'Just a few ideas I read somewhere; I thought you might like to try them out with me.' She grinned. 'And how!'

He rubbed his nose against hers. 'Speaking of ideas, there's something else that I'd really like to do with you. Seeing that Aidan went to all that trouble to get us a kinky black ribbed condom, we really should use it, don't you think?'

'Mm.' Helen lay back on the bed, adopting an inviting pose with her knees bent, her feet flat on the mattress and her thighs wide apart; Mark's cock swelled instantly at the sight of her exposed quim. 'If I had anywhere near your talent with a pencil, I'd sketch you like that,' he said softly. 'You look so beautiful: glistening with arousal, your labia all soft and puffy because you've just come. I almost wish my mouth and my cock were in the same place, so I could suck you and fuck you at the same time.'

Helen grinned. 'Which gives me a fantastic idea for an obscene drawing . . .'

He laughed. 'Don't tell me – a bit like a male version of the Indian temple dancers?'

'I'm not with you.'

'They were women who were specially trained – from birth, I should think. They used to lean back into a crab position.'

Helen groaned. 'God, I remember doing that at junior school. Well, I could never do it – I used to just fall over.'

'These women went a bit further than that. They must have been virtually double-jointed, because they could wrap their arms round their legs and put their head between their thighs. The idea was, the man would give her one stroke in the mouth, and one in the quim, then in the mouth again.'

She pulled a face. 'I don't think I'm quite that supple!'

'I don't think I've ever met anyone who was,' he said.

'So how do you know about it?'

'I borrowed a book of beautiful drawings from a friend – that was one of them. I fantasized about it for weeks afterwards.' His hand slid down to curve over her buttocks. 'I suppose the nearest you could get to it would be with two women who knew each other very well, found each other attractive, and wouldn't mind performing together or tasting the other one's juices on the man's cock.'

'Say, one sitting on the edge of a very high bed, leaning back, and the other sitting on the floor, beneath her?' Helen asked.

'Yeah. Though I think it would be more fun for the man than for the women.' He smiled. 'Anyway, threesomes and whatever don't really appeal to me. I prefer making love one to one. It's more intimate, more special.' He grinned. 'Though there is one exception to that – something that would make one hell of a drawing for you.'

'Oh?'

'This,' He climbed off the bed, and walked over to her cheval mirror. He moved it nearer to the bed, adjusting the angle, then smiled at her. 'I want to watch myself fucking you. I want to see my cock sliding into your beautiful wet cunt. And I want to see that condom glistening with your juices.'

His words sent a delicious thrill through Helen: she could see it as he described it – his beautiful powerful body pushing into hers, the black condom stretched over his cock and disappearing into her with every thrust.

Smiling, he unwrapped the condom and rolled it over his cock. Helen was the one who was going to get the most sensation out of this, but it didn't bother him; if anything, it meant that he'd be able to bring her to a series of climaxes, rather than just one. Though the idea of watching themselves make love in the mirror made his cock twitch and his heart beat faster. He had a feeling that Helen would be even more inventive than Selena, when she lost her reserve and let her imagination take over – being a painter, she had an eye for form and patterns. And her mind could dream up beautiful positions . . .

Mark stroked her face, then took the two spare pillows from his side of the bed, using them to prop up her buttocks. 'It means that I'll penetrate you at a different angle – it'll feel good, and you can see it better,' he explained, seeing the question in her eyes. 'And I'm going to take it slowly, so you get the most out of the condom.'

He knelt in front of the pillows, holding her ankles and lifting her legs gently so that they were stretched out fully. 'Look in the mirror,' he said softly.

Helen did so, and the pulse in her quim began to beat hard. What she saw was a good-looking and athletic man kneeling on the bed, his cock rigid and encased in black rubber. He'd positioned his lover so that they could both see what was going on; her pelvis was tipped up, and the angle of his penetration meant that his cock wouldn't be hidden from view as he pushed into her. She'd be able to see everything, from the first moment his cock pressed against her entrance until he was all the way inside her. Her internal muscles flexed, and she longed to feel Mark's cock filling her.

'Mark. Please,' she said huskily.

He moved his hips so that his condom-encased glans rubbed along the length of her quim; Helen gasped as he touched her clitoris, the rubber nodules on the condom giving her extra sensation. He repeated the action once, twice, three times, until she was shaking and about to beg him to fuck her properly.

As if anticipating her words, he let the tip of his cock slide down to her vaginal entrance, and pushed very gently inside her. He kept the movement slow and steady, so that Helen could feel every single rib on the condom; her gasp of pleasure made Mark smile and quicken his pace just a touch.

Helen kept watching their reflections in the mirror. The sight, she thought, was beautiful: the way Mark's cock slid so deep inside her, the way his buttocks moved as he thrust. It beat the occasional pornographic films she'd seen by a long way; and it was beautiful. Mark was right – it made her itch to paint the scene. Maybe with a mirror the other side, reflecting the scene again and again, tiny lines of lovers fucking . . .

He began to move his hips in small circles; Helen gasped, and drew her legs up to clasp his waist. 'Oh, God,' she said. 'That's so *good*!'

He smiled, and continued moving, his thrusts alternately quick and hard, then slow and very light. Helen's mouth opened, and she began to moan with pleasure; Mark, seeing the familiar rosy mottling spread over her neck and breasts, gently guided her face to the side. 'Watch yourself,' he said softly. 'See yourself as I see you, when you come.'

His words, combined with the way his body fused with hers and the pictures in the mirror, made Helen orgasm sharply. She cried out, her body convulsing round his; her reaction was so strong that it took Mark by surprise, tipping him into his own climax. He let his body relax over hers, keeping his weight supported on his own hands and knees, and kissed her lightly. 'What a way to wake up,' he said softly.

'Mm, and it's the sort of breakfast in bed that I'd like more often,' she said, stroking his hair back from his forehead.

He smiled. 'That can be arranged . . .'